"Bill Hall's audacious fantasy thrusts Oregon's mythic political hero Tom McCall in the Presidency with the simple twist of being President Nixon's 'outside of the box' choice to replace Spiro Agnew as Vice President in October 1973 and becoming President of the United States when Nixon resigns the following August. McCall aficionados will be thrilled with McCallandia, as their champion, who always harbored national ambitions but never acted upon them, changes the arc of US and world history for the better. One can imagine Governor McCall's large spirit looking over the reader's shoulder, smiling and chuckling, his face beet-red with embarrassed pleasure."

CHARLES K. JOHNSON
Portland writer, author of Standing at the Water's Edge: Bob Straub's Battle for the Soul of Oregon.

"Great read, excellent craftsmanship. Realandish or Outistic, the genre is difficult to peg. My personal recollection of Tom, leads me to accept your premise as real, and the situations, as plausible."

DON JARVI
Former McCall energy adviser and father of odd-even gas rationing

"Tom McCall made it so cool to be an Oregonian. Bill Hall's McCallandia imagines what it would have meant for the entire country if McCall had made his way into the presidency after Nixon's resignation. The Governor might have made it cool to be an American during a rough time in our nation's history. It's a story that never was but should have been."

BRYCE ZABEL
Author, TV Academy CEO, Creator of five primetime TV series

"Bill Hall's fantasy on what might have been for "the Oregon Story" is so true to the sense of the Tom McCall era that when you finish this work, you wonder how the rest of the nation could have missed out on what Oregon takes for granted as a way to live. A truly pleasurable read for an Oregonian."

DORIS PENWELL
Former executive secretary to Governor McCall

"It was arguably Oregon's 'Camelot' moment: those few years in the early 1970s that Governor Tom McCall helped fashion Oregon into a national laboratory for progressive and innovative policy ideas. Bill Hall's evocative, page-turning book—a first-rate political "What Might have Been?" tale—imagines a President McCall bringing that same vision to a larger canvas. Given the otherwise dreary decade we actually lived through think—Ford, Carter, oil embargoes, Reagan, and disco, though not necessarily in that order—Hall's spirited romp through a McCall-centric political universe provides readers with a compelling, alternative reality that isn't just more heartening. It's also one that's just a helluva lot more interesting."

PHIL KEISLING
Former Oregon Secretary of State and McCall campaign aide

"McCallandia is simply the best political novel ever written about Oregon."

MATT LOVE
Publisher

McCallandia is a novel about an America that might have been and should have been. The central figure is Tom McCall, legendary two-term Governor of Oregon, and it is based on a simple premise: that McCall, not Gerald Ford, was appointed vice president in 1973 and became president the next year when Richard Nixon resigned. See what happens when McCall brings his vision, candor and environmental ethic to Washington. Follow the three-way 1976 presidential election, one of the most memorable in history, as McCall seeks a term in his own right. With a supporting cast of outsized personalities, including Ken Kesey, Steve Prefontaine, Richard Nixon, Hunter S. Thompson, John Lennon and more, McCallandia takes you on a journey to a place you won't soon forget...and where you may wish you lived!

“Some men see things as they are and say why. I dream things that never were and say why not.”

—Robert Kennedy

“There was something goofily, marvelously Lincolnesque about him. More than a governor, he would have been an ideal candidate for president — what a wonderful one he would have been.”

—Studs Terkel to McCall biographer Brent Walth

nestuccaspitpress.com

Published by Nestucca Spit Press in Astoria, Oregon
An Independent Press Publishing Books About Oregon
Printed by Dave at Pioneer Printing in Newport, Oregon.

First Edition. ISBN 978-0-9906775-0-5
Cover illustration: Alex Turner
Photograph of McCall and Reagan: Gerry Lewin
Political cartoon: James Cloutier
Book design: James Herman

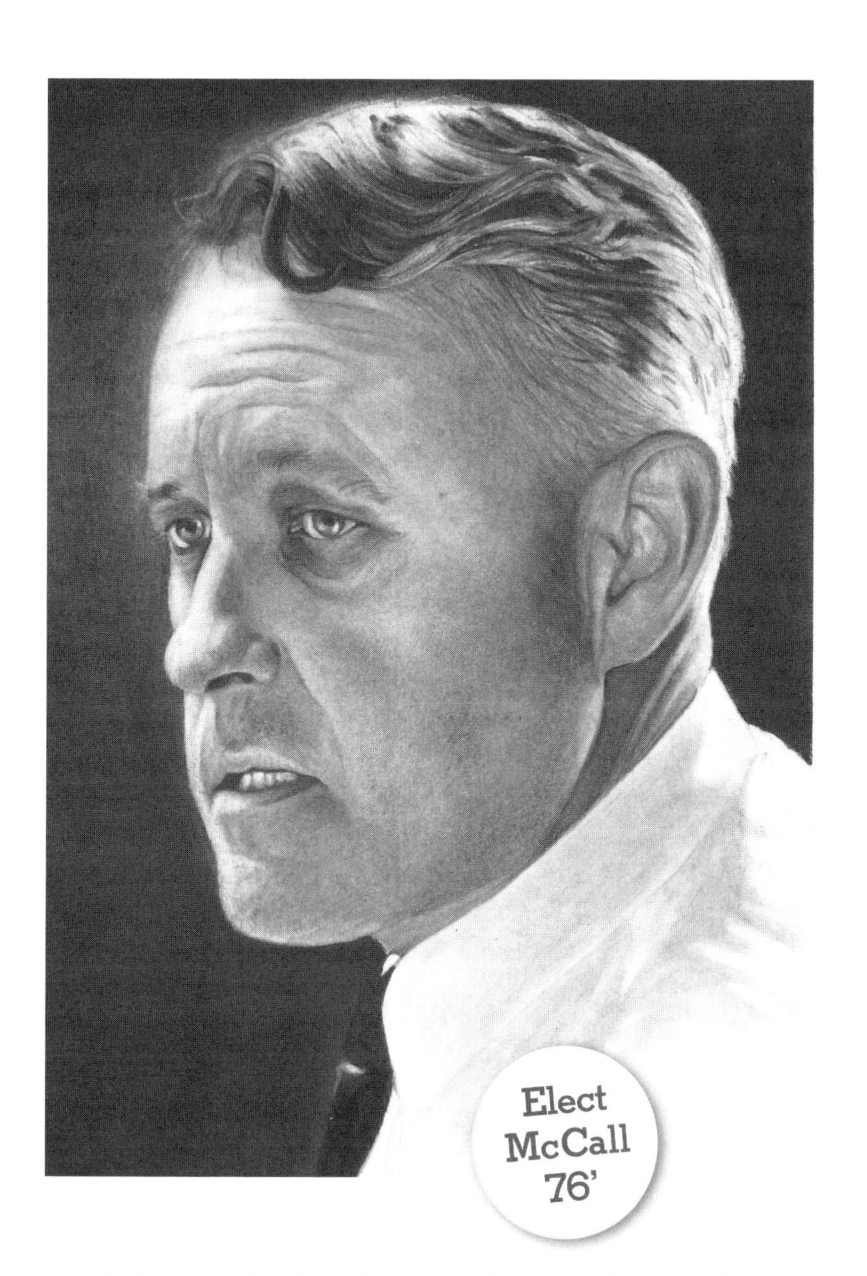

McCALLANDIA

by Bill Hall

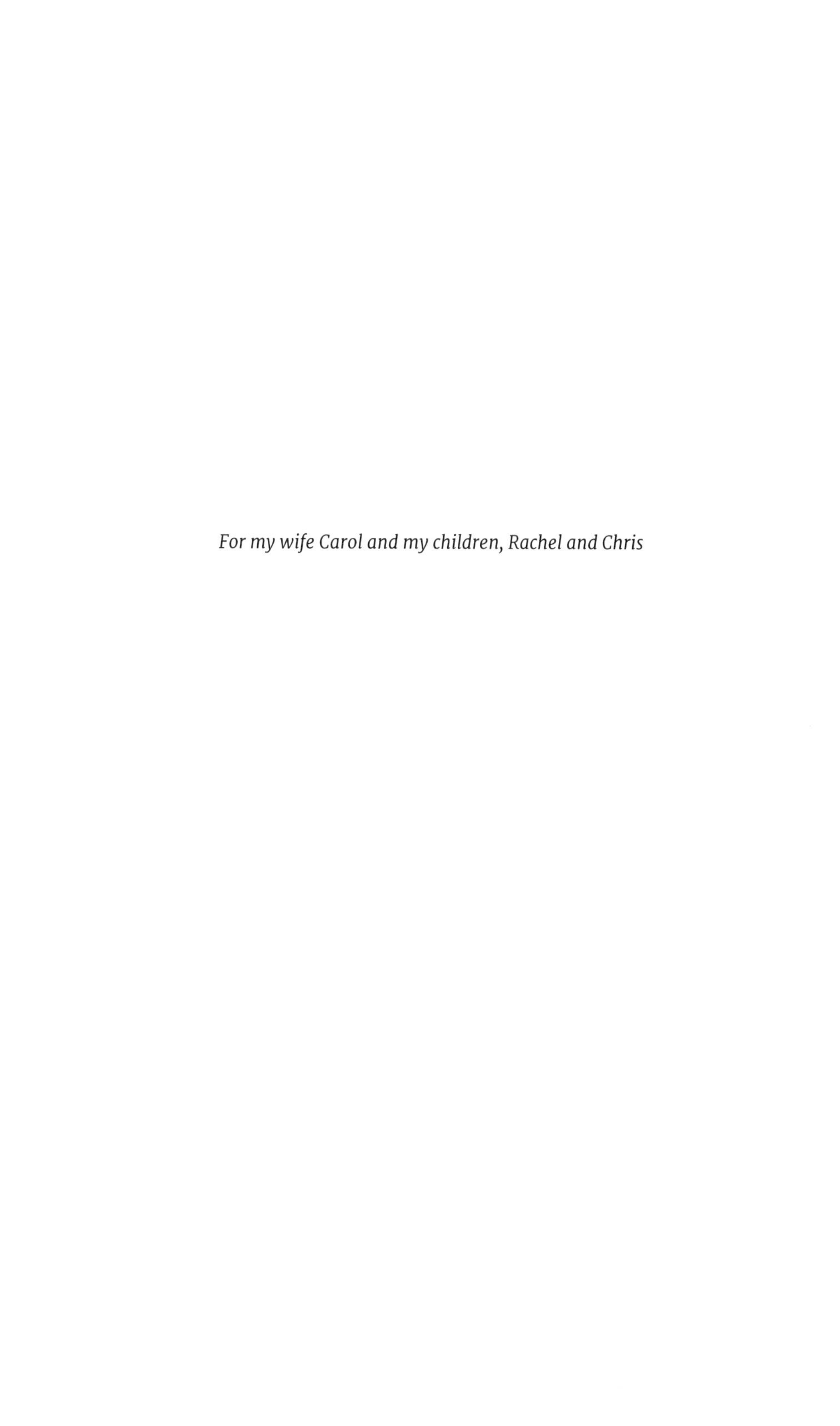

For my wife Carol and my children, Rachel and Chris

Introduction: Tom McCall and Me

Most people see their childhood heroes diminish in stature as they get older. I'm lucky. My hero, former Oregon Governor Tom McCall, has only grown to be a larger presence in my life across the decades.

I've had the honor of serving as an elected Lincoln County Commissioner since 2005. A large part of the reason I'm in politics today is the example set by Tom McCall. More than thirty years after his passing and forty years after he left office, Tom McCall continues to be a commanding presence on the Oregon landscape.

I wasn't your average kid. When I was five, and my Kindergarten classmates were aspiring to be astronauts or firefighters, I was telling my parents I wanted to grow up to become President of the United States. Washington, Lincoln and the Roosevelts were real people to me, not just names in dusty history books.

I was seven years old when McCall was elected governor in 1966. I was already reading both of Portland's daily newspapers by then, so I'm sure I knew who he was; but my first vivid McCall memories are from 1970, when he ran for re-election and made the memorable decision to hold the Vortex rock festival (Officially known as Vortex I: A Biodegradeable Festival of Life)—the first and only state-sanctioned rock festival in history. I remember watching him on a statewide television and radio broadcast announcing the decision, the first time a governor had used this platform to communicate with the entire state at once.

Soon I was learning about the other things McCall had accomplished, like the Beach Bill, and watching other remarkable things unfold, like the Bottle Bill, statewide land use planning, the odd-even gas rationing system, the outdoor lighting ban...and the list went on and on. I saw Oregon being recognized as a national leader and innovator. It made me proud to call this place home. By the end of McCall's second term, I was an unabashed disciple of this man who had done so much to define the Oregon spirit.

Although McCall's popularity was at a peak in 1974, the state constitution prevented him from seeking a third consecutive term. He accepted a part-time teaching position, began writing a newspaper column, and was soon back in front of the cameras as a television news analyst. Yet speculation began almost immediately that McCall would seek to reclaim the governorship in 1978. I spent the next three years hoping that would happen; I still remember the thrill I felt when I heard KATU anchor Richard Ross open an 11 p.m. newscast one mid-February night with the words, "Tom McCall will run for governor." I heard the same excitement in Ross' voice that I was feeling.

Most of McCall's former staffers had urged him not to run. They told him his heart would be broken. Sadly, they were right. McCall himself later conceded he had doomed his chances from the start by running as a Republican instead of as an independent. Although the Oregon Republican party of 1978 was more tolerant of diverse views that the GOP of today, it had already moved considerably rightward in the eight years since McCall's last electoral victory. McCall finished a distant second in the primary to State Senator Victor Atiyeh, the eventual November winner.

I didn't know any of this at the time, of course. I was just thrilled to have an opportunity to help get Tom back into office. I was a freshman at Pacific University, and organized a campaign appearance on the campus. The first time I visited McCall headquarters, they were handing out orange stickers that read: "Tom McCall: Back by Popular Demand." But these were soon replaced by new literature using the familiar green-and-white color scheme from past McCall campaigns and bearing a new slogan: "The Best is Yet to Come." If only.

My main contact in the campaign office was a 22-year-old Yale graduate named Phil Keisling. Phil would go on to serve as Oregon's secretary of state from 1991 to 1999, a job once held by McCall. As of this writing he's director of the Center for Public Service at Portland State University's Mark O. Hatfield School of Government.

The campaign team asked me to invite the University president to introduce McCall when he came to the campus, but as Washington County was Atiyeh country, he declined, and the opportunity fell to me. I was fired up to say the least. My introduction ended this way: "And so it's my privilege and high honor to present to you Oregon's greatest governor, and Oregon's next governor. Ladies and gentlemen, please welcome Tom McCall."

McCall stepped to the podium and quipped, "Bill Hall! The last of the firebrands!" A pause and some chuckles followed. "What an introduction!"

I went out canvassing for Tom a couple of weeks later. He was on hand at the campaign headquarters to thank us and give us marching orders: "Tell them we're going to thrash William Jolley!" (The jug-eared Jolley, a refrigeration contractor from Willamina, showed up on the ballot every couple of years in this era, but never won an office.)

I was at the Benson Hotel on election night for what we all believed would be a victory party. McCall had seen the trend in the polls, his lead steadily shrinking as the election neared, and probably already knew what was coming. The rest of us were stunned when the early numbers showed Atiyeh in the lead. It appeared Jolley, who finished a distant fourth, was the only contender who would be thrashed by the McCall team that night. (I exaggerate slightly. Tom was also comfortably ahead of the third-place finisher, State Representative Roger Martin.)

Have you ever held onto a dream for years, been certain that it would become tangible, only to see it dissolve in an instant? I was heartsick; we all were. When Tom entered the ballroom, he immediately picked up on the sense of melancholy that enveloped the crowd. Like any good general, he felt a duty to rally his troops, even if the battle was lost. We formed a protective circle around him. He stepped to the center of that circle and thrust one leg forward, dipped his trailing leg, and pumped a fist in the air like a boxer delivering an uppercut. He shouted one magic word: "Oregon!" We answered as one: "Oregon!"

Tom was a master of political theater, and he was going to wring all the emotion he could from the scene.

"Oregon!" he shouted again.

"Oregon!" we answered once more, this time with greater fervor.

The message I took away from that moment was that the cause of our beloved state was even more important than the individual. On more than one occasion McCall had declared the message to be more significant than the messenger. But it's important that we remember and celebrate this remarkable man. He reminds us of what is possible with imagination and courage.

There would be other memorable moments that night; a conciliatory visit from Governor Bob Straub; a testy exchange with Atiyeh; media interviews and endless handshakes; but that scene brought down the curtain on the career of Tom McCall, candidate.

I only saw Tom McCall one more time after 1978. Sadly, it was after his death from cancer at the beginning of 1983. I sat next to my own state representative in the House of Representatives chamber for the celebration of life. Although the ceremonies were carried live on statewide television, I felt compelled to be there in person. McCall had insisted that the ceremony be open to all on an equal basis. I listened to the wonderful tributes. As McCall's casket was carried from the chamber for the final time while a choir sang *What the World Needs Now,* I cried.

Tom McCall remains a daily presence in my life, as I suspect he does for thousands of others. I'm surrounded by tangible links to him, including one of the most treasured books in my library, a copy of his autobiography signed: "Merry Christmas to Bill Hall from Tom McCall." A friend attended the estate sale held when Audrey McCall moved from her home into a retirement center, and he bought several items for me, including McCall's rolodex, which sits in my office. The well-thumbed typewritten cards, many with additions and corrections in McCall's own hand, represent a who's who of Oregon in the 60s and 70s. I sometimes show it to visitors as if it was a holy relic, which in a sense it is.

These objects are important to me, but more significant is my commitment to upholding his values in my public work. When dealing with a complex or controversial issue, I often find myself asking: What Would Tom Do?

I had always hoped to find a way to celebrate the McCall legacy. Journalist Brent Walth published the definitive McCall biography, *Fire at Eden's Gate*, in 1994. I didn't have an idea for a project until I read a blog post by fellow Newport resident Matt Love in March 2013, just before the celebration of the centennial of McCall's birth. McCall had toyed with the idea of running for president as an independent in 1976 to help spread what he called "the Oregon story," but that never moved past the talking stage. But what if it had? What if history had taken a different turn? A photograph of McCall with California Governor Ronald Reagan, taken by photojournalist Gerry Lewin at the 1967 USC-Oregon State football game in Corvallis (one of the legendary games in Oregon college sports history) helped spur Matt's imagination:

"Just think where this country would be today after two of his terms in the White House as opposed to Reagan's. I do all the time. In fact, I'm going to write a historical science fiction novel with that exact premise. I'm going to call it *McCallandia*. "

I saw Matt at a reading he presented in Newport a couple of nights after I read that blog post, and we briefly discussed the concept, which had struck me like a bolt of lightning. I went home and wrote preliminary versions of a couple of scenes that appear in the book you are holding and sent them to Matt via Facebook. I said I hoped I wasn't being too presumptuous. Matt generously responded that he probably would never get around to writing the book and bequeathed the concept to me. He provided feedback and suggestions throughout the writing process, and encouraged me to let my imagination soar and take some risks in the narrative.

You are holding the result of Matt's inspiration and my lifetime of devotion to Tom McCall. I hope you enjoy it.

Bill Hall

March 2013-April 2014

Oregon artist James Cloutier capitalized on the iconoclastic reputation McCall created for the state during his governorship with a series of "Oregon Ungreeting" cards, bumper stickers, T-shirts and books, featuring the everyman character Hugh Wetshoe. When McCall became president, Hugh Wetshoe also made the transition to the national stage.

LOOKS LIKE WE'RE A LONG WAYS FROM HOME, HUGH!
CLOUTIER 2014

1

A crisp January day in the nation's capital, January 1983.

The network news cameras focused on the prototype all-electric car pulling up in front of the National Cathedral in Washington, D.C., where the state funeral of the thirty-eighth president would soon begin. Tom McCall, who had stepped into the Oval Office after Richard Nixon's resignation and then won a term in his own right two years later in one of the most tumultuous elections in U.S. history, had died the week before following a recurrence of prostate cancer.

McCall's vice president and his successor in the White House, Barry Commoner, stepped from the electric vehicle and walked into the cathedral. He was followed by Vice President LaDonna Harris—a prominent Native American activist and the first female vice president in the country's history. The broadcast networks—ABC, CBS and NBC, plus Ted Turner's fledgling Cable News Network—were carrying the proceedings live.

CBS anchor Dan Rather noted that the car President Commoner arrived in was one of the tangible signs of how McCall had transformed American life.

"The Energy Independence Act of 1979 mandated that at least 25 percent of all vehicles sold in the United States would be gas-electric hybrids by 1984," Rather reminded his audience. "That percentage will rise to 50 percent by 1989, with an additional 25 percent being all electric. Ford and Chrysler are beating the deadline, rolling out their hybrids a year ahead of schedule, and the powers-that-be at General Motors assure us they're right behind."

Rather had forsaken the V-neck sweaters he had been wearing on the CBS Evening News for a simple black suit and tie. "No doubt they'll be telling the stories for decades to come," Rather declared. "When the auto industry lobbyists lined up outside the Oval Office to tell the president and Energy Secretary Bob Davis it was impossible to meet the deadlines in the bill. 'Damn it,' McCall shouted, his raspy Massachusetts accent echoing off the walls. No doubt he was pounding his fist on the desk for emphasis, 'Don't tell me it can't be done. We built the atom bomb in two years. We put a man on the moon in eight years. It can be done.'"

"It's too early to write the definitive story of President McCall's life and career," said retired CBS anchor Walter Cronkite, who had joined his successor to co-host the funeral coverage. "But it seems clear that history will remember Tom McCall as one of those rare transformative figures in American political life—the arrival of the right man at the right time, allowing the American people to rise above the petty squabbles of the moment and accomplish something real and lasting.

"We're still sorting it out: what Tom McCall called the Oregon story, and how he took that story to the national stage when the presidency was thrust upon him in the dark summer of 1974. Certainly the accomplishments in his home state that he was able to replicate nationally—a Beach Bill, a Bottle Bill and a land use planning law—are major elements of that story, but they are pieces of something larger; the McCall administration represented a turning point in the way Americans viewed their government, their environment and their world."

Rather chimed in: "The national psyche was scarred, some would even say it was broken, by a decade of crises—assassinations, Vietnam and Watergate. Many were questioning whether Americans would ever have faith in their government again. President McCall managed to restore that faith. One elderly woman who approached me as I entered the studios this morning summed up the feelings of many when she said, 'Thank God for Tom McCall.'"

Rather paused. "Tom McCall was beloved not just for his achievements, but for his candor and his colorful way with words. His most memorable utterance came in an interview with our own Terry Drinkwater in 1971"—and the film clip played, McCall imploring:

"Come and visit our state of excitement again and again. But for heaven's sake, don't move here to live."

"Although he didn't utter the exact words, this was forever remembered as McCall's admonition to 'visit but don't stay.' To this day, there are Oregonians who say this was the best thing their governor ever said, summing up the iconoclastic Oregon spirit with humor and style. But there are also those who put the blame for Oregon's current economic slump squarely on the late governor and president's broad shoulders. Yet the facts are undeniable: during his governorship, Oregon outstripped the national average and other West Coast states in population growth, new employment and total and per capita personal income. If he was trying to keep people away from Oregon, the message may have backfired."

The cameras continued to show scenes around the majestic cathedral, but they steered clear of another visible aspect of how McCall's administration had changed American life. In the group of smokers congregated to one side of the crowd outside the cathedral's entrance, only slightly more than half were using tobacco. The rest were smoking marijuana, the possession and use of which had been decriminalized by another act of Congress championed by McCall.

The picture on millions of television screens switched from outdoor scenes to an indoor view as a Marine Corps color guard carried McCall's casket into the cathedral. The casket was followed by the honorary pallbearers, McCall's sons Tad and Sam, and the men who had been closest to him during his time in office, his former Chief of Staff Ed Westerdahl and his former Press Secretary Ron Schmidt. Tad McCall wore his Navy dress uniform and the other three were clad in black suits. A fifth honorary pallbearer trailing behind them was also clothed in black, but in this case, it was a black track suit. Unlike the others in the procession, he was jogging slowly. Dan Rather made note of the man in the tracksuit:

"There's one iconic symbol of the Beaver state, Oregon, Olympic gold medalist Steve Prefontaine paying tribute to another Oregon icon, Tom McCall. The two men became friends shortly before Prefontaine's record-setting run in the Montreal Olympics, and they remained close until the former president's death." Rather paused, and turned to his right. The camera zoomed out to reveal a smiling, balding man who looked a little uncomfortable in what appeared to be a brand new suit.

"And joining us now with his observations on the late president, yet another Oregon icon, novelist Ken Kesey." Kesey would have been more comfortable in tie dye or flannel and suspenders. His bald scalp, framed by a ring of curly grey hair, shone under the harsh studio lights; he had stubbornly refused an offer of powder to cut the glare; if CBS wouldn't let him wear a cap, they could take him as is. "Mr. Kesey served as the nation's first, and so far, only, secretary of counter-culture for three years during the McCall administration. Mr. Kesey, that was a great experience for you, even though it ended in controversy."

The smile momentarily disappeared from Kesey's face. "Was there a question there, Dan?"

"So. Can you tell us how you got to know then-Governor McCall?"

Kesey's soft, low-key delivery, betraying just a slight Midwestern drawl, belied his avant garde image, something he addressed in answering the anchorman. "A lot of people look at me as some sort of colorful character, a hippie pied piper. They forget that I'm a farmer, an artist, and foremost, a husband and a father. I was concerned about some things related to education, so I decided to go right to the top—the governor's office."

"Did your relationship have anything to do with the President making a cameo appearance in the movie version of your novel, *One Flew Over the Cuckoo's Nest*?"

The grin left Kesey's lips once more. "No, Dan. I had nothing to do with that film." The CBS anchorman was apparently one of the few people in media circles who was unaware of Kesey's disdain for the filmed version of his most famous work.

Seeking to recover, Rather plowed on: "Please give us your thoughts on what President McCall meant to the country."

"When Nixon went out, I knew we had won."

"Well. What, in your view, was the secret behind Tom McCall's success? How would you sum it up in one word?"

"Well, asking a writer to choose just one word is a challenge. But if I had to do that, I'd say it was his vision. I tried to talk him into dropping acid a couple of times to expand that vision even more, but he refused. But he still had a greater vision than anyone else I've ever seen in politics."

Rather wrapped up the conversation as President Commoner stepped to the pulpit of the cathedral.

"As governor of Oregon, Tom McCall became the living embodiment of a people's love of their state. As President of the United States, he taught us all the importance of cherishing our entire planet. Make no mistake about it—Tom, to his dying breath, was an Oregon chauvinist through and through. In one of his more memorable statements, he declared that Oregon was 'demure, and lovely, and ought to play a little hard to get.' But he realized that a healthy Oregon was ultimately dependent on a healthy planet." The cameras lingered on a close-up of Secretary of Peace George McGovern as a tear trickled down his cheek.

McCall's widow Audrey sat in the front row. She was composed, but the anguish of her loss was etched on her deeply-lined face; friends and loved ones said it was as if she had aged a decade overnight. Her sons had joined her at the conclusion of the procession. They were surrounded by the usual array of world leaders, members of Congress and the prominent and powerful. Nothing less was to be expected with the first presidential funeral since Lyndon Johnson's passing almost exactly a decade earlier. But a lot was different. A good number of ordinary Americans, chosen by a lottery, were interspersed in the audience.

This had been McCall's idea. A couple of days after Christmas, as he lay dying in Portland's Good Samaritan hospital, he waited for his wife and younger son to step out for a bite to eat in the cafeteria, leaving older son Tad as the sole visitor.

The soft hum and steady beeping of the equipment monitoring the former president's vital signs filled any silences in their conversation. Tom McCall had been waiting for this moment to be alone with Tad. But it was really only an illusion of privacy they enjoyed, for a Secret Service agent sat on the other side of the curtained glass wall. Unfortunately, cancer was one killer even the Secret Service couldn't defeat.

As if the burden of losing their spouse and father wasn't enough, the McCall family also had to cope with the constant presence of the news media, which was engaged in a prolonged death watch. A row of trucks from the networks and the Portland and Seattle television stations lined the street in front of Good Sam, and radio and print reporters took turns hanging out in the hospital's briefing room, just in case there was a sudden significant change in McCall's condition.

Tom McCall saw a certain sense of irony in it all, since he had come to politics through the media, and after he had made the transition from news reporter to news maker, TV, radio and newspapers had provided him with the bully pulpit that allowed him to accomplish so much.

Though his body was wasted, McCall's mind was still alert. Just a few nights before he left his home for what he knew would be the last time, he had noticed that Audrey had awakened and was looking at him with concern. She knew he was now in constant agony as the cancer advanced through his body. She asked if the pain was keeping him from sleeping. No, he had replied, the painkillers were working their magic for the moment. He just couldn't stop thinking about the days ahead and how he could guide Oregon and the world toward a better tomorrow. A rational corner of his mind was telling him he was in his final days. But that restless, urgent part of his spirit that had driven him to accomplish so much in his sixty-nine years couldn't stop trying to see how the pieces would fit together ten, twenty, a hundred years from now.

The local press corps kept a respectful distance, another sign of their affection for the man who had risen from their ranks, but it was a different story with the national reporters, who followed Audrey, Sam and Tad's every movement in and out of the hospital. McCall Library Director Ron Schmidt tried to run interference for the family, and joined the hospital in issuing periodic updates on the former president's health, even if they simply indicated no change.

The most unnerving incident for the family came on Christmas Eve, when the Secret Service stopped a freelance photographer on assignment for the *National Enquirer* who was attempting to sneak into the hospital to snap a picture of the former president on his deathbed.

Agent Robert Sulliman, who had been part of McCall's presidential detail and asked to stay on after he left office, was fiercely protective of the man he considered a friend. Sulliman was a no-nonsense kind of person, rarely given to flights of fancy. In the rare moments that he did let his imagination roam, he saw himself stopping an assassination attempt; somehow, he hadn't envisioned pouncing on paparazzi when he signed up for the job. While the young woman hadn't been trying to take McCall's life, she was attempting to steal something almost as precious: his dignity and his privacy.

Asked by reporters how he had recognized the woman as a fraud, he quipped, "It was pretty easy, really. She was in a nurse's uniform, yes, but she was wearing way too much makeup, she was in heels, not tennis shoes, and she was carrying a purse, which hid her camera. What nurse carries a purse when she's on duty?"

For now, at least, all the media was at bay, medical personnel were busy elsewhere, wife and brother were getting coffee, and father and son were alone.

"Tad," the former president croaked, his voice barely rising above a whisper. "I want you to make sure there are regular people at the funeral, not just the stuffed shirts. I…."

"Now, Dad!"

"Tad, you know as well as I do I'm not getting out of here." The family had already had this conversation; Tom McCall had insisted that no artificial means be used to prolong his life, but he could understand the reluctance of his loved ones to let him go. ("Aud, dying is just part of life," he had told his companion of forty-three years.) Now he chuckled softly. "Well, not the way I'd like anyway." He closed his eyes for a moment as he grimaced in pain. The morphine could only do so much. "This is important to me, son. Will you promise that you'll take care of it?"

Tad nodded and squeezed his father's hand. Tom McCall smiled.

"Remember right after my cancer surgery, about ten years ago, when they found the bomb in the restroom on the floor below, and they rushed me out of that hospital on a stretcher?"

"How could I forget that, Dad?"

"Find the guys who carried my stretcher that night. Maybe we can get them to sneak me out of here and take me home."

Despite the sadness he felt, Tad McCall couldn't help smiling.

It was later reported that at least one Supreme Court justice who showed up late for the president's funeral was denied a seat in the overfull cathedral and wound up in a side room where a closed-circuit feed of the proceedings was offered.

The cameras scanned the crowd. Canadian Prime Minister Pierre Trudeau sat next to a truck driver from Atlanta. A teacher from

Chicago was shoulder-to-shoulder with Indian Prime Minister Indira Gandhi. A logger from the town of Cottage Grove, Oregon rubbed elbows with German Prime Minister Helmut Kohl.

Some pairings seemed eminently logical. House Speaker Tip O'Neill was with Senator Ted Kennedy. But the contrasts were also striking. Former Beatle John Lennon and acting legend Jimmy Stewart sat side by side. Her Royal Majesty, Queen Elizabeth the Second, shared a pew with Don Henley of the Eagles, who was beginning to emerge as a leading advocate for environmental causes.

The camera settled on the three men who McCall defeated in the hotly-contested 1976 presidential election—Republican nominee Ronald Reagan, Democratic candidate Jerry Brown and Independent Eugene McCarthy. The commentators pointed out the notable absence of McCall's predecessor, Richard Nixon, the only living former president. Nixon had stayed at his home in Saddle River, New Jersey. Although his office issued a brief statement pleading illness, everyone knew Nixon had never forgiven McCall for his betrayal in calling for his resignation as the Watergate scandal intensified, and then refusing to pardon him after he left office. Nixon had avoided trial with a plea bargain, but would go down in history as the first president who, despite his protests to the contrary, was a crook.

All of this particularly galled Nixon because McCall was his handpicked vice president. When Nixon had held the same job during Dwight Eisenhower's presidency, he had been fiercely loyal to his boss, even when it cost him personally and politically. Nixon may have prized expediency above truth, but he cherished loyalty.

On ABC, David Brinkley was reflecting on how McCall had spent the two years since he had left the presidency, approving plans for the McCall Library in Eugene, launching the McCall Institute in Portland and finishing his memoir, *Maverick*. "McCall seemed like a man possessed, especially after he suffered a recurrence of prostate cancer a few months after he left office. He knew his days were numbered, and he wanted to do all he could to secure his legacy. As he told a reporter shortly after his diagnosis: 'You're dead for a long time.'"

NBC was showing film clips from the previous fall when the gravely ill McCall had campaigned around his home state against a ballot measure that would have undone what he considered his most lasting accomplishment: the state's land use planning system. Other efforts to roll back the land use laws had failed, but this one was polling favorably among potential voters as of September. The language was deceptively simple, asking, "Shall the state's land use authority and goals be advisory only?" That single sentence would have taken all teeth out of the system. The same poll showed only one man had the power to potentially change that outcome: Tom McCall.

A gaunt, white-haired figure by then, stooped and using a cane, McCall summoned his great persuasive powers one last time in an appearance at Portland's University Club in early October. He held the audience spellbound with something close to his old power as he appealed to Oregonians to defend the state's livability. Then his message became intensely personal: "You all know I have terminal cancer—and I have a lot of it. But what you may not know is that stress induces its spread and induces its activity. Stress may even bring it on. Yet stress is the fuel of the activist. This activist loves Oregon more than he loves life. I know I can't have both very long. The trade-offs are all right with me. But if the legacy we helped give Oregon and which made it twinkle from afar—if it goes, then I guess I wouldn't want to live in Oregon anyhow."

The usual shuffling and background noise of a public event had been replaced by a wall of complete silence as the impact of these words sunk in. A few sniffles and sighs were all that broke the quiet. Men and women reached for handkerchiefs to blot tear-stained faces.

Millions of Americans watched this clip and shared in the collective mourning for the former governor and president. But for those who had been in the room that day barely three months earlier, it packed a particular emotional resonance. Among them was Judge Jacob Tanzer, who had recently stepped down from the state's Supreme

Court. Tanzer had been Oregon's solicitor general when McCall tapped him in 1971 to lead the newly-created state Department of Human Resources. Tanzer was later named to the state Court of Appeals by McCall.

By the time of the speech, McCall had started refusing his Secret Service guard. "If they're going to shoot me at this point, well...." he had told a friend, leaving the conclusion unfinished. "I'm not going to live in a cage anymore." Tanzer approached McCall following the talk and offered his congratulations. He asked McCall if he needed a ride home, and the former chief executive happily accepted.

McCall's cancer had advanced so far into his bones he couldn't climb into a car seat. Refusing Tanzer's offer of help, he crawled into the back of his Volvo station wagon and made the trip lying down. When they reached the McCall residence in Portland's West Hills, the ex-president once more declined assistance, and slowly, painfully, crawled out of the car and began hobbling up the curved walkway that led to his front door. As he reached one of the curves in the path, McCall stopped, smiled, and waved goodbye to Tanzer. It was the last time Tanzer ever saw McCall alive.

The land use repeal failed by a 55 to 45 percent margin. "It was President McCall's final victory," Chancellor said. A month later, McCall entered a Portland hospital as the cancer's advance spread throughout his body; two weeks after that, he was dead.

This ceremony would be the first of two official funerals for McCall. After the pomp and circumstance was done, McCall's body would be loaded on Air Force One for a final trip home to Oregon. A second funeral would take place at the Capitol Building in Salem, where the powerful would sit shoulder to shoulder with the anonymous before McCall's remains reached their final resting place at Redmond Memorial Cemetery. Some had suggested that McCall, who was a Navy veteran, should be the third president to be buried at Arlington National Cemetery. (Kennedy and Taft were the others.) But Audrey dismissed that idea with a wave of the hand and the first chuckle she had managed since her beloved husband's passing. "Tom would never forgive me if I let him be buried anywhere but Oregon," she said with a sad grin.

Before leaving Washington, however, the McCall family had one more task. The next day, they would visit the White House for the unveiling of McCall's official portrait. The State of Oregon had commissioned it as a gift to the nation; Dutch artist Henk Pender, a Portland resident since the mid-sixties, was chosen to capture McCall in oils. McCall had several sessions with the artist in the final months of his life, but did not live to see the result. If he had, he might have reveled in the fireworks.

The television footage showed what was a routine ceremony until the moment Audrey McCall pulled the rope that removed the cloth covering the painting. The cameras zoomed in on her face, highlighting a wide-eyed, open-mouthed look of surprise. President Commoner also appeared taken aback for a moment before regaining his composure. Tad McCall remained stoic, but Sam couldn't hide his grin.

Although Pender sometimes tailored his work to popular tastes, he wasn't afraid to take risks and make statements. A 1969 exhibit by Pender at Portland State University, featuring works reflective of the conflict-driven, sexually revolutionary times, had been attacked as "pornographic" and "depraved." Portlanders "were aghast at nudity, skeltonized animals, bodily functions, sex acts and pubic hair in the works," according to the *Oregonian*.

The canvas presented McCall sitting at the foot of a hillside with solar panels and a windmill perched on it. McCall was alongside a river. None of this was controversial; what had caused jaws to drop was the portrayal of the president himself. He was seated on the grass, his long legs pulled up in front of him, his arms folded and resting on his knees. One of his feet was immersed in the water in front of him, apparently symbolizing McCall's oneness with nature.

What shocked and outraged people about the McCall portrait was the fact that the thirty-eighth president appeared to be naked. Some commentators noted that with the way McCall was posed, he might be wearing swim trunks. Pender was silent on that question when contacted by reporters at his studio the next day, though he did tell them, "More than any other figure in public life, Tom McCall was willing to display himself honestly and openly to the world. I hope this portrait reflects that honesty."

After the second funeral, Tom McCall's earthly remains were laid to rest, and a chapter in American life was closed. Now he would exit the front pages and the magazine covers and pass into the pages of the history books. The reporters tucked away their collections of notes and clippings in their reference files, to be pulled out on significant anniversaries and milestones. One article that was prominent in almost every clip file was a celebrated piece that appeared in *Rolling Stone* in the fall of 1975, a year into the McCall presidency.

2

The head of *Rolling Stone*'s National Affairs Desk, the great gonzo journalist Hunter S. Thompson, decided the time had arrived for him to take the president's measure.

Thompson had written one of the frankest, funniest, strangest books of political coverage in history, *Fear and Loathing on the Campaign Trail '72*, a compilation of his *Rolling Stone* reportage. In one memorable piece, he had declared that Sen. Ed Muskie, the early Democratic front-runner, was addicted to Ibogaine, a plant-based hallucinogen. According to Thompson, this was the true explanation for Muskie's wild emotional swings (from tears to rage) in the early stages of the race and his quick descent from front-runner to footnote.

Thompson wrote: "It was noted, among other things, that he had developed a tendency to roll his eyes wildly during TV interviews, that his thought patterns had become strangely fragmented, and that not even his closest advisors could predict when he might suddenly spiral off into babbling rages, or neocomatose funks." Of course, as Thompson later admitted, there wasn't a shred of truth to the claim; it was something he had made up.

Examples like this (and a thousand more) might have caused many White House press secretaries to be wary of Hunter S. Thompson. But not Ron Schmidt. He saw the beautiful potential of a *Rolling Stone* profile that would reach millions of young people—and more importantly, young voters. Nineteen seventy-six would be the second presidential election since eighteen-year olds were given the vote, and although McCall wasn't of their generation, they seemed to be as attuned to him as their mothers and fathers were.

Schmidt had suggested that the interview take place at the White House, but Thompson insisted on meeting McCall on his home turf. He would spend nearly a week with him in Oregon. The press secretary was relieved that Thompson's frequent partner, artist Ralph Steadman, wouldn't be able to make the journey with him. Steadman's illustrations had done as much as Thompson's prose to create the new literary form known as gonzo journalism. While Schmidt privately enjoyed Steadman's work, he found it suggestive of a crazed Picasso...he was glad a Steadman portrait of McCall wouldn't be gracing the *Rolling Stone* cover. Instead, the magazine commissioned famed photographer Richard Avedon to capture the president on film.

Although Thompson had notoriously clashed with *Rolling Stone* Publisher Jann Wenner over his expense accounts, he could have easily secured a plane ticket to Portland. But Thompson decided to drive himself in his red 1971 Chevrolet Impala Convertible, which he had dubbed The Shark. He went roaring out of his home at Aspen, a tumbler of Chivas Regal in his hand and a carton of Dunhills at his side.

In a memorable prologue to his article, Thompson told of crossing the Idaho border into Oregon:

> *The Shark hides 454 cubic inches beneath its hood. It was conceived and built long before the current Energy Crisis had invaded Detroit's nightmares. It's a serious machine designed for drivers who like to move, including yours truly. As I crossed into the Beaver State, I realized that I was now in the president's territory. As governor, McCall had imposed the first 55 mile per hour speed limit in the nation to help encourage conservation.*
>
> *Much to my astonishment, I discovered Oregonians were almost universally still obeying their former governor's edict. To my even greater astonishment, I found that I was as well. I briefly thought I might be in the grip of Al Haig's Sinister Force, but quickly concluded it was a far more benevolent power.*

The main body of the piece represented Thompson's attempt to explain McCall's appeal, as well as offering a speculation on his political future:

Fear and Loathing on the Oregon Coast, Rolling Stone #195, September 11, 1975

By Hunter S. Thompson

President Tom Lawson McCall is not a flesh-and-blood human being.

No, the six-foot-five McCall, tallest president in the nation's history, is a figure larger than life, a creation of Central Casting, or maybe the Gods Themselves; they are the only ones who could have envisioned such a perfect antithesis to the man he replaced in the White House a year ago.

The strange and terrible saga of Richard Milhous Nixon reached its end with his resignation on a hot August day, the sight of him entering the presidential helicopter on the White House lawn forever burned into our collective consciousness. Nixon—indeed, his entire family, never seemed human either; they must have been rejects from a doll factory, stamped from defective molds, life breathed into them by a depraved assistant to Doctor Frankenstein.

McCall's humanity is in doubt for just the opposite reason. He seems too great, too heroic to be believed, especially in a country still reeling after a decade of assassinations, Vietnam and Watergate. And while Tricky Dick lusted after power like a vampire lusts after blood from the time his eyelids fluttered open in the morning until well after they had closed for the last time at night, McCall appears to be the first leader ready to voluntarily relinquish power this great since Cincinnatus, the Roman dictator who fled back to his farm in relief as soon as the empire was secured from outside threats.

Not long before he was killed, Robert Kennedy told a crowd that Richard Nixon represented the dark side of the American character. Of course, Bobby was right...and that had something to do with why they pumped a bullet into his brain. But while Nixon may have been our Prince of Darkness, he's fought off plenty of contenders for the title in recent years. Lyndon Johnson,

Spiro Agnew, George Wallace...we've had no shortage of men willing to lie, cheat, steal, and practice human sacrifice to advance their own greedy and selfish ends. All the more reason that McCall feels like a cold splash of water in the face after an all-night bender...not just your usual drunken revel, but the kind that leaves your liquor cabinet empty, your girlfriend whimpering quietly, the dog fleeing for its safety, and your home a smoking ruin. But I digress.

With McCall, the country hasn't seen such a plain-talking straight shooter in the White House since the days of Harry Truman. Almost a year into the new administration, the honeymoon between the President and the people shows no signs of wearing off.

McCall is single-handedly credited with saving this country from a dictatorship, or worse. (My last bad acid trip was a dark vision of a parallel universe where Watergate went undetected and the Nixon presidency rolled on. The last thing I remember was that I was locked in a concentration camp; after that I collapsed into complete madness.) McCall's popularity during his first year in office has only rivaled Johnson's in the dark bloody days following Dallas.

It seems to take a crisis to bring out people's love for a President these days.

Still, McCall does seem like the genuine article. Republican chieftains haven't forgiven him for his manhandling of Nixon, but the party rank and file, who had lost hope that their team would ever win another election in their lifetimes, now see him as the savior of not only the nation but their party. It's hard to avoid drawing parallels to the last Republican president of similar stature, a Kentuckian who guided us through the Civil War. That choice worked out pretty well for the country too.

Abraham Lincoln is remembered for his lack of pretense. He was a self-educated product of the backwoods, and while many celebrated him as a man of the people then and now, several of his contemporaries called him a baboon, a gorilla...and some less complimentary things.

McCall has generated similar reactions. Forget the D and R labels for a moment and remember that Washington, first and foremost, is a company town. You can't swing too far from accepted protocol in one direction or the other without there being consequences from the ruling class. Nixon raised eyebrows about five years ago when he outfitted the White House Secret Service detail in uniforms that featured double-breasted white tunics, gold piping, draped braid and high plastic hats. The charitable observers said they were reminiscent of old-time movie ushers; the cynics insisted they evoked the Praetorian Guard.

The storm of ridicule forced Nixon to mothball the outfits after two weeks. Delusions of monarchy aren't acceptable, but too much informality isn't exactly welcomed either. You just can't please everybody, especially these days.

"You know when it really sunk in that I was president?" McCall asks. "Not when I put my hand on the Bible and took the oath of office. Not when Audrey and Sam and I spent our first night in the White House. It was the first time that big black limousine delivered me to Andrews and we pulled up alongside Air Force One. I got out of the car and looked up at that big blue and white 707 with 'United States of America' splashed across it, the American flag on its tail, and I realized it was there for me. Me. Tom McCall. I was amazed. In fact, I'm still amazed."

While most of the country remains as astonished by the unlikely meteoric rise of the nation's thirty-eighth chief executive as does the man himself, there's at least one person who seems to believe the position was nothing less than his due—eighty-seven year old Dorothy Lawson McCall, the First Mother.

President McCall's mother is the daughter of Thomas W. Lawson, "The Copper King," who once controlled every scrap of copper in the United States. McCall's paternal grandfather, Samuel Walker McCall, served as governor of Massachusetts after spending a couple of decades in the U.S. House of Representatives. That's a pretty heavy duty lineage on both sides of the family tree. It's not a surprise that the president's father yearned to break free from the shadow of his forebearers, and decamped for the great west.

In those vast plains, Hal McCall became a moderately successful rancher and Dorothy preached to the future president and his four siblings about the specialness of their family line and their obligation to give back to society. Sort of a western version of the Kennedys, sans the guns and booze and Mafia whores.

If there's one thing the American People love even more than a rags-to-riches story, it's a riches-to-rags-to-riches story. At the turn of the century, Thomas W. Lawson was worth forty or fifty million bucks, which was real money in those days....and still isn't a bad wad to be walking around with today. But at some point, the river of gold ran dry, and by the 1930s, power at the McCall ranch in Central Oregon was being shut off for non-payment of bills and the children wore hand-me-downs instead of new clothes. The McCalls let the hired help go, and Dorothy learned to cook, as well as keeping the rambling five-fireplace, five-bath structure clean by herself.

By the time young Tom McCall entered college during the depression, the family's fortunes were at their lowest ebb; Thomas W. Lawson the multi-millionaire had gambled big in the stock market, won big and lost big, and had the misfortune to meet his maker during a down cycle, dying penniless. As a result, mother McCall had to hock some jewels and other heirlooms to pay her son's tuition at the University of Oregon. But Dorothy McCall has never lost her Brahmin accent or her regal bearing, despite sixty years in Oregon and rising and falling bank accounts.

"Of course Nixon did the right thing by choosing my son," she declares, a double Manhattan adding high color to her cheeks. "It was one of the few good things that horrible man did. The country is lucky to have Tom. They should have had him sooner." It's as if she knew her son was destined for the presidency one day.

"He's the perfect person to follow a crook like Nixon," Dorothy—Baba to her grandchildren—declares. "If he has a fault, it's his candor. Most politicians are sly. Tom has never been sly."

All who know mother and son say they are clearly devoted to each other, but the relationship is not without its strains. The tale is told that at one point early in his governorship, McCall changed his home phone number and didn't let his mother know. He was sitting at his desk when he was told the president was on the phone.

"Tom?" Lyndon Johnson drawled. "I just had a nice chat with your mother. She wants you to call her."

Dorothy McCall's voice, is, no doubt, even more familiar to the White House switchboard these days.

The President has also kept his mother at arm's length during his campaigns, something that's not surprising when you realize she puts even her famous son to shame in the candor department. With the slightest prompting she will volunteer stories like the one from the summer of 1917, when the future president was four. She sent him out into the garden of Westernwold, the McCall estate in central Oregon, to plant sweet peas with his older brother Harry. Dorothy shared the gem with Portland magazine writer Tom Bates:

"Harry was my little businessman. He was just digging away. Tom, that round, curly-haired little rascal, just sat there. Then all of a sudden he picked up a worm, held it up like that, dropped it in his mouth and swallowed it. And my sister said to me, 'Oh, Dote, don't try to make a farmer out of that boy. He's an artist.'"

It's clear that Dorothy McCall will go down in the history books alongside Sara Delano Roosevelt and Nancy Hanks Lincoln as one of the most influential First Mothers. As I down one more Manhattan with the First Mother, I can't help but think the country got lucky. But isn't it what we deserved after Nixon?

As the hard edges of the room start to blur, I begin to realize much to my horror that an 87-year-old woman is about to drink me under the table. My admiration for the McCall family takes another quantum leap upward. I contemplate petitioning the president to give his mother a significant role in the administration. She toyed with running for the statehouse in Salem herself last year, but sadly backed away from the idea, allowing a conventional Republican hack to claim her son's chair. No matter; she could be an ambassador. Imagine the president sending his mother to Paris, Moscow or Peking....

Her temper is legendary; she is rumored to have once threatened to blow up the headquarters of The Oregonian, the state's largest newspaper. On second thought, her son might want to choose another emissary if he wants to continue on the path of normalizing U.S.-China relations...

McCall's detractors—and you can find them in this green paradise—are quick to note that he's shown feet of clay on occasion. They point to the first time he ran for Congress, back in 1954. He knocked off the Republican incumbent, Homer Angell, in the primary, but then made the mistake of bowing to pressure from Republican bosses and running as a conventional conservative in the fall.

His opponent was Edith Green, a lobbyist for the Oregon Education Association. In what he now calls the most shameful moment of his life, McCall attacked Green as a puppet of labor and mocked her for being a good homemaker. The speech backfired badly; although the race had looked close, McCall went down in flames. (Green went on to hold the seat for two decades and voluntarily retired from Congress just last year.)

It's a testament to McCall's innate likability that the day after that election, Green told reporters, "I really don't think he has a mean bone in his body," and today considers him a friend.

McCall had given up a steady position as a political commentator on local radio to make the race. Now his career and his reputation were in tatters. It took him a decade to rebuild, but when he ran for Oregon Secretary of State in 1964, he was determined to do so as his own man. It's been a pretty impressive run in the decade since.

Yet speculation abounds in Washington that McCall will not be a candidate for a term in his own right in 1976, that like Cincinnatus, he is ready to lay down his sword and return to his plow. The president himself, rarely known to play coy with the press, insists on being taken at his word when he says, "When I say I don't know if I'm going to run next year, that's exactly what I mean. I don't know."

McCall speaks in what one Oregon journalist calls a "raspy Massachusetts cowboy drawl." Some of his critics accuse him of using a phony English accent. McCall himself likes to quote a friend who coined the phrase "Ivy League Barnyard." Dorothy McCall, who has known him the longest, insists his unique voice is the product of the Central Oregon drawl mixed with the Massachusetts accent. The sprawling central Oregon estate where Dorothy and the president's late father Hal raised the future president and his four siblings still belongs to the family, though Dorothy spends most of the year in a Portland apartment smaller than Westernwold's servant quarters.

The President agreed to take me through the old house, much of it frozen in amber from shortly after old Tom Lawson built it for his daughter and son-in-law more than sixty years ago. Televisions and radios are conspicuous by their absence. Most of the lights are wall-mounted and covered with glass flower-printed shades. The light switches are still of the old push button kind, white on, black off.

The bookshelves are still filled with the volumes shipped across the country along with fine linens, crystal and china. "Mother would read to us for hours every night," McCall says, pulling a book from the shelf. He points to the title. "Letters and Speeches of Oliver Cromwell, with Elucidations by Thomas Carlyle" he reads, peering at the cover. "How'd you like to dig into that when you're seven years old?"

There was plenty of fare to feed a youngster's imagination as well: Beatrix Potter, "The Wonderful Wizard of Oz," the stories of King Arthur, Howard Pyle's "Book of Pirates," Stevenson, Dickens, Milne, Lamb's "Tales From Shakespeare" and Scott's "Waverly Novels." The magic of words was infused into his bloodstream from the beginning, or maybe before the beginning; both Grandfather Lawson and Grandfather McCall had several books to their credit, and a stream of journalism issued from both their pens.

Baba continued the reading habit with her grandchildren, something first son Tad McCall fondly recalls. "My grandmother is a powerful influence on us all," he told me. "She's the power in the family. It's the finest reward a person could have, to sit on the bed with grandma as she read. She has this tremendously sharp New England accent, which she passed on to my father and his siblings. The words were pure as water."

Presidential nephew Sandy McCall still remembers his childhood introduction to the great house's playroom, a huge loft on the third floor, ruled by the rocking horse Pegasus and giant stuffed animals, including a bear, camel and elephant.

Dorothy McCall sternly admonished him: "All these were shipped out from F.A.O. Schwartz in a private boxcar. They were the gifts of the Copper King to his grandchildren. Have a care you treat them as well as they did."

The McCall clan continued to gather at Westernwold for holidays and significant milestones even as the children reached adulthood and started families of their own. Tad McCall says his grandmother would cook for the entire clan as well as keeping house. Once learned, the ways of thrift can be difficult to unlearn.

In the sagebrush surrounding the house, McCall and I took turns shooting at a series of targets I had set up, and while he was at pains to make sure I knew it had been years since he had picked up a rifle, he did not embarrass himself. I asked him if he could remember his first shooting experience.

"My mother had been given a pair of custom-made pearl-handled revolvers by her father. They're still hanging on display on the living room wall. One day, when I was about ten, I took them down, loaded them and took them outside." There the future President saw a couple of neighbor boys and proposed a game of cops and robbers. The boys went to hide behind some nearby boulders. When one of them popped out of his hiding place, young Tommy McCall fired and nicked him. It was a long time before he was allowed near another loaded weapon.

We then retired to the porch of the house as the sun was going down to partake of a bottle of Gordon's gin I had stashed in the kit bag I always carry with me. Audrey McCall produced a couple of martini glasses and a small bottle of vermouth. One of the Secret Service brigade surrounding the president toted the briefcase with the nuclear launch codes McCall could use to rain destruction down on the Godless Commies. That thirty-pound black case is known as "the football." I prefer to score in a different manner, and McCall seemed to appreciate the distinction.

He had shooed away the agent who approached when I produced the bottle, but the goon was right back on top of us when I pulled out some high-grade pot and a pipe. Being the gracious guest that I am, I wanted to share all my good fortune with my host. Once more, the president waved off the gorilla in the black suit.

"Thank you Hunter, but no thanks," McCall said, lifting his martini. "This will stay my drug of choice." No evil Nixonian rants on the dangers of illicit substances. But this wasn't a surprise from the man who testified before the National Commission on Marijuana and Drug Abuse in San Francisco four years ago and had the balls to tell the assembled Wise Minds:

"Those whose minds are made up, and who accept no facts and no discussion on legalization remind me of the scholars who refused to look into Galileo's telescope, fearing the Devil might lead them into the effort of believing the earth was round.

"And those who would rush headlong into legalization immediately cannot claim to be any better informed.

"The studies we need now should have begun in 1938 when marijuana was first banned. We suffer from that long and trouble-breeding gap. Let us suffer no longer. Let us study....Let us get the best scientific and medical heads in America into this issue. Let us find out what the facts are. Let's reason with this question. Let's act from wisdom and examination—not from prejudice or panic."

Brave words in 1971. Still brave today. But will he be willing to translate them into action?

We watched the sun set against the Cascades that evening. I gazed up at the Rimrock, the great basalt formation that rises two hundred feet above the ranch and runs for miles, and I could see where the future president developed his love of nature. The Crooked River is just a short hike from the front door. No wonder he's already developing a reputation for wanting to escape to home as frequently as possible.

As the last light of the day began to fade, I asked the president if he missed anything about life before the White House. "It would be the height of ingratitude for me to complain when I'm living like an Arab Sheik in one of the most beautiful homes in the world," he said. "But there are some things I miss. Like Audrey's cooking."

The First Lady is an accomplished home economist, and the McCalls have been a classic meat and potatoes family. The president fondly remembers his wife preparing rare rump roast for Sunday dinner, "so tender and delicious." He carved it on the sideboard, and all four McCalls enjoyed hearty portions. Ham, chicken, roast beef, legs of lamb, wild duck (courtesy of brother Harry, an avid hunter), and of course the salmon, steelhead and trout that the leader of the free world brings home from his labors at water's edge all graced the McCall table. In the White House, it wouldn't do for the First Lady to don an apron and prepare a meal herself. Just one more reason the McCalls look forward to their escapes to home.

As I gaze up at the clear canopy of twinkling stars, I realize that this place is the headwater of the river of McCall's life. Everything began here—the passion for public service, the love of words, the symbiotic relationship to the environment. This is the kind of setting—the beauty, the isolation—ideal for nurturing a rich inner life. Coming from a line of high achievers, especially grandfathers Lawson and McCall, could have been a crushing burden for a lesser youngster; but young Tom McCall managed to lift that burden and carry the family name to a glory even his most illustrious ancestors could have envisioned. But it didn't come easily.

The calm starlit night put the President in a particularly expansive mood, and he let his guard down to a degree unusual even for him.

Although the family homestead holds countless warm memories, there are other ghosts of a less pleasant nature lurking about; ghosts that bring memories of a shy, frightened child to the forefront. He still shudders as he recalls being locked alone in an attic for punishment. As a child he also feared the dark and being in a room with one person. Even into adulthood, air travel and speaking in public can bring knots to his stomach.

He points to the slough and recalls a childhood moment with his Aunt Bunny (Jean Lawson Edwards) who, "One cold sunset in winter, took my tiny trembling hand and said, 'How will God take care of this frightened child?"

But gradually the future president emerged from his shell, especially after older brother Harry graduated from Prineville High. Tom was student body president, coached the baseball team, played the saxophone in the band and sang, and even went out for football, though he carried just 130 pounds on his six-foot three frame at the time. He says his knees still provide painful daily reminders of that rash decision.

He became daring enough to smoke in front of the school where the principal could see him. As I affix another Dunhill in my holder, he tells me that he finally kicked tobacco a few years ago after a bout with pneumonia. I light up, nod, take a deep drag and say, "Good for you, Mr. President."

Continuing our theme of exploring the state's Great Outdoors, after a night at Westernwold, we decamped to the North Umpqua River. The North Umpqua is renowned for some of the most challenging steelhead fishing in the world, in part because that's the truth, and in part because a dime novelist helped spread the word.

Zane Grey, who wrote some of the purplest prose ever immortalized between hardcovers and got rich in the bargain, loved to fish the North Umpqua. He discovered it in the early thirties after his own writings made the Rogue River too popular—something he then proceeded to complain about. A classic example of chutzpa, fitting the best definition of that phrase I've ever heard—the tale of the man who murdered his parents then pleaded for clemency from the court because he was now an orphan.

Although Grey is credited with creating the modern fishing industry on the north Umpqua, he is not fondly remembered by the locals. He didn't endear himself to them when he would send out his stooges in the predawn hours to shoo the natives away from his favorite spots, a cardinal breach of fishing etiquette that says first come, first served.

I'm a deep sea fisherman myself, but in the interests of getting closer to my subject, I agreed to climb into hip boots and waders and venture into the frigid Oregon waters. McCall had shown me a photo of an eight-pound steelhead he landed a couple of years ago. He said it was the first he had ever caught on a fly, and only the eighteenth he had landed by any means in almost a half century. "It took me almost an hour to land her, and she was so exhausted she died in my hands. I was so sorry I'd ever caught her."

Almost all of the McCall family vacations have been fishing trips, exploring the lakes, streams and rivers of the Beaver State. It's clear the President cherishes every opportunity to fish he gets and is determined to make the most of it. Outdoors reporter Jim Conway, a onetime colleague on Portland television, remembers: "When we'd get a heavy shower some us might park ourselves under a tree, but Tom would grab his rod and keep right on fishing in the rain."

Conway affirms that McCall's angling skills aren't more polished because of a lack of enthusiasm but because of a lack of time.

Although it is the duty of every good fisherman to spin tall tales about his adventures, I have to follow the example of brutal, open candor set by my fishing partner (and acknowledge there were too many witnesses) and admit that neither of us brought any North Umpqua steelhead to the point of fatal exhaustion that day.

This trip was planned as a vacation for the president, without any official business or public appearances, but he couldn't resist an invitation to throw out the first pitch at a Portland Mavericks baseball game, so we made a quick swing through the state's largest city. I should have let my friend and colleague, Raoul Duke, handle this part of the assignment, since the Sports Desk is his territory, but he graciously agreed to let Yours Truly stay on the story.

The Mavericks, who play in an aging concrete bunker in the heart of downtown, are the Dead End Kids of professional baseball; they have no major league affiliation, and they regularly dominate the league with a ragtag collection of castoffs from the bigs.

It was fitting that the starting pitcher this night was Jim Bouton, who made himself a pariah in the cloistered, prudish world of baseball five years ago by publishing Ball Four, *a diary of his 1969 season that revealed players using amphetamines to boost their performance, playing under the influence of intoxicants, and (gasp) engaging in sexual intercourse with women who were not their wives.*

Bouton has been making a nice salary reading the sports scores on New York television news, but he's taken a leave of absence to see if, at the ripe old age of 36, he can resurrect his pitching career with the Mavericks. He and the president posted for photos prior to the first-ball ceremony.

"They say I'm a maverick, too," McCall told the pitcher as he shook his hand.

"Then you should feel right at home tonight, Mr. President," Bouton responded.

In the early days of his career, Bouton relied on an overpowering fastball to get opposing hitters out. Then his arm went dead, and he turned to the knuckleball, a mysterious pitch that dances on the currents of the wind. A good knuckleball forces a hitter to guess at its destination, and he usually loses. McCall has unleashed the political equivalent of the knuckleball on Washington, and The Establishment hasn't caught on yet. And yes, the President heartily enjoyed the game, even though the men in black suits and mirrored sunglasses made him watch from the security of the press box. The beer was cold and the hot dogs were hot and Bouton and the Mavericks sent the Walla Walla Padres home in shame; they were on the losing end of a 9-2 drubbing.

We had to make one more stop before our journey through Oregon's scenic wonders was complete: we had to visit the president's beloved Oregon Coast.

McCall and his wife Audrey bought a weekend retreat several years ago in Road's End, an unincorporated community on the central coast of Oregon about ninety minutes southwest of Portland. Although the setting offers access to miles of open beaches and postcard vistas, the homes themselves are rustic, shoehorned side by side, and very human in scale....nothing like the walled compound at San Clemente which the taxpayers spent millions to convert into a fortified bunker for Tricky Dick.

Once McCall became president, the Secret Service declared Road's End off limits to him. The McCalls have rented another beachfront house in Salishan, a gated community a few miles to the south, and have steadfastly refused any proposals for security upgrades. No sniper's nests, spotlights or booby traps.

The president is reported to be an enthusiastic but moderately skilled golfer. Inside sources say he shows a lot of strength off the tee, and works on his game when the opportunity presents itself. He declined my invitation to go out on the links of Salishan's golf course. "Too much of a hassle these days," he says with a sad sigh and a nod toward the gorillas in black.

While the image of Nixon striding down the San Clemente beach in business suit and wingtips will haunt the collective American psyche forever, McCall loves to put on an old plaid quilted jacket and actually explore the rugged beachscape, clambering over rocks and splashing through tidepools.

It's a joy he rarely indulges in these days due to his sense of guilt over the Secret Service goons shooing away any visitors who come within eyesight of the chief executive. As governor, McCall rammed through a measure guaranteeing the public's unimpeded right of access to these sands, and is on the verge of pushing a similar measure through Congress that would do the same nationally. He'll be damned if he'll let anyone, including himself, keep people off of them.

The irony of it is not lost on the thirty-eighth president. Most of the time, he and Audrey sit on the deck of the house and watch the tides from a distance. Audrey McCall seems content to relax and breathe in the invigorating salt air so different from the damp blanket of humidity that hangs over D.C. much of the year, but the president paces the weathered boards like a caged lion. A plate of crackers and cheese remains untouched. A frosty cold bottle of beer sits for a long time before the Leader of the Free World downs half of it in a single long gulp.

McCall resumes his pacing. He gazes at something unseen in the distance. He broods in silence for a bit before blurting out a statement you could never imagine coming from the mouth of Richard Nixon: "It is the damndest life you ever knew."

3

The door to the Oval Office swung open and Richard Nixon's chief of staff, retired General Alexander Haig, strode in with a sense of purpose.

The thirty-seventh president of the United States was a man under siege. For more than a year, the Watergate affair had been building until it dominated the front pages of the nation's newspapers and the nightly network news. What had started with the discovery of an attempt to plant wiretaps at the Democratic Party's national headquarters had mushroomed into an abuse of power scandal that now threatened to end his presidency.

"General," Nixon said with a forced smile. "Good to see you."

Haig, his military-straight posture intact in civilian life, nodded slightly. "Good to see you, Mr. President."

Nixon pointed Haig toward the couch in front of his desk. As Haig sat, Nixon moved to a chair opposite the couch, and close to the fireplace. Nixon liked the warmth of a fire, no matter what the time of year; he would have the White House air conditioning turned up if needed to keep things comfortable.

The relationship between the two men was formal, stiff and a bit distant; neither liked informality in working relationships. It had been just a little over five months since Haig had replaced H.R. Haldeman as Nixon's chief of staff, Haldeman having been sacrificed as the stain of Watergate seeped deeper into the president's inner circle. Although the Nixon-Haldeman relationship had stretched back to Nixon's 1956 vice presidential campaign, the two men had never been close personally.

Now, as October began, a second, totally separate scandal was reaching a fever pitch; Nixon's vice-president, Spiro ("Ted") Agnew, had accepted bribes from contractors doing business with the state while serving as Governor of Maryland. It looked like Agnew would have no choice but to become the second vice president in U.S. history to resign. It was a situation without precedent. The only other vice president to step down, John C. Calhoun, had done so 141 years earlier to accept appointment to a seat in the U.S. Senate.

"Well, what about the Agnew situation?" Nixon said.

Haig shuffled through a pile of papers on his lap. "It's not looking good, Mr. President. The most likely scenario is resignation and a negotiated criminal plea."

Nixon shook his head. "Ted was foolish, absolutely foolish. Well, this means an appointment. For obvious reasons, we have to be very careful with this one."

"I understand perfectly, Mr. President. We've already been sounding out the Congressional leadership. They seem to be very strong for Representative Ford."

Nixon snorted. "Jerry Ford? You have got to be kidding me. He still hasn't lived down Lyndon Johnson's crack about playing football without his helmet too long. No, not *Jerry*." Nixon sighed. Although Agnew still clung to the job, the speculation about his replacement was already in full swing. Some Congressional Democrats had already declared they wouldn't support any replacement who was a potential presidential candidate, saying they only wanted to consider a caretaker to keep the seat warm for the remainder of the term. Republicans found themselves doing a difficult dance. They didn't want to concede that Nixon was such badly damaged goods his survival was in question, but felt they had to make the case that any vice president needed the qualifications and stature to assume the presidency if the need arose.

"There will be lots of conventional choices floating around, I'm sure,"

Nixon said."Reagan, Rockefeller....but I think this is a moment that calls for the unconventional."

It didn't surprise Haig that Nixon brushed aside Reagan without a second thought. There had been speculation about Reagan as a potential running mate for Nixon in 1968, but he had squelched the idea, calling him a "know nothing" in foreign policy and telling Tom Wicker of the *New York Times* that he wouldn't put the California governor next in line for the presidency. Although Nixon liked Reagan personally, his opinion of his political acumen hadn't improved in the ensuing years. Rockefeller had been a long-time political rival, and Nixon wasn't enthusiastic about handing him the opportunities that would go with the vice presidency. As for Haig, he considered himself a serious man, and was grateful for the opportunity to serve a true statesman like Nixon; he couldn't *ever* see himself in the employ of someone as vapid as the movie star-turned governor.

Haig showed just the hint of a grin. "I think I've got a name that will appeal to you Mr. President. The Oregon Governor. McCall."

"Tom?" Nixon seemed taken aback at first. McCall was increasingly seen as a maverick in a Republican party that was moving rightward. McCall and Agnew had clashed famously; McCall, never shy about sharing his opinions, had once described the vitriolic Agnew as being "like a man with a knife in his shawl." In 1970, McCall had generated headlines when he called an angry tirade by Agnew at the Republican governor's conference a "rotten, bigoted little speech." Part of McCall's ire, no doubt, had been sparked by the fact the outburst was largely directed at him. It had been an attack on Republicans who Agnew thought hadn't shown sufficient loyalty to the administration.

The statement immediately went public; the next day, as the conference continued, Agnew confronted McCall, clutching a crumpled piece of copy from the Associated Press newswire. "Tom," he demanded, not trying to hide his exasperation. "Did you really call it a 'rotten, bigoted little speech?'"

McCall looked thoughtful, then slightly sheepish.

"I'm not sure I said 'little.'"

It wasn't the first time McCall and Agnew had clashed over the vice-president's tactics. Agnew's response to McCall on that earlier occasion had represented what McCall considered to be politics at its worst: "There's only one way to campaign and you're very naïve if you don't know it. You've got to chew your opponent's nuts out before he chews out yours."

Nixon wasn't a man to live in the past, except for his own, and he had already consigned Agnew to a footnote in his story. He considered Haig's proposal carefully. McCall had clashed with the administration in 1970 over a proposal to store outdated chemical weapons at the Umatilla Army Depot. The Defense Department's plans had been stymied when McCall led a public crusade that flooded the Pentagon and White House with tens of thousands of petition signatures opposing the idea. That same year, the governor had annoyed the White House by agreeing to the first and only state-sponsored rock festival in history, Vortex I, a "biodegradable festival of life."

Nixon had been scheduled to address the American Legion's 1970 national gathering in Portland, and less than two years after the bloody riots at the Democratic Party's Chicago convention, anti-war protesters were threatening to converge on the city for a violent confrontation with authorities that would make Chicago seem like "a tea party." McCall, who was in a tough battle for re-election as governor, agreed to the unorthodox plan, famously telling his staff he had "committed political suicide." About 100,000 young people went to Vortex, which took place at a state park 30 miles south of Portland. The music, food, drugs and sex were all out in the open and free. The mass protest in the city never materialized. Apparently making love was more appealing than making war.

The only mischief in the city during the convention, McCall later said, was a broken window. By supporting this safety valve, McCall provoked the wrath of the White House, where some staffers like speechwriter Pat Buchanan were eager for violence; Nixon's appearance was cancelled and the hatchet man Agnew was sent in his place.

But McCall had remained a loyalist to the administration's Vietnam strategy even as anti-war protests intensified nationally, just as he had backed Lyndon Johnson's prosecution of the war. McCall had walked a fine line on Watergate up to this point. The previous June, when Wisconsin Governor Patrick Lucey, a Democrat, had called on Nixon to resign to avoid impeachment, McCall had responded: "There's no question the president has been severely damaged by the affair. But if the president is guilty of anything, it's misfeasance. That's not an impeachable matter."

The nation's tallest governor had also provoked the White House's ire when he vetoed legislation that would have reined in farm workers' rights to unionize following the 1971 Legislative session. The administration had planned to use the Oregon bill as a template for national legislation. The Undersecretary of Labor, Larry Silberman, gave McCall a tongue lashing for derailing that opportunity.

Grudgingly, Nixon admitted to himself that McCall had shown foresight on occasion. In the fall of 1970, he had come out publicly for wage and price controls, which led to a tongue-lashing from Federal Reserve Chairman Arthur Burns who warned McCall that step would put the United States on the road toward socialism. Of course, Burns had helped steer Nixon to just such a move the following summer.

As Nixon weighed the totality of the McCall record, he was willing to forgive incidents like Vortex and the confrontation over the nerve gas. As a consummate politician, Nixon understood the necessity of playing to the home crowd. He realized some of McCall's more liberal acts would provoke the ire of the most conservative elements of the party, but Nixon felt confident in his ability to contain any backlash.

"Yes," Nixon finally said. "I think McCall is an inspired choice. No one will be able to say the President chose a yes man."

"Very good, Mr. President," Haig said with a nod. "We'll begin a full background check."

On the opposite end of the continent a couple of hours later, Ed Westerdahl was speeding down Interstate 5, approaching Oregon's state capitol of Salem. Westerdahl and his friend Ron Schmidt had helped McCall become Oregon's secretary of state in 1964 and then win the governorship two years later. Westerdahl had functioned as McCall's chief of staff during the first term, but had left shortly after the 1970 election to take over management of the Port of Portland. Both men had yet to reach the age of forty; but McCall depended on them above all others who had worked for him, and they commanded respect both inside and outside the government. They won regard for their intelligence, their capacity for hard work, their vision and their ability to help their boss keep his prodigious energies focused. Both were driven, focused and articulate; their dress and their speech were extremely precise.

Westerdahl was puzzled by the phone call he had received from McCall, all but ordering him to come to the Capitol building. He found it strange that the normally voluble McCall refused to drop even the slightest hint about the reason for the call. Westerdahl was a straightforward, no-nonsense sort, but he wasn't above baiting his ex-boss a little, saying it was lucky he had filled his gas tank the day before, since he couldn't buy gas today. Normally, McCall would have had some sort of pointed response about Westerdahl's ability to plan ahead, but he had merely said, "Ed, please. Just get down here."

Under the ingeniously simple plan that McCall had advanced to deal with the Arab oil embargo and the resulting gas crisis that had generated long lines at filling stations, people could only buy gas every other day, based on whether their license plate ended in an odd or even number. It was the brainchild of one of his advisers, Don Jarvi, and it had taken less than twenty-four hours for it to make the journey from inspiration to reality.

Westerdahl parked in front of the late-thirties marble edifice that served as Oregon's capitol. He stepped through the heavy revolving door at the building's entrance and found himself in the rotunda, the bronze great seal of the state set into the center of the marble floor. Although he had been in this building every day for almost six years, it still filled him with a sense of awe. These surroundings were a reminder of the state's rich history and its future promise. His gaze traveled upward from the seal to the soaring dome above. He paused briefly to glance at the huge murals portraying Oregon's pioneer heritage, then hurried to the governor's office on the second floor.

"What the hell is going on, Doris?" Westerdahl asked Doris Penwell, the governor's executive secretary.

She arched an eyebrow. "All I know is he got a call from the White House first thing this morning. You'll have to find out the details yourself. He's got Ron in there with him, waiting, but I don't think he's even told him yet."

Westerdahl nodded, hesitating momentarily before pointing at Penwell's legs. "Slacks, Doris?" he asked. He wasn't used to seeing a woman wearing something other than a dress in a state office.

"New dress code," she said with a slight grin. "You notice how *cold* it is in here?"

Westerdahl stepped into the cubbyhole where McCall did most of his work. The big office visitors saw was mainly for public ceremonies. The governor's back was turned toward his guests; he was looking out the window. Schmidt stood to greet his old colleague and friend.

Schmidt nodded slightly in McCall's direction as he anticipated Westerdahl's question. "No, I don't know what's going on. He said he wanted to tell us both at the same time."

McCall swirled around in his chair. Westerdahl could see that his old boss' prominent jaw was set tight.

"What's this all about, Tom?"

McCall almost growled: "Sit down, Ed. You're not going to believe this."

Tom McCall had arrived at this moment because of his unique personality, skills and achievements, but it didn't hurt that he *looked* the part of a governor. As a young man, McCall had been something of a stringbean—friends teasingly called him Ichabod Crane—but until not too long before he had topped the scale at 230 pounds, which he wore well on his six-foot-five frame.

The governor was sixty years old and still looked to be in his physical prime, despite having survived a very recent and very public bout with prostate cancer. He had broad shoulders, silver-gray hair, an engaging smile and penetrating blue eyes that truly reflected his state of mind at the moment, whether it be animated, restless, or troubled. Westerdahl was looking into the eyes of a man who was processing many things at once.

Most politicians did a good job of hiding their feelings behind a face of false cheerfulness; McCall had never mastered that art, and this was one of the reasons Oregonians embraced him so warmly. He was candid—genuine.

Westerdahl settled into the chair and waited. He realized Penwell was right; the office *was* cold. The governor, who had ordered the heat turned down in all state buildings to help conserve energy, was wearing a tweed jacket over a blue cardigan. When the silence became uncomfortable, Westerdahl finally spoke: "Well?"

When McCall spoke, he almost spat out the words: "Al Haig called this morning. He wanted me to know they're considering me for vice president if Agnew resigns."

Both men blanched. Once he absorbed the initial shock, Schmidt blurted, "My God, Tom, do you know what this means?"

"It means they want to stick me in the job Jack Garner said wasn't worth a bucket of warm piss."

"I thought he said warm spit," Westerdahl said.

"They sanitized it," McCall said, grinning. "You know, that man spent eight years as vice president under Roosevelt—being a real pain in the keister to FDR, by the way—but do we remember him for anything other than that statement?"

Schmidt couldn't help but smile as well, but he didn't want the conversation to stray off course. "That's not what I meant Tom, and you know it. This means that you could be the next president of the United States."

McCall turned so his back was to the two men again; he gazed out at the street below. Westerdahl and Schmidt sensed he needed to sort out the thoughts that were churning through his head.

"Ed, Ron, you know the only way Nixon is leaving the White House before the end of his term is in chains or in a pine box." McCall turned to face them once more: "Oh, and Haig asked for my tax returns for the past ten years, even though I'm sure they could get them from the IRS themselves. And they want complete medical records. Want to make sure I'm clear of cancer." A pause. "Why me? Why me?" McCall demanded.

Westerdahl knew that McCall expected and appreciated candor above all else. "Well, Tom, you know how they've been calling Agnew Nixon's insurance policy for years. No one would ever impeach Nixon or try to kill him for fear of what they'd unleash with an Agnew presidency. I imagine they're looking at you in the same way. You are too much of a wild card."

McCall nodded in apparent agreement. He hunched forward and scowled as he furiously scribbled notes on a legal pad.

Westerdahl understood the turmoil that his friend and former boss was feeling. He knew McCall was already restless with the end of his second term as governor in sight. The state constitution barred him from seeking a third consecutive term in 1974. Some were suggesting McCall run for Congress, but Westerdahl knew McCall's heart wasn't in Washington; it was right here, in the state he loved with a deep and lasting passion.

"Tom, if the offer comes, you have to take it. I know you love this job, and I'm sure you hate the thought of leaving before your term is finished, but let's be realistic. The Legislature is done until after you're out of here, unless you need to call a special session. Your record is written—and it's a hell of a record. Next year will basically be your victory lap. Very nice, but not a chance to accomplish a lot.

"If you take this appointment, and Nixon is impeached or resigns, it means that *you*, Tom McCall, become the thirty-eighth president of the United States. If Nixon somehow rides this thing out, it still positions you as a front-runner for the Republican nomination in 1976. And even if that doesn't happen....two-plus years as vice president of the United States isn't a bad way to cap your career and write your name into the history books."

"History books? Oh come on, Ed, you remember Thomas Marshall?"

Westerdahl was silent for a moment. "Woodrow Wilson's vice president?" he said hesitantly.

McCall nodded. "Remembered today for two quotes. He's the man who said what this country needs is a good five cent cigar. He also told the story of the woman who had two sons. One went to sea. The other became vice president. Neither was ever heard from again." At that moment, the serious cast of McCall's expression vanished, replaced by the winning grin that had endeared him to thousands of Oregonians.

"If the offer comes, I'll take it. On one condition."

"What's that, Tom?" asked Schmidt.

"That you both join me."

Westerdahl shot back: "Tom! We have lives here!"

"So do I, Ed. So do I. But if I'm going to wade into that viper's nest, I'm not doing it without you two. And I'm going to let Doris know I need her, too."

Westerdahl nodded. It would mean a major upheaval in all their lives, and in the lives of their families, but he didn't doubt they would join McCall if the opportunity came. He began wondering where he could find a suitable renter for his Portland home while he was in D.C., however long that might be.

Schmidt walked back to his desk, already mentally generating a list of phone calls he needed to make. One of the first would be to his friend John Phias. He, Phias and Westerdahl had been taking about establishing a public relations agency in Portland when McCall left office; obviously, those plans would be shelved indefinitely if this appointment came to pass. He leafed through his rolodex, picked up the phone, lit a cigarette, took a deep drag, and started dialing.

He should also call Gerry Frank, Senator Mark Hatfield's chief of staff and a member of one of the founding families of the Meier and Frank department store. Frank was known for his impeccable taste and Schmidt figured he would have a lead on good clothiers and tailors in the Washington area. Schmidt, who had earned a reputation as the office clothes horse, was always frustrated that McCall looked like he selected his suits off the rack at Sears. His outfits were timeless and appropriate to his position, but they didn't convey the fashion flair that Schmidt craved. McCall's wife Audrey had been his secret conspirator in trying to upgrade the governor's wardrobe; but now that effort would have to move to another level. A vice president often greeted visiting heads of state and other dignitaries, and appearances were important.

The relationships among those closest to Tom McCall were complex. Audrey liked Schmidt, almost thought of him as a third son, but there had been tension with Westerdahl at times; on more than one occasion she had accused him of working her husband too hard.

Audrey McCall had been a part of every major decision during their thirty-four years of marriage; so of course, they would talk this through as soon as the governor could get home. Tom McCall was a twenty-six year old sports reporter for the Moscow, Idaho daily paper when he was assigned to cover a cooking school sponsored by the local power company at the community Grange Hall. Idaho Power wanted to show off how easy it was to prepare a meal with modern electric appliances.

"When I walked in, there was this darling blonde girl seating old ladies and cooking roasts, steaks and cakes," McCall wrote in his memoirs. "She was Audrey Owen...and I was completely enthralled with her." McCall towered over the young woman, who stood just five-three. Years later, Audrey described the tall man who had shown up at her class as "a very hungry reporter," who sat down and ate her work.

They were married three months later, just a day after she had accepted his proposal. They tried to keep the marriage a secret so that the new bride could keep her job with the power company; two incomes in the same household were frowned on in this depression era. Word soon leaked out though, and the new Mrs. McCall joined the ranks of the unemployed. The newspaper gave her husband a $2.50 a week raise to help cushion the blow.

Audrey had been at his side through the decades, making a home wherever journalism or politics had taken them, raising their two sons, and offering wise counsel on any decision impacting Tom's career and their lives.

One of the major issues of discussion in the McCall household the night of the vice presidential offer was the impact on their two sons. Tad, twenty-nine, had been in the Navy since 1967. After distinguished service in Vietnam, he had considered leaving the military, but decided to stay in. He was stationed in San Diego and had just entered law school, the next step in a promising career. He was more than a thousand miles away, but at least he was in the same time zone, which wouldn't be the case if this move took place. But both parents were confident in the course of Tad's career and life.

But twenty-three year old Sam was a different story. He had struggled with drug addiction for years and was still seeking a stable path in life.

He still lived with his parents, and they wondered whether it would be wise to expose him to the glare of the Washington media spotlight.

"What about your mother?" Audrey asked. "She is going to be so proud!"

Tom smiled. It was a sly grin. "Well, I suppose so, Aud. But I don't have enough time to give her now. What's it going to be like if we go to Washington?"

As the McCalls settled in to discuss what was potentially the biggest transition of their lives, the appointment was still the main subject of discussion in the White House. Secretary of State Henry Kissinger joined Nixon for "a drink" in the second floor residence. Only a few lights were on and the curtains were drawn, adding to the air of gloom.

Kissinger was becoming concerned by Nixon's increasingly erratic behavior, including bouts of heavy drinking. Just a couple of nights earlier, he had refused to allow a call from the British Prime Minister to be put through to the president, telling a staffer that Nixon was "loaded." Kissinger thought it was an odd experience to play nanny to the most powerful man in the world. He barely touched his scotch and soda. He let Nixon ramble on that evening, offering just a few interjections as the president downed multiple martinis and railed against Agnew's stupidity. "Ted fucked up royally, Henry, do you realize that? He took crumbs from those contractors, absolute crumbs, and now his whole career, his whole goddamned life, is in the crapper." Nixon sighed deeply. "Well, at least this takes the focus off of Watergate for a while."

Kissinger nodded in agreement. "What about this new man, Mr. President, McCall?"

"A non-entity, an absolute non-entity. He's a newsman for God's sake, and you know how much love I have for them." Nixon tried to laugh, but it came out sounding stale and forced. "But he's an unknown, unlike Jerry Ford, who they wanted to shove down my throat." Nixon shook his head, and displayed just the hint of a grin. "That's part of the beauty of this. Kate Graham at the *Washington Post* and our Jewish friends at the *New York Times* won't know what the hell to make of McCall, because none of their goddamned liberal friends will have had time to tell them what to think." Nixon paused as he finished the thought and his third martini.

"If this goddamned Watergate thing doesn't go away, they might actually decide they can take the president down, and they'd probably be happy to have good old Jerry in here. But McCall? They don't have any idea what they'd be getting into, and that's exactly what I want."

Manalo Sanchez, Nixon's white-jacketed Cuban valet, delivered another martini on a silver tray, slipping in and out of the semi-darkness as quickly and as unobtrusively as he could. Nixon offered just the slightest nod of acknowledgement. Sometimes the president liked to make small talk, but Sanchez had learned to read his boss' moods, and he knew this was not one of those nights.

"And this will placate the environmentalists for a while," Nixon said, his scowl deepening. "Though it was probably a mistake to go too far down the road with them in the first place. John (Ehrlichman, Nixon's former chief domestic policy adviser) always pushed their agenda. He insisted it won us more friends than it cost us. He's a good man, damn it, but a little fuzzy headed when it comes to the outdoors." Nixon paused to drink.

Kissinger knew Nixon was seeking affirmation, and he was more than ready to offer it. "You didn't get to this place by being stupid, Mr. President. It is a brilliant feint, worthy of an Olympic fencing champion or a chess grand master."

Nixon nodded.

Kissinger didn't know a thing about McCall. "Where is he from? Oregon? Not exactly a place that's produced a lot of national leaders, is it?"

"Not a lot of men of substance," Nixon agreed. "Charles McNary, the senator, was on the ticket with Wendell Wilkie back in '40. The state mainly seems to produce peaceniks—Wayne Morse, Hatfield. McCall was always right on the war, though."

Nixon smiled. "But someone like McCall is absolutely no threat for the nomination in '76. Oregon has six votes in the Electoral College. Six. That's not a strong base for a winning campaign. As soon as things die down a bit, we can start laying the groundwork for Connally. I should really be sending his name up to the Hill, but there are issues that are better avoided at the moment. His change of party is too recent, for one thing. To use your chess metaphor, Henry, I don't want to expose my queen too soon. McCall will keep the chair warm, and that's all."

Kissinger understood Nixon's thinking. John Connally was Nixon's treasury secretary and the man he most wanted to see succeed him, but he had been a Democrat until May of 1973. He recalled Nixon had even toyed with dumping Agnew in 1972 and making Connally his second-term running mate, but had been talked out of the idea.

Nixon signaled for another drink. "We've done a lot to make the world a safer place, Henry, but we have to have a man in here with the balls to stand up to the Russians and Chinese if they suddenly decide they've got to prove their manhood. John will be the man, when that time comes."

A strange thought popped into Kissinger's head. Though the hour was approaching 11 p.m. Nixon was of course still in his suit jacket and tie; his perfectly polished wingtips remained on his feet. Kissigner had removed his jacket and loosened his tie, and wished he could kick off his shoes. Did Nixon ever actually undress? He pictured the president climbing into bed, still in business attire; in his minds' eye, he saw him walking into his morning shower dressed the same way. Was paranoia contagious?

He began mentally calculating how many days Nixon had left in office.

The conversation on the other side of the country in the McCall residence was very different from the talk on the second floor of the White House. No dark Machiavellian plotting; Tom McCall was mainly concerned if this was the right thing for his family. The weighing of options continued inside the governor's head late that night as he lay next to his sleeping wife. McCall was proud of what he'd achieved in his sixty years. The governorship had been a grand adventure, and his sense of destiny had always told him that something just as grand, or even greater, was still ahead. Now that the door was opening, the first tentacles of doubt came creeping in.

As he stared at the ceiling of the darkened room, he admitted to himself what he hadn't wanted to acknowledge to his friends, or even his wife: this really could be the beginning of a path that led to the presidency. He had been talking for a while about becoming a candidate as a way to tell his cherished "Oregon Story" from coast to coast and spread his concept of a Third Force—not just a third party for alienated Republicans and Democrats, but a broader movement to energize and engage Americans in building a better country. Would the opportunity be tainted if it came at Nixon's hand? Was it something he really wanted at all?

What rational man, he asked himself, truly lusted after that kind of power? What kind of man welcomed the authority to order young men into battle? What man wanted to be in a position where he might have to issue orders to launch nuclear weapons....orders that could lead to an exchange of missiles that could actually wipe humankind off the face of the Earth?

What man indeed?

It was nearly 3 a.m. before an exhausted Tom McCall finally drifted off to sleep.

4

Word that Oregon's popular governor might be headed to Washington spread rapidly. On a farm at Pleasant Hill, the state's greatest living novelist carried his copy of the *Eugene Register-Guard* inside the converted barn that was home to himself, his wife and three children, stomping the mud off his logging boots as he opened it. It had been a beautiful Indian summer, but the morning dampness and chill signaled that fall was taking hold. The headline splashed across the front page trumpeted the news: "McCall Said to Be V-P Pick."

"Faye!" Ken Kesey called to his wife as he read the headline. "There might be hope for this country after all." Kesey wasn't a fan of most politicians; he hadn't allowed a political leader to stir feelings of hope within him since John F. Kennedy's murder. But McCall was different.

The file photo accompanying the *Register-Guard* article featured the prospective vice-president alongside the embattled president. It had been taken in September, 1971 at the Portland airport. The president had stopped in Portland on his way to Alaska and a meeting with Hirohito, the Japanese emperor. Nixon, in the foreground, was turned to his right and smiling in the direction of McCall, who was about a foot behind him. McCall appeared to be looking at someone or something to Nixon's left. His grin appeared to be slightly pained. Although it was a compelling shot in its own way, many others thought another photo of the two men that appeared in several papers in Oregon and across the country better captured the reality of the moment.

That one was taken at the midwinter Republican Governor's Conference. There, Nixon and McCall shook hands. Both were flanked by their wives. The governor's grin was broad, his gaze direct; the president looked like he wanted to disappear into the floor, but there was already no escape from the web of deceit he and the men surrounding him had created.

Oregon's two United States Senators had very different reactions. Mark Hatfield, who had preceded McCall in the governorship and had a sometimes testy relationship with him, couldn't help but reflect on the irony that he had been on Nixon's short list of potential vice presidential running mates in 1968. Had Nixon chosen Hatfield, he would be the Oregonian a heartbeat away from the Presidency. But Hatfield was a man of deep religious faith, and was serene in the belief that things were developing according to a higher plan.

Bob Packwood, the state's junior senator, quickly issued a press release congratulating McCall and applauding the potential choice. Packwood, who had ousted Wayne Morse from the Senate in a close, bruising race in 1968, was publicly statesmanlike but privately jubilant. Packwood was up for re-election in 1974, just as McCall's term in the statehouse was ending. McCall had passed on challenging Hatfield in 1972, but there was growing speculation he would take on Packwood when the opportunity came.

McCall and Packwood had a complex relationship, born of mutual self-interest. McCall had been the only statewide officeholder to help Packwood organize the first Dorchester Conference, a gathering of progressive Republicans, in 1965. When the 1972 election approached, Packwood offered McCall covert support if he would take on Hatfield in the primary. McCall realized Packwood's motives weren't entirely altruistic; if McCall won, he would be removed as a potential opponent for Packwood, who would become the state's senior senator, with the additional prestige that entailed. But in the shifting sands of politics, a potential ally could just as quickly become a potential enemy.

Although Packwood didn't practice bare-knuckle politics with the intensity of an Agnew, he had already made it clear to McCall he was willing to wage an all-out fight for his own political survival if McCall chose to challenge him; nothing would be off the table, including Sam McCall's struggles with drug addiction and Tom's own use of alcohol.

Packwood briefly toyed with contacting the White House to make sure Nixon's staff was fully aware of McCall's maverick inclinations. Packwood was a student of history, and he remembered that Mark Hannah, one of the most powerful Republican bosses at the turn of the century, had tried a similar gambit in the 1900 election, when he engineered the selection of New York Governor Theodore Roosevelt as President William McKinley's second term running mate.

At the time, the choice of Roosevelt was seen as a crafty strategic move; shunting Roosevelt aside to the vice-presidency removed him from the New York statehouse, where he had been an unpleasant obstacle to powerful business interests that were the backbone of Republican support. But it backfired badly six months into McKinley's new term when he was assassinated.

"Now that damned cowboy is President!" Hannah had famously cried.

Packwood sat alone in his Senate office late at night contemplating the political landscape. He poured another glass of wine. As he sipped, Packwood weighed the growing possibility that Nixon would not serve out his second term. He shuddered at the thought of a McCall presidency; but he decided the odds were still in the president's favor, and that supporting the appointment was a gamble worth taking to make sure his most formidable potential rival was off the Oregon stage.

The news continued to filter its way around Oregon. For some, who weren't closely attuned to political happenings and the deeper motives behind them, it took a while. A 22-year-old graduate of the University of Oregon with a bushy mustache and an intense stare didn't hear about it until one of the customers at the bar he was tending (the Paddock, his own favorite hangout) pointed the bold headline out to him the following night. That part-time bartender, Steve Prefontaine, was living in a trailer with his German shepherd Lobo, devoting all of his energies toward vindication. Prefontaine picked up the paper, already wrinkled and stained from spilled beer, and tried to make out the story in the dim light and the haze of cigarette smoke.

"Pre" owned every major distance record in the American running record books, but he had failed in his quest for the top prize at the 1972 Olympics in Munich, finishing a disappointing fourth in the 5,000 meters. He gave back to the community, spreading the gospel of fitness, lecturing at local schools and organizing a sports club at the state prison. But his laser focus was now on preparing for Montreal and the 1976 summer games. Still, he found the news about the governor to be intriguing. Prefontaine was noted for his bluntness and had little use for most politicians. McCall was an exception, though; in Pre's mind, McCall was different.

That summed up most Oregonians' feelings toward their governor. McCall was different. Young and old, rich and poor, rural and urban, black and white, Republican and Democrat, Oregonians from every walk of life loved Tom McCall.

Even those who found his ego to be as outsized as his six-foot-five frame and his size twelve shoes. Even those who disagreed with him from time to time.

They loved his candor. Nineteen seventy-three was the year historian Arthur Schelsinger published his famous study, *The Imperial Presidency.* No one ever applied the term "imperial" to McCall. McCall loved to amble through the Capitol Building, engaging friends, colleagues and total strangers in conversation. He seemingly knew everyone in the building by name, including the custodial staff. He would eat lunch with whoever he found at the first open table in the basement cafeteria. If one of his staff didn't accompany him, they had to make sure someone gave him a few dollars; he didn't carry money, a trait he shared with another of the state's most powerful men, Highway Commission chair and utility executive Glenn Jackson. In McCall's case, it had been a discipline imposed by Audrey at the beginning of their relationship to help rein in his free-spending tendencies.

He'd then be likely to drop in on the press room unannounced, which wasn't a surprise. He had been a journalist, and was still a newsman at heart. He reveled in contact with school kids who visited the Capitol. He wasn't above helping give a push to a car in need of a jump start, reminding the young driver, "Never let them tell you I'm not a man of the people."

Oregonians loved his willingness to try daring and unusual things, like Vortex, the Woodstock-like rock festival.

Most of all, they shared his deep and abiding love for the state itself. If Oregon had a living, breathing soul, it was Thomas William Lawson McCall.

McCall's term in office still had fifteen months to run, but people already sensed he was feeling at loose ends. Although his popularity was at its peak, he couldn't run for governor again and other political options didn't look promising. He toyed with ideas of what he might do after his time in the governorship ended. Perhaps he would teach, or return to journalism. Colleges were putting out feelers to see if he would be interested in their presidencies. Although flattered by the attention, he told confidantes that it was unlikely he would wind up in charge of a campus; he said it was the type of position that demanded "you chase money until your tongue is hanging out," and raising campaign funds had been the thing he had liked least about running for office. Ultimately, nothing looked to be remotely as satisfying as the governorship.

Now it appeared that McCall had found that next chapter and the love affair between the man and the state would be drawing to a close, sooner than expected. Oregon would have to share McCall with the entire country. But the rest of the country would have to get to know him first.

Reporters Jack Germond and Jules Whitcover were first to break the news that McCall was on Nixon's short list as a possible replacement for Agnew in their syndicated column, "Politics Today." They probably didn't realize how close they had come to understanding Nixon's true motives in putting McCall at the top of his list:

> *The most intriguing prospective replacement for Vice President Spiro T. Agnew, according to administration sources, is Oregon Governor Tom McCall. If McCall emerges as Nixon's choice, he's likely to be assailed for his lack of foreign policy experience; yet many recent vice presidents, including Agnew, have also lacked any first-hand knowledge of the world beyond our shores.*
>
> *McCall has shown a willingness to sanction, or at least look the other way, when it comes to activities that would generate stern disapproval of American conservatives. The Vortex rock festival of 1970, the first and so far only state-sanctioned event of its kind, was decried by some as an orgy of drugs and free love, so it may be difficult for Nixon to reconcile McCall with his law-and-order, tough on drugs image. But the President has accomplished far more challenging political feats.*
>
> *The McCall selection makes sense only in the context of Nixon wanting to control the choice of his successor but delay showing his hand. The choice of someone like Ronald Reagan, Nelson Rockefeller, or Nixon's presumed heir apparent, John Connally, would set off an early battle for succession that Nixon probably wants to avoid. He may be counting on the Congressional leadership wanting to postpone that as well.*
>
> *The shadow of Watergate looms over this choice, of course. And there we may find the ultimate reason for this act of political sleight-of-hand. It's one of the first tricks any magician learns: distract and confuse. Because McCall is not a conventional choice, the attention of the Congress, the public and the press will be distracted for weeks—weeks when the focus will shift away from Watergate, and momentum toward impeachment may be lost.*
>
> *If Nixon does choose McCall, the man who has dominated the American political landscape for more than a quarter century may show he has one more trick left up his sleeve.*

Once Agnew entered his no contest plea to charges of tax evasion and money laundering, Nixon knew there were some phone calls he had to make. He asked his secretary, Rose Mary Woods, to get

House Minority Leader John Rhodes on the line. His next call was to Gerald Ford. Nixon's conversation with Ford was brief; he sensed the Michigan congressman was almost relieved to learn he was out of the running.

Nixon then got down to business with Speaker of the House Carl Albert. There were already rumblings that some Democrats wanted to drag out the nomination process and keep the job vacant long enough so that if Nixon were forced to resign or be impeached, Albert, who was next in the line of succession, would become president. Nixon didn't accept the possibility that he would be forced from office, but he also didn't want a lengthy battle over this nomination, which could further weaken his political standing.

Carl Albert was only five feet, four inches tall, but the Oklahoman was regarded as a giant among his colleagues in the House—a man of absolute integrity and fierce dedication to the institution of Congress. Nixon knew he would have to play to those values, rather than attempt the crass horse trading of federal dollars for favors and votes that made up so many of the dealings between presidents and members of Congress.

Although the infamous White House taping system had been removed several months earlier after its existence was exposed during the Senate Watergate hearings, Nixon had Woods listening in on the call and taking notes in shorthand.

NIXON: Mr. Speaker! Thank you for taking my call.

ALBERT: Of course, Mr. President.

NIXON: Well, you know how things are going these days. I'm not the most popular man on the Hill right now, I imagine.

ALBERT: Now, Mr. President....

NIXON: Let me get to the point, Mr. Speaker. It's about this Agnew thing, and the appointment I've got to make. I know you and the rest of the leadership are big on Jerry Ford, but I really don't think he's the right man. Not that I don't have the highest respect for Jerry, exactly the opposite is true. I think he's a true man of the House, and, and, with the difficult times ahead, I think we, I think the country needs his integrity and good old fashioned common sense right where he is, right now.

ALBERT: I see your point, Mr. President. Did you have someone else in mind?

NIXON: Yes. The Oregon governor. Tom McCall.

ALBERT: (A long pause) That's an interesting choice. I have to admit I don't know him well at all, but I've heard good things about him. I'll have some conversations with the rest of the leadership team. I assume you'll be talking to Jerry?

NIXON: I already have, Mr. Speaker.

When Albert hung up the phone, he called for Charlie Ward, his chief of staff. The speaker thought he had heard McCall was a former newsman; Albert had hired Ward away from the Oklahoma City paper more than a dozen years previously. He hoped Ward would have some insights about McCall, or at least have some connections in the business who could explain what the man was all about; he didn't doubt that people all over Washington would soon be asking similar questions.

Editorial, the New York Times, October 10, 1973

President Nixon has made an unconventional choice in selecting Oregon Governor Tom McCall to be the next vice president. If McCall is confirmed by the Congress, he will earn a place in the history books: for the first time in almost 200 years of our nation's history, a vice president will move into office without being elected to the post.

The twenty-fifth amendment to the Constitution, ratified in 1967, gave the President the ability to appoint a second-in-command with Congressional approval. Until then, if the office of vice president became vacant for any reason, it stayed vacant until the next election. The momentum for the measure began to build after John F. Kennedy's assassination nearly a decade ago, when the seventy-two-year -old Speaker of the House, John McCormack, stood next in line for the presidency for more than a year.

The appointment takes on added significance due to Mr. Nixon's precarious position in the Oval Office. Although the President insists he will serve out his term, there is growing speculation that he could face the first Presidential impeachment in more than a century, or be forced to resign. Should that scenario play out, Thomas William Lawson McCall could become the next president of the United States.

All of this no doubt has most of the country asking: Who is Tom McCall? He generated national headlines a couple of years ago when he invited people to come and visit his state but told them not to stay.

Ron Schmidt stopped reading aloud and put the paper in his lap.

"Tom, they don't have any idea what to make of you," he said. Although the appointment wasn't confirmed yet, Westerdahl and Schmidt had already made arrangements to move their households to D.C. Neither could pass up the opportunity to be part of history. Schmidt glanced down at the page. "Beach bill, bottle bill, Vortex, land use planning. The standard clip file stuff."

"You'd expect more out of the *New York Times*," McCall said with a grin that bordered on a smirk.

Former Nixon aide William Safire had recently joined the *Times* as a columnist, and began working his Congressional contacts for insights into the process. After spending the better part of two days on the phone, he concluded that McCall would be headed for easy approval. Neither Republicans nor Democrats saw him as a threat in any sense; certainly not as a major player on the national and international stage.

Safire was soon proven to be a prophet.

McCall didn't have a difficult time with the hearings before the Senate Rules Committee and the House Judiciary Committee. Even though the congressmen knew they were potentially vetting the next president, they seemed disarmed by McCall's candor. This exchange was typical:

FLORIDA SENATOR EDWARD GURNEY: Governor, How is your health? You had surgery for prostate cancer last year, and thanks to the information you provided to the public, everyone in your home state was made aware that it was a pretty serious situation.

McCALL: You have my records, Senator, but I can say with confidence that I am in the best shape since the cradle.

GURNEY: Governor, you were very open about....the, uh, extent of your surgery and the follow-up treatment. In fact, someone wrote in a letter to the editor that they found it distasteful to be served your glands for breakfast with the morning newspaper. What would you say in response to that?

McCALL: Well, senator, I have been accused of going overboard on more than one occasion in my life. But if I'm going to make a mistake, I want to do so on the side of candor. We've learned in recent years about the lengths many of our presidents have gone to in order to conceal illnesses and disabilities. I want the American people to always know they will have access to the latest information about my health....though there may need to be a warning to wait to read your newspaper until *after* breakfast.

The executive editor of the *Washington Post*, Ben Bradlee, watched the proceedings with fascination. He was having a difficult time getting a handle on McCall. He had called one of the paper's west coast correspondents to ask if he had found any skeletons in McCall's closet.

Since becoming managing editor of the *Post* in 1965, Bradlee had continually pushed his newsroom to new levels of achievement. His hunger became his reporters'; he loved young turks like Bob Woodward and Carl Bernstein, who many saw as singlehandedly responsible for uncovering the misdeeds that had collectively become known as Watergate. But success hadn't abated Bradlee's hunger; it had only intensified it. He lived by the credo that the only thing tougher than getting to the top was staying there.

He paced back and forth in his office as he conversed with his reporter over the speakerphone.

"There are people who say he drinks too much," the correspondent said. "Some old duffer who worked with him in his newspaper days back in Moscow—Idaho, not Russia, by the way—swears there were days he came to work so soused he couldn't see a hand in front of his face and had to sneak off behind the newsprint rolls to sleep it off."

When Bradlee heard this story was more than thirty years old, he sighed audibly. "They say his fondness for drink hasn't diminished, either," the reporter said, trying too hard to prove he had dug up something relevant.

"So what?" Bradlee snapped. "Does it affect his performance on the job? Unless he pulls a Wilbur Mills, I don't see that as an issue." Bradlee paused in his pacing, closed his eyes and pictured the scene from just a few weeks earlier he wished he could have witnessed first-hand: the powerful chairman of the Ways and Means committee, stopped by D.C. police in the predawn hours because he was driving without headlights, a stripper with the stage name of Fanne Foxe fleeing his car and jumping into the Tidal Basin. You couldn't make stuff like this up, Bradlee told himself. He found himself envying the young guys, the Woodwards and Bernsteins of the world, still out there on the beat, digging up stories instead of being doomed to sit in a glass office and play the ultimate traffic cop for the newsroom....The droning voice on the other end of the line brought him back to the present.

"And people say he enjoys slot machines..." The correspondent paused, and Bradlee heard the rustling of paper that indicated he was shuffling through a pad of scribbled notes. God, Bradlee thought, maybe it was time to look for someone else in that part of the country. "In fact, when he was in Moscow—"

"Ida-friggin-ho," Bradlee chimed in.

"Right," the correspondent said, unnerved. "He dropped so much money in the slot machines and at the poker tables, he was a year's salary in debt. Not the best judgment or self-restraint for a future president, maybe."

"He was what, twenty-three? Give me a break. I was throwing down a lot of bucks in poker games at that age, too."

"You know, it may be a trait that runs in the family. Did you know that old Tom Lawson actually broke the bank on a trip to Monte Carlo in 1907?"

"Interesting, but not relevant to the task at hand."

The correspondent pressed on as he grew increasingly desperate to please his boss. "Uh, that's really about it. Oh, some people say he's got a big ego, even for a politician. And that he's mastered the art of taking credit for other people's ideas."

"Jesus H. Christ, they say those things about every politician. Is that really all you've got?" Bradlee asked with an exasperated sigh. It looked like he was going to have to send one of his regular staff out to Oregon for a few days to see if he could find anything of substance. On the surface, this McCall looked too good to be believed. "What is he, some kind of overgrown Boy Scout?" he muttered to himself as he hung up the phone.

A day or so later, Bradlee decided to send his young Los Angeles bureau chief, Lou Cannon, to explore McCall's territory. The tenacious Cannon spent several days in the state, conducting interviews and plowing through files. He heard Bradlee's barked orders to find something fresh about McCall, to not just plow the same over-tilled ground that every other reporter in the country seemed to be turning over, and he succeeded in that task, although the result only added to McCall's stature.

Cannon's first big career break had come with his hiring by the *Post* from the *San Jose Mercury-News*. He was proud to be heading up the *Post's* biggest west coast bureau, but felt he had even bigger career goals ahead. Impressing Bradlee with his coverage of McCall might help him realize his goals. Who knows, he thought, if by some fluke McCall actually winds up in the White House, Bradlee might see the value in having a fellow westerner covering him.

All these thoughts were swirling through Cannon's head as he flew into the Portland Airport and made his way toward the Hertz counter. He had spent the flight poring over the material he had collected from the Post's files and other sources on McCall. The portrait of the man that began to emerge from Cannon's interviews was complex. People saw McCall as amazingly passionate about the state and its people; it was a relationship almost unique in politics.

Cannon thought he might have a fresh lead when a contact in Cesar Chavez's United Farm Workers called his attention to McCall's veto of farm worker legislation following the 1971 session in Salem. It was an issue that had generated plenty of political theater and a few national headlines.

By the late sixties, farmers across the country were becoming increasingly alarmed by boycott movements on behalf of migrant workers and by the efforts of those same workers to organize. They decided to fight back through the legislative process. In Oregon was one of ten states to see similar bills introduced. Although the details differed, the thrust was the same. Farm workers would be given the "right" to organize, but it was a hollow right, with severe limits on collective bargaining, arbitration, pickets, boycotts and strikes. No strikes would have been allowed during harvest season, when they would carry the most impact. Discussions of issues like use of pesticides were put out of bounds from the bargaining table.

The bill worked its way through the session, attracting little attention, including a puzzling lack of opposition from organized labor and Chavez's own group. Although the United Farm Workers Organizing Committee was aware of the Oregon bill, they were distracted by the fight against similar legislation in California. The Oregon bill passed both houses in May and headed to McCall's desk, and the widespread assumption was that he would sign it. That's when the real fight began.

By the end of June, Cesar Chavez had come to Salem to join hundreds of supporters at a candlelit nighttime prayer vigil in front of the Capitol building. Church groups, hippies, students, and Portland liberals had joined farm workers, Chicano activists and others to appeal to McCall's moral conscience and urge him to veto what they were calling "the slave bill." But Chavez was also flexing his organization's muscle inside the building; one of his top assistants had met with McCall to threaten a national boycott of Oregon products if he allowed the bill to become law, a threat that Chavez publicly repeated at the rally.

McCall was uncharacteristically quiet as the drama unfolded, though he did say he was facing greater pressure over a single bill than any Oregon governor had ever faced. When he appeared at a news conference to announce that he was vetoing the bill because he considered large portions of it to be unconstitutional, the howls of outrage quickly began. The Farm Bureau accused McCall of caving in to blackmail. At the news conference, McCall had vented his outrage at being subjected to pressure from outside the state, saying this had almost boomeranged and caused him to sign the measure.

The incident had led many to question McCall's commitment to the challenges facing minority populations. But those who studied the record a bit more deeply, and especially those who knew him best, knew differently. This was the same governor who had created an Advisory Council on Chicano affairs in 1969. But his record on the issue reached back much further.

A long-untouched file folder in the state archives eventually led Cannon to the town of McMinnville in the upper Willamette Valley, a business and government hub in the middle of rich farmland. There, in a modest downtown coffee shop near the county courthouse, he met a quiet, unassuming man named Ruben Contreras. At first Contreras politely declined Cannon's request for an interview, but changed his mind when he realized this could help the country to better understand the man he considered a friend.

Sitting across from Cannon in the red naugahyde booth, Contreras sipped his coffee and spoke with quiet passion about a man he knew was committed to the cause of society's underdogs.

Contreras has been born into a life of privilege in Mexico in 1921, but felt a calling to take his life in a different direction. That had led him to the United States after World War II, where he became a guest worker under the Bracero program. Contreras eventually came to McMinnville, married a local girl, and settled into a career as a refrigeration technician at a local bean farm's processing plant. He was the first permanent Hispanic resident of the county.

After suffering a serious on-the-job injury while protecting a fellow employee from a piece of equipment that had broken loose, Contreras faced a lengthy convalescence. It was during this time he felt a calling to help workers without the education and skills to speak up for themselves. That led him to the Oregon Council of Churches and Migrant Ministry, which was organizing volunteers to talk with migrant workers and compile first-hand information on their plight. Contreras organized the group's Yamhill County chapter, and it was this work that eventually brought him and Tom McCall to the same table.

In the fall of 1958, McCall, still employed as a political reporter and commentator at KGW, accepted the task of chairing and organizing the Oregon Committee on Migrant Affairs, which would help craft a package of proposals for the 1959 Legislature to consider. Contreras was one of the members of that panel, which also took on the challenge of educating the public about the realities of migrant life. It was more than two years before distinguished CBS journalist Edward R. Murrow produced "Harvest of Shame," the first significant journalistic work credited with bringing the plight of migrants to the attention of the broader public.

McCall showed his instincts for translating passion into tangible results even at this stage of his career. In a call to action, he emphasized the need for an organized effort. "Several years ago a similar awakening of interest in Michigan resulted only in meaningless resolutions, not in effective action. Michigan's opportunity to act was lost. We can learn from this example."

There had been no federal legislation on behalf of migrant workers, and only a handful of eastern states had enacted legislation. The package of bills that passed the 1959 Oregon legislative session were seen as the most comprehensive in the nation to that time. More than a decade later, McCall retained his credibility as a friend of migrants when he vetoed the controversial farm bill.

Contreras, who considered McCall to be a friend, remained steadfast in his support of the governor as he moved into full-time advocacy on behalf of migrants in the 1960s. Another member of the McCall committee, Tom Current, said the pioneering legislation helped boost standards for sanitary field conditions and decent housing, but didn't go far enough. "In other words, we didn't cure the disease," he told Cannon.

Cannon spent a couple of days at KGW-TV, McCall's home base for the eight years prior to his move to Salem. He didn't just settle for screening McCall's most celebrated documentary, "Pollution in Paradise," but also watched many other noteworthy projects, including "Crisis in the Klamath Basin," which focused on the land grab in the making following the termination of the Klamath Indians' tribal status. Their million-acre pine forest was a rich prize potentially headed for the auction block.

McCall's work not only examined the environmental threat of clear-cutting if the forest went to the highest bidder, he also brought focus on the human plight of a people who had suddenly lost their anchor, their culture, their way of life. Oregon Senator Richard Neuberger used "Crisis" as a tool to secure $120 million in federal funding to preserve the land as a national forest, and McCall won an award from the Issac Walton League.

Those who could read census numbers pointed out that Oregon still had one of the tiniest minority populations in the country, and remained uneasy about the nomination. New York Congressman Charles Rangel reportedly grumbled to a staff member that "Nixon couldn't have picked a guy from a whiter state if he tried." Still, the publication of Cannon's story would help ease fears of many minority members of Congress who wondered about McCall's commitment to disenfranchised populations. They saw he was as much a champion of the people as he was of the land.

Bradlee shook his head as he read through the story before sending it to the composing room. "I guess we're joining the Tom McCall love fest," he muttered.

There were some who raised the question of McCall's lack of foreign policy credentials as the confirmation process moved forward, but that issue didn't gain any real traction, and a handful of southern Democrats grumbled about Vortex, but McCall hit back by selling it as a public safety measure. "We were looking at the prospect of a bloodbath in the streets of Portland that would have made Chicago look like a picnic," he told one panel. "Desperate times call for creative and courageous responses."

McCall was supported by an 88-10 Senate vote on November 7th; he sailed through the House a little over a week later on a 367 to 25 margin. Although he was watching the voting on television, the call from Haig made it official: Tom McCall was the next vice president of the United States.

5

A crowd of reporters, photographers and television cameramen filled the Governor's ceremonial office. Tom McCall had participated in countless bill signing events at this desk during his time in office. Usually, he attacked the paper with a series of quick, forceful strokes. But the piece of paper sitting in front of him was different. He hesitated before putting his bold signature on his letter of resignation as governor. His six years and ten months in the office had been the most satisfying of his life. Now he was headed into an uncertain future.

He forced a smile as he looked up at the television cameras and newspaper photographers who had gathered to record history. "My parents always taught me not to be a quitter," he said.

He was ready to hand the reins in Salem to his successor, Secretary of State Clay Myers. Just the year before, the state's voters had approved a constitutional amendment to put the Secretary second in line for the governorship, instead of the president of the State Senate. Oregon was one of the few states without a lieutenant governor; it made sense to put another statewide elected official at the head of the line if the governor died, quit, or was incapacitated, instead of someone who had been chosen from a single local district.

But no one had expected to see the provision put into play so soon. The jokes about Myers having impossibly large shoes to fill started as soon as word of the appointment began filtering out.

There were some Mutt and Jeff jokes about the relationship between the two men; the six-foot-five McCall towered almost a foot above Myers, and wore his heart on his sleeve while Myers was cordial but reserved; yet the two men shared a common vision and goals for the state. If McCall was going to hand his cherished job to anyone, he was glad it would be Myers. When he had been elected governor, McCall had chosen Myers to fill out the remainder of his term as secretary; he had been elected to the job twice since then. When he forced himself to think about it, McCall acknowledged this passing of the baton would happen one day, but he thought it would be in 1975, not at this moment.

After signing the resignation letter, he made the short walk down the marble hall to the House of Representatives chamber for the official swearing-in ceremonies for the new governor. His family, staff and close friends were already waiting for him there. The photographers trailed several feet behind him, so for this brief distance, Tom McCall was alone.

A Gerry Lewin photograph for the *Capitol Journal* captured the essence of that feeling; the viewer saw McCall's long frame from the rear, his head bowed slightly. It was a classic Lewin shot, a wide angle capturing the sweep of the scene, the sharp contrast in the print making the details stand out crisply.

Lewin was about a foot shorter than McCall, and used that contrast to his advantage here, making McCall appear to loom large over the panorama. Even from behind, it was unmistakably Tom McCall. The packed chamber was visible in the distance, with many peering toward the man heading their way. The photo was evocative enough to inspire an editorial, "Tom McCall's Lonely Walk," which read in part:

> *Tom McCall is without a doubt the most outgoing governor in our state's history. It's said that he's met more Oregonians than any of his predecessors, and everyone who had crossed his path knows how much he thrives on contact with people.*
>
> *That made his walk from the Governor's ceremonial office to the House of Representatives chamber yesterday especially poignant. In front of a bank of cameras, he signed his letter of resignation and walked out of the office*

as governor for the final time. A short time later, he was at the podium of the House Chamber, addressing an overflow crowd of family, friends, colleagues, reporters and well-wishers.

But what thoughts must have been in his head as he made the lonely walk between those two destinations?

Did he wonder if he had done the right thing by stepping down and accepting Richard Nixon's invitation to come to Washington? If he had the option of seeking a third consecutive term as governor next year, would he have been tempted to stay put?

That's one of the many wonderful things about Tom McCall, and one that the Salem press corps will particularly miss. We didn't have to wonder. All we had to do is ask. Tom rose from our ranks, and we have always thought of him as one of our own. Our new governor, Clay Myers, is a known quantity, having served as secretary of state since 1967, and he shows all signs of being up to the job. But as he's the first to admit, he's no Tom McCall. But that's okay. No one else is, either. Tom's a true original, the likes of which we will not see in Salem again.

Best wishes in Washington, Tom. If anyone can keep this administration honest, you can.

The overflow crowd rose as one to applaud and cheer for McCall. When he reached the area in front of the podium, known as the well, McCall stopped, overwhelmed by emotion. Friends, colleagues, rivals all came together to thank McCall and wish him well. He turned, smiled, and spent several moments acknowledging the outpouring of adoration before he quickly ascended the podium to deliver his farewell address.

Although he had stood in this spot many times before in the past few years, gazing out at similar gatherings of legislators, journalists, family and friends, none of those moments had carried the same import that this one did. McCall was proud of his skill with words and hoped the remarks he had prepared for this day would be worthy of the occasion.

He knew it was a speech that wouldn't reassure those who questioned his selection for the second-highest office in the land, especially those who thought his vision was too narrow, too parochial, not broad enough. But he felt he had to stay true to his values. It was a valedictory to the state he loved and a signal to those who would listen about the values he would carry east.

"This Chamber has been the scene of many battles for the Oregon cause. At the same time, working in this building is a delicate responsibility and deep honor for all of us who have had the opportunity. In all honesty, though, I must say the entrance is more invigorating and pleasant than is the exit. But it is not in the Oregon style to dwell on goodbyes. Though we fully understand that the past gives us our foundation and our generating guidance, we are most ardently concerned with the future and how to get there."

Once again, McCall felt the emotion washing over him. As he looked around the packed chamber, he saw so many faces that meant so much to him; close allies, like State Senators Hector Macpherson and Ted Hallock; the reporters who had covered him for the past six years and who he still thought of as old colleagues; and up front, Audrey, Sam and Tad. A part of McCall hated to be leaving Oregon, yet when he looked at his family, he knew he would be taking the best part of it with him. He fixed his gaze on Audrey for a long moment before continuing. The outgoing governor held up his cherished state as a beacon of hope as he headed for the storms in the east.

"I feel certain that Oregon has a place in the destiny of world leadership . . . that this state is a lodestar for the wavering pace of the American society. Let us continue to be that star. If there is a single hallmark of the Oregon character, it must be citizen initiative. We in Oregon do not wait for answers to be handed down to us . . . We assess the ever-changing situation and respond with our own action. We do not celebrate a problem. We set about to make things better by trying solutions. We are creative, and we trust our intuition. We do not like to wait for the inevitable . . . we send scouts to stalk its approach.

"Throughout the nation now there is a faint, cold fear that veins to haunt the shadows. This mood must not be allowed to fasten and grow. So let's export the Oregon system, now when it's needed most.

"At a time when most Americans no longer believe or trust their government, it is worthy of note that --- here in Oregon --- the Legislature, and our citizen boards and commissions operate in the light, day and night . . . the level of public participation remains high . . . the two major parties continue to debate and cooperate amicably . . . and the people continue to believe and trust themselves and their chosen representatives.

"That is a quality worthy of export." The standing ovation that followed lasted more than two minutes.

The coverage of the day was focused on the man departing from Salem, although Henny Willis, the *Eugene Register-Guard's* veteran Salem reporter, wrote a poignant piece about the man who stayed, Clay Myers. Willis was a journalist by trade, but also enjoyed a passion for community theater. As an actor, he carefully studied the expressions of those he observed on stage, in both the theatrical and political arenas.

As McCall spoke, Willis found his eyes straying toward Myers. He saw Myers' mouth was smiling, but his eyes were not. Did they convey anticipation for the opportunities that would go with the top job? Dread for the challenge of following one of the most dynamic figures in state history? Some combination of these? Willis' piece began: "Clay Myers today must have understood how John Adams felt on March 4, 1797. It was Inauguration Day for the second president, and Adams, like Myers, was following a predecessor who cast a long shadow over the political landscape, even setting aside the fact he was also physically much taller."

After his address to the Legislature, McCall was joined by Audrey and Sam for a drive to the Hilton Hotel in Portland, when a ballroom overflowing with admirers awaited him. McCall fed on the upbeat energy that coursed through the room. Many of the same people who had listened to his farewell address in Salem had also made the journey up Interstate 5 with him; it was as if they weren't ready to surrender him to Washington just quite yet. The former governor was upbeat throughout the evening of tributes and good-natured roasting. He only betrayed the sadness lurking below the surface just once, when a display of photos by Gerry Lewin moved him to tears.

After his emotional sendoff in Salem and Portland, the vice presidential swearing in ceremony felt like an anti-climax. Nevertheless, McCall sensed the eyes of the country were on him as he stood in the chamber of the U.S. House of Representatives, facing Chief Justice Warren Burger. Audrey stood between them, holding the McCall family Bible, bursting with quiet pride in her husband and partner. Nixon, looking stiff and shifty-eyed, was off to the side.

Living in the nation's capital was going to be a major transition for the McCalls, who were lifetime westerners (Although Tom had actually been born in his parents' home state of Massachusetts, due to his maternal grandfather's insistence that his daughter give birth at a hospital that met his standards.) It would be a change of lifestyle, a change of climate, as well as a move away from friends and family.

Audrey had only put a couple of requirements on their selection of a temporary home: it had to have a garden, for she found joy and refuge in working with plants and flowers, and it had to be dog-friendly, since Duffy, their ten-year-old wire-haired terrier, would be making the cross-country move with them. All three of the McCalls involved in the move put a fireplace high on their wish list, and that wish was granted when they found a rambling old house in Virginia, only a half-hour's drive from downtown Washington, that had a large stone fireplace in the living room. Tom looked forward to the therapeutic value of splitting wood and stacking it in the garage for the coming winter; it also took him back to his childhood days at Westernwold, when family members had to take shifts to keep the wood-burning furnace going through the bone-chilling winter nights.

Audrey also agreed to Tom's insistence that they hire a full-time housekeeper to help with her official duties as hostess, though she said she wouldn't give up her time in the kitchen. She eagerly jumped into the challenge of researching which flowers thrived in the Washington-area climate; her gardening skills were as renowned as her homemaking abilities. As with her cooking, precision and attention to details had brought her success. Tom, knowing roses were her specialty, said with a wry grin, "Well, Aud, you know at least one famous rose garden thrives back there." Both McCalls thought back to a rented Portland home they had occupied a couple of decades earlier; when they had moved in, there were already fifty rose bushes on the property.

There was also an economic impact that had to be weighed in considering the move. The McCalls didn't have any significant income beyond Tom's $35,000 a year salary as governor, so the bump to the vice president's pay of $62,500 per annum would be welcomed, though they weren't sure if it would fully offset the expenses associated with the move and the new position. (Unlike Agnew, McCall hadn't done anything legal or illegal to supplement his gubernatorial salary.)

The McCalls hadn't finished unpacking their belongings at their rented home in the D.C. suburbs by the time they headed back to Oregon to celebrate Christmas 1973. The new vice president made the rounds of the state's media outlets, including his former employer, KGW-TV, the Portland NBC affiliate. McCall had been the station's news analyst for eight years prior to his election as secretary of state, so he truly felt at home there.

McCall taped an appearance on *Viewpoint,* the station's weekly public affairs program. He had hosted the program during his time at the station and had returned many times since as a guest. Here, he wasn't the vice president—he was Tom, their old friend and colleague. This was a place where news anchor Richard Ross could gently tease him with a reminder that when their desks sat side by side, McCall's was so covered in papers and books that he didn't have room for his telephone, which sat on the corner of Ross' desk.

"You won't be able to get away with that trick in the Oval Office, Tom," Ross joked as McCall sat in the makeup chair. "There aren't any other desks in there." Ross remembered that a colleague had once measured the piles on the McCall desk and found they averaged seven and a half inches in height.

"True," McCall agreed. "But that desk is bigger." He paused and reached for the makeup bib on his chest. "It's good to see you, Dick, but I better not keep Floyd waiting."

Host Floyd McKay asked McCall if he had his eyes on the White House in 1976—or sooner. He noted that grassroots "McCall for President" groups were starting to spring up. Although the interest was highest in the vice president's home state, there were also committees forming in Washington, Idaho, Colorado and the New England states. McCall admitted he was flattered by the interest, even if it might be premature. He made no effort to hide his feelings, though: "There's no point in being coy about it," McCall said. "Yes, I'd like to be president. Hell, yes."

Questioned by the host, McCall insisted he wasn't a ghoul hovering over a terminally ill patient; he fully expected Nixon to complete his term. He also said expressing a desire to be president wasn't necessarily the same as a declaration of candidacy; he said launching a campaign was a backbreaking, expensive task, and he would need some time to assess whether he had the resources to mount the effort. Privately, though, his course of action was becoming clear, whatever happened to Nixon. He felt a growing sense of restlessness following his return to Washington in early January, 1974.

"I feel like the goddamned Maytag Repair Man," McCall groused over his evening martini with Audrey. This was one of their shared rituals they both looked forward to. "Garner was absolutely right. This is the most pointless job in the world." McCall had tried presiding over the United States Senate, the one official duty assigned to the vice president by the Constitution, but he quickly grew bored with the task, as had virtually every one of his predecessors. He was happy to hand the gavel back to the president pro tempore of the senate, Mississippi's James Eastland. McCall was an executive at heart, not a legislator, and he had no enthusiasm for what was essentially a ceremonial role.

Nixon, meanwhile, had shown little interest in his new vice president's counsel.

Audrey McCall suggested that her spouse get himself out among the people. Why not some speaking engagements and television appearances, she asked. "Nixon could use some positive P.R. right now."

Tom McCall's eyes lit up. He realized he needed to be back in his element. The national press, still preoccupied with Watergate, had paid scant attention to the new vice president. Well, if they weren't interested in learning what he was thinking and doing, he'd just have to let them know. McCall did exactly that over the next few weeks, but the results weren't to the White House's liking. Any doubts about that were erased one afternoon when he was called to a meeting in the White House press office.

By the time he got home that evening, McCall's anger had dissipated, and he was able to laugh as he related the story to Audrey over dinner.

"I got called in to see Ron Zeigler today," he began. "Being Nixon's press secretary makes that little man, that little pipsqueak, think he's actually important. You know what he was doing a few years ago?" McCall asked, the irritation starting to creep back in.

Audrey knew the answer to the question, but she also knew that her husband wanted her to play along. "No, Tom. What?"

"He was skipper of the boat on the Jungle Cruise at Disneyland, that's what!" he said, slapping his hand on the dining room table for emphasis. "And that was the peak use of Mr. Zeigler's skills." He still loved his nightly martini, but every now and then liked to experiment with other mixtures, and he was trying one out on this evening. He paused to take a drink of his rum-and-tomato-juice concoction he called the "maverick."

"So Mr. Zeigler actually decided he would set me straight about my recent public appearances. He told me I wasn't conveying the proper message. He said I'm supposed to clear everything through his office from now on."

"What did you tell him?"

"I told him I was only interested in acting on those instructions if I heard them directly from his boss. Then I told him to go to hell."

"Tom! You didn't!" Audrey exclaimed.

The vice president smiled and downed the rest of his drink. Audrey let a small sigh escape her lips and said, "Of course you did."

Audrey told herself it wasn't the first time her advice hadn't produced quite the result she intended.

From the "Washington Merry Go-Round" column by Jack Anderson, February 20, 1974:

> *Confidential sources say the Nixon White House is already second-guessing its choice of Oregon Governor Tom McCall as Vice President Spiro Agnew's replacement.*
>
> *McCall has been all over network television in recent weeks, appearing not only on traditional venues such as Meet the Press and the Today Show, but also on programs that see prominent political leaders much less frequently, such as the Tonight Show and the Phil Donahue program.*
>
> *McCall generated plenty of laughs when Johnny Carson asked him if he was worried about finding a comfortable bed in the White House, an obvious jab at Nixon's increasingly perilous position in the wake of the growing Watergate scandal.*
>
> *'I'm not too worried,' McCall said. 'I know Lincoln's bed is still there, and he was almost as tall as I am.'*

The VP even exchanged quips with Jack Benny, who was also a guest of Carson's that night, asking the comedian who has built a persona around being tight with a dollar if he would consider becoming secretary of the treasury in a McCall administration. Benny said he might take the job if it paid well enough.

The television audience may have loved it, but the reception in the West Wing of the White House was decidedly different. A highly placed source says McCall was the recipient of a furious tongue-lashing from Nixon's press secretary, Ron Ziegler, who demanded that McCall clear future television appearances with the White House in advance.

Ron Schmidt paused in his reading, put the *Washington Star* in his lap, and looked at his boss with just a hint of a grin. "Tom," he demanded. "Would I lose any money betting that YOU are Anderson's 'highly placed source?'"

McCall looked at the ceiling with an expression of feigned innocence. It was a rare lighthearted moment in what was becoming an increasingly dark time.

6

Vice President McCall was noted for his level of comfort with the press corps, having risen from their ranks himself. So the assembled reporters immediately sensed something was wrong when McCall entered the room for his announced press conference. Instead of his usual ease, McCall radiated a real sense of anxiety, as if he wanted to be anywhere else on earth at this moment.

Which was exactly the case.

McCall had bitten his tongue when, just days after his swearing in as vice president, the infamous "18 ½ minute gap" in a key Watergate tape had been revealed. It was all he could do to contain his sense of outrage when Al Haig had suggested a "sinister force" might have been responsible for the erasure.

Schmidt could see the strain of events was weighing on McCall. He was coming to the office later and later in the day, and the dark circles under his eyes were more pronounced. He wondered if McCall was drinking more than usual. He was strangely subdued, only showing his usual fire in brief flashes; one of those moments came in a morning meeting with Schmidt and Westerdahl the morning Haig announced the "sinister force" theory.

"Sinister force, *hell*," McCall thundered. "The only sinister force is Nixon himself."

McCall walked into the vice-presidential office in the Old Executive Office Building one day carrying a copy of the *Washington Post* and handed it to his secretary, pointing to a strange photo on the front page. "Doris," he said gravely. "No matter how bad things get, I give you my solemn vow that I will never, ever, do to you what they've done to poor Rose Woods."

Penwell examined the photo, which showed Woods, who was been Nixon's devoted secretary for decades, doing her best to mimic a contortionist. In the photo, Woods was sitting in her office chair, reaching behind herself to answer the phone while her right foot was stretched in the opposite direction, resting on a wooden pedal.

The explanation? When the "sinister force" concept generated ridicule, the White House decided to sacrifice Woods. She had been tasked with making transcripts of some of the tapes, using the foot pedal to start and stop the recorder. Woods loyally suggested that she might have accidently caused the erasure by hitting the foot pedal while answering the phone.

Penwell shook her head in disbelief. She didn't doubt that McCall would always reciprocate her loyalty, but she still found it hard to absorb that politics could be so cutthroat.

Nixon had released hundreds of pages of highly edited transcripts in response to the House Judiciary Committee's subpoena for his secret tapes of Oval Office conversations. Nixon said the transcripts offered proof of his innocence of criminal wrongdoing, but McCall disagreed. He had spent several days agonizing over his next step, but once he had set a course, there was no turning back. And although he knew many would claim he was acting out of his own self-interest, he could remain silent no longer. The ache in his gut was something he hadn't felt in a long time; decades in front of a microphone, whether in a broadcast studio or behind a podium, had taken care of any traces of stage fright. But the stakes had never been as high as they were at this moment.

Rather than accept a ride to the National Press Club building, McCall had walked the half-mile from the White House complex with Schmidt in hopes of calming his nerves. He stepped in front of the bank of microphones and rows of cameras. He looked around the ornately-paneled room and took a deep breath.

"Today I am calling on the President to resign," McCall began. Schmidt, who stood a few feet away from the podium, heard someone inhale deeply in the silence that followed; he was also sure someone near the back of the room gasped. An explosion of camera flashes followed and the heat from the bank of television lights suddenly seemed more intense.

Schmidt sensed the slight hesitation in his boss' voice, but figured that most people wouldn't notice. The press corps was getting used to bombshell after bombshell with Watergate; this, though, was something of a wholly different magnitude. Not since Thomas Jefferson and Aaron Burr had a president and vice president been so completely at odds.

McCall continued: "It is clear that his ability to lead the nation has been fatally, irrevocably damaged by more than a year of revelations of White House misdeeds. The profanity-laden transcripts released last week show a President more concerned with avoiding perjury and raising blackmail money than ferreting out the truth. For the good of the American people, a change in leadership is absolutely necessary.

"Let me make one more thing clear," McCall declared, his old self-assurance reasserting itself and his voice returning to its full strength. "I do not make this statement out of any personal ambition or lust for power. If the American people demand it, I am happy to resign the vice presidency and allow the country to start over with a clean slate."

More than half a million phone calls, letters and telegrams poured into Washington over the next several days imploring McCall to remain in office. Most of the country was still getting to know the vice president, but people liked what they had seen, and they instinctively understood that the open, honest, approachable McCall was stamped from wholly different cloth than the increasingly isolated president, and those who cared about the environment and had taken the time to look into the Oregon record, realized they now had a potential champion in D.C.

The small office suite McCall and his team occupied was soon overwhelmed with paper, and much to the chagrin of Nixon's staff, the West Wing was soon buried in a blizzard of correspondence as well. The same story was true in Congressional offices. The official silence from the White House was complete. A one-sentence statement said there would be no comment on the vice-president's remarks. When Helen Thomas of UPI asked Zeigler for a reaction at the morning press briefing, Zeigler walked away from the podium without a word.

Stories about Nixon's angry drunken tirade the night of McCall's press conference soon took on the quality of legend, fueled by a controversial *National Enquirer* article. Members of the Secret Service and the White House domestic staff sign oaths of silence; yet the *Enquirer* published a detailed account, which it claimed was based on multiple sources, that told of a butler finding Nixon passed out face down on the floor of the Oval Office, a golf club in hand. He had left a trail of destruction in his wake.

"That club was a gift to him from Eisenhower," one of the sources told the tabloid. "He used it to smash statuary and flower pots, knocked books off of shelves. It was a real mess. When a Secret Service agent revived him, he almost went careening through the windows behind his desk and into the bushes. He was even more incoherent than usual when he's drunk. He was calling McCall a bleeping Jew, which made no sense because he's not Jewish....and a lot worse. It took three agents to restrain him."

Nixon exploded when the article hit the newsstands and checkstands. His fury was fueled in part by the fact that almost every word of it was true. He ordered the FBI to question every member of the staff who had been on duty that night. He threatened to replace the entire domestic staff with non-English speakers, until the impracticality of that idea was pointed out. He briefly considered replacing the Secret Service detail at the White House with members of the U.S. Marshals.

In the end, the identity of the leakers was never uncovered. Although the mainstream media outlets wouldn't touch the story, it somehow found its way into the collective consciousness. The rapidly dwindling number of Nixon loyalists left in Washington began muttering about "Judas" McCall.

At the end of the month, McCall was back home to wait out the Oregon primary election results with his handpicked successor, Governor Clay Myers. Myers had been aggressively challenged in the Republican primary by State Senator Vic Atiyeh, who presented himself as "Oregon's Next Great Governor," yet promised a break with the direction McCall had set for the state. "My God," he had muttered to Audrey as he read a file of campaign coverage Schmidt had prepared for him. "How can he run *on* my record and *away* from it at the same time?"

The Benson Hotel in downtown Portland was supposed to be the site of a victory party on Election Day; the ornate old brick and terra-cotta hotel had a tomb-like aspect, which seemed fitting on this night, because it hosted what turned out to be a wake.

Myers and McCall's hearts were broken when Atiyeh claimed victory in the Republican primary, rendering Myers a lame duck. As great as McCall's personal popularity might be, it apparently couldn't be shared. They watched the returns in disbelief; the polls had shown Myers in a narrow lead, but Atiyeh was out front of the vote tally from the start, and by 11 p.m., the results were clear; the McCalls joined Myers for a painful concession speech.

McCall then rode with Myers to the Atiyeh campaign headquarters, where the two candidates were able to exchange strained pleasantries, but the vice president wasn't in a conciliatory mood; his frustration over Atiyeh's campaign tactics boiled over. As he shook Atiyeh's hand, with TV cameras rolling, McCall declared, "All the little minefields that you laid for Clay, that he was a creature of the 1960s, that he was an I-5 candidate--..." Atiyeh tried to protest, but McCall cut him off. "Well, there's no use bickering. You apparently have a sufficient number of votes to win the Republican primary, which is about eight percent of the votes of the state of Oregon. Good luck to you."

After offering words of comfort to Myers, the vice president, his wife Audrey and mother Dorothy were left alone in their suite at the Benson.

"A prophet is without honor in his own country," McCall declared sadly as he poured himself a drink.

"Oh, Tom," Dorothy Lawson McCall snapped. "I hope you're not comparing yourself to Christ." McCall's tart-tongued mother had sensed Myers' vulnerability long before her son did; she had generated headlines early in the year by announcing her candidacy for the job her son had just vacated, saying she would continue his policies but without "his foot in the mouth." But she withdrew without ever actually filing, saying she had decided to steer clear of the muck of politics.

Atiyeh now looked to have the momentum going into his November race against Bob Straub, who had won the Democratic party's nomination for a third consecutive time. McCall began weighing what once would have been unthinkable: endorsing Straub in the general election. He was dealing with a mass of conflicting emotions. It was looking more and more likely that he could end up as president, and he had to focus his energies on Washington. Yet he couldn't forsake his legacy in Oregon and everything he had spent so much energy to build. Could a Republican vice president openly endorse a Democrat for the governorship? Oregon media outlets began to speculate on the possibility.

McCall and Straub had engaged in one of the great political rivalries of the era. Straub was a farmer from Lane County who had twice been elected state treasurer. The two men had faced off for governor twice, with McCall winning both races. Now Straub was taking one last shot at winning the job, and with McCall no longer in Salem, he harbored hopes that the outcome would finally be different. Although McCall was a Republican and Straub was a Democrat, the two had more similarities than differences in their positions; the press had dubbed their matchups "the Tom and Bob Show."

Both men loved the environment. Both were tall enough to start on most basketball teams. Both believed that government could be a force for good in people's lives. Both genuinely liked people and had deep empathy for those seeking to overcome life's challenges. But there were differences. McCall was a rare natural on the stump and had an innate gift for self-promotion. Straub was almost painfully awkward, fighting a stammer, and was self-effacing to a degree that drove those closest to him to frustration; yet his decency and humanity always shone through in one-on-one encounters.

The McCall-Straub rivalry was friendly for the most part, though they were as willing to engage in heated campaign rhetoric as anyone, and the attacks were sure to generate headlines. During the first race, in the fall of 1966, Straub had been startled awake by a 1 a.m. phone call from Dorothy Lawson McCall. He picked up the phone:

"Mr. Straub, I am shocked by the reports I heard on the radio. Did you really say those things about my son?"

"Well, yes, Mrs. McCall..."

"Mr. Straub, I understand you went to Dartmouth College," she said, her uppercrust Brahmin accent dripping heavy sarcasm. Her "a"s were even more elongated than usual. The name of his alma mater came out Daaaahtmuth.

"Yes, Mrs. McCall, I did..."

"Well, I come from Boston, and I know something about Dartmouth. And Dartmouth men are supposed to be gentlemen!" Mother McCall punctuated her anger by slamming the phone back into its cradle.

Straub related the story to McCall at their next joint campaign appearance, expressing fear that he had irreparably damaged his relationship with Dorothy McCall.

"Oh hell, you're lucky she hung up so quickly," McCall said with a bemused smile.

The vice president's dealings with other leaders of his home state remained prickly at best. There was a longstanding divide between McCall and Senator Hatfield. Many traced the breach back to 1958, when Hatfield, then the secretary of state, was elected governor. McCall believed Hatfield had pledged to appoint him to the two years remaining of the secretary's term. The position was widely seen as the stepping stone to the governorship. Hatfield chose businessman and party activist Howell Appling instead.

In 1972, McCall boasted to Hatfield that polls showed his personal popularity at such a peak that he could defeat any other political figure on the landscape, including Hatfield, who was running for re-election to the Senate that year. McCall had no serious interest in the race, but couldn't resist tweaking Hatfield with the news, who responded with a huffy, "Bully for you, Tom."

The clash was about more than egos: it was also about values. By 1971, Hatfield's opposition to the war in Vietnam had become so great that he co-sponsored an amendment to the federal budget with liberal Democrat George McGovern to cut off all funding for the conflict. McCall, whose son Tad was a naval officer who had done service in Vietnam, remained a defender of the war effort. He wasn't a true believer in the mode of those who thought the U.S. had to take a stand against Communism in Vietnam to prevent its spread across Asia and eventually to our own shores. He didn't consider himself a hawk or a dove—he was a self described duck, believing that once the U.S. had made the commitment to South Vietnam, it needed to be seen through for better or worse.

The complexity of McCall's relationship with Oregon's junior senator, Bob Packwood, had made it difficult for the two men to trust each other. When McCall moved into the White House and home state issues came up, he increasingly found himself dealing with the state's Democratic members of the House of Representatives—Les AuCoin,

Al Ullman, Edith Green, and Bob Duncan, who was elected to replace Green after her retirement.

If anything was clear, McCall couldn't be defined by party labels. Although most politicians talk about getting things done above partisan interests, McCall was one of the few who actually lived that ideal.

The White House took on a siege mentality as the summer of 1974 rolled on. Nixon had told his press secretary to "stonewall it," and Garry Trudeau showed a block wall being built in front of the White House in his comic strip *Doonesbury*. The House Judiciary Committee voted out three Articles of Impeachment against Nixon. The next steps would be a vote in the full House of Representatives, followed by a trial in the Senate. Speculation that Nixon would quit intensified, but he still vowed to fight on to the end.

But when the U.S. Supreme Court unanimously voted to direct the President to obey a Congressional subpoena and turn over White House tapes that Nixon still held, the endgame had arrived. The infamous "smoking gun" tape of June 23, 1972 proved that Nixon had masterminded the cover-up from the beginning, and the last of Nixon's support crumbled.

Uncharacteristically, McCall made himself unavailable to the press as Nixon's final days began. Cut off from the inner circle, the vice president watched along with the rest of the nation as the last chapters of the scandal played out. His staff found him to be moody and preoccupied, and they weren't able to penetrate his protective veil. The man who thrived on human contact like others thrived on food and water took to spending long periods alone behind the closed door of his office.

Schmidt asked him if Audrey had ordered new drapes for the White House yet, the kind of jab that would usually get a rise out of McCall, but he refused to take the bait, muttering something that Schmidt could only half understand. Even Audrey found it difficult to break through the shell her husband had built around himself.

She came closest during a series of long drives they took through the Virginia countryside, where they could escape the congestion and clamor of Washington. These trips had been Tom's idea; he wanted to get away from having to turn away reporters' calls or say "no comment" over and over. And though he couldn't articulate it for his family, an inner voice was telling him that these days represented their last opportunity to enjoy a freedom they would never know again. So Tom, Audrey and Sam climbed into their leased Lincoln Continental as their Secret Service detail followed at a discreet distance, and headed down the back roads.

Audrey admired the beauty of the rolling green hills, and while her husband nodded in agreement, he couldn't but help blurt out a dismissive comment: "The Blue Ridge *Mountains*? They call those *mountains*? We call those hills back home, you know."

"Yes, Tom," Audrey said, reaching for her husband's free hand. "I know." Audrey had to acknowledge that the countryside was lovely, but couldn't begin to match the sweeping beauty and variety of Oregon: the vast deserts, soaring mountain peaks and rugged coastal headlands. No wonder a larger-than-life figure like her husband was having difficulty feeling at home in a landscape that seemed so constrained.

"And don't even get me started on what they call beaches out here..."

It finally dawned on Audrey McCall why the last days of Richard Nixon were taking such a toll on her husband. It literally sickened him to be so close to such cynically corrupt men. It made his stomach hurt, it made his head hurt, it pained him to his very core. He had been brought up to believe that words like honor and freedom were more than slogans; they represented core values of what it meant to be an American, what it meant to be an honorable human being. He had gone to Washington understanding that Agnew, the exponent of nut-chewing politics, was not an aberration in the Nixon camp. Presidential aide Chuck Colson had once said he would walk over his own grandmother if necessary to help Nixon win (not run over her, as usually reported, but the truth was bad enough). But until McCall had been confronted with the ugly coarseness first hand, he couldn't absorb the depth of the moral decay at the center of the Nixon White House.

McCall's political instincts told him where things were headed, even while many commentators refused to believe the end was finally at hand for Nixon. McCall would have appreciated any kind of an overture from the White House at this point; but the communication channel between the West Wing and the office of the vice president remained silent.

John Adams had once said, "I am vice president. In this, I am nothing, but I may be everything." Schmidt had framed those words and hung them in McCall's office weeks before, a reminder to all of them that they could be crossing that chasm that separated 'nothing' from 'everything' any day now. As the August heat hung heavy over Washington, they all began to sense that moment was at hand.

It wasn't until the morning of August seventh that McCall received a phone call from Al Haig as he and Audrey finished their breakfast at their rented home in Arlington, Virginia.

Congress had recently approved the purchase of the first official vice-presidential residence, which was being renovated at this moment with the expectation that the McCalls would be its first official occupants. Audrey McCall had even visited the property a couple of times and had some input on paint and decorations. By the time McCall had finished speaking with Haig that morning, he knew that he, Audrey and Sam would never be moving into the vice-presidential estate. Audrey McCall only heard snatches of her husband's end of the conversation, but she could pick up enough from his tone of voice to know that it was something momentous.

McCall hung up the phone, sighed heavily, and turned to his wife.

"That was Haig. The son of a bitch is resigning tomorrow." Audrey McCall thought she saw her husband's eyes misting up. He shook his head in disbelief. "My God, Audrey, what have I gotten us into?"

7

Before the McCalls could absorb the enormity of what was happening, Haig called back. McCall was being summoned to a meeting at the White House later that day. He had expected to see Nixon face-to-face, but that didn't happen. When the limousine delivered him back to his house, he stormed in. Audrey later told her sons she had never seen their father so angry.

"The S.O.B. asked me to promise to pardon the other S.O.B.!" he said, his voice rising theatrically.

"Tom, what are you talking about?"

"Nixon! Haig wanted me to promise to pardon Nixon! I said, pardon him for WHAT? You don't pardon a man unless you know he's guilty of something!"

McCall snatched the phone. He needed more of his "Oregon mafia" at his side, people he knew and trusted, if he was going to take up this burden. Westerdahl and Schmidt arrived within the hour to form an emergency transition team. Penwell had beaten them by a few minutes, and had a portable electric typewriter set up on the McCall dining room table. She was screening incoming phone calls, which were almost non-stop. It took some effort to keep the line clear long enough to place an outgoing call.

The television set in the living room was turned on, but the continuous coverage leading up to Nixon's live address to the nation was only background chatter with the flurry of activity unfolding. Tom, Doris, Ron and Ed only paused and redirected their attention when the presidential seal flashed on the screen. Audrey and Sam stepped to the vice president's side.

"Look at him," McCall said as Nixon's face appeared on the screen. "You'd never know he was about to walk the plank."

"In all the decisions I have made in my public life, I have always tried to do what was best for the Nation," Nixon intoned gravely. Westerdahl snorted and Schmidt shook his head. "Throughout the long and difficult period of Watergate, I have felt it was my duty to persevere, to make every possible effort to complete the term of office to which you elected me. In the past few days, however, it has become evident to me that I no longer have a strong enough political base in the Congress to justify continuing that effort. But with the disappearance of that base, I now believe that the constitutional purpose has been served, and there is no longer a need for the process to be prolonged."

"What did he just say?" a disbelieving Sam McCall asked. "That he's quitting, not because he did anything wrong, but because he needed to get out of here before Congress strings him up?"

Tom McCall laughed. "That's exactly what he said, son."

Nixon pressed on until he spoke the words that sent a shiver down all their spines: "Therefore, I shall resign the Presidency effective at noon tomorrow. Vice President McCall will be sworn in as President at that hour in this office." It was real at last.

On the other side of the country, in a Portland apartment, Dorothy McCall watched the speech with a growing sense of righteous indignation at the man who had put the country through hell for two years and pride in her son at his moment of destiny. Nixon tried to convey some sense of humanity at this moment: "As I recall the high hopes for America with which we began this second term, I feel a great sadness that I will not be here in this office working on your behalf to achieve those hopes in the next two and a half years. But in turning over direction of the Government to Vice President McCall, I know, as I told the Nation when I nominated him for that office 10 months ago, that the leadership of America will be in good hands."

Dorothy McCall snorted. "The first honest words out of that man's mouth in ages," she declared as she hit the mute button on the television's remote and reached for the telephone. She had a long list of people in her head she knew would want to hear from her right now. She had declined Schmidt's invitation of a flight to Washington to see her son sworn in. She wasn't feeling her best, she had told her son's aide. Though she wouldn't voice the thought aloud to anyone, she knew this was her son's moment, and it would be an act of grace to leave the spotlight all to him.

In Washington, another Grande Dame was also relishing the downfall of the man she always thought of as Tricky Dick. The man had put such a stain on the name of the Republican Party her father had loved so much; he deserved all of this shame and more. In the third-floor bedroom of her Massachusetts Avenue townhouse, Alice Roosevelt Longworth was also thinking about which reporters might be interested in hearing from her at this pivotal moment in history.

Theodore Roosevelt's daughter was ninety, and as much as she hated to admit it to anyone including herself, she was getting old, and it was a sad thing just when Washington might be fun again. Fun had been an alien concept here for a long time, ever since poor Jack Kennedy was shot. Although they called her father a cowboy, she was proud of the Roosevelts' aristocratic Dutch heritage. She wondered what the McCall era would bring. Her memories raced back across the decades. She remembered crossing the path of the president's grandfather, old Tom Lawson, at many social gatherings. Lawson had aroused the ire of many in the uppercrust when he turned his pen loose on them; it was father himself who coined the term "muckraker" to describe Lawson, Ida Tarbell and others of that ilk. It seemed worse coming from Lawson, who was branded a traitor to his class.

Lawson had written a twenty-month long series about stock market abuse and insurance fraud for *Everybody's Magazine* in 1904, later published as a book and titled *Frenzied Finance.* He hoped the articles would inspire the president to "shake the largest trusts and corporations until their teeth chattered and their backbones rattled like hung dried corn in a fireplace when the wind gets at it." Father had taken on the trusts, but he hadn't needed Lawson's help, or any of the other muckrakers, to get the job done.

Alice didn't know much at all about the president-to-be, but she was aware he had risen from the ranks of journalism. Well, look at what those damn kids at the *Post* had done, she thought. The muckrakers were in charge at last. Maybe it would be fun again. Where was his wife from, though? Idaho? Alice hadn't spent much time there. She knew it was part of the region of the country father had loved best, but it was so wild, so uncivilized. She just hoped the new First Lady would know how to arrange a decent party. Well, his mother was still alive, and that gave her hope. Dorothy McCall was just four years younger than she, and had grown up in elegance; Alice hoped she would take her daughter-in-law by the hand if needed to show her how to entertain.

The White House East Room was chosen as the location for the swearing-in ceremony. Although the room only seated 275 people, millions would be able to watch the proceedings on television. Schmidt began scrawling notes for an Inaugural Address even as he worked to track down Chief Justice Warren Burger, who was vacationing in the Netherlands. He also made sure that Tad McCall was on a military jet from the west coast in order to reach Washington in time for the ceremony. None of the McCalls liked using the authority of the vice president's position for any sort of personal benefit, but Schmidt felt strongly enough to set this in motion without clearing it with his boss.

"Very few men ever get to see their father sworn in as president," he told Penwell. "If there's any flak about this, I'll take it."

There was no requirement that the Chief Justice administer the oath; Federal Judge Sarah Hughes had sworn in Lyndon Johnson before he left Dallas on the day of Kennedy's assassination. Calvin Coolidge had taken the oath from his own father in the middle of the night when he had received word of Warren Harding's death in 1923. But with the country teetering on the edge of a constitutional crisis, McCall thought it was important symbolically to have the Chief Justice oversee the transfer of power, and Burger agreed to cut his vacation short. A military jet was sent to bring him back to Washington.

The reality was starting to sink in: the transfer of the power of the presidency, which is a process that stretches over several weeks in normal circumstances, would happen in a matter of hours. McCall's anger at Nixon grew. He wasn't a scholar, but he knew history, and he thought about Harry Truman taking over for Franklin Roosevelt in the waning days of World War II. During the twelve weeks that Truman served as vice president, he and Roosevelt met face-to-face just two times. Truman hadn't learned that the United States had developed the first atomic bomb until after he became president.

McCall's instincts told him Nixon hadn't been keeping any secrets quite that big, but he had done almost nothing to prepare his vice president for the possibility of stepping into the top job. McCall thought about Truman, and the famous story about him being called to the White House one gray Thursday afternoon in 1945. Truman had been in the Capitol Building when the summons came, and even though he wasn't told the reason, he intuitively knew something big was up; he sprinted toward the car that would take him to the White House, where his destiny awaited him.

Truman soon found himself in the second floor residence of the mansion, where Eleanor Roosevelt laid a hand on his shoulder and informed him the president was dead.

"Is there anything I can do for you?" Truman asked.

"Is there anything we can do for you?" Eleanor answered. "For you are the one in trouble now."

McCall took a deep breath. He thought some more about the situation Truman had walked into; his first major decision had been whether or not to use the bomb on civilian populations. Next to that, what McCall was facing was a piece of cake. He could handle this. He picked up the phone and made another call.

By the time midnight rolled around, McCall had commitments from his legal counsel, Robert Oliver, and his second term executive assistant, Bob Davis, to join his White House staff. Many back home had expected Davis to make the move the year before, but McCall had encouraged him to stay on and help Myers keep things on course in Salem. But now that Myers had just a few months left in the governorship, McCall didn't hesitate to issue the summons.

McCall took the oath of office from Chief Justice Burger shortly after noon the following day. Nixon had been carried off the White House lawn in a Marine helicopter, giving a final salute to gathered supporters. McCall watched the spectacle, which followed a strange, rambling, at times tearful, farewell message Nixon delivered to his staff in front of network television cameras.

Audrey McCall once again held the family Bible. This time her pride was leavened by a heavy dose of foreboding. She was sure her spouse was up to the task, yet she was sobered by the thought of how her husband's predecessors had departed the office: Nixon, forced out in disgrace; Johnson, hounded from office by hatred of the war; Kennedy, assassinated. Eisenhower was the last man to exit the job more or less whole. McCall seemed grimly determined as he addressed the nation's leaders gathered before him, and the millions more watching on television from coast to coast:

"We have emerged from the darkness of deceit," the new president declared. "Let us now throw open the windows of the White House and let the light of openness and truth come shining in." A survey by the *Columbia Journalism Review* determined that one-quarter of the nation's newspaper editorial cartoonists used some variation on McCall's "windows" metaphor at some point in the days following the inaugural.

McCall promised a new level of candor with the press and the

American people, including weekly media availabilities. Many doubted the sincerity of the pledge, but not the reporters from his home state who knew him best. They had joked that despite the presence of the able Ron Schmidt, McCall really was his own press secretary. He even allowed an NBC crew to follow him from morning to night for several days the following week, though he did point to the remote microphone clipped to his lapel as he headed to the bathroom on the first morning of shooting and ask, "How do you shut this damned thing off?"

The new president asked Nixon's cabinet to stay on, with one exception. McCall accepted the resignation of Rogers Morton, the only easterner to serve as interior secretary in the twentieth century. In his place, McCall tapped Morton's predecessor, former Alaska Governor Wally Hickel. Nixon had chosen Hickel for his original cabinet, but had unceremoniously fired him in late 1970 after Hickel openly criticized the administration's "lack of appropriate concern for the attitude of a great mass of Americans – our young people."

Although the Sierra Club and many environmentalists had opposed Hickel's initial appointment, he had won over his critics during his two years in the job, supporting legislation to impose new liabilities on oil companies operating offshore rigs and other environmental protections.

Writing in the *New York Times*, pundit James Reston called McCall's decision to bring back Hickel "inspired." Reston declared: "In one bold move, McCall signaled that his administration will be about both change and continuity. He also sent a pointed rebuke to his predecessor."

While praising McCall for his candor in his first days in office, Democratic National Committee Chairman Robert Strauss also sounded a note of caution in a news release the following week.

"As Oregon's governor, President McCall urged people to 'visit but don't stay.' Will President McCall send the same message to the world, 'visit America, but don't stay?' Like it or not, the United States has a key role on the international stage. We cannot afford to enter a new era of isolationism as the country begins to heal from the wounds of Watergate."

Strauss' statement was widely seen as the opening shot in the 1976 presidential race.

Nixon quit on a Friday morning. McCall was presented with his first great challenge exactly one week later. Attorney General William Saxbe had pushed for a face-to-face meeting sooner, but Westerdahl had put him off, saying McCall needed some time to sort out priorities and be brought up to date on foreign affairs. When Saxbe walked into the Oval Office, he only spent a couple of minutes on pleasantries before laying out the question: was he, Tom McCall, ready to order the Justice Department to move ahead with the prosecution of Richard Nixon, or did he want to consider a pardon?

Saxbe carried a memo Watergate Special Prosecutor Leon Jaworski had prepared the previous Friday. He had laid out a persuasive case for going after the ex-president; the need to reach a final disposition in the case; the fact that Article 1, Section 3, Clause 7 of the Constitution specifically called out that impeached officials would be liable for criminal prosecution after their removal; that surrender of the office should not alone be considered sufficient punishment; that forgoing prosecution because of publicity would effectively grant any president immunity from prosecution; and first and foremost, the principle that no one is above the law.

McCall absorbed this document in an Oval Office that still had a barren feel to it. Nixon's books, pictures and personal mementoes had been boxed up in preparation for being shipped to San Clemente, and lighter rectangles and squares were visible on the walls where his pictures had been removed. Only one item in the room signaled the heritage of its new occupant: a scale model of the *Thomas W. Lawson*, the only seven-masted schooner ever built, and named for the new president's maternal grandfather. The model had been proudly displayed in the governor's office, and had been carefully packed for the move east. Audrey was already working with the staff, overseeing plans to redecorate the Oval Office, but that work hadn't started yet.

McCall listened impassively as Westerdahl scribbled notes. Bob Oliver had promised to come to Washington, but needed time to make arrangements; both men wished he was there already. The President indicated Saxbe should lay out the case against prosecution. He was doing his best not to openly signal where his thinking was headed, no sighs, frowns or head shakes, as much of a poker face as he could manage, although his heart was already steering his head in a clear direction.

"Well, it's pretty simple, Mr. President," Saxbe said. "An awful lot of people, including me, think the president, uh, the former president, has been punished enough. That a prosecution would only prolong the anger and division. That it's time to put Watergate behind us and move on with the business of the country."

McCall thanked Saxbe for his time and promised to have an answer for him by the end of the day.

When Saxbe left, McCall asked Westerdahl to summon Schmidt. The three men spent the next hour in a furious debate. It became clear that Schmidt was for prosecution and Westerdahl was against it. McCall asked questions and poked and prodded both men, but didn't show his hand until the end. With a theatrical wag of his finger he declared, "Gentlemen, I am about to commit political suicide. I am going to order the prosecution of Richard Nixon!"

There was just a hint of a smile of Schmidt's lips. "Political suicide? Where have I heard that one before?"

McCall grinned, "It was a good line last time, and it still fits. It may cost me the election two years from now—if I even decide to run, but damn it, it's the right thing to do."

"Tom, uh, Mr. President," Schmidt corrected himself. "You may have just won the election right here and now."

"Oh come on. The Republicans will never even think of nominating me after this. Hell, they'll probably lock me out of the goddamned convention."

McCall's decision touched off a firestorm that didn't abate for days. The first reverberation came that very night, when a courier delivered Saxbe's letter of resignation. The message was respectful in tone and wished the new president well, but made it clear that he could not stay on to support a decision he absolutely believed was "wrong for the country."

The next morning, McCall told Westerdahl he had a candidate in mind to run the Justice Department: Elliot Richardson. Richardson had resigned from the job the previous October after refusing Nixon's direct order to fire the first Watergate prosecutor, Archibald Cox. The "Saturday Night Massacre" had turned Richardson into an overnight folk hero, and he was being talked up as a potential presidential candidate in 1976, something Westerdahl was quick to point out. McCall brushed that argument aside.

"Damn it, Ed, I know that. But I don't care. If we don't restore people's confidence in the country—if they don't believe the system can actually work—then there might not even be an election to worry about in a couple of years."

Richardson accepted McCall's request to come to Washington that afternoon, and his return to the Justice Department was announced by Schmidt that evening. The move won almost universal applause in the press and from the general public, although the sardonic Nicholas Von Hoffman, writing in the *Washington Post*, couldn't help but note, tongue firmly planted in his cheek, that with the return of Hickel and Richardson the McCall White House was beginning to look like "the son of the Nixon administration with the original cast, but without the break-ins, wiretapping, bribery and paranoia." Von Hoffman was as much a fan of McCall as anyone in his position could be; he had praised McCall during his governorship for being "unmistakably forthright."

Von Hoffman was about the only Washington journalist to "get" McCall from the start. While most of the Eastern press corps had pegged the Oregon Beach Bill as McCall's defining moment as governor, when his leadership gifts took full flower, Von Hoffman surmised that the Vortex rock festival marked the emergence of the real McCall. In the journalist's view, McCall's championing of the Beach Bill was actually something that was completely aligned with his values and the values of his party. His gift for political theater may have been on display, but at heart it was a conservative measure, in the classic sense of the word, for it was involved a literal act of conservation—the preservation of public rights that dated, in lawyer's terms, "from time immemorial."

Vortex was different. Vortex wasn't conservative; it was revolutionary. In an era when passions were at their highest—between young and old, war Hawks and peacenicks, hipsters and squares—McCall had made an extremely risky decision, totally without precedent, and he had done it when he had everything to lose politically. It would have been quite easy to lock down and arm Portland as the American Legion arrived. Even though it might have led to bloodshed, it was an absolutely safe decision politically and personally. McCall had served in the Navy himself and his own son was serving honorably in Vietnam at the time. How could anyone argue with a stance for law and order? McCall ultimately trusted his gut, decided it was the right thing to do. That moment, in Von Hoffman's view, represented the true crucible of Tom McCall's career and set the stage for all the accomplishments that followed in his abbreviated second term.

Yet even Von Hoffman was skeptical that the Oregon model could be scaled to fit the national stage. In the midst of Vortex, he wrote:

> *Portland could come to be regarded as a model for other places and situations. That would be a mistake. Tough talk and procrastination with parade permits doesn't always cut down the size of the crowd as the Washington moratorium last fall showed; an alternative rock festival wouldn't have averted Chicago; finagling with dope enforcement is too transparent and ineffective because people in large numbers can safely*

smoke it anywhere and are as likely to at a demonstration as at a rock festival.

The mood here (Oregon) is wrong for massive manifestations. The country is too beautiful, the Oregonians too polite and civilized, the Legionnaires too well behaved to irritate their would-be opponents. Excluding a few incidents, there will be peace in Portland. First Amendment rights will be protected. Thanks to some benign manipulation by public officials and a happy conjunction of the stars, we will have gotten over another hump, but hump jumping isn't the same as problem solving.

Von Hoffman thought McCall had a deft political touch, even if he categorized him as more of a hump jumper than a problem solver. Like most of the Washington press corps, though, he harbored serious doubts whether he could successfully negotiate the transition from Salem to Washington. These first few months of the McCall presidency had done little to dispel those doubts.

Another *Post* columnist, George Will, offered his readers an intriguing slice of history: there might have been a President McCall decades earlier if Tom McCall's maternal grandfather had his way:

In 1916, Thomas W. Lawson wrote a small book he titled A Path Pointer. *Lawson was boosting Theodore Roosevelt for the Republican presidential nomination. Four years earlier, TR's attempt to reclaim the presidency had split the party and he had run under the Progressive Party banner. But as the United States headed for the brink of war, the more militant wing of the GOP was eager to welcome TR back into the fold.*

The full title of the extended essay was, "A Path Pointer for Delegates to the National Republican Convention," and Lawson had five thousand copies printed for distribution to the delegates and other influential individuals.

Lawson used the slim volume to boost Roosevelt's candidacy and to blast the apparent front-runner (and eventual nominee) Charles Evans Hughes. If Roosevelt wouldn't run, Lawson had an alternative: Samuel Walker McCall, who had been elected governor of Massachusetts the previous year following two decades of service in the U.S. House of Representatives.

What makes this interesting is the fact that Lawson's daughter was married to McCall's son. Imagine Black Jack Bouvier penning a tract in 1956 boosting Joseph P. Kennedy for president.

Lawson envisioned a McCall presidency:

"Samuel Walker McCall, Governor of Massachusetts, twenty continuous years congressman from the most typically American district in the United States, the Harvard University district, author, lecturer, orator, and all-round greatest statesman in America. One could write on and on, filling volumes and volumes with glowing pictures of his great ability, his profound learning, his splendid oratory, his superb pen, his rugged honesty, his simple, spontaneous courage, his subconscious fearlessness, his retiring modesty at medal-giving time, and his may- I-to-the-weak-I-will-to-the-strong all-round, manly good- ness...

President McCall would not enter the White House to the bass-drumming of 'The Conquering Hero Comes,' rather to the sweet bag-piping of "Auld Lang Syne." He would not set the White House afire or turn it into an ice factory, neither would he bathe on the roof or bag his trousers kowtowing to the embassies of foreign or American royalties, but shades of the nation's earlier days! What lawn minuetings and quilting bees the American people would have with as true a type of American as ever occupied the historical home of presidents. And then, too, it would be decades and decades before the Presidents who would follow would lose the habit of atmosphering in the Yankee sweetness which Sam McCall and his wife, sons, daughters, and grand-children, would have left behind to distinguish the days when the Executive Mansion held the sort it was built to hold."

Lawson's grandson and namesake was three years old at the time these words were written. Undoubtedly, the Copper King couldn't foresee that there was indeed a President McCall in the country's future, but not in his lifetime.

"What if" historical speculations may be amusing, if not scholarly; it is intriguing, though, to imagine the McCalls as another American political dynasty, taking their place alongside the Adamses and Harrisons.

8

The latest developments in the Nixon case seemed to take Jaworski by surprise. Richardson carried word to McCall that the prosecutor, despite laying out a strong case for moving ahead, harbored doubts about whether he could assure Nixon the prompt, fair trial guaranteed to any criminal defendant by the Constitution. "If pressed by the court, his answer would be no," Richardson said.

The tide of public opinion was heavily in the president's favor, but as McCall predicted, he was strongly lambasted by the Republican establishment. One of the milder rebukes came from Congressman Gerald Ford, who, in an appearance on ABC's *Issues and Answers*, declared, "This is not a time for retribution. This is a time for healing." Earlier in the week, Ford had announced plans to step down from Congress at the end of the year. Sitting in the historic St. John's Episcopal church the following Sunday morning, he heard the minister read Jesus' words on the cross: "Father, if you are willing, take this cup from me." Although he wasn't entirely pleased with McCall's actions, Ford offered a silent prayer of gratitude that fate had spared him the burdens of the presidency. He would go home to Michigan thankful for the opportunity to have served his people for a quarter-century; if he had any disappointment, it would be that his one true ambition, being speaker of the house, had gone unfulfilled. But a call from the White House following that broadcast would derail Ford's plans.

The McCalls were also Episcopalians, and had sometimes shared a pew with the Fords, but this was a working Sunday for the president. Betty Ford interrupted her preparation of the family's lunch to call her husband to the phone. "It's the president," she whispered as she passed the receiver to her husband. "Jerry?" McCall asked. "I'd like to talk with you. I don't think your service to your country is finished yet."

When Ford hung up the phone, he looked at his wife and smiled. "I may be headed to the White House after all," he said.

McCall and Ford appeared at the Monday morning press briefing to announce that Ford was stepping down from the House immediately in order to go to work in the White House as deputy chief of staff, chief Congressional liaison, and chief domestic policy adviser. Audrey McCall had asked her husband whether he really needed to introduce an outsider into his inner circle at this point, but the President explained: "Jerry is beloved up there (Capitol Hill). Hell, a lot of those Congressmen still think it should be him, not me, sitting here right now. And he knows how to count votes. You know, that's the first rule of politics. Count the votes."

Westerdahl welcomed the appointment. "We need another pipe smoker around here," he quipped.

McCall told Westerdahl and the rest of the team that they desperately needed a Washington insider. "You know, I think there's a side of Jerry he's kept hidden from the public," McCall observed. "The man was on the Warren Commission. He probably knows what really happened to Kennedy. I think Jerry's not going to be afraid to bring the hammer down up there when it's necessary."

The public furor over Watergate died down for a few weeks as Jaworski and Nixon's personal lawyer, Herb Kalmbach, began the behind-the-scenes business of criminal negotiations. A criminal prosecution often resembles a poker game: more often than not, one side or the other folds its hand before anyone bets. Both men hoped they could still spare the country the spectacle of a former president on trial. McCall found himself torn over what outcome he wanted to see. Although his head was telling him a trial was the only way to assure that Nixon would have to account for his actions, he had to acknowledge there was truth to Saxbe's argument that a trial would rip the country apart. But he realized that things were out of his hands now. Nixon, like any other criminal defendant, had the right to negotiate a plea deal.

There was another unexpected twist that suddenly sent an emotional tide of sympathy Nixon's way, something that would have seemed impossible a few weeks earlier: the former president was hospitalized with a serious, potentially life-threatening attack of phlebitis which would require surgery and an extended rehabilitation.

"Damn," Westerdahl muttered when he heard the news on John Chancellor's nightly report. "We're going to really look like we're kicking a man when he's down." Schmidt, who was standing next to him said evenly, "Ed. Remember 'I am not a crook?' The country would never forgive Tom, or any of us, if we let him get away with that."

On Friday, September 6, the front page of the *New York Times* carried the news in type usually reserved for declarations of war and presidential assassinations: Nixon to Plead to Obstruction of Justice. The story, based on unnamed sources, said Nixon would enter a no contest plea to two counts of obstruction of justice. (While technically not a guilty plea, this means the accused chooses not to offer a defense.) The expectation was that Nixon would receive a suspended sentence. McCall breathed a sigh of relief. That relief would be short-lived, because none of the other players in this drama had factored in the heart and mind of John J. Sirica.

"Maximum John" Sirica was the federal judge presiding over the Watergate cases. He had earned the nickname for his tendency to impose the longest sentence allowed under the law when a defendant was convicted; it also underlined his stern appearance. His strong jaw and carefully combed black and steel-grey hair made him a formidable presence in the courtroom.

His career had been largely undistinguished until now, but he was writing his name into the history books with the Watergate case. He was about to show one more time why he had earned his nickname.

And the most famous team of reporters in the country were about to deliver one more exclusive. Bob Woodward, as usual, was working late at his desk at the Washington Post building on 15th Street Northwest when his phone rang.

Woodward and Carl Bernstein had their story in Executive Editor Ben Bradlee's hands by noon the next day. They had risked Sirica's wrath before when they had approached members of the Watergate Grand Jury for interviews, and they knew that the volatile judge would be angry now, but it was a story important enough to be worth the risk; the pair was extra-eager for an exclusive, after having been beaten by the New York Times on the news of the plea deal. The *Times* and *Post* were locked in a fierce battle for preeminence in American journalism.

The clock was ticking toward the deadline for the first edition of the Sunday paper. Bradlee, who was eager to get out of town for a weekend on Martha's Vineyard with his wife Sally Quinn, quickly satisfied himself the reporting was solid. He did look up from the typewritten pages to ask Woodward and Bernstein, "You boys are ready to go to jail, this time, right? You can poke the bear only so many times." Two heads nodded in unison. "Just checking." Bradlee had rolled the sheets of copy into a tube, and he slapped Woodward on the shoulder with it before unfurling the pages and handing them back to him, saying, "Go with it."

Sirica Considering Prison Term for Nixon
By Bob Woodward and Carl Bernstein

> *Highly placed sources close to Federal Judge John J. Sirica say he is prepared to sentence former President Richard M. Nixon to a prison term. Nixon, who became the first president to resign, last week pleaded guilty to two counts of obstruction of justice.*
>
> *Most observers believed the former president entered the plea with an expectation that he would not be sentenced to any form of incarceration.*

The news that he may in fact be facing prison time has unleashed speculation about how the federal government could cope with the situation.

"You obviously can't put him in a standard federal facility," said one member of the prosecution team. "You might have to put him at a military prison, or place him under house arrest, although I doubt that Sirica would agree to that one."

When the story appeared, Sirica was predictably furious, but he didn't order Woodward and Bernstein to disclose their sources, a move that could have led to them facing contempt charges and jail time. The real reason the judge gave the reporters a pass wasn't disclosed until years after McCall's death: the president had attempted to contact Sirica directly in an effort to persuade the judge not to impose the prison sentence, and the judge was more focused on that fact than any newspaper story. Only Audrey McCall, Westerdahl and Schmidt knew about the approach; all three had counseled against it.

"You're treading on dangerous ground, Tom," Westerdahl had warned.

"I understand that Ed, but damn it, this will absolutely tear the country apart," he said, picking up the phone and dialing. "Third world countries throw their deposed dictators in jail; we don't do that. The man has admitted he's a crook; we don't need to make him into a martyr." Westerdahl listened with trepidation as McCall asked to be put through to Sirica. He saw confusion, then surprise on his boss' face as he muttered a brief "thanks," and hung up.

"Well, so much for the power of the imperial presidency," McCall said with a rueful smile. Westerdahl looked at the president quizzically, waiting to hear more. "He refused to talk to me."

"It's probably for the best." Sirica passed word through a Justice Department contact that he would consider citing the president for contempt if the effort was repeated.

If word had leaked out that the president had attempted a direct intervention in the case, it would have been one more Watergate bombshell, but there was still plenty of fallout from the Woodward-Bernstein story. Political cartoonists raced to their drawing boards, eager to portray the thirty-seventh president wearing stripes behind bars. Comedians sharpened their jokes. McCall, still in his bathrobe as he read the Post in the private residence of the White House, knew he had to act, and he had to do it quickly and decisively. He summoned Richardson, Westerdahl, Schmidt, Ford and Oliver to the Oval Office "as fast as you can get your butts over here."

Audrey McCall silently shook her head as she watched her husband hang up the phone. She had done her best to establish the White House as a true home for the McCall family, though she was sure one of the nation's great landmarks would never really feel like it was theirs. Still, she had tried to focus on the positives, like the fact that her husband was only a short walk away from his office. That meant they were only minutes away from each other. She had tried to preserve whatever private routines of theirs that she could. She still mixed the gin, vermouth and ice that constituted their nightly martin and put it in the freezer of their living quarters to await Tom's evening return from the Oval Office.

But when a crisis like this erupted and he had to run out on an otherwise peaceful Sunday morning, it seemed like it wouldn't make a difference if he was three thousand miles away. The president gave his wife a quick peck on the cheek before hurrying to their bedroom to change.

The First Lady worried about the stress the job was placing on her husband. Even though he had negotiated the Washington minefields successfully so far, she still saw the toll the past months had taken on her husband. She had recently approached Westerdahl, pleading that he try to get McCall to cut back on his schedule, but Westerdahl had brushed those concerns aside, saying the president was thriving on the challenges and would let everyone know when he needed a break.

The six men met in the Oval Office forty-five minutes later. The Oregonians were dressed casually; Richardson was in a London-tailored suit, having been summoned right before he was to leave for church. Ford was in golf pants and sweater, having planned to skip church for a day on the links.

McCall told his aides he wasn't opening up a debate; he had already made up his mind. He was going to grant Nixon executive clemency if the proper arrangements could be ironed out. Westerdahl and Schmidt exchanged knowing looks.

"I ticked off half the country by refusing to pardon him," McCall said. "Now I'm going to tick off the other half by refusing to let him go to jail."

"If no one is happy, that's often the sign of a just decision," Richardson said.

Ford offered an enthusiastic, "Good call, Mr. President!"

"I'll get started on a draft," Schmidt said. Their usual procedure for a speech of this magnitude was for Schmidt to produce a preliminary version, which McCall would then revise. But not this time.

"No Ron," the President said. "I need to do this one myself. I hope you understand." Schmidt nodded; he knew McCall the wordsmith would want to make sure every word of the speech conveyed his personal convictions. Even before his love of the environment and his love of public service, Tom McCall had developed his love of words. Words mattered deeply to him. He wanted to make sure that he chose every one of them with extraordinary care on this occasion.

Soon McCall was ensconced in the small study he had established just off the Oval Office. This was reminiscent of his working office in Salem, the desk piled high with books and papers, his trusty Royal manual typewriter sitting in the center of the desk, a well-thumbed dictionary within easy reach. He prided himself on never needing a thesaurus; the dictionary was the tool he used to make sure he chose exactly the right word.

"Don't touch anything or I won't be able to find anything," he sternly told his professional colleagues when they veered too close to his workspace. The same warning applied at the McCall home, where Tom's messy study stood in sharp contrast to the otherwise neat house that Audrey kept. Neatniks would never understand, but most people recognized that McCall's desks were a perfect reflection of his mind; forever overflowing with facts and ideas, passion spilling over the edges, an overarching vision that was too great to be contained in neat, orderly piles.

Woodrow Wilson was the last president to write all his own speeches. Given the modern demands of the job and with someone who understood his thought processes as well as Schmidt close by, McCall wasn't going to try to revive that tradition. But this address was of singular importance. The president spread out the notes he had scribbled, rolled a piece of paper into the well-worn platen, and began hammering away with two fingers. This initial draft would be filled with strike-overs (the lowercase "m" hammered repeatedly with the president's strong right index finger) and covered with additions and corrections in his scrawl; it would go through several iterations before a finished product was ready to be loaded on the Oval Office teleprompter. He worked late into the evening; Audrey finally called the White House kitchen to make sure a soup and sandwich tray was delivered to her husband.

Four days later, the United States ventured into uncharted territory once more as the networks carried live coverage of Nixon's guilty plea. The broadcasters were disappointed by the lack of theatrics and good visuals. Of course, no cameras were allowed in the courtroom, and reporters were only able to capture the most fleeting glimpses of Nixon being helped into a wheelchair from his limousine and being whisked in and out of the Courthouse. Woodward, whose sources had told him Nixon had been up and around for weeks, was appalled by the theatrics of it all. Kalmbach had all but begged to be allowed to enter the plea on Nixon's behalf, but Sirica had been unyielding on that point. Woodward was convinced that was all for show; he doubted that Nixon would have missed one more opportunity to play the victim, something he had been doing masterfully since the Checkers Speech.

The television views of the crowd outside the Federal Courthouse were replaced by the Presidential seal, and then a shot of McCall seated at his desk. The model of the Thomas W. Lawson sat on the table behind the president. Although McCall had been a frequent television presence in the weeks since taking over, this was his first address from the Oval Office. Schmidt thought his boss betrayed just the slightest hint of nervousness.

"Fellow citizens," he began. "I want to explain to you today why I have agreed to offer clemency to my predecessor, Richard M. Nixon. It is my firm belief that no man, up to and including the President of the United States, is above the law. When President Nixon resigned, many believed he had suffered sufficient punishment, and some urged me to pardon him. They said prosecuting a former president would further divide the country. I disagreed. I believed that if we were to ever completely close the book on Watergate, it would be imperative for us to have final resolution of any and all charges that might be brought against Mr. Nixon. That has now occurred. Mr. Nixon has appeared before the bar of justice to answer for his misdeeds." McCall paused and swallowed hard.

"However, there is no need to subject the country to the spectacle that would ensue with Mr. Nixon's imprisonment. I have consulted with federal officials who say that any effort to incarcerate him would pose great and probably insurmountable obstacles. The plea agreement that Mr. Nixon just signed includes a pledge of complete cooperation with Congressional and Department of Justice investigators on all matters and a stay of the prison term imposed by Judge Sirica. When the Attorney General and the Congressional Leadership inform me that all pending investigations are concluded, the stay of sentence will be removed and my order of clemency will take effect. This could take months and it could take years. The American people deserve nothing less than an opportunity for a complete review of the prior administration's conduct."

He closed with these words: "Richard Nixon will never again wield authority or influence over the affairs of this nation. History will forever remember that the American people bequeathed to him their ultimate gift, and he squandered that gift. Future presidents will ignore that lesson at their peril. Thank you, and good night."

The red light atop the camera went dark, and McCall let out an exhausted sigh.

The television crews had just exited the Oval Office and McCall was eager to get to the private residence to unwind with a drink, but he was stopped by Doris Penwell with words that caused his gut to tighten. "Your mother is on the phone." For years, the rule for all members of the McCall staff was that Dorothy McCall was never to be given any private or backdoor numbers to his office, or be put directly through to him, for she had the ability to consume an entire day; but when he became president, he had relaxed that rule. He never really explained why; most assumed it had to do with the fact that mother and son were now separated by three thousand miles instead of fifty, but there was speculation that he simply wanted to spare the White House press corps and staff the kind of hectoring their Oregon counterparts had been subjected to.

Mother McCall wasn't beyond cultivating a friendship with a young reporter covering the governor, then calling that journalist late at night to ask her to deliver a message the next time she saw her son. When the bemused reporter would pass the message along, the governor would shake his head and say, "Better you than me." Most of the time, staff was still able to run interference for McCall. Even the imperious Dorothy conceded her son was kept busy by the demands of his job. But there were also moments like this when it was hard to pretend he wasn't available.

With a sense of the inevitable, McCall settled back into his chair. He closed his eyes and rubbed his forehead with his right hand as he picked up the phone with his left; the strain of events on her boss seemed clear to Penwell. "Son!" Dorothy Lawson McCall cried, loud enough for Penwell to hear. "You should have let the son of a bitch rot in jail!"

As Penwell slipped out of the Oval Office, she heard her boss say with a heavy sigh, "Oh God, Mother, not you too." She gently closed the door.

9

The McCalls' spirits were buoyed by Tad's first visit to the White House. It was a welcome diversion from the strain of the ongoing Watergate drama. Tom McCall particularly enjoyed giving his eldest son the grand tour of the building and grounds. Tad had majored in history at the University of Oregon and had dreamed of a career teaching at his alma mater before Vietnam sent his life in a different direction. He would have been thrilled to get a first-hand, behind-the-scenes look at one of the country's most historic sites; the fact that his own father was now at the center of history in the making made it so much more special.

When they got to the tennis courts near the West Wing, Tad challenged his father to a match. Tom McCall had been an avid, self-taught player in his younger years, developing lots of unorthodox but effective strokes, cut shots and trick shots. Father and son would engage in titanic battles, but the competitive spirit in Tom made it hard for him to accept it when his son matured enough to start beating him.

"I'm going to take a pass, son," he said. "But let's plan on going fishing at Camp David the next time you can make it out here." Now it was Tad's turn to smile. He had many happy memories of fishing with his father. Perhaps one of the sweetest was a trip Tom planned to celebrate his son's return from Vietnam. The governor hired a guide and they drifted down a coastal stream. Tom senior snagged one steelhead and his namesake landed two. It was a wonderful, shared moment between father and son, which the entire state learned about as well when by sheer coincidence, a newspaper photographer happened to be fishing a short distance away on the same river and was able to capture the scene for posterity.

The president would find time with his family and time in his beloved outdoors to be even more precious as he grappled with the challenges and burdens of the presidency.

McCall had the good fortune to come into the Oregon governorship at a time when the national postwar economic boom was at its peak. He had the misfortune to become president just as the party was ending.

It had been a heady quarter-century since the end of World War II as the American standard of living reached unprecedented heights. A suburban ranch house with all the modern appliances in the kitchen and a color TV in the living room; two long, sleek powerful cars in the driveway; it was the American dream made tangible. Madison Avenue had done a superlative job of creating desires for products that were newer, shinier, somehow better than what had come before.

But it couldn't last forever. Any student of economic history knew that there are broad cycles to prosperity, and there was no question the U.S. economy was on a downhill run as McCall took office. Lots of theories were advanced as to why: Lyndon Johnson's refusal to seek a tax increase to pay for the Vietnam War; the steady escalation of oil prices from the Middle East; Nixon's fiddling with the economy (wage and price controls, keeping interest rates artificially low) in a desperate effort to keep inflation in check and unemployment from rising.

Whatever the cause, the reality was that inflation was speeding toward double digits and unemployment wasn't far behind.

McCall was no economist, but he was a bright man, and where he lacked deep knowledge, he listened to the experts. But he ultimately trusted his instincts.

He had been in office less than a month when he, Westerdahl and Schmidt had a meeting scheduled with an overly-enthusiastic young man from one of the top ad agencies in the country, Benton and Bowles. B and B lent some of its talents to the Ad Council, the nonprofit that used talent from the leading Madison Avenue agencies to produce public service campaigns. The Ad Council had been approached by staff for the President's Council on Economic Advisers to develop a program to enlist the public in the fight against inflation. Schmidt recalled the incident in his memoirs:

The President, Westerdahl and I walked into the Cabinet Room, where a nervous-looking young man stood next to an easel. A posterboard display, its back turned outward, sat on the easel. The young man was nervous; I could see beads of sweat on his upper lip. No doubt it was what I came to think of as the White House jitters. I worked there for six and a half years, and I still felt a sense of the majesty of the place every time I walked into the West Wing. I'm sure it was overwhelming for most first timers.

Although the President was one of the friendliest men I've never known, I could sense he took an almost immediate dislike to our guest. I later learned I was correct, in part because of his striking resemblance to the recently-departed Ron Zeigler, right down to the sideburns and the cheap polyester suit.

Our guest, who shall remain nameless, introduced himself and launched into his pitch, which he had tailored for a typical Republican. Unfortunately, he didn't know Tom McCall very well.

"We know the American people don't like to be told what to do. We know they want to do the right thing. Often it's as simple as just being asked. We know they understand that unchecked inflation can have devastating consequences." The tremble in his voice was starting to subside; I thought he might pull this off after all. Then he reached for the corkboard and turned it around.

"That's the thinking behind the campaign we're proposing—WIN, or whip inflation now." The board displayed a large red button with WIN spelled out in white block letters. I immediately caught the President's eye. We had been together on an almost daily basis for ten years at this point, and I thought I could read him pretty well. At the moment, what I was reading was distaste and disbelief. Westerdahl looked like he wanted to bolt from the room.

The ad man went on with his spiel. It got worse. He had a red-white-and blue gym bag with the "WIN" logo emblazoned on it sitting on the table in front of him; he now unzipped it. I began to wonder if he was going to pull out buttons reading, 'place,' 'show,' and 'scratch,' but instead he had stickers, buttons and pins with variations on the theme, a sweater, and earrings. For god's sake...Whip Inflation Now earrings. He was about to start explaining an 'inflation fighter' pledge form he wanted to have people sign and send back to the White House. I caught the president's eye. His brief nod told me I had license to interrupt. I stood up, walked to the easel and took the posterboard in hand and turned it upside down so it now read NIM.

"What's this going to stand for?" I asked. "Need Immediate Money? No Immediate Miracles? Non-stop Inflation Merry Go-round?" I could see the young man was trembling and looked ready to cry; the President was doing his best to stifle a laugh. He composed himself and told our guest: "I appreciate the effort here, but I just don't think this is the answer. It's going to take more than slogans and gimmicks to deal with the economy. Thanks for your time."

After the kid from B and B left, Tom could no longer restrain his urge to laugh. "They really thought that gimmicks were the answer? I think, as painful as it may be in the short run, we are going to have to let nature take its course. That means no more fiddling around to try to fix things. How many times have we seen the result with nature? Sometimes, it seems we have a gift for making things worse when we try to make them better."

He was right; once Nixon lifted wage and price controls, both businesses and their employees launched desperate efforts to catch up. Although McCall had favored the controls initially, he now realized they were too blunt an instrument. No, Tom reasoned, better to ride this thing out. He directed the Federal Reserve to gradually ease up on the brake on interest rates. He also pushed Congress for incremental tax increases, managing to appeal to that same spirit of "doing the right thing" the man from Benton and Bowles wanted to tap into. It didn't involve sloganeering as much as leading by example. For instance, Nixon had generated unwanted headlines (something he had a chronic gift for) by failing to pay income *tax; McCall made his returns public, showing that he was paying the full 70 percent tax rate on his presidential salary of $200,000 per year.*

A footnote: Gerry Ford saw the discarded WIN displays later that day as he arrived for the next scheduled meeting. "Looks like a good idea to me," he muttered.

One of the great political parlor games involves reading the results of an election as if they were tea leaves. Reporters, politicians themselves, and the public at large all delight in taking one night's results and seeing if there's a larger trend to be found.

On the night of November 5, 1974, readers of the tea leaves were ready to write President McCall's political obituary. Although McCall wasn't on the ballot, the election in the middle of a presidential term is seen as a crucial barometer of the public's opinion of the man in the White House.

Leaders of the Republican Party might be excused for thinking of their president as radioactive after they've absorbed the magnitude of the disaster they suffered in Tuesday's midterm elections," Nicholas Von Hoffman wrote. "The loss of three seats in the Senate and forty-six in the House is, to put it bluntly, a disaster for the GOP, mirroring the debacle the 1966 midterm elections represented for the Democrats.

"Some are faulting President McCall for not being more active on the campaign trail for Congressional Republicans in recent weeks. The more fair-minded might point out the blame for this ignoble result should not be laid at the feet of the president, but rather at the doorstep of his predecessor, private citizen Richard M. Nixon of San Clemente, California.

"In 1966, the team on the field for the Democrats absorbed the full wrath of the public that had decisively turned against Coach, or rather President Johnson's conduct of the Vietnam War. This time it was the Republican Congressional players who took the whipping voters would have preferred to administer to former Coach Nixon.

"As true as this might be, there's one fact that does turn the results from

the political to the personal for President McCall. The one Republican he did oppose—Vic Atiyeh, the party's candidate to replace Clay Myers in the state capitol in Salem—emerged a winner.

Ron Schmidt crumpled his copy of the *Washington Post* when he read those words. As a result, he missed Von Hoffman's take on whether the outcome had fatally damaged any chances McCall had for a term in his own right (the answer: too soon to tell). He was galled by the reference to the Oregon governor's race; galled, because it did hit home. He reached for a cigarette, and as he took a deep drag, tried to let go of his frustration.

Not surprisingly, the mood wasn't the brightest at the first post-election staff meeting in the Oval Office. Westerdahl suggested they head out into the Rose Garden and get into an om circle.

"Om circle?" Ford asked, his brow furrowing.

"You know. You get in a circle, join hands, and chant om. It's a mantra. Tom, uh, the president, did it after the close of Vortex. I was part of several om circles, too, you know."

McCall smiled at the memory. "It was after all but a few of the young people had cleared out of the park. The final cleanup crew was all that was left. I came in by helicopter to survey the scene and thank them. Some of them were still afraid that the National Guard would arrest them, but I gave them my vow that they would be safe. We recited the Lord's Prayer together and some lines of William Blake's poetry, and then we chanted." He paused and turned, looking out the window toward the Rose Garden. "Maybe we could have the staff build a fire for us. You know, we could use a barbecue pit out there."

Ford momentarily wondered if he had made a mistake by coming to the White House. But the moment did represent a minor epiphany for him; he realized that the McCall administration signaled a shift not just in degrees, but in magnitude, from the Nixon years. Never, in his wildest imaginings, could Ford picture Nixon, Al Haig, or H.R. Haldeman in an om circle.

It had been a rough fall for McCall. As he had predicted, one major constituency was angry with him for offering Nixon clemency, while another was furious with that he had refused to grant the former president a pardon. ("The middle of the road gets damn lonely on occasion," he had grumped to Audrey). Unfortunately, the latter group still was in control of the machinery of the Republican Party, and those with an interest in dusty historical precedents were already trotting out the name of Chester Alan Arthur. Arthur, the largely forgotten twenty-first President. He'd been the last vice president to ascend to the highest office and then be denied his party's nomination. This was back in 1881. Skeptics and critics were beginning to predict the same fate for McCall.

McCall had made a campaign swing through the Midwest and West in mid-October, supporting progressive Republicans like California Congressman Pete McCloskey, who had challenged Nixon's 1972 bid for renomination. But during a visit to Portland, he appeared at a news conference with Bob Straub to endorse him; he also filmed a pair of commercials on Straub's behalf. Because the weather cooperated, the filming took place outdoors, next to the Willamette River both men had done so much to clean up. In the first spot, McCall appeared alone, speaking directly to the camera and the unseen voters on the other side; in the second, he and Straub were standing together.

"Tom and I had a couple of memorable races against each other," Straub said. "He was a great governor. Not perfect (he glanced at McCall and cracked a small smile, which McCall returned), but great, and if I'm elected, it will be my honor to continue the work he's started." Straub looked over his shoulder, toward the deep blue waters of the Willamette, and said, "We've started the job; now we need to finish the job." Perhaps in a play on his reputation for loquaciousness, McCall was silent throughout the ad; he simply held up a "Straub for Governor" lawn sign and grinned.

The public never got to see these spots. They would end up in a closet at Ted Hallock's ad agency, not to resurface until the original film was donated to the Oregon Historical Society many years later. The

McCall-Straub commercial never aired because Straub rocked the political landscape with the news on September 30th that he was dropping out of the race. His campaign staff issued a statement that the decision was health related, but didn't elaborate. Despite a heavy clamor from the media, he declined for what he called "personal reasons" to hold a press conference to explain.

Like the unfinished commercials, the full story wouldn't surface for several years.

Straub had since January been prescribed lithium and anti-depressants to help him manage bi-polar disorder and a severe bout of depression brought on by the death of his youngest son. *The Los Angeles Times* had gotten wind of the story and was ready to go to press with it. Some of Straub's staff thought he could turn the situation to his advantage, but the candidate knew otherwise. It was just two years earlier that Missouri Senator Thomas Eagleton had been forced to resign as George McGovern's vice-presidential candidate after a newspaper revealed he had undergone electro-shock therapy in an effort to combat his depression. Straub knew that public attitudes toward depression and mental illness were still mired in the dark ages, and rather than put his family through the inevitable media firestorm, he decided to bow out.

There wasn't much opportunity for Oregonians to reflect on the end of a remarkable, if underappreciated career of public service. With less than a month to go before the general election, Democrats scrambled to find a replacement candidate. State Senator Betty Roberts had almost gotten the call a few months earlier when former Senator Wayne Morse, mounting a comeback effort against Bob Packwood, suffered a mild stroke; but after a few days in the hospital, Morse climbed out of bed and returned to the campaign circuit, more determined than ever to unseat Bob Packwood. Now the Democratic Central Committee gathered in an emergency session at Pendleton to anoint Roberts as their substitute candidate. Roberts had unsuccessfully challenged Straub for the Democratic nomination in the May primary. This time, she fended off a strong challenge from

Senate President Jason Boe to become the first woman in the state's history to stand for the governorship.

It had been daunting enough to contemplate a ten-week campaign; now Roberts was faced with putting on a four week blitz. Fortunately for her, most of the Straub team was ready to move over to her as a unit. One key consultant, Len Bergstein, had actually been on her primary staff.

The polls had shown Straub with a steady lead over Atiyeh; now the governorship was up for grabs. The pundits pointed out that if the announcement had come forty-eight hours later, counties wouldn't have had enough time to remove Straub from the ballot and substitute Roberts' name.

Roberts hit the campaign trail hard, shaking hands outside of mills at dawn, talking to Rotary clubs at noon, giving speeches in every venue that would offer her a platform at night. She was quick to assert that she, and not Atiyeh, was the true inheritor of the McCall mantle. "The greatest achievements of Governor McCall's tenure came when he had a Democratic legislature to work with," she pointed out. Atiyeh was working almost as hard, and the race appeared too close to call going into the final stretch.

Morse hammered hard at Packwood through the fall, painting him as a pawn of the disgraced Republican Party. Packwood hit back equally hard, stressing his record as a champion of women's rights. Packwood declared, "I'll put my record with women's issues up against any candidate, of any gender or any party." He reminded the audience that Republicans were still working to pass the Equal Rights Amendment, and said he hoped President McCall would be able to push it through during his time in Washington.

The two faced off the Friday before the election at a memorable Portland City Club debate, which echoed their 1968 face-off before the same venue, also carried live on statewide radio and television. Six years earlier, Morse seemed unprepared for the poised, articulate young foe he faced. This time, Morse was ready to hit Packwood hard on Watergate, Vietnam, energy policy and a host of other issues. The Oregon press corps was informally scoring it like a boxing match, and while they agreed neither candidate had scored a knockout, most agreed Morse was ahead on points.

But then came the closing statements. Morse, to the anguish of his supporters, suddenly lost his train of thought. "We can do better! We have to do better! We, we...." His remarks became rambling and confused; the fire in his eyes vanished, replaced by a look of confusion. Morse finally had to be helped to his chair without the opportunity to deliver what he had hoped would be the knockout blow.

A trip to the doctor confirmed that it was fatigue and dehydration, rather than another stroke, that had been responsible for the episode, but the incident was the turning point of the campaign. Too many Oregonians feared the 74-year-old Morse wasn't up to the demands of six more years in Washington. Even the *Oregon Journal*, one of the most reliably Democratic papers in the state, withdrew its endorsement in an anguished editorial.

The results of the Oregon governor's race were close—Atiyeh ended up with just over 51 percent of the vote. Despite her late start, Roberts had dominated the Portland metro area and most of the Willamette Valley, but she had not fared well in the state's rural regions. Some blamed it on her gender. Even after decades of women in politics, there was still a minority who resisted the idea of a female governor. Others said it was simply a reflection of the state's economy, which was settling into a recession; others read something deeper into the results, noting the amount of resentment that seemed to be building toward McCall's policies in rural Oregon, especially his land use planning program, which was still in its infancy.

The one bright spot for Oregon Democrats was in the races for the U.S. House of Representatives, where newcomer Les AuCoin claimed the first district seat vacated by Wendell Wyatt's retirement, and Jim Weaver unseated fourth district incumbent John Dellenback.

Straub faded from the scene quietly in the weeks following the election. His spirits had been at a low ebb on election night when he saw the tide going against both Roberts and Morse, but they had been buoyed by a lengthy call from his old rival and friend, the president. "Bob, I know you're going to need some time to sort things out, but I'd love for you to consider coming to Washington. I can always use another good man like you back here. Keep these Washington insiders on their toes, you know."

Straub managed a soft chuckle. "Thanks, Tom, but I don't think so. I'm just too rooted here. Frankly, I'm still surprised you made the move."

Now it was McCall who laughed softly. "Sometimes I am too, Bob. I am too."

Straub and his wife Pat retreated to their huge ranch in Central Oregon after he dropped out of the race to spend a few days out of the glare of the spotlight and chart the course for the rest of their lives. He had been out of office for almost two years, so in some ways it wouldn't be a difficult transition to leave elective politics behind; still, as he and Pat surveyed the rugged acreage and the abundant wildlife that called it home, reminiscent in so many ways of the McCall childhood estate, he admitted to feelings of disappointment, but also voiced a sense of relief in being able to step away from the public stage.

"It's going to be nice to be able to spend more time outdoors," he told Pat with a smile. He had been relieved when the *Times* had decided not to publish the story of his use of lithium. There had been a furious debate in the highest reaches of the paper. The Wilbur Mills episode and Watergate had redefined the boundaries of what was considered in-bounds for journalists. But since Straub was no longer an office holder or candidate, the paper decided there was no longer a justification to publish. Now, Straub didn't have to worry about what anyone thought of him beyond his family. In the end, he told himself, they're the ones who mattered the most anyway

McCall managed to shake off the multiple disappointments of Election Day and he stood by with pride later in November as Nelson Rockefeller was sworn in as the new vice president. The president quietly reflected on the fact that he had urged Nixon to choose "Rocky" as his running mate in 1968, but the New York governor had brushed the idea aside. The resistance remained when McCall first approached him about the position just days after his swearing-in as president.

"Damn it, Tom, I'm not built to be standby equipment," Rockefeller had grumbled down the phone line. McCall was sitting at his desk in the Oval Office, and Rockefeller was four hundred miles away at the New York Capitol building in Albany, but his voice boomed down the line with as much presence as if he was in the room. Rockefeller was quickly swayed by McCall's pleas that he would bring an added level of public confidence to the fledging administration—something McCall considered to be absolutely critical as the healing from Watergate began.

"Nelson, there are millions of people who think I'm some kind of woodsy weirdo from the West," McCall pleaded. "They need the reassurance of knowing a responsible adult is around." Like most politicians, Rockefeller wasn't immune to flattery; it didn't matter that he was a the son of the world's first billionaire, a member of one of the wealthiest families in America, and that he wielded power in New York far greater than he would in Washington. This move meant attending parties at embassies and at the White House, instead of arguing with legislators about whether Syracuse or Rochester was entitled to the next big highway construction project. After a dozen years of marriage, Rockefeller's second wife was getting tired of socializing with legislators, agency directors and their spouses in Albany; she longed for the glamour of Washington. She belonged with ambassadors, senators and network television personalities. The choice of Rockefeller wasn't popular with conservative Republicans, but McCall had already written off that wing of the party. He also thought bringing another eastern political heavyweight into the White House would be a wise move. Unlike Nixon and most other presidents, who had shunted their vice presidents off in a corner, McCall planned to make Rockefeller an active part of the team.

In announcing the nomination, McCall told the public, "I have never known a more able, courageous and public man than Nelson Rockefeller." Unlike McCall's relatively quick vice-presidential confirmation, the process for Rockefeller dragged on for several weeks, despite McCall's plea for quick action. No smoking guns were uncovered, and he won confirmation from the Congress. President McCall was all smiles at Rockefeller's swearing in; it was a rare bright spot in what had been a bruising first year in Washington.

10

By the spring of 1975, the American public and the press corps were still trying to figure out their new president. One thing that many were struggling to understand was how this man who was so progressive on environmental and social issues was also a pretty conventional Republican when it came to foreign policy, including his support for the ill-fated American participation in the Vietnam War.

Foreign policy was far from McCall's first interest or driving passion. Even as governor, though, McCall had been outspoken on issues far beyond Oregon's borders. He had staunchly defended the U.S. position in the Vietnam War. Some who knew McCall well said this stance was a natural outgrowth of his own patriotism. Some noted his clashes with Oregon's U.S. Senators, Mark Hatfield and Wayne Morse, who were both outspoken doves, and suggested there was a personal motive driving McCall. Still others agreed there was indeed a personal motive, one stronger than anything political—his eldest son, Tad, had followed his father into the Navy and found himself commanding a swift boat in Vietnamese waters in early 1969.

It was a complex issue for McCall, one that had produced divisions within his own family. His sister Jean Babson was an outspoken critic of the war and had chaired a Republicans for McGovern group. When McCall's name had first been put forward for vice president, Westerdahl had wondered if that fact alone might be enough to sink McCall's chances, but Schmidt pointed out that Nixon was enough of a realist (and a sexist) not to hold McCall accountable for his sister's actions.

Vietnam had also been at the root of the only serious rift between

McCall and his eldest son. The younger McCall had opposed the war, and he and his father had some heated discussions about it. Yet when Tad McCall saw the military draft looming in his future, he decided to confront reality and follow in his father's footsteps by signing up for the Navy. Ultimately "the crucible of Vietnam brought us much closer," Tad reflected later.

Tom McCall shared the desire of many young men of the World War II generation who came of age in the waning days of that great conflict—he was desperate to experience combat before hostilities ceased. That finally happened in March of 1945, when his ship, the *St. Louis*, participated in the shelling of the Japanese island of Okinawa. The lanky McCall found life on board the claustrophobic ship to be a challenge, constantly bumping his head on the low doorways. He was assigned as a combat correspondent, and had plenty of opportunities to experience the violence of war up close. He was struck by the impersonal nature of the killing.

Though he harbored no illusions about the nobility of war, McCall had also grown up in an era when the country as a whole and political leaders in particular coalesced around the president on foreign policy. Domestic issues might be open to debate, but there was still a predominant belief the nation had to speak with one voice overseas.

In July, 1967, after an argument with his staff over the war, McCall had let his feelings pour out onto the typewritten page. Westerdahl, Schmidt and most of the rest of the team were a generation younger than him; too young to remember World War II; too young to have sons old enough to serve. They just didn't get it. In this memo to himself, he said: "A governor owes his support to the people his nation sends overseas...It would be unthinkable for him to cast doubt on his commander in chief's motives or fault the cause that sends out men into history's most brutal and frustrating combat..."

As McCall biographer Brent Walth later concluded: "His support of the war was no mystery after all. McCall had surveyed war's ugly landscape and come to a true-to-form conclusion. Whatever the issue, McCall sought out—and embraced—the underdog. In this case the underdog was the soldier fighting the war."

In September of 1967, Lyndon Johnson was desperate to shore up sagging support for the war. He pushed the military regime in charge in South Vietnam to hold open elections, and send McCall to Saigon with twenty-one other prominent Americans as part of a team to make sure the elections were conducted in an aboveboard manner. The experience gave him personal insights into the civil war that had divided the Southeast Asian nation for decades, but his support for the American troops remained firm.

When Johnson stunned the nation the following March by announcing he would not stand for re-election, McCall called the decision "tragic" and said it was a sad day when the commander in chief was forced to lay down his sword in the middle of battle. He warned against "a stampede toward appeasement."

McCall drew on those insights when the South Vietnamese regime collapsed with stunning swiftness less than a year into his presidency. The last United States ground troops had exited the country more than two years earlier. Now, in April 1975, the endgame had arrived for the Saigon regime. McCall presided over the meetings of the National Security Council as the U.S. establishment struggled to respond.

"What the hell is going on over there?" McCall snapped. Just weeks earlier, Army Intelligence and the C.I.A. had insisted the Saigon government was secure at least into 1976. But the offensive by the Peoples Army of Vietnam (North Vietnamese army) that began right after the New Year rolled toward Saigon, seemingly unstoppable. U.S. Ambassador Graham Martin was pushing for more aid to General Thieu and the Saigon government, and Secretary of Defense James Schlesinger, another Nixon holdover, tried to push the president to make one last effort to stop the juggernaut.

Henry Kissinger emerged as the realist, telling McCall it was time to negotiate the withdrawal of the last Americans in the country and offer humanitarian aid.

"It goes against my grain," McCall declared.

"Mine too, Mr. President," Kissinger replied. "Mine too."

U.S. citizens watched in fascination and horror on their nightly newscasts as overloaded helicopters carried the last refugees off the roof of the U.S. embassy in Saigon. McCall had earlier authorized "Operation Babylift," the evacuation of 2,000 Vietnamese orphans. Audrey McCall flew to San Francisco on Air Force One to greet the first planeload of children, some three hundred in number. Penwell accompanied her on the trip and she later wrote of the deep emotional impact the experience had on Audrey McCall in an article for *Redbook* magazine:

> *Seeing one or two of those children, so sad, so alone in the world, thousands of miles from the only home they had ever known...that would have been tough enough. But to see three hundred of those children, all at once, so dirty, so ragged, so scared...they had seen horrors no child should ever have to see, and it was still reflected in their eyes...such haunted looks...it was just overwhelming. Audrey hugged as many of them as she could. It haunted her for months. It became her cause for years afterward, making sure those children had homes...had people to love them.*

The final tragic act of war came in May, less than two weeks after the fall of Saigon, when the Khmer Rouge seized an American container ship in international waters claimed by Cambodia. The SS Mayaguez was soon the focus of an international incident. When the ship slowed after a Khmer Rouge swift boat fired across its bow, a group of sailors boarded it and took the crew hostage.

The entire state and military apparatus urged a quick and decisive response, saying it was critical to the country's reputation. Kissinger pressed for an immediate rescue operation and bombing of the Cambodian mainland. McCall acquiesced, against his better instincts. The hostages were released less than twenty-four hours later, but the price had been steep; forty-one U.S. soldiers were killed, including twenty-three in a helicopter crash. Yet the operation was hailed as a success, and McCall's approval rating jumped by seven percentage points.

The *New York Times* editorial typified the consensus: "The United States will be sorting out the painful lessons of Vietnam for decades to come. Many questions need to be answered, and many painful and shameful moments deserve to be addressed. But it seems clear that the Mayaguez incident will be seen as a moment when the country showed that it could still act decisively and courageously to protect its citizens."

There were a few dissenting voices. An editorial in the liberal magazine *The Nation* bore the title, "Imperialism's Friendlier Face." It contrasted McCall's progress on the environment with what it called "continued old-school, eastern establishment thinking" about foreign affairs.

McCall, who was haunted by what he saw as unnecessary deaths for the rest of his life, stayed quiet publicly, but the experience represented a turning point in his attitude toward war and diplomacy. The inner circle of his staff realized it before the diplomatic and military establishments became aware, but as always, his wife was the first to know.

Audrey had awakened in the middle of the night not long after the incident had concluded and realized her husband wasn't in bed with her. As her eyes adjusted to the semi-darkness, she saw the numbers on the digital clock by her bed: 3:14 AM. She wondered if some new international crisis had caused him to be summoned away. Then she realized he was in the room with her. She turned and saw the president in his bathrobe, sitting in an armchair, drinking a martini. His hair was askew and his eyes were red-rimmed. "Tom?" she asked. "What's wrong?"

"Johnson had two daughters," he whispered. "I wonder if he would have felt differently about sending all those boys to Vietnam if he had a son. When I heard about that helicopter going down, I couldn't help but think about the families of those boys...and about Tad."

11

McCall's first major legislative initiative came in early 1975—a national Bottle Bill.

As Governor, McCall had championed Oregon's Bottle Bill four years earlier. It was a simple idea; in order to reduce roadside litter, charge a five-cent deposit on soft drink and beer containers. Returnable containers had once been the norm in the beverage industry, but the postwar years had seen a dramatic rise in the use of nonrefundable bottles and cans. It made sense economically for the industry to dispense with the handling costs associated with collecting containers, washing them and refilling them. But the consequence was a sharp increase in roadside litter.

Oregon's Bottle Bill had led to a dramatic improvement in the cleanliness of roadways while helping to engender a broader environmental ethic as well. As he told one correspondent, the bill "can also be a most visible move to start us generally along a path of managing materials for continued use instead of our curious idea of 'throw it away and get a new one.'" The state was already emerging as a national leader in recycling of all types.

McCall saw the Oregon Bottle Bill as the essence of the larger Oregon story he was now trying to spread from coast to coast. It involved simple ideas with larger consequences. It involved cherishing our surroundings. It involved innovation. It was quintessentially Oregon. And even though it wasn't his idea initially, it was quintessentially McCall.

He wanted to take it national.

In an Oval Office session designed to map out a strategy, Westerdahl warned, "It's going to be like that wise philosopher, Yogi Berra once said—déjà vu all over again, but on a much bigger scale. This is going to be one of the rare cases where big business and big labor line up against you together. You could say we snuck it past them the first time. But this time they know what's coming."

"And the stakes are a hell of a lot higher," Schmidt chimed in.

"We're going to have to fight like hell for this," McCall agreed. "You remember the Four Ds from last time—Distortion, Deceit and Dollars equaling Defeat. But I'm ready to take the case to the people." He recycled a line from the first effort, saying it was time to "put a price on the head of every beer and pop can and bottle in the United States."

Alcoa, the Aluminum Corporation of America and the single biggest producer of disposable cans, poured tens of thousands of dollars into a lobbying and public relations campaign, as did other industry giants like Kaiser Aluminum. The Coors family targeted the bill for defeat, as they had done in Oregon. Coors Beer wasn't even sold in Oregon, but they had correctly perceived the bill to be the opening shot in a larger war. Now with the prospect of a bottle bill in the three dozen-plus states where their product was available, they redoubled their efforts.

The opposition trotted out every one of the arguments mustered against the Oregon Bottle Bill—that retailers would be overwhelmed by mountains of filthy empties, that distributors would be burdened by millions in added expenses, that bottling and manufacturing plants would be bankrupted.

The industry fight was staged at many levels. Besides the in-your-face, bare-fisted approach, they weren't above using more subtle P.R. appeals. The nonprofit "Keep America Beautiful" had been responsible for one of the most celebrated campaigns of all time, giving the nation the iconic image of a Native American who looked like he might have just stepped off a buffalo nickel. As he stands by a busy highway, a passing motorist throws a bag of trash out the window of a speeding car; the bag lands at his feet; a tear trickles down his cheek. The memorable tag line: "People Start Pollution. People can stop it." Environmentalists couldn't dispute the truth of the statement, but they did point out that industry was conveniently left out of the loop of responsibility.

In response to this public relations onslaught, Ford began quiet, behind-the-scenes lobbying with his old colleagues. This was the part of the process McCall found the most distasteful: trading favors for votes. Sometimes it was a promise to support a representative's pet bill; sometimes it was something as simple as a promise of a presidential visit to the lawmaker's district; sometimes it involved something more substantial, like millions to build a bridge or keep a military base open. But McCall understood this was the way politics worked. This was the way things got done.

Rockefeller was also a key behind-the-curtain player with the business community. Although large pockets of resistance remained, Rocky helped blunt some of it by pointing out that other states were starting to follow the Oregon lead with their own bottle bills. Though bottling and retailing were still primarily local operations, there was a growing trend toward regionalization, and it would be easier for the industry to deal with a single national standard instead of a series of conflicting local laws.

There was also a public side to the crusade, of course. Schmidt devised one of his most memorable efforts, a nationwide campaign aimed at school children, who were asked to collect and mail bottle caps and pull tabs to Congressional offices to indicate their support for the measure.

"It was pretty hard to give a fair hearing to an anti-bottle bill lobbyist when your office was filled with bags of bottle caps from school kids," said Oregon's First District Representative, Les AuCoin, who called the bottle bill fight the most memorable one of his first term.

AuCoin appreciated the symbolism of the bottle cap campaign, but not all of his House and Senate colleagues did. Westerdahl came into the Oval Office one morning with this story: "You're going to love this. Some kid on (Nebraska Senator) Roman Hruska's staff is, or rather was, a closet environmentalist. He tried to talk to him about it, but could never get through to him. He apparently came in at about 4 this morning, buried Roman's desk in bottle caps and pop tops, laid his letter of resignation on top of the pile, and walked out."

"Jesus," Schmidt said with a chuckle.

"I think the kid even rounded up some of the caps and tabs from neighboring offices," Westerdahl said. "Roman couldn't get to his desk until someone found a shovel. Lord, he was ticked off."

McCall, with as much of a deadpan as he could muster, said, "So I take it we still count Roman as a 'no?'"

The Sierra Club, Audubon Society, National Wildlife Federation and other environmental groups lined up behind the measure, recruiting expert testimony and orchestrating letter-writing and telephone campaigns; it was seen as one of the first times the movement flexed its growing political muscle.

McCall himself was responsible for the other masterstroke that made the national Bottle Bill a reality. He picked up the phone one afternoon and placed a call to former First Lady Lady Bird Johnson.

Lyndon Johnson's widow had made highway beautification one of her main causes. She had been a key advocate for legislation in the 1960s that led to removal of thousands of billboards along interstate highways. One of the big drivers for Oregon's bottle bill had been the high proportion of bottles and cans littering the state's roadsides. Lady Bird's effort was broader, involving organized clean-up efforts and the planting of wildflowers. "Ugliness is so grim," she had once said. "A little beauty...can create harmony that will lessen tensions."

Not only did Mrs. Johnson go on television to stump for the bottle bill, she also flew into Washington and touched down on Capitol Hill "like a gracious whirlwind," in the words of Texas Senator John Tower, who had succeeded Johnson's husband in the Senate. Johnson testified in a committee hearing that drew heavy media coverage, but that was mainly for show; her real work was in one-on-one private meetings with Tower and other southern Democrats, a constituency where McCall was at his weakest.

When the Bottle Bill passed, McCall thanked Johnson for her efforts by flying to Texas for the bill-signing ceremony. The setting was a rest area adjacent to a stretch of an interstate highway that had been identified as especially prone to littering; several garbage trucks were lined up in the parking lot to represent the amount of trash collected along that mile of highway in the preceding year.

There was one man who should have been present for the event, but sadly, he had died the year before of colon cancer at the age of fifty-two. Richard Chambers was an Oregon logging equipment salesman and the true father of the legislation. His name was not widely known because he never courted publicity, but those who crossed his path would never forget him.

Chambers was a big man—about six feet, four inches tall and well over 200 pounds, with the build of a wrestler or a linebacker. His deep, resonant voice added to his commanding presence. But what truly left a lasting impression was his single-minded focus on accomplishing a goal. Once he set his mind to a task, he would let no obstacle stand in his way. Yet these were intensely personal milestones; his work involved extensive travel, so he decided he would climb the tallest peak in every state. Did he actually accomplish that? No one in his family ever knew. Bragging rights weren't the point; the goal itself was.

He loved the outdoors, and relished challenging himself with goals that tested his skill and endurance. If there was also an element of danger involved, so much the better. He climbed mountains, hiked difficult trails and rode rapids. All the time he spent outdoors helped engender a deep love of nature and respect for her resources. He could not abide waste in any form; the non-returnable bottles and cans that increasingly littered the trails he walked were an affront on many levels.

The Chambers family lived in Salem and owned a cabin at Pacific City, in southern Tillamook County. One Sunday morning in 1968, Chambers read an item in the *Sunday Oregonian* about a proposal to ban non-returnable beverage containers in British Columbia.

At that moment, a crusade was born.

Chambers picked up the phone and called Paul Hanneman, the state representative for the county. He insisted that Hanneman meet with him that morning, but that was only the first step in a three-year crusade. Chambers set up a command center in his home office, where he gathered reams of research materials and organized a letter writing campaign. He used a typewriter that produced big blocky capitals; he put his missives on colored paper; anything to grab the recipient's attention. The letters were buttressed by personal visits with as many lawmakers as he could get to. They quickly learned it was all but impossible to say "no" to Richard Chambers.

His hatred of waste included a distaste for wasting time (he drove fast and considered speeding tickets part of the cost of getting to where he was going as quickly as possible), so he didn't squander it on pleasantries when he met with a legislator in person; he immediately got down to business, burying a hesitant lawmaker in an avalanche of data.

Hanneman introduced the bill in the 1969 session of the legislature. McCall initially refused to support it, and there was plenty of speculation about the reason. Some pointed to enmity between McCall and Hanneman because Hanneman, like most coastal legislators, had opposed the 1967 Beach Bill championed by McCall. Whatever the reason, McCall came on board in 1970 and threw his full persuasive powers behind passing the bill in 1971. And now, just four years later, it was the law of the land from coast to coast.

As Chambers' widow Kay, daughter Vicki and son Lee looked on while

McCall signed the historic legislation with a series of bold pen strokes, they wished their husband and father could have lived to see this moment. Yet Vicki wondered if her father would have been willing to attend. Chambers had famously shunned publicity during and after his crusade, granting only one interview, and that was to a journalist who happened to be a fellow hiker.

Once the measure had become law in Salem, talk of a national bill began. But if that was going to happen, others would have to carry the crusade. Chambers had already moved on to the next task, asking his daughter to help him research the issue of nuclear waste.

The previous spring, when his terminal illness had been diagnosed, Chambers almost refused a hastily arranged public acknowledgement of his achievement. Chambers and Don Waggoner of the Oregon Environmental Council, another key player in the campaign, would receive the CUP (Cleaning Up Pollution) award. Arrangements were made for Vice President McCall to make the presentation at the beginning of May while he was in the state to campaign for Clay Myers.

Chambers wasn't interested in the slightest. He wasn't a particular fan of McCall, or most of those he had encountered in the political realm. It wasn't anything personal; for someone who was used to dealing in hard facts, the transactional nature of politics, where votes for an idea often become bargaining chips, was completely outside his value system. He had been raised a Republican, but had a strong libertarian streak. The Watergate scandal demolished any lingering shards of faith in politics and the system he might have still harbored.

Only a plea from his mother led Chambers to relent. He had been diagnosed with colon cancer just weeks earlier. The doctors said the malignancy might have been growing for as long as a decade; by the time the pain became severe enough to make a visit to the doctor unavoidable, there was nothing to be done.

And so, because his mother wanted to see him honored, Chambers climbed out of his sick bed, got dressed, and headed to the Capitol

Building one last time. He hadn't been in the building since the Bottle Bill had passed three years earlier. The event was held in the governor's ceremonial office. It was also a homecoming of sorts for McCall, who hadn't been in the building since his resignation more than six months previously.

The photos taken that day show a gaunt Chambers, his suit hanging loosely from a once-robust frame that had already shed fifty pounds, accepting the commemorative bowl from McCall, and surrounded by his family. After a stop at his parents' house, he returned to his own home after the event and went back to bed, never to leave it until his passing just a few weeks later. The man who had courted danger to such a degree that his family had spent years steeling itself for a knock at the door from a policeman bearing bad news, slipped away quietly. Yet his legacy lived on; decades later, his daughter Vicki served as a State Representative in the same halls where he had once fought a good fight. She represented her district with distinction for a dozen years, and one piece of her legacy was a measure to expand the scope of the Oregon Bottle Bill.

With the national Bottle Bill under his belt, McCall was ready to build on the momentum by pushing a pair of measures that would extend his Oregon legacy nationally and which he saw as having even more far-reaching impact: national land use legislation and a national Beach Bill. For the latter proposal, he recruited the help of another Texan: U.S. Representative Bob Eckhardt.

As a Texas state representative in 1959, Eckhardt had written and spearheaded passage of the Texas Open Beaches Act, which had served as a model for Oregon's 1967 beach law. Once he arrived in Congress in 1969, Eckhardt had introduced a national version of the bill. He rounded up a handful of sponsors but could never piece together a broader coalition to support it. Like so many measures, it was referred to committee, where it languished. Eckhardt had reintroduced the measure in every session of Congress, with the same result. But with Tom McCall in the White House, he had a feeling that things might be different.

Eckhardt had actually been pushing for an Oval Office meeting with the president for several weeks, and it had even been scheduled a few times, but it kept getting postponed, usually due to issues associated with the Nixon case. When the two men were finally able to meet shortly after the mid-term elections, they hit it off famously. They found they had a lot in common. Both men were born in 1913 and both grew up with the trappings of wealth, including household staff, on vast rural estates. Both had ties to the media. (McCall had his newspaper, radio and TV reporting background, while Eckhardt had been a founder of the influential *Texas Observer* and drew cartoons for the liberal paper.) Both spoke with distinctive regional drawls. Both enjoyed strong drink. Both had a passion for the environment. Both enjoyed using words to shape opinions and actions. Both had a reputation for being outside the political mainstream. Eckhardt's fellow Texan Maury Maverick had once described him as "ninety-eight percent genius, two-percent village idiot."

Of course, there were also differences: with his thick, often unkempt hair, bow ties, panama hats and rumpled seersucker suits, Eckhardt's personal style could best be summed up as flamboyant; a true contrast to McCall's understated, classic style of dress. Eckhardt had been through a string of relationships with women, while McCall was faithful to Audrey first, last and always. But their commonalities outweighed their differences, especially in the crucial area of the beaches.

Eckhardt's national Open Beaches Act had attracted the support of a few eastern liberal Democrats and scattered others like Morris Udall, one of the most environmentally progressive members of the House, before being shunted off to oblivion. Now things would be different; now the bill had a champion at both ends of Pennsylvania Avenue.

When Eckhardt was ushered into the Oval Office, he was pleasantly surprised to discover a selection of his favorite whiskies and a bucket of Shiner beer on ice. Shiner was a local Texas brand, and Eckhardt had to regularly bring a supply to D.C. during his trips home. He had never seen it on sale outside of his home state. "Shiner?" said a surprised Eckhardt, said, pulling a bottle from the ice bucket. "How—"

"Rex (White House Chief Usher Rex Scouten) and his staff are amazing. Just amazing," McCall said. "I wasn't here very long, when I happened to mention I missed Mo's Clam Chowder, one of the Oregon Coast's favorites. They had some for my lunch the very next day."

The two men strategized deep into the night, their soaring vision fueled by strong drink and shared passion.

Eckhardt often darted through the busy Washington traffic on a bicycle, and it took his wife Nadine to persuade him that it wouldn't be dignified for a Congressman to arrive for a White House meeting with the president on two wheels. Bob Eckhardt pointed out that a few years earlier, McCall had signed the first state law setting aside funds for bike paths, but his wife prevailed, and he had shown up in his Volkswagen Beetle, the back seat piled with whiskey boxes containing books and files pertaining to the beach law. But he wouldn't be driving home on this night. Neither man was feeling pain as the conversation wound down and midnight approached. Schmidt, who had sat in on the meeting to take notes, called a cab and bundled Eckhardt into it.

As McCall exited the West Wing and ambled down the colonnade toward the residence, the press secretary smiled at him, wished him a good night, and quoted the closing line from a famous film: "I think this is the beginning of a beautiful friendship."

Oregon Governor Oswald West had staked a pioneering position for public beach access with his 1913 bill that declared all of Oregon's beaches a public highway from the Washington to California borders. Although he sold it at the time as a means to provide a road to coastal residents in an era when Highway 101 wasn't even a distant vision, West later claimed it was a stealth measure to insure public ownership of the beaches.

But half a century later, that right of public access to Oregon's shoreline was threatened by court rulings that declared the 1913 law only applied to the "wet sand" area of the beaches. A measure was drafted in the 1967 legislature guaranteeing public access of the "dry sand" area up to the vegetation line. It was bottled up in committee, on the brink of death, until McCall led the charge to get it passed.

One of the measures consulted in drafting the 1967 Oregon law was Eckhart's Texas Open Beaches Act, which he had written and passed as a freshman legislator in Austin in 1959. He was spurred to action by a Texas Supreme Court ruling that property owners had taken as a green light to block access to beaches that had been open to the public for decades.

Eckhardt's exhaustive legal research reached back to English common law and civil, or Spanish law, documenting centuries of traditional open access to the beaches for both commerce and recreation. Eckhardt had also shown a flair for the dramatic gesture in stumping for his measure, at one point dropping a four-thousand signature petition, fan style, from the balcony of the house chamber to underscore public support for the measure.

In the fall of 1973, his national Open Beaches Act had received a hearing in the House Committee on Merchant Marine and Fisheries. The measure asserted the public's right to use the beaches, gave the Attorney General power to sue to protect that right, and created a state-federal partnership, supported with federal dollars, to support state measures protecting beach access.

The bill had gone nowhere in Eckhardt's first sessions in Congress; the elevation of McCall to the vice presidency that fall gave him a renewed sense of hope. But as McCall learned first-hand, the gulf between the number two and number one offices is immense. The equation changed with McCall's move into the White House.

The two men realized they were facing a fight far more challenging than the Bottle Bill. This time, it wouldn't be just a handful of industries lined up in opposition; now they would be doing battle with powerful property owners and developers in every coastal state. They worked with the White House team to craft a strategy that "sold" the

Open Beaches Act not as a revolutionary measure that represented a "taking" of property, as opponents had portrayed it, but as a profoundly conservative law that protected rights that had belonged to the people for centuries.

Eckhardt had a real sense of déjà vu, as the fight in many ways mirrored his battle in Texas sixteen years earlier. Now that the White House had put its weight behind the bill, it had real traction, and it would be too politically risky for members of Congress to try to kill it outright. It would be too hard to explain come election time a vote to bar a child with a plastic pail and a shovel from enjoying an afternoon at the seashore. No, it was far better to try to gut the bill, rendering it toothless while still appearing to support beach access.

"A snake's a snake, whether it's a Western Diamondback (a common Texas rattlesnake) or a Northern Brown Snake (one of most common species in the District of Columbia)", Eckhardt warned Ford during one strategy session.

In the end, all the public and backroom wrangling paid off. Republicans and Democrats in the Congress actually found themselves vying to present themselves as the greater protectors of the environment. McCall was pleased, yet he also realized the bill, historic as it was, had its limitations. It guaranteed the public's use of the beach unless existing state law already limited it in some way, but it did nothing to guarantee access. Oregon was already an anomaly with a network of state parks and wayside that provided a chain of access points to its public beaches. Far more common was the type of development seen from Miami Beach to Honolulu; unbroken rows of high rises that stood between the people and the beaches like a fortress wall.

There was no way to unring the bell, to remove these structures, but there might be a way to put the brakes on further development of this type. But that would take another bill. For now, it was time to celebrate this victory.

"Are we going to sign this one in Texas, too?" Schmidt asked.

"Nope," McCall declared. "We're going home for this one. Although we do owe Eckhardt a lot. We'll fly him out for the ceremony. I think maybe doing it at Seaside, end of the Lewis and Clark Trail and all, would be fitting."

"Two down, one to go," the president told his inner circle after signing the Open Beaches Act at Seaside. He didn't have to explain; they knew that land use was the third leg of the trifecta.

On the face of it, a national land use planning law didn't look like the kind of issue that could ignite the passions of the public. McCall knew it would take the kind of sales job the Oregon Beach Bill and land use bill had needed: people had to understand that nothing less was at stake than their way of life and their quality of life.

The concept of a national land use measure actually predated Oregon's landmark law. In his 1970 State of the Union message, Nixon had put the idea on the national agenda, but didn't have specific legislation to roll out. Washington Senator Henry M. Jackson, a Democrat, jumped into the issue with a bill of his own a few weeks later that called for federal financial incentives for states to develop planning programs. In addition to the carrot of federal dollars, there was also a stick: states that failed to get on board within three years could face cuts to their entitlement programs at the president's discretion.

It wasn't until the beginning of 1971 that the administration finally introduced a bill of its own. It dangled the incentives before the states, but didn't carry the penalties that had raised the ire of conservatives. And while Jackson's bill required statewide land use plans, the Nixon bill limited the program to "environmentally sensitive" areas. The presence of two competing bills on Capitol Hill led to a stalemate and lack of action for months. Still, many considered it remarkable that the concept was on the table at all.

Many in the environmental community doubted Nixon's commitment to the cause; they saw him as driven by political expediency. Public demand for action was reaching a tipping point, to use a term that hadn't been coined yet. Nixon took office a few days before the infamous Santa Barbara oil spill, the largest incident of its kind in the U.S. to that time.

The images of tar-coated shorebirds, whales that had suffocated after their blow holes were plugged by oil, and bulldozers attempting to clear the mess off the beaches seared themselves into the American consciousness. Even if cold, hard politics were driving Nixon's agenda, the environment stood to benefit. Although some real things were accomplished on the environmental front during the Nixon presidency, the land use bills got stuck in muck of a different sort: the muck of politics.

Several federal agencies fought over who should have jurisdiction over any land use program. Meanwhile, things remained stalled in Congress. Jackson finally pulled his bill in early 1972, believing that a flawed measure was better than no law at all. By the fall of that year, Congress approved the Coastal Zone Management Act, which provided for an incentive-based grant program to encourage state planning for coastal areas.

Nixon privately considered vetoing the bill because of the impact on the federal budget, but he didn't want to risk backlash from environmentalists so close to the election. In a statement issued by the White House after the signing, he even renewed his call for broader land use legislation, saying "coastal zones are not the only areas which need this sort of long-range attention." But the idea remained stuck in neutral.

By early 1974, Nixon agreed to support a version of the legislation that was watered down to a greater degree than his original proposal, but even that measure was stillborn, and angry environmentalists charged Nixon had sold out to conservatives in an effort to stave off impeachment. McCall, sitting in the vice-presidential chair by this point, bit his lip and remained silent, hoping that the window of opportunity for a national bill wouldn't close before he had a chance to do something about it.

Debate raged in the environmental community and other quarters about the depth of Nixon's commitment to the cause; the consensus was that he was driven more by expediency than passion. McCall shared that view.

Something deeper, more fundamental was driving Nixon's successor. The man who had stood at the podium of the Oregon House chamber and denounced the "grasping wastrels of the land" couldn't let the opportunity fate had given him slip away. He had condemned "coastal condomania" and "sagebrush subdivisions" in his beloved home state; this was his chance to draw the line against unchecked development in the rest of the country.

Less than two weeks after signing the Open Beaches Act, McCall stood on the ocean shores at Santa Barbara to announce that he would make passage of a national land use bill his next priority. He faced a row of television news cameras, and the wind made it difficult for him to grasp the typewritten pages in front of him. McCall said he was using the original Nixon and Jackson bills as a template to craft a measure that would provide states with strong financial incentives to participate, but also hold the potential for penalties for non-compliance, though they were weaker than what McCall would have preferred. To address jurisdictional issues in the federal bureaucracy, he set up a council with representation from all the relevant agencies to oversee the program.

"We're talking about more than preserving natural beauty," the president told the national media and the millions from coast to coast whose awareness had been elevated by the developments of recent years. He knew that the idea would be pronounced dead if it was seen as simply the desire of misty-eyed tree huggers. People had to understand that it wasn't a question of stopping building completely, but rather what kind of development would shape the beginning of America's third century. "We're talking about growth, and how that growth can be accomplished in a sane manner. We're talking about the economy and the environment....we're talking about balance. In short, we're talking about the People and the Land."

McCall had battled the perception that land use legislation was a liberal cause in Oregon, and had to battle the same thing on the national stage. One of his strategies was to quote from a campaign speech by 1936 Republican presidential nominee Alf Landon. The Kansas governor had carried only two states against Frank Roosevelt, but remained a GOP hero almost four decades later. Landon told an audience: "The Republican party also proposes a sound long-term program of conservation and land use. This is the only permanent solution of the farm problem and is essential to the preservation of the nation's land resources. We propose to stop muddling and meddling and to begin mending."

Privately, McCall vowed to his team that he would not let bureaucratic infighting and Congressional foot-dragging get in the way of success of the measure. "We can't let this opportunity slip away, we just can't," he said over and over. Environmental groups organized a grass-roots lobbying campaign, buying unprecedented amounts of television time to hammer the public with pictures of oil-covered birds, endless freeway traffic jams, the Cuyahoga River on fire and other arresting images. They decided to marshal every ally they could find, including fiscal conservatives. The six-year old national flood insurance program gave the federal government a stake in limiting coastal development, and Eckhardt suggested recruiting insurance experts to project the potential costs of the program to taxpayers based on unchecked coastal development versus a more restrictive approach that preserved public access.

The environmentalists grabbed the moral high ground and the headlines, but analysts later said two groups really were responsible for putting the bill over the top: the farm and forest industries. The national trade groups, like the American Forest and Paper Association and the American Farm Bureau, came to a realization that their Oregon counterparts had grasped a few years earlier: that land use planning was good for the economic health of their businesses.

Without land use planning, the postwar sprawl threatened to force land values so high that family farms and forests within any distance of an urban area would be unable to remain viable economically. Sure, there were some farmers who were tired and eager for a quick payout. Some were exhausted from decades of hard work and didn't have children who wanted to carry on the business to the next generation, but countless others did. And they didn't want to have to deal with complaints about noise, truck traffic, spraying and other realities of farm activities as they were slowly encircled by ranch houses.

"Once the Farm Bureau was on board, the Congress fell into line pretty quickly," said one veteran lobbyist.

The bill was through both the House and Senate and on McCall's desk before Congress recessed for the Christmas holiday.

Although he was president of all fifty states, McCall was still an Oregonian. Right before leaving Portland after spending his Christmas at home, he appeared at a news conference announcing the formation of 1,000 Friends of Oregon, an organization devoted to advocating for the state's land use planning program. The previous summer a young lawyer, Henry Richmond, had written to McCall to propose formation of the organization and invited him to become honorary chair of its advisory board. Richmond understood that in the political realm, passing legislation was only the start of the battle; making sure there was implementation and follow-through was even more important.

Joining McCall on the advisory board were Oregon heavyweights, including Pacific Power and state Transportation Commission Chair Glen Jackson; developer and businessman John Gray; photographer Ray Atkeson; newspaper publishers Eric Allen Jr. of Medford and J.W. Forrester Jr. of Astoria; and State Senator Hector MacPherson, the Linn County Republican and farmer who had shepherded Senate Bill 100 through the Legislature.

McCall was feeling good about the success of the Bottle Bill, the Open Beaches Act and the land use legislation, but he wanted to make one more bold statement of intent in the environmental field. The opportunity came when the director of the Environmental Protection

Agency, Russell Train, left the post to return to his former position with the World Wildlife Fund. McCall told Westerdahl he had the perfect nominee, and wanted to see if his chief of staff could figure it out.

"Bill Ruckleshaus, since you seem to like Nixon retreads?" Westerdahl said. Ruckleshaus had served as the first EPA director before moving to the Department of Justice as Richardson's deputy; he had also lost his job in the Saturday Night Massacre.

"Not Ruckleshaus. I'd love to get him back, but I don't think he's ready to return to government service yet." After a couple of more futile guesses, Westerdahl gave up. McCall grinned. "Me. Remember when I put myself in charge of the sanitary authority?" McCall had indeed appointed himself to the board of the state agency, the predecessor of Oregon's Department of Environmental Quality, in an effort to galvanize attention to pollution issues.

"Tom, this is a little different. This is a cabinet-level position. I am sure a president has never appointed himself to his own cabinet before. I don't know if that's even legal. You're really breaking precedent here."

McCall didn't say a thing at first; his expression of feigned innocence, like a child caught red-handed stealing cookies but still denying culpability, said it all. Finally he spoke. "Well, it should make for some interesting confirmation hearings, shouldn't it?"

It did.

Theodore Roosevelt was the first man to describe the presidency as a "bully pulpit." That was T.R.'s colorful phrase to refer to the president's unique opportunity to focus the nation's attention on a cause. McCall wanted to be remembered as the most environmentally active president since Roosevelt. What better way to make the statement?

Richardson hoped his sigh wasn't too obvious when McCall conveyed his plans via a phone call. He knew the President wouldn't be able to see his eye roll. As directed, the Justice Department did exhaustive research, but could find no precedent to prevent a president from putting himself in his own cabinet.

Nicholas Von Hoffman, though a steadfast admirer of McCall, couldn't resist capitalizing on the absurd dimension of this appointment. He wrote a memorable column that featured an imaginary meeting in the Oval Office between President McCall and EPA director McCall:

> *"How are things at the agency, Mr. Director?" McCall asked from the presidential chair. He stood up and strolled in front of the big desk, taking a seat in an armchair.*
>
> *"Oh, just fine, Mr. President," EPA director McCall replied. "I think we're starting to shake some of the cobwebs out of the place, but we're going to have a hard time getting some of your current legislative agenda through Congress."*
>
> *The EPA director moved back behind the presidential desk. "Oh really, Tom? Fill me in...."*

Good-natured teasing from a sympathetic columnist was one thing, but McCall faced plenty of critical skepticism from senators when he appeared before them to make the case for himself. He was asked what would happen if the country came under attack while he was presiding over a staff meeting at the EPA. They wanted to know what department he would take over next. They wanted to know why the EPA was more important than any other agency.

Of course, McCall had answers for them.

"When I became governor of Oregon not quite ten years ago, I told the people of my state that the overriding issue of the decade was quality of life. That is also true for the entire country. If we don't have clean air and healthy rivers, nothing else matters very much. I shudder when I envision the day a mother has to strap an oxygen mask on her child before sending him off to school in the morning. We cannot continue to despoil our land, senators. The price will simply be too great."

McCall was also frank in admitting that the appointment was largely symbolic; his deputy would have charge of the day-to-day affairs of the agency, and he would not neglect any of his other duties. Still, he said, sitting in the administrator's chair would give him a unique opportunity to give the agency direction and establish priorities in a way he couldn't otherwise.

He even had a bone for Republicans who were skeptical of heavy-handed environmental rule-making, saying, "It's my suspicion that we don't need a whole new portfolio of laws and regulations; we simply need smarter, more effective enforcement of what's already on the books. Policy is made in the halls of Congress and in the White House, but it's implemented at the ground level, and I want to get a good feel for how effective we really are in this area."

McCall won confirmation by a relatively close 55-47 vote. Most of those who landed in the "no" column said they didn't question McCall's vision and purpose, but were wary of setting a new precedent.

Privately, he was a bit more expansive with his own team, telling Ford, Davis, Westerdahl and Schmidt that he looked forward to using "the old ramrod" to shake things up at the EPA. He reminded the trio of his ability to "ramrod" a meeting. "You see a lot of fat old bureaucrats sitting around...they need the animation. They need the old ramrod." He smiled and smacked his fist into his open palm for emphasis.

Nine months later, Ruckleshaus finally agreed to return to his old job; although practicing law was far more lucrative, he could recognize McCall's zeal for the environment, and decided he couldn't pass up what he knew would be a once-in-a-lifetime opportunity.

"I draw the line at bringing back Agnew," Schmidt told McCall when he asked him to draw up an announcement. McCall just smiled.

12

From the Website of the Sam McCall Center

OUR HISTORY

When Sam McCall, the twenty-five year old son of President Tom McCall, drove his car into the Washington Tidal Basin in the early morning hours of April 12, 1975, it appeared that his father's worst fears had been realized.

After McCall was pulled from the car and treated at a local hospital, he was arrested for drug possession and driving under the influence of intoxicants.

Two great loves had almost held the senior McCall back from accepting the call to duty from the east. There was his love for Oregon itself, and just as significant, his love for his family.

Tom McCall had been especially concerned about the impact of the move on his younger son Sam. Since his early teen years, Sam had struggled with addiction issues following abdominal surgery. The president later explained that his son had been given painkillers "like candy," and his brushes with the law had generated a few headlines during McCall's governorship, though many incidents were handled quietly.

Sam McCall had a stint in the famed Menninger Clinic in Topeka, Kansas, as well as multiple stays in the Oregon State Hospital. None of these resulted in a successful outcome. Today, Sam McCall says some people will blame his parents for coddling him; but he says people need to understand that only one person was responsible for his failures.

"At Long Beach, I finally learned to blame the man in the mirror. He's the only one who is responsible."

After the younger McCall's crash and arrest, his parents persuaded him to undergo treatment for chemical dependency at the U.S. Naval Hospital in Long Beach, California. The treatment was successful, and the younger McCall later spearheaded the creation of the Sam McCall Center. The entire McCall family spoke frankly about Sam's struggles in a famous Mike Wallace interview on 60 Minutes *that was credited as a turning point in changing public attitudes toward addiction.*

In the decades since, Sam McCall has continued his recovery journey, sometimes suffering setbacks, but always persevering and always offering encouragement to those traveling the same path, as well as their loved ones.

The non-profit Sam McCall Center is located at Gleneden Beach on the beautiful Oregon Coast and has become known for treating celebrities and the unknown side-by-side without regard for their status or ability to pay.

Although the McCalls had never hidden Sam's struggles, the conversation with Mike Wallace marked a new level of candor for the family.

"I've caused my family a lot of pain," Sam McCall said, his voice breaking. He admitted to pawning the family's best silverware to generate cash for drugs; Tom McCall related the tale of tracking it down with the help of his secretary's husband. He had been about to go charging into the pawnshop himself when a firm hand on the shoulder stopped him, accompanied by the words, "Governor, you probably don't want to go in there."

The president also talked about never asking for favors or using his position to open doors for personal reasons with one exception: to help Sam. He opened up about the time and emotional energy he had invested in finding jobs for his son and making sure he got to those jobs (which often involved driving him there and picking him up). Things would go well for a time, but the pull of his addiction always proved to be too strong. The move to Washington, which Tom and Audrey had feared would make things worse for Sam, actually led to temporary improvement, because he was cut off from his old friends (and dealers); but eventually the old patterns reasserted themselves.

"I'm lucky I didn't get myself killed," Sam said with a sad shake of his head. "The president's son, wandering into some pretty dangerous neighborhoods in the middle of the night? If that wasn't a recipe for disaster..."

A tearful Audrey McCall told Wallace the hardest moment of her life came when she had to tell her son one simple word: No.

She clutched a handkerchief tightly, as if she was trying to wring the residual emotional pain from her body. "Every other time Sam was hospitalized, he would call me, begging to be allowed to come home. It broke my heart to hear how much pain he was in...emotional pain and physical pain. So I always said yes. But I finally realized that I was killing him with kindness. Literally killing him. So this time I said no."

The president told Wallace: "There's one very important thing our family understands, and I think any family dealing with this understands, and that is the fact that this isn't a weakness of character. It's a disease. We have to treat it like any other illness."

"Except that there is no cure," Sam interjected. "Recovery is an ongoing process, something I'm going to have to work at for the rest of my life."

Among those watching the McCall family interview that night was Steve Prefontaine. Prefontaine was still struggling with the disappointment of his fourth-place finish at the 1972 Olympics, and some friends were concerned about his increased drinking and partying, though no one thought he had developed an alcohol abuse problem.

Seeing the McCall interview triggered some deep soul-searching on Prefontaine's part and he finally concluded he should rein in his consumption. He briefly toyed with seeking out Alcoholics Anonymous or some other kind of program, but finally decided he had the inner resources to master it. Nothing, absolutely nothing, was going to keep him from gold in Montreal in 1976.

•

Emily Palmer slipped into a West Wing restroom to give herself one more going over. The new White House intern was about to meet President McCall for the first time, and she wanted to make sure everything was right. Hair? Check. Makeup? Check. No lipstick on her teeth. She anxiously smoothed her sleeveless navy blue dress, and glanced down at her heels to make sure there wasn't a piece of toilet paper stuck to one of them. She nervously popped out her left contact lens and immediately stuck it back in place; she still was adapting to the lenses after having worn glasses since third grade.

The twenty-one year old rarely wore makeup before her arrival in Washington the week before, and she would have been a lot more comfortable in her usual jeans jacket, peasant skirt and Birkenstocks, but she figured it was wise to dress the part. She wasn't back home at Portland's Reed College any longer.

McCall had established a practice of meeting with newly-arrived White House interns. These were some of the top college students from around the country, and he was eager to learn what interests and passions were driving them. He would stay in touch with many of these interns and be a friend and mentor to them for the remainder of his life.

Some who watched McCall closely noted his tendency to reach out to younger people and place them in positions of significant authority. Schmidt and Westerdahl were both a generation younger than the president, and they weren't isolated cases. Some read into this a desperate desire on McCall's part to cheat death and extend his reach beyond his time on earth by leaving an imprint on the next generation; others, like aide Don Jarvi, had a different take.

Jarvi recalled a trip on Air Force One during the 1976 presidential campaign, when he and McCall had started off by talking about new satellite technology that would allow for better use of finite resources by measuring the moisture content of the earth from space. For example, it would be possible to avoid watering crops that didn't really need it. The far-ranging discussion eventually evolved into a spirited debate over how to balance idealism and pragmatism in the making of public policy. Jarvi had even coined a term, idrealism, to reflect this.

In the midst of the conversation, the sixty-three year old president had looked at Jarvi, who was more than three decades his junior, and said, "Jarvi, you probably just think I'm an old guy, but I think about things like this all the time."

Jarvi realized McCall was right; the president was constantly envisioning the world of the future, trying to anticipate the problems and develop solutions even before they became problems. Though McCall might be physically older, and have more life experience to draw on, they were, in a real sense, contemporaries. It was a lesson another young staff member was about to learn.

Penwell ushered Emily Palmer into the Oval Office, where McCall greeted her warmly and invited her to sit on one of the couches facing the fireplace. Unlike in the Nixon days, the fireplace went unused in warm weather. Even though the president loved a good fire, he couldn't in good conscience waste energy the way Nixon had, blasting cold air into a room with a roaring blaze.

McCall asked her about what led her to the internship. "I'm not a political science major or anything like that, Mr. President. I'm working on a dual degree in history and literature. Frankly, I probably wouldn't have applied if anyone else had been president. But our whole family has always admired you. You know, my older sister was at Vortex."

McCall smiled, "And?"

Emily took a deep breath, and continued. "And she had a great time. Nothing too wild—at least that's what she told our parents....though she did confess to a bit more to me. You know how it is between sisters? Some skinny dipping, pot smoking, and well...let's just say my parents sensed they weren't getting the full picture. But they were cool about the whole thing. They thought you did something daring and brilliant by giving it the go-ahead."

"I figured it was either going to be my biggest success, or it was going to blow up in my face. I guess the fact that I'm sitting here right now shows that it worked." McCall pointed at a volume sitting in Emily's lap. "You bought a book to show me?"

Emily nodded. "Mr. President, I know you must be incredibly busy, but I hope you will take the time to read this book. I apologize for its condition." She handed him a well-worn paperback. It was held together by a couple of rubber bands because several pages had become separated from the binding.

McCall cradled the battered volume in his hands. "*Ecotopia*," he read. "Is this an old book?"

"No, Mr. President, it was just published at the beginning of this year. It's in bad shape because I've read it so many times."

"So what's it about?"

"It's a novel, set in the future. It's 1999, and it's been almost twenty years since Oregon, Washington and northern California broke off from the rest of the United States and formed their own country."

McCall chuckled. "Some people said that's what I wanted to do as governor, but they would have said I wanted no part of California, even the northern half. That's an interesting premise. I wonder if Mr. Callenbach is aware that in the thirties, there were people in northern California and southwest Oregon who wanted to break off from Salem and Sacramento and form the state of Jefferson. But no one was talking about a new country." He opened the book and read a quote aloud from the title page: "In nature, no organic substance is synthesized unless there is provision for its degradation; recycling is enforced." He paused and nodded. "Barry Commoner."

"You're familiar with Dr. Commoner?"

"Familiar with him? I've read his books. I've met with him several times over the past year. He's given me wise counsel on environmental issues."

"I guess that shouldn't surprise me. I heard you talking about E.F. Schumacher at the National Press Club recently. I was sad to hear that he had passed away."

McCall nodded. "A good man. 'Small is Beautiful.' What a simple, powerful idea. So you heard the talk?"

"Yes," Emily said. "It was quite a thrill, after all of those years listening to National Press Club talks on NPR with my parents, to actually be there...and for the president, no less! And it means so much to me that the president is from my own state, and he's actually talking about concepts like 'spaceship earth.'"

"Well, it's an idea whose time has come," McCall said, tapping a finger on the coffee table in front of him for emphasis. "It's gained currency in the past few years, thanks to everyone from Adlai Stevenson to Buckminster Fuller, but the scholars tell me it first surfaced as far back as the 1880s."

Emily reached for a notepad she had placed on the table. "I loved it when you talked about John Muir, and his theory of interconnectedness." She opened the pad and read the words she had taken down: "We surely cannot do much for our children without facing the hard fact that everything in this universe is interconnected, that the fate of a hungry child in Bangladesh is somehow bound up with the limousine of a wealthy matron on Park Avenue." She fanned herself with the pad; she felt herself blushing. She hadn't intended to let herself get so emotional, but it was so wonderful that the most powerful man in the world shared her deepest values.

"I'm very proud to have a bright young person working for me who cares about these things," McCall said gently. He picked up the book sitting in his lap. "So, Emily, I will read this. But can you tell me more about it, and why it's made such an impression on you?"

"I think you'll see some of Schumacher and Commoner's themes reflected in there. It's a society built around strong citizen participation in a government that's driven at the local level. There's no cult of the presidency, no offense—"

"None taken, young lady."

"People in *Ecotopia* are very conscious of the environment. There are free bicycles everywhere, recycling bins on trains. There's a focus on using less energy and on eating locally produced foods. There's also a real live-and-let live kind of atmosphere. Drugs are legal. People do right by the environment not because it's forced on them, but because they're persuaded it's the right thing to do."

McCall leafed through the book, careful to make sure none of the pages fell out. "Sounds like the kind of place I might like to live."

"Me too, Mr. President. Me too. But I think you're helping us get there."

Later that afternoon, Schmidt met with McCall. The president was scheduled to appear on *Meet the Press* soon. It would be a special hour-long edition marking the retirement of Lawrence Spivak, who had co-founded the program twenty-eight years earlier and been its moderator for the entire run. Spivak had a reputation for being a fair but relentless interviewer, and Schmidt wanted to make sure McCall was thoroughly briefed on all the potential issues that could come up during the discussion. He quickly sensed his boss' attention was elsewhere.

He was right. Tom McCall was thinking about a lovely young woman in a blue dress. He was devoted to his wife and only his wife, and that would be true until the day he died. But he was also a man. In his mind, it was the mid-nineteen thirties once more and he was a young man striding across the green lawn of the University of Oregon, gangly in the extreme, all arms and legs, trying desperately to act the part of a Big Man on Campus, doing his best to impress pretty young coeds like Emily.

"Earth to the President," Schmidt finally said when he caught McCall gazing out at the White House lawn.

"Eh? I'm sorry Ron," he said. Then, he smiled slightly and looked directly at Schmidt. "You know, it's a myth that only the young think they're immortal."

McCall would soon have his mortality brought home to him in a painfully vivid way.

13

From Maverick: The Memoirs of Tom McCall

September Fifth, 1975 was one of the most harrowing days of my life. It was a day that I confronted the mortality of those closest to me, as well as my own; it was a day that forced me to make some very difficult choices.

It was a day that started with so much promise. We were in Sacramento, California, having flown in from Portland the night before. I freely admit that once I got to Washington, I looked for any opportunity I could find to get back to the West Coast, and especially back to Oregon. There is something peculiar about the Washington mindset; my greatest fear during the seven years I spent on the East Coast was going native. Spending as much time at home, or at least close to it, was absolutely essential to keeping me grounded and keeping me sane.

As our traveling party made its way from the airport to the historic Senator Hotel downtown, I couldn't help but reflect on how the presidency isolates its occupants. We were taking over two hundred rooms, about half the capacity of the nine-story structure. President, White House staff, Secret Service, reporters; we were a traveling community of our own, much like a circus rolling into town. In the year that I had been on the job at this point, I had tried to find ways to reach outside that protective shell; but the events of that day were destined to increase my isolation.

The following account is drawn from the diary I kept while in office. I usually typed up the entries myself right before bedtime. It was a means of capturing things while they were still fresh.

September 5, 1975, 11 p.m.

Today started out with such promise. Audrey and I got up early. The

Senator's Presidential Suite is pretty modest, just a couple of rooms, and that's just fine with us. Audrey stayed behind while I headed out to a breakfast with a group of more than twelve-hundred Sacramento business leaders. A lot of people say if I want to run for this job next year, I might as well write off California already. Ronald Reagan is making pretty loud noises about running for the Republican nomination whether or not I'm in the race, and I'm willing to wager he won't be able to resist the siren's call. There are even some people talking up Governor Brown as a potential candidate for the Democrats. He's only thrity-seven, but he's an exceptionally bright young man and is surely headed for bigger things.

The breakfast went about as well as could be expected. I did my best to persuade them that I'm not their enemy, despite what they may have heard about "visit but don't stay." I reminded them that the beautiful climate, the endless beaches and great forests had been what had drawn their forbearers to the west in the first place. I could tell the message resonated with at least a few of them. I felt good on the drive back to the hotel. Audrey and I had a couple of precious minutes alone together, then it was time for Ron Schmidt to join me for the walk across the street to the Capitol, and a meeting with Governor Brown.

It was such a beautiful morning; sunshine and temperatures headed toward the 80s. There were probably five hundred people along our route, no doubt most of them state employees wanting to catch a glimpse of the president. They had the message drilled into them that the president didn't like Californians too much; I laughed when one young woman asked me about that. I told her, "I love your state. I hope you love it too."

As we crossed onto the Capitol grounds, I noticed the crowd was two and three people deep in places. One young woman caught my eye. She stood out among the conservatively dressed crowd. Her red bandana, flowing red dress and red shoes matched her fiery red hair. She looked like she was about to take a step toward me; I assumed she wanted to shake my hand, maybe exchange a couple of words. I was puzzled when she stopped. She then reached down to her leg; when she straightened up, I saw she had something in her hand.

A gun. Things took on a slow-motion quality at that point, though it was over in moments.

They say your life flashes before your eyes when the end is near. All I could see in my mind's eye at that moment were Audrey, Tad and Sam. Before I could react, before anyone could say or do anything, the young woman pulled the trigger. There was an explosion and a flash, and I heard Ron, who was just a couple of feet to my left, cry out in pain.

As I set this down twelve hours later, I'm still not sure what I really saw and what my mind has filled in. I saw the grimace on Ron's face and the splatter of blood on his arm, as bright as the woman's dress. I heard Larry Buendorf, part of my Secret Service detail, shout "gun" as he lunged toward the woman. At that point, other agents grabbed onto me and whisked me away, so I didn't get to see Larry wrestle the woman to the ground even as he had jammed the meaty part of his hand into the trigger mechanism to prevent the woman from getting off a second shot.

It wasn't until about an hour later that I learned that the woman kept mumbling repeatedly, "I can't believe it went off" as she was lead away. I also found out something chilling: her name was "Squeaky" Fromme, and she's one of Charles Manson's disciples. I understand she's told the police she's passionate about the California redwoods, and while she appreciates what I've done on behalf of the environment, she thinks I should be doing more. Try to figure that out.

I didn't know any of this at that point. All I cared about was Ron. I rarely issue demands, but I told the agents to take me to whatever hospital Ron was being treated at. I also made sure someone had let Audrey know I was unhurt. By the time my limousine pulled up at Sutter General Hospital a couple of miles away, I was told, much to my relief, that Ron had only suffered the most superficial of flesh wounds and was about to be sent back to the hotel. I finally caught up with him there, but there was one other stop I had to make first. I knew my wife would be wanting visual reassurance of the news that I was unhurt. Audrey and I embraced, silently. No words were spoken at that moment; they were not needed. Then we headed down the hall toward Ron's room.

The door was open slightly, and I could hear him in conversation with my secretary, Doris Penwell. We had been treading as lightly as possible, not wanting to disturb him if he had managed to find sleep. But Ron was in full voice.

Doris said something I couldn't quite make out; then it sounded like she was fighting back tears as she said, "Larry told me that after Dallas, they swore they'd never lose another president. Oh, Ron..."

I could tell he was choked up as well as he said, "Thank God they didn't, Doris."

Audrey and I knocked to announce our arrival. Ron was sitting up in an overstuffed chair, wearing pajamas, and his arm was in a sling, but his color was good. I felt a wave of relief wash over me.

"Hello, Tom!" was his cheery greeting. "Have you seen a proof of the Hunter Thompson piece yet? It's supposed to be out next week. I still haven't seen it, but word is, Hunter fell in love with you. That's not surprising, is it?"

It was one of the few times in my life I've ever found myself to be speechless. "Oh, Ron..." Audrey managed, before choking up.

Ron laughed. "Tom, I always said I'd take a bullet for you, but I never thought anyone would take me quite this literally."

I had already cancelled my meeting with Governor Brown; as wrenching as this had been for all of us, I felt I needed to keep my scheduled appointment to address a joint session of the state legislature. Sometimes personal considerations have to take a back seat to official duty, as painful as the choice might be.

The Secret Service insisted I drive across the street to the Capitol Building this time; no strolling through the crowd. When I entered the chambers, the legislators rose to their feet in a prolonged ovation. "We're not Democrats or Republicans, Californians or Oregonians today, Mr. President," Governor Brown said in introducing me. "We're all Americans. Grateful Americans."

Another ovation followed when I stepped to the podium. Anything I had to say after that was pretty much an anti-climax.

As soon as I finished my talk, I returned to the hotel. Audrey and I only had only been able to spend a few moments together, and I knew how awful this had been for her. After we checked on Ron again, who was now groggy from painkillers, we went back to our suite. She told me, or rather implored me, to accept a greater degree of protection.

I tried to reassure her. "That poor disturbed girl is obviously not in her right mind. I don't think she really wanted to hurt me, and even if she did, I don't think she had the wherewithal to follow through on her intentions. The agents said she was surprised as anyone that the gun actually fired."

Audrey wasn't in a mood to be placated. I think it must have hurt her too much to look at me at that moment; she was gazing out the window toward the Capitol, and the park below where I had almost met my maker.

"But don't you see Tom? Don't you see? What if the next person with a gun is sane? What if they're willing to trade their life for yours, like Oswald was willing to do with President Kennedy? What if we had lost Ron today?"

At that moment, I knew I didn't really have a choice. I love contact with people; I thrive on it. But for the sake of those who matter most, I know I'm going to have to accept greater precautions. I embraced Audrey and told her I'd do whatever the Secret Service asked from now on.

I couldn't help but allow my thoughts to drift back in time. It had just been a few years earlier in Salem, when I was a newly-elected governor. I needed to shop for a present for Audrey's birthday, and rounded up Ron to accompany me. Of course, he was happy to come along, but I sensed his puzzlement. I think he caught on fairly quickly that he was there to make the purchase when I found myself dealing with a steady stream of friendly and inquisitive faces.

Just seven years ago. But tonight, it feels like a lifetime away.

The attempt on the president's life put an end to periodic public open houses that McCall had conducted during his first year in the White

House. In order to alleviate the concerns of the Secret Service, the events didn't take place on a set schedule and weren't announced in advance. On days when his schedule would permit it, staff would go up and down the line of those waiting for a White House tour and offer a selected few an opportunity to meet with the president. They had to go through a search, but were not screened otherwise. "I've got to keep in touch with regular people, or I'll go nuts," the president had told Audrey. "There's more to this world than Congressmen and businessmen."

•

The White House press corps was buzzing with the news that President McCall would be making what Press Secretary Ron Schmidt described as "a major announcement." The consensus among politicians, journalists and the public was that McCall would be running; no one could picture him voluntarily relinquishing the authority of the most powerful job in the world. Days earlier, Vice President Rockefeller had declared that whether McCall ran or not, he would not be part of the 1976 ticket; speculation was that McCall would also be naming a new running mate at the news conference.

"Tom," Schmidt had said sternly the night before. "You've got to promise me, no leaks on this one!" Schmidt was thinking back to an incident a few years earlier in Salem. He had stormed into McCall's office, furious over a news story prematurely disclosing information the governor was scheduled to announce to the capitol press corps later that day. Schmidt had vowed to track down the responsible party. McCall sheepishly admitted that he was the guilty party.

The president held up his right hand, two fingers extended skyward. "Scouts honor, Ron."

When McCall stepped to the podium, Schmidt offered a small sigh of relief. He couldn't believe his boss' self-restraint. As far as he could determine, the news that was coming would surprise everyone except for the handful of people directly involved.

"I am announcing today that I will not be a candidate for the Republican nomination for President in 1976."

No surprise there, thought David Broder of The *Washington Post*.

"I will, however, stand for election to a full term, but I will be doing so as an Independent. I—"

Okay, big surprise, Broder said to himself. This will really make things interesting.

McCall was halted by an eruption of shouted questions and popping camera flashes. He saw several reporters bolt for the door in the back of the auditorium. He held up his hands, almost in supplication. "Gentlemen, ladies, please! I'll be glad to answer all your questions, but I would like to finish my statement." He cleared his throat, and continued:

"I have been a Republican all my life. My family has been Republican for generations. I have been proud to be a member of the party of Abraham Lincoln, Theodore Roosevelt and Dwight Eisenhower. The two-party system has served our country for most of its history. But we are at a crossroads. Increasingly, as I travel this land, I hear from Americans who no longer feel a sense of connection with either party. They see both parties as more concerned with winning elections than addressing their needs.

"That is why it's time for a third alternative. Not just a third party, but a movement to address our needs in a more effective and rational way. As our country moves into its third century, we need to, in Lincoln's words, 'think anew and act anew.'"

McCall was more candid with family and friends. He made it clear that he relished the prospect of "having conventional party hacks all frothing at each other and running against each other." He paused and smiled. "And then you take the middle right out as an independent and leave them sidelined." But that conversation came later, after the decision was made. What no one but the President and First Lady knew was that they had engaged in some very spirited discussions (some might have called them arguments) over the choice. Audrey McCall had pleaded with her husband to remain loyal to the Republican Party, but this was one of the rare times when Tom McCall went against his wife's wishes. In early 1974, Vice President McCall was still able to generate laughs by pulling a letter from his pocket and reading it to Johnny Carson: "You may be a Republican, but you're a good man." But any humor in the relationship between the president and the party he had called home had long since vanished.

"The Republicans have been *tolerating* me!" he told her. "I have to leave them before they leave me."

Over their evening martini in the second-floor private residence of the White House, Audrey told her husband that running as an independent was tantamount to conceding the election. "We might as well start packing to go home right now," she said.

The president, drink in hand, walked to the window and gazed out at the vast lawns below. "Damn it, Audrey, that wouldn't be the worst thing in the world." He paused and turned to his wife, "Don't you remember '54?"

Audrey immediately knew what her husband meant. It was the first time he ran for office, seeking Oregon's third Congressional District seat. Against his own instincts, he bowed to the pressure of party leadership and ran as a conventional conservative. He suffered a humiliating loss and didn't resurface as a candidate for a decade.

The First Lady sighed. Her shoulders slumped slightly. "You have to do what you think is right, Tom. I'll be behind you, no matter what. You know that."

The president put down his drink, walked to his wife, and put his arms around her. "We'll do what Teddy Roosevelt couldn't do," the President said with a chuckle. "Show 'em that a renegade Republican can win."

Those who had spent their lifetimes in politics did their own private chuckling. They said in one move, the idealistic McCall had doomed himself to defeat. They said building a national political organization from scratch in a matter of months was too daunting a task for anyone, even a figure as charismatic and popular as McCall. Just the task of qualifying for the ballot in fifty states as an independent would be too formidable, as the other well-known outsider in the race, Eugene McCarthy, would learn in the months ahead.

McCarthy, the former Minnesota senator who had mounted a challenge to Lyndon Johnson's renomination in 1968, had left the senate in 1971, but he retained an almost romantic following among tens of thousands of Americans. In early 1975, he had announced that he would seek the presidency as an independent.

Westerdahl, who would take a leave of absence from the White House to organize the fledgling campaign, saw that there were a number of tasks that had to be addressed. First and foremost was assuring McCall a ballot slot in all fifty states and the District of Columbia. In some jurisdictions, it would require as little as twenty-five signatures; but in California, it would require more than 100,000 names on paper.

Finances would be a huge challenge as well. Under the Federal Elections Campaign Act, the two major party nominees automatically qualified for millions in taxpayer financing; each party had the fundraising apparatus in place to supplement that. A third party or independent candidate could only get financing after the fact, and only after meeting the thresholds of qualifying for the ballot in at least ten states and finishing with at least five percent of the popular vote. Few doubted that an incumbent president would be able to achieve those benchmarks, but it would still be necessary to have lots of cash on hand to pay the bills; broadcasters, printers, landlords controlling office space and other vendors seldom extend credit to political campaigns.

Westerdahl was soon able to return to the White House when McCall approved the hiring of top political strategist David Garth to run the campaign. Garth had mostly worked for Democrats, beginning with Adlai Stevenson's short-lived 1960 presidential run, though his greatest success to date had been with a liberal Republican, New York Mayor John Lindsay. Garth had masterminded Lindsay's successful re-election bid in 1969 when most experts had called Lindsay's candidacy a lost cause.

The pairing of McCall and the blunt New Yorker, a practitioner of bare-knuckle politics, seemed odd to many; but David Broder suggested in the Post that the president could have sent no clearer sign that he was in the race to win. McCall liked Garth's reputation for honesty, even if their styles differed.

If there was any doubt that McCall's 1976 campaign would be unconventional, those doubts were erased at his New York City news conference on the third day of the New Year. This time, he was ready to name a new candidate for vice president. There had been growing speculation in the press and among political insiders that McCall would go outside the standard political realm with this choice; CBS anchor Walter Cronkite was the name most prominently mentioned, and one rumor said consumer advocate Ralph Nader would join the ticket. But the name of the man who was McCall's actual choice never popped up once beforehand, on the air or in print.

It was a selection that produced widespread surprise and head-scratching: Barry Commoner. There were more than a few muttered cries of "Barry who?" from the crowd of reporters. But for those who knew anything about the country's environmental movement, the selection immediately resonated. In his 1971 book, *The Closing Circle*, Commoner had proposed the four laws of ecology—everything is connected to everything else; everything must go somewhere; nature knows best, and; there is no such thing as a free lunch.

Commoner had another book coming out in the year ahead, *The Poverty of Power*. He had been on the cover of *Time* magazine in early 1970, a few weeks ahead of the first Earth Day; the newsweekly had hailed him as the "Paul Revere of the environmental movement." He was emerging as the leading thinker and spokesman for the nascent crusade, and had even mulled over the possibility of launching a political career with friends and associates. *Time* had called him a "professor with a class of millions." Now he might be leading that class, not just teaching it.

With his strong face, heavy eyeglasses, black eyebrows and a thick head of hair that was turning white, Commoner presented a professorial presence, not something the public was used to in a political leader; but he showed a knack for conveying complex ideas in terms the larger audience could understand.

Writing in the *Washington Post*, David Broder declared: "President McCall's selection of Dr. Commoner as his running mate signals that he's serious about permanently transforming the political landscape in this Bicentennial year. While most of the speculation about his choice had centered on the political affiliation of his VP selection, few expected him to reach entirely beyond the political realm."

Although he had never sought office before, Commoner proved to have a knack for translating complicated issues into a message that public and press could understand. He was nonplussed, however, at the campaign stop in Albuquerque when a reporter asked him, "Dr. Commoner, are you a serious candidate, or are you just running on the issues?"

Many challenged the choice of someone without political expertise for the second highest-office in the land. One of the skeptics was William F. Buckley, who said Commoner was a brilliant biologist, but the skills necessary to understand nature weren't necessarily those needed to succeed in politics. "We did okay with Eisenhower, and he didn't hold an elective job before he became president," McCall reflected. "Of course, anyone who says the military isn't political doesn't know what they're talking about."

The new campaign chief quickly settled into the task, assembling a team and building a fund-raising network. Garth worked the environmental community very heavily in the early stages, telling representatives of organizations like the Sierra Club, the National Wildlife Federation and Greenpeace that corporations were increasingly pouring big money into campaigns and sending armies of lobbyists to Capitol Hill. His set speech went something like this:

"This is the big time now, ladies and gentlemen, and either you're in it to win it, or you're out. McCall may not be able to deliver everything you want, but he's the closest you're going to see in your lifetime or mine. How many years has it been since Teddy Roosevelt rode off into the sunset? Eighty? Don't miss this chance. Don't miss it."

The cash soon began pouring in, and armies of volunteers began fanning out to collect signatures for ballot petitions.

14

The thirty-eighth president was determined to make women a priority in his administration. He had been one of the first governors to declare that the days of women facing the butchery of back-alley abortions had to end. Although the family was remarkably candid, few people knew that Dorothy McCall had undergone three abortions as well as bearing five children.

Maybe the country would be ready for a female president someday, but not yet. Women had achieved leadership positions in Congress and had held seats in the president's cabinet. McCall wanted to make a strong statement that it was time to welcome women into full equality in society.

The president's first opportunity to fill a seat on the Supreme Court came toward the end of 1975 with the retirement of veteran Associate Justice William O. Douglas. Douglas had grown up in Washington State and was a noted conservationist, and as much as McCall was tempted to put another westerner on the court, he thought breaking down the court's gender barrier carried even more importance.

"Doris," he asked his secretary . "This country is almost two hundred years old. Isn't it about time that a President put a woman on the Supreme Court?"

Penwell smiled and set in motion the process of screening potential candidates. McCall's choice turned out to be Sandra Day O'Connor, a mainstream Republican who had been elected to a judgeship in Arizona the previous year. She had also served in the state senate and as assistant attorney general. In his appearance in the White House briefing room announcing the appointment, McCall declared:

"As president, I have the privilege of picking thousands of appointees for positions in the federal government. Each of these nominations is important, but some have a more lasting influence on our lives. Among these is an appointment to the United States Supreme Court. Those who sit on the highest court in the land interpret the laws of our land, including the Constitution itself. Long after members of Congress and presidents are forgotten, their impact remains.

"For this reason, I have given extraordinary consideration to my choice to replace Justice Douglas. Today I am proud to nominate the first woman to our highest court in history, Judge Sandra Day O'Connor of Arizona. Judge O'Connor's story is the American dream personified. She grew up on a cattle ranch and attended public and private schools before earning both her economic and law degrees at Stanford. After she earned her law degree, at least forty firms refused to interview her, simply because she was a woman. She eventually was given a position as a deputy county attorney after offering to work without a salary and without an office, sharing space with a secretary.

"Judge O'Connor's selection represents a milestone in the path of women to full participation in the affairs of the nation. But please understand that I have not chosen her solely because she is a woman. I have chosen her because of her intellect, her work ethic and her temperament. She will approach her work on the court with the seriousness it deserves."

Conservatives in the Republican Party slammed McCall for the appointment because of O'Connor's pro-choice record; they feared, correctly as it turned out, she would not support overturning the landmark Roe vs. Wade decision that had legalized abortion. As a state senator in 1970, she had voted in favor of overturning Arizona's statute outlawing abortion—a year before the Roe decision. The wave of outrage following the announcement confirmed in McCall's mind the rightness of his decision to jettison the Republican label.

The flap over O'Connor also helped to push McCall toward greater activism in support of the Equal Rights Amendment. The proposed

Constitutional amendment had been approved by Congress in 1972, and declared: "Equality of rights under the law shall not be denied or abridged by the United States or by any State on account of sex." The legislatures of two-thirds of the states would have to ratify the amendment in order for it to become part of the Constitution.

The ERA had been drafted in 1923, just three years after women had been given the right to vote in federal elections by the nineteenth amendment. Although it was introduced in every session of Congress through 1970, it was usually left to languish in committee. Until the late 1960s and the blossoming of the modern feminist movement, the main support for the ERA had been among middle-class Republican women; the party's national platform supported it four times. Nixon had endorsed it after it passed the Congress.

The measure approved by Congress in 1972 gave the states seven years to complete the ratification process. The momentum was rapid at first, with thirty of the thirty-eight states needed acting affirmatively. But then things slowed dramatically, with only three more states signing on by the end of 1974. A conservative backlash was gaining steam with the message that ratification of the ERA would lead to the complete unraveling of traditional society. Its leader was Phyllis Schlafly, a lawyer and conservative activist, who gave voice to the anti-ERA movement, saying it would lead to women being drafted for combat and unisex public bathrooms.

"Just five states," McCall told his cabinet. "Don't tell me we can't get just five more states on board with this. If we don't stop this anti-ERA movement that's starting to build, if we let the reactionaries win, I shudder to think what the consequences will be. They'll think they can keep women barefoot and pregnant, push blacks to the back of the bus again...." He let the thought trail off, but the implications were clear. Society had to keep moving forward, not retreat into a hazy nostalgia for a reality that never really existed.

Every member of the cabinet, as well as the President himself, made advocacy for the ERA a priority. In speeches, television appearances, meetings with governors and state legislators, the push became relentless. The normally apolitical Audrey McCall also went on the stump for it.

"I have been the proud wife of Tom McCall for more than thirty years. I am the proud mother of two sons, and it's been a wonderful, fulfilling life," the First Lady told a gathering of Republican women. "But if I had been blessed with a daughter, I would want to be able to tell her that all the wonderful possibilities this country has to offer are just as open to her as to her brothers. We can't do that if we don't have the Equal Rights Amendment. Please, don't believe the outrageous claims that are being made against this measure, which is only designed to secure one of the principles we all hold dear—equality. Please, don't abandon the fight now." She was received with a prolonged standing ovation. More significantly, the speech was seen as one of the major turning points in the struggle for the ERA; if a traditional wife and mother like Audrey McCall believed in the ERA, many women reasoned, it must not be so scary after all.

The focused effort paid off; with a vote by the Illinois legislature on May 23, 1976, the ERA became the twenty-seventh amendment to the Constitution of the United States.

It had been a rough battle with plenty of political theater on both sides. Anti-ERA activists baked pies and delivered them to members of the legislature. They hung "don't draft me" signs on baby girls. Pro-ERA demonstrators chained themselves to the door of the State Senate chamber. Cooler heads prevailed, though, and a plan by a radical faction of women to buy pig blood from a slaughterhouse and use that blood to spell out the names of key opponents on the capitol's marble floor was stopped.

In a celebratory event the National Organization for Women held that summer at Seneca Falls, New York, the historical birthplace of the women's rights movement, McCall was a keynote speaker. He told his audience:

"It is simply amazing to realize that it's only been fifty-six years since all women were given the right to vote in our country. Although we formally abolished slavery a century ago, it's only been twenty years since we decided black Americans no longer needed to sit in the back of the bus or be relegated to second-class schools. As we approach our bicentennial in a few weeks, we rightly celebrate the fact that this nation has held the torch of freedom aloft to the world. But we must also acknowledge how far we still have to go before every American has the opportunity to enjoy the full bounty of that freedom; not just freedom from want, but freedom to develop to her or his fullest potential. Let it be our goal that by the time our descendants celebrate this nation's tricentennial, every American will be an equal participant in the blessings of life in the United States of America."

15

McCall felt it was a special honor to be the nation's Chief Executive during the Bicentennial celebrations. He threw himself into the festivities with characteristic gusto. He presided at a ceremony at the Capitol shortly after New Year's Day to mark the arrival of one of four original copies of the Magna Carta, on a year-long loan from the British Parliament. He accepted a request to pose in costume for the cover of *Newsweek* magazine in a re-enactment of the famous painting, the "Spirit of '76." McCall took the role of the tall soldier in the middle; he was flanked by House Speaker Albert on drums and Senate Majority Leader Robert Byrd on fife. He threw out the first pitch at the major league baseball All-Star game, held at Philadelphia that year in commemoration of the signing of the Declaration of Independence.

Time magazine also put the president in costume for a series of portraits in which he became some of his more famous predecessors. His height helped him evoke Washington and Lincoln; his prominent jaw was the key to making his FDR portrayal evocative of the original. Although there were a few grumbling voices—William F. Buckley said McCall was supposed to be Commander-in-chief, not Model-in-chief—most Americans seemed to enjoy having a leader who entered into the spirit of the national celebration.

The President led specially-selected groups of school children from around the country on tours of the White House. As in Salem, McCall found a real sense of joy and renewal in interacting with children. The McCalls welcomed Queen Elizabeth II and Prince Phillip to the White House for a state dinner in conjunction with the festivities. At a photo opportunity before the event, the normally affable McCall glared at a photographer who asked the president if he had told the Queen she was welcome to visit the United States but please don't move here to live.

Audrey McCall had asked the pop music duo the Captain and Tennille to provide after-dinner entertainment. The president wasn't familiar with them, but the First Lady enjoyed their variety program on ABC television. McCall found the bouncy charm of their mega-hit "Love Will Keep Us Together" to be catchy, and he smiled broadly at their recent hit, "Muskrat Love."

McCall had been enchanted by the vivacious Toni Tennille, who stood over six feet tall in heels. "I'm not used to women who can come so close to looking me in the eye," he said with a broad smile.

There was a minor flap a couple of days later when one of the dinner guests was quoted as saying it was "inappropriate" for a song about muskrats to have been performed in front of the Queen. A White House reporter tried to tease a statement out of Schmidt at the daily press briefing, but his only response was, "The White House has no official position on muskrats. But the President and Mrs. McCall were charmed by Ms. Tennille and Mr. Dragon and appreciate them being their guests."

In an address at Philadelphia's Independence Hall on the morning of July 4, 1976, McCall began by noting that King George III had written in his diary exactly two hundred years earlier: "nothing happened today." After the laughter died down, the President used his national platform to tie the country's birthday to his great passion for conservation: he announced he would send Congress a proposal to spend at least $50 million to acquire prime open space in every state. He declared:

"In this 'year of the eagle' and the Bicentennial, it is truly a national endeavor to reach beyond the martial music and the plastic decals to our real heritage—the land."

The wave of nostalgia and good feelings engendered by the

Bicentennial festivities, with the charismatic President front and center, gave many hope that the country was beginning to heal from the twin blows of Vietnam and Watergate.

The President took special pleasure in an East Room ceremony that August to honor the team that had represented the United States at the Summer Olympics in Montreal. Decathalon winner Bruce Jenner had grabbed headlines, along with Michael and Leon Spinks, the boxing brothers. McCall was cordial with them and the rest of the group, but he couldn't help but focus extra attention on the home state hero, Steve Prefontaine, who had taken the gold in both the 5,000 and 10,000 meter races.

It had been the sweetest of moments for Prefontaine, who had been unable to shake the memory of his experience at the Munich Olympics four years earlier. The 5,000 meter final of 1972 was already being remembered as one of the great races of all time. Against his deeper instincts, Pre had remained in the middle of the pack for several laps ("a tight, worried clump" as runner-turned-writer Kenny Moore later described it), absorbing the punishment of his competitors' elbows and spikes, before putting on a surge that carried him to the front in the late going. But it hadn't been enough to overcome the eventual gold medal winner, Lasse Viren of Finland. Pre had poured on one final heroic burst of speed in the last lap, when he could have assured himself of the third place medal ("the horrid bronze," as he referred to it) by maintaining a steadier pace, but he was spent too soon and died at the finish, crossing the line a heartbreaking fourth.

He had spent four hard years training to avenge that humiliation. At twenty-five, he was in his physical prime. There had been an even more difficult challenge he had to overcome this time: changing his fundamental mindset toward racing.

"I have to go out hard and just about lead from the start," he once told a television interviewer. On more than one occasion he had groused to his coach, the University of Oregon's Bill Bowerman, that he hated others breathing down his neck. The legendary coach and his young legend in the making engaged in an epic struggle of wills throughout Prefontaine's four years in Eugene.

McCall had met Bowerman and Prefontaine almost a year earlier. Bowerman had brought three of his former runners to the Oval Office meeting: Phil Knight, who was his partner in a fledgling shoe company called Nike; Prefontaine, who was working for the company on a very part-time basis, and the former miler Roscoe Devine. McCall listened with fascination and something bordering on horror as he heard how the young runners had to live in near-poverty in order to retain their amateur standing and remain eligible for the games.

"The Amateur Athletic Union and the International Olympic Committee hold all the cards, Mr. President," Bowerman explained. "The I.O.C. Chairman, Avery Brundage, has an almost obsessive belief in competition for competition's sake alone, and that the athlete should remain untainted by money. Of course, what that really means, is plenty of money in the pockets of promoters, and nothing for our young men."

"Brundage is a big-time developer. He's made his millions," Devine added. "He was actually one of us, once. He was a member of the 1912 Olympic team, along with Jim Thorpe. He competed in the pentathlon and the decathlon. But he is so out of touch with the life of the average young person today, it's almost pitiful."

"Avery Brundage is an old—"

"Steve!" a chorus of voices shouted, cutting Prefontaine off.

"Jeez, guys," he said with a rueful grin. "I was just going to say 'fossil.'"

Knight had brought along a gift for McCall: a pair of Nike Bruins. "I hope we got the correct size, Mr. President," he said, handing him the box with a pair of size 12s with the distinctive red swoosh on them. McCall nodded affirmatively.

"You really think there's money in athletic shoes?" McCall asked, his finger tracing the outline of the swoosh.

Knight smiled and nodded. "A LOT of money," he said.

Now, years of preparation were coming down to a few crucial moments. Whenever a reporter asked Prefontaine his strategy for the great rematch, Pre would say, "If you know me at all, you know I only run one way. To win."

McCall flew to Montreal aboard Air Force One to witness Prefonitaine's historic race. The brand-new Olympic Stadium was being hailed as a showpiece of modern architecture, but it had been plagued by multiple construction issues and a workers' strike and had barely opened in time for the games. All that was forgotten amidst the festivities of the moment, which had so far managed to erase the dark stain of Munich, where Arab terrorists had murdered a group of Israeli athletes. The Olympics were on the verge of redemption; but what about Prefontaine?

McCall had invited Phil Knight to be his guest in his VIP box. The president wasn't a great track and field fan, but he watched with intense interest as the race began and Prefontaine settled into the middle of the pack. This didn't look like the kind of race Prefontaine had promised to run. The commentators immediately began to speculate: was Prefontaine hurt? Or was this really a strategic move? McCall looked at Knight with growing alarm but the shoe executive just offered a slight grin and nod along with a soft, "Don't worry, Mr. President."

At the beginning of lap three, with Pre still in third place, Viren nervously glanced over his shoulder, expecting to see a grimace on Prefontaine's face. It was a quick gesture, not seen by most, but Prefontaine was aware of it; a still photographer captured the slight smile that crept across his face. He remained ten yards back of Viren, keeping pace with Dick Quax of New Zealand who was in second place.

Then he made his move.

"It was as if Joe Louis suddenly started punching with his left hand, or Sandy Koufax began firing 100 mile per-hour fastballs with his right arm," *Los Angeles Times* columnist Jim Murray wrote later. "That's how remarkable Prefontaine's transformation was. Pre showed that he had the soul of a gambler by waiting until the seventh lap to turn on the afterburners, and he was finally on Viren's heels. It was all the more amazing because Viren was on a record pace, but that didn't matter now. The hunted had become the hunter."

When the last lap arrived, the bell lap, Prefontaine had more than enough gas left in the tank to put on a burst that carried to him victory at 13.08.2, obliterating Viren's own world record set four years earlier and a mark that would stand for the next five years. He told reporters after the event that it had almost felt like riding in a car, his body was such a fluid machine. He was more than ready for another race.

Prefontaine broke away from the media crowd when he spotted McCall and Knight on the edge of the field. The president had gone against the wishes of the Secret Service in order to offer his personal congratulations to the Oregon star. Multiple cameras captured the moment when a smiling McCall raised a beaming Prefontaine's arm in a gesture of victory; the photo was on the top of almost every newspaper sports section the next day, but it made the front page of most Oregon papers.

By the time Pre had claimed victory over Viren in the 10,000 meters (and downed a celebratory beer, his first in more than a year), he had written his name into the Olympic record books, and had achieved a sense of inner peace. As Murray concluded: "Viren was, and is a great runner, but Munich was his moment. Montreal belonged to Prefontaine."

As the crowd mingled in the East Room, the president towered over Prefontaine, who stood just five-nine and weighed 145 pounds. He took note of Pre's barrel chest and sensed the surging energy he could barely contain; he reminded McCall of a caged lion, pacing in tight circles. Yet McCall sensed something was different than during their first meeting; an inner demon had been tamed, at least for now. McCall had promised to speak out on behalf of amateur athletes after that first meeting a year earlier, and he was good on his word, helping to set in motion changes that made life easier for those who followed in Pre's path.

When the program was ready to begin, McCall had a surprise at the ready. It was one more step in fulfilling his promise to the Oregon coaches and athletes. He had pushed and goaded the International Olympic Committee into a rule change that would make the steps he was announcing a reality. "Today, I am announcing an Executive Order that creates a national program to support and train our future Olympic-caliber athletes. It is simply wrong that some of our most gifted young women and men be forced to take a vow of poverty in order to compete at the highest levels in the world. This program will provide financial stipends for living and training expenses, including but not limited to food, living quarters, travel, training and medical care. I congratulate the International Olympic Committee for recognizing the changing realities of our time and permitting this to take place."

The athletes in attendance applauded vigorously; Prefontaine offered the loudest cheer.

Cynics contended that Olympians in the Soviet-bloc countries had been benefiting from state support for years, and this step simply represented a leveling of the playing field. But McCall knew what others did was beyond his control. He was happy to do what he could to right a wrong.

16

From the Making of the President 1976 by Theodore H. White:

It would forever be remembered as the twentieth century's version of a great Wild West shootout.

The 1976 presidential election pitted three Westerners against each other:

--Democrat Jerry Brown, the chief executive of California, derisively nicknamed "Governor Moonbeam" for his eccentric policies and who, at age thirty-eight was bidding to become the youngest Chief Executive in the nation's history.

--Republican Ronald Reagan, Brown's predecessor in Sacramento, who had come to politics after a career in the movies and even after eight years at the helm of the largest state in the union viewed politics as just another stage.

--The incumbent, Tom McCall, the first man to succeed to the presidency after the resignation of his predecessor, the first un-elected president in the country's history and the first man to forsake his political roots to seek election without the endorsement of a major political party.

Because McCall had ascended to the Oval Office with almost two years and six months left on Nixon's term, he was only eligible to a single term in his own right under the provisions of the twenty-second amendment to the U.S. Constitution, which had imposed a two-term limit for future presidents. The exception was for anyone who completed more than half of another presidential term.

There had been other presidential races in the twentieth century where a third candidate had claimed a share of the spotlight and at least some degree of consideration as a potential spoiler, siphoning off enough electoral votes to influence the outcome—Robert LaFollette in 1924, Henry Wallace in 1948 and George Wallace in 1968. But everyone quickly agreed that 1976 would be the most dynamic three-way contest since 1912, when Theodore Roosevelt, wearing the Progressive Party banner, tried to wrest the White House from his Republican successor, William Howard Taft. Ultimately, all Roosevelt had done was to deliver the keys to the White House to Democrat Woodrow Wilson. But while Roosevelt was running as a former president in 1912, McCall was the incumbent.

Reagan cruised to the Republican nomination, easily holding off challenges from Attorney General Elliot Richardson and former Treasury Secretary and Texas Governor John Connally. Connally's relatively recent conversion to the GOP, and his close identification with Nixon, doomed his candidacy at the beginning. Richardson started off with promise in his native New England, but faded quickly after that; many Republicans were still Nixon loyalists, and they had no use for the man who had stood up to him.

Meanwhile, the Democrats provided a rough-and-tumble battle for their prize that included a large cast of colorful characters. It would be the last hurrah for the Happy Warrior, former Vice President Hubert Humphrey, who had been pursuing the presidency since 1960. The field was largely dominated by westerners: Utah Congressman Mo Udall, Washington Senator Henry "Scoop" Jackson and Idaho Senator Frank Church. Though he was confined to a wheelchair after being shot during the 1972 campaign, fiery Alabama Governor George Wallace put himself into the fray one more time. The race eventually narrowed to two contenders: Brown and former Georgia Governor Jimmy Carter.

Carter had served a single term in the Georgia statehouse; the state's constitution had prohibited him from seeking re-election. Carter had never established much of a national profile, but he had been working steadily since leaving the governorship in 1974 to build a campaign organization. Carter was banking on the nation's post-Watergate revulsion with politics as usual to carry him to the White House.

For several months, it looked like Carter's unaffected manner and simple slogan, "Why Not the Best?" was resonating with Democratic voters. But as the campaign moved west, Carter's star began to dim at the same time Brown's started to ascend. As Carter's team searched for ways to restore momentum to his candidacy, someone suggested a more prominent role for the candidate's mother, Miss Lillian Carter. A widow for decades, at age sixty-eight she had volunteered for the Peace Corps and been sent to India. She had developed a reputation for sass, once telling a reporter: "When I look at all my children sometimes I say to myself, Lillian, you should have stayed a virgin." Miss Lillian didn't fit the image of the typical political mother.

The young staffer who tossed out the idea looked to Carter pollster Pat Caddell for reassurance. "Pat, isn't it true that one of the candidate's issues is that people see him as a bit of a, forgive me, self-righteous stiff? A little more of Miss Lillian might help counteract that."

Carter's campaign manager, Hamilton Jordan, squelched the idea. "Not a bad idea, in theory," he said. "The only problem is in the general election Miss Lillian gets mowed down by an unstoppable force named Dorothy Lawson McCall." A round of head nods and sighs followed. "O-K, on to the next big idea."

Jerry Brown had been a late entrant into the race, not declaring until the deadline to enter several key early primaries had passed. Many thought he had doomed his candidacy because of the delay, but he soon displayed an impressive ability to energize Democrats, who began to sense the opportunity for their first victory in a presidential race in a dozen years. McCall's surprising popularity had left some Democrats discouraged, but many of the faithful were convinced that the president would show a lack of staying power by the end of the campaign.

By the time the dust had settled after the final round of primaries on June 8, when voters in California, Ohio and New Jersey all went to the polls, the only thing that was certain was that the Democratic nominee would not be anointed until the party's convention in New York City in July.

One long-time Democratic strategist predicted the party would choose Brown as the nominee. "Reagan is a movie star, and McCall packs plenty of charisma. You don't put a Georgia peanut farmer up against a couple of stars." But another was equally insistent that Carter would prevail: "After a crook, this country is ready for a Boy Scout." Brown's youth and the fact that like McCall and Reagan, he hailed from the west, were obstacles that many thought were too great to be overcome; but in a year that seemed to involve a constant rewriting of the conventional wisdom, nothing seemed impossible.

The next month saw rumors flying across front pages and on the evening news:

--Carter had brokered a deal that would give him the nomination.

--Brown had sewn up the nomination by promising cabinet seats to Udall (interior), Jackson (defense) and Church (state);

--Ted Kennedy would make a dramatic announcement of his candidacy the day before the convention opened, banking on the magic of the Kennedy name to allow him to steal the nomination;

--and a hundred other scenarios.

In the end, the fact that the convention was the first not to pick a nominee on the initial ballot since 1952 seemed almost anti-climactic. Brown fell 181 votes short of the prize on the initial vote, but the second ballot saw a stampede to the inevitable nominee begin as soon as the roll call unfolded. Bowing to the urging of party leaders who wanted to see a Washington insider on the ticket, Brown chose Minnesota Senator Walter Mondale as his running mate.

NBC's David Brinkley summed up the brief drama at the close of the inconclusive first ballot in his trademark style: "Just when the national conventions were in danger of turning into a coronation ceremony, the Democrats here in 1976 have gone back to their original purpose—choosing a presidential candidate."

Party chairman Strauss worried that the Democrats were about to repeat the disastrous mistake of 1972, when the start of nominee George McGovern's acceptance speech was pushed past 2. a.m., but the quick second ballot resolution allowed Brown to take the stage before the prime time television window closed on the east coast.

Reagan's nomination was a foregone conclusion going into the GOP convention, so the only drama there was over the announcement of his running mate. Pennsylvania Senator Richard Schweiker was seen as a choice who could help reassure those concerned about Reagan's complete lack of experience in the nation's capitol.

There was no clearer indication that the nation's population center and political balance was moving than the fact that two Californians and an Oregonian were contending for the presidency. It had been more than a century since Horace Greeley said, "Go west, young man, and grow up with the country." Most of the postwar growth in population had been in the south and west, with the industrial northeast in decline. It's expected that the 1980 census numbers will cost New York, Pennsylvania and Ohio several seats in the House of Representatives. By putting westerners at the head of their national tickets, both major parties appeared to be trying to get ahead of the curve.

McCall and Reagan seemed the outsized figures, but few were counting Brown out, something that was reflected in a cartoon by the Washington Post's celebrated editorial cartoonist Herbert L. Block. It was classic Herblock, broad black strokes highlighting each man's most prominent features: McCall's chiseled jaw, Reagan's pompadour. It showed McCall and Reagan as giant figures in the foreground, dressed in cowboy gear, scowls on their faces, hands reaching for their holstered guns. Brown was a tiny figure in the distance, holding the reins of their horses. His caption balloon read: "I just might win this thing yet."

One of the many milestones of the campaign was the first presidential debates since 1960. The matchup between McCall, Reagan and Brown provided plenty of colorful moments that would resonate for some time.

The Kennedy-Nixon debates of 1960 had been the decisive moment of that campaign. The image of the tanned, self-assured Kennedy contrasted sharply with the sweaty, shifty-eyed Nixon who seemed to fade into the background. Johnson and Nixon had refused debates in the years since, *but all three of the 1976 contenders embraced them. The first face-off took place September 23 in Philadelphia's Walnut Street Theater. NBC's Edwin Newman was moderator.*

In their opening statements, each man did their best to carve out their positions for the American people, cognizant that first impressions are the most lasting ones.

Brown may have had the greatest challenge. At thirty-eight, he had to persuade the public that he was mature enough for the burdens of the Presidency. If he stressed his role as Governor of California, a state so vast that it would be the seventh-largest economy in the world if it was a separate country, he ran the risk of having Reagan point out that he had done the same job—and for a full eight years. The Democrat decided on a risky gambit—positioning himself as the one candidate willing to speak the hardest truths. He told Americans their gas-guzzling sedans were only rolling down the highways because the nation imported forty-five percent of its oil from overseas, and the purchase of that oil was financed by arms sales to countries that could threaten our security at some point.

He talked about signing legislation in California that created tax deductions for solar energy installations, that mandated a halving of water use in new toilets, and slowed nuclear power development in the state. He asked why McCall, the "so-called environmental president," hadn't taken similar measures to strengthen safeguards on nuclear plants in the rest of the country.

Reagan knew that not every citizen was ready to concede that it was time to rein in the growth of the economy in order to protect the environment.

He told the audience that the American Petroleum Institute had filed a lawsuit against the EPA, asserting that the agency had suppressed a study that revealed eighty percent of air pollution came from "plants and trees." Newman did a visible double-take, and pressed Reagan for further details, without success. Even after reporters failed to produce any tangible evidence of the study or the lawsuit, Reagan doggedly stuck to the story.

McCall's opening statement acknowledged the unusual circumstances that had led to him sitting in the White House, but his focus turned to the future. "People with narrow minds and narrow fields of vision will tell you that this country is facing an either-or choice; that we must either sacrifice growth to maintain and improve our quality of life, or forsake a healthy economy in order to have a healthy environment. What they fail to see is that the two are inextricably linked; you cannot have one without the other."

For many viewers, the most memorable thing about the debate was not anything that was said but the twenty-seven minutes of silence from the stage caused by a technical failure. For a few moments, all three men remained behind their podiums, but McCall was the first to step out. He ambled over to Reagan and struck up a conversation. Brown soon joined in. Asked afterward what the three men discussed, Newman said, "Football. They argued about who was going to win the Pac-8 this year."

Once the sound was restored, the three men went back to trading jabs at each other. Soon it was time for closing statements.

In a not too subtle poke at the two men in their sixties he was facing, Brown closed by saying: "This is still a very vital country. We don't need to concede anything to any country in the world. My candidacy can symbolize a new vitality that can move us into the rest of the century."

Reagan grinned broadly and promised not to make Governor Brown's youth and lack of experience a campaign issue. He said he was proud to be carrying the banner of the Republican Party in the bicentennial year. He asserted that the party of Lincoln was still the party of freedom, and in one of the best-remembered lines of the campaign, declared, "It's morning in America. Our best days are still ahead." As governor and presidential candidate, Reagan had shown a gift for appealing to people's sense of optimism and hope. It drew people to him in an almost magical way, but skeptics said he too often seemed detached from reality. McCall experienced the Reagan worldview not long before he left the governorship when he called the Sacramento statehouse to see if Reagan would consider adopting the ban on outdoor display lighting McCall had imposed in Oregon.

"Oh no," Reagan told McCall. "California would be too dreary." The two men also fundamentally differed in their view of the natural environment.

McCall's conservationist credentials were rock solid; Reagan had never shown much regard for nature. While campaigning for the governorship in 1966, he had weighed in on proposals to protect the California redwoods: "I think too, that where the preservation of a natural resource like the redwoods is concerned, that there's a common sense limit. I mean, if you've looked at a hundred thousand acres or so of trees—you know a tree is a tree, how many more do you need to look at?"

Although they stood far apart on the political spectrum, some observers noted that McCall and Reagan shared common skills and temperament. They saw both men as visionaries; both as big-picture thinkers, not encumbered by fine details; and both as optimists by nature. Both had found their path into politics largely through their abilities to articulate a vision and persuade others to share it; one commentator even called them "The Great Communicators." But it was an idea not universally shared by all. As one California editorial writer quipped to me, "McCall actually thinks. He reads. Reagan just watches old movies."

The "morning in America" line seemed to resonate with the Philadelphia audience and with viewers across the country. But then Reagan made what many later saw as a fatal misstep.

When Reagan looked into the camera and declared, "Government is not the solution to the problem. Government is the problem," McCall shook his head sadly.

"Oh, Ron," he said wearily as he began his own closing statement. "There you go again." Then McCall turned, drew himself up to his full six foot-five inch presence, and looked squarely into the cameras: "Governor Reagan would have you believe that government is your enemy. Government is not an alien force out to enslave the people. The government is not our master, but our servant. It is our collective tool to enhance our lives in ways small and great. It was written long ago, 'where there is no vision, the people perish.' An intelligent, forward-looking government can help the people to realize their collective vision. It can help them to thrive."

When Reagan had accepted the GOP nomination in Kansas City that summer, he had harkened back to one of his most famous film roles and urged the delegates to go forth and "win one for the Gipper."

In the post-debate analysis, NBC's John Chancellor summed up the impact of McCall's response: "The Gipper fumbled just short of the goalposts tonight." Reagan's campaign never recovered. With McCall and Brown generating most of the excitement, especially on Reagan's own home turf, and the shadow of Watergate looming heavily over anyone wearing the Republican label, his campaign appeared doomed.

"Brilliant line Tom. 'There you go again.' Brilliant," Schmidt said that evening as Air Force One hurled toward one more rally. McCall just smiled and asked for a drink.

The final blow to the faltering Reagan campaign may have been delivered by Richard Nixon; just two days after the debate, he refused a request to appear in person before a special Senate committee investigating the Central Intelligence Agency and its role in the 1973 coup that ousted Chilean President Salvadore Allende. Nixon offered to provide written response to the committee's questions instead.

"Has Mr. Nixon learned absolutely nothing?" Democratic Vice Presidential nominee Walter Mondale thundered at a rally in New York City. "Will he have to go to jail before he realizes he is not above the law?"

Nixon had refused to slip quietly into political obscurity; a few weeks earlier, it was announced that he had signed to do a series of videotaped interviews with British television personality David Frost that would be shown the following year.

Reagan attacked McCall from the right, quoting a talk the future president had given to a League of Women Voters chapter in Eugene, where he assailed "the exploiters who don't give a damn about tomorrow as long as they can wallow in their wealth of today." Reagan said this was the sort of thinking "that threatens to cripple the American spirit of free enterprise." Meanwhile, Brown continued to assail McCall for talking a better game on the environment than the results justified. This unintentional triangulation helped the president claim the middle ground, and ultimately, a plurality of the popular vote.

As the Reagan team's desperation increased, a scenario played out that Westerdahl and Schmidt had feared, and things really got nasty. McCall had a reputation for having a thin skin, and with the opportunity to make up lost ground dwindling, the Republican's team decided to exploit that perceived weakness.

Reagan's chief strategist, Roger Ailes, denied responsibility for the mailers and leaflets that denounced McCall as a peacenik with a drug addicted son.

"If he can't manage his own son, how can he manage the country?" one radio spot asked. Meanwhile, a flyer showed a picture taken in the Portland television studio in 1970 when McCall had delivered a statewide address to announce his decision to hold the Vortex rock festival. McCall could be seen in profile. A large peace symbol hung on the wall to his left. Although the peace symbol had been a leftover from a prior program, the juxtaposition proved irresistible for the creators of the brochure that accused McCall of sanctioning a pot party while brave American boys were putting their lives on the line in Vietnam.

"My God," McCall railed. "Don't they know my son was over there on a Swift Boat?" After a particularly ragged day on the campaign trail, when the president snapped at a heckler and a reporter at successive stops, his closest aides made the decision to pull him off the campaign trail for the weekend. Perhaps it was inevitable that the meltdown came in California, the state that was convinced the president hated it. Responding to a reporter who had heard Interior Secretary Hickel wouldn't be staying on, McCall said he planned to appoint Smokey the Bear to the job. "I don't hate Californians!" he told a student on the Berkley campus who repeatedly interrupted his talk. "But I don't care much for jerks!" McCall had never concealed his fondness for drink; now rumors swirled that his alcohol consumption had veered out of control.

Although the official word was that the president was ill with a bad cold, Campaign Manager Garth privately told close aides that "We've got to get him away from the pressure for a couple of days. No man should have to withstand this kind of abuse." McCall was physically and emotionally exhausted and had turned angry and churlish, snapping at his family and closest advisers in a way that was uncharacteristic even before the public incidents. Even this break didn't come without a furious internal debate. White House Chief of Staff Ed Westerdahl and First Lady Audrey McCall reportedly exchanged harsh words over it, though neither would confirm or deny that.

The opening presidential debate, along with its two follow-ups, had been a three-man show, though McCall would have personally preferred to add Eugene McCarthy to form a quartet. McCall and McCarthy had real affection for each other, to the point where, when Governor McCall began first talking about running for the White House as an independent, McCarthy had suggested to him they team up, "and I don't care who is at the top of the ticket." The former senator had also been on McCall's short list of potential running mates a few months earlier.

The Democratic and Republican National Committees had squelched the inclusion of McCarthy, which was not surprising, since they had each worked in concert to keep him off the ballot in as many states as possible. Although the McCall team had pushed the door open to loosen the laws that had made it impossible for many outsiders to claim ballot spots, the major parties wanted to make sure the bar remained high.

Although he went on to garner more than 300,000 votes, McCarthy's failure to win ballot slots in several key states cost him any chance of being a major player in the final result. The ex-senator's own lack of organization and aggressive challenges from the DNC delivered a one-two punch that left the McCarthy campaign stranded on the launching pad.

He might have been a former seminary student, but Governor Brown proved he wasn't too pure of heart to deliver some hard blows to the president, especially when Brown was on his home turf.

"When he was governor of the fine state to your north," Brown told a rally in Oakland one early fall day, "President McCall said the only way California would ever get a drop of Oregon water is if we learned to blow or suck." There were scattered boos. "Tell me, do you think the interests of our great state can get a fair hearing in the McCall White House?" The shouted chorus of "nos!" threatened to shake the Bay Bridge from its foundations.

"They even have bumper stickers up there," Brown declared, his voice rising to a crescendo, "bumper stickers that say, 'We shoot every other car with California plates.' The president says Oregon's model of civility is worthy of export. Tell me, does that bumper sticker represent civility?"

One more thunderstorm of "nos" followed. The tape of Brown's speech was shown on all three major networks that night. No one was surprised when McCall finished a distant third in the Golden State that November.

An Associated Press reporter in Portland generated an amusing feature story simply by making a phone call to First Mother Dorothy Lawson McCall and asking her reaction to Brown's blast. "My son does have a gift for putting his foot in his mouth from time to time," she said.

McCall shook his head when he read the story and muttered, "And some people wonder why I don't have her campaigning for me."

His mother's sometimes tart tongue aside, if McCall was looking for adoring fans, he needed to look no further than his own backyard. It was the Monday night before the vote. The last rally ever for Tom McCall, candidate, was held on the banks of the Willamette River he had done so much to clean up. A crowd conservatively estimated at two-hundred thousand turned out to hear the President declare:

"No matter what happens tomorrow, we can take pride in the fact that we've been able to carry the Oregon Story from coast to coast over these past two years. We've planted seeds. Some seeds take time to germinate; some never do; but a few of them are already bearing fruit, and we can all celebrate that."

After the rough-and-tumble campaign, few Americans were surprised that election night, November 2, 1976, failed to produce a clear winner. Reagan was left at the stage door, finishing third in total electoral votes, while McCall claimed a plurality over Brown, but failed to achieve the magic 269 electoral vote total that would have guaranteed him a term in his own right. McCarthy had garnered some headlines during the campaign, but his exclusion from the debates, his failure to win ballot slots in key states like New York and lack of money doomed him to a distant fourth place finish; he didn't carry a single state.

McCall had carried twenty-four states with a total of 195 electoral votes, dominating New England and the west. Brown's "big state" strategy saw him taking just eight states, plus the District of Columbia, but they were prizes rich in electoral votes, including California, New York, New Jersey, Ohio, Florida and Pennsylvania, and his total stood at 183. Reagan prevailed in 18 states, mainly in the south and Midwest, with 160 electoral votes.

One of the most memorable political spectacles of the century would unfold in the weeks that followed. For the first time since 1824, the House of Representatives would elect the President. Under the Twelfth Amendment, each state would cast a single vote, so it came down to basic math: twenty-six votes would be needed to win.

The "big state" strategy might have made perfect sense for Brown in a normal year, when the final outcome was simply a matter of taking a majority of electoral votes; but with the new playing field of one state, one vote in the House, things were suddenly turned on their head and Brown was in the mathematically weaker position. McCall, meanwhile, needed to win over just two states to claim a majority.

The phrase "corrupt bargain" was in the headlines for the first time since that year of so long ago. The original corrupt bargain allegedly struck that year, saw Henry Clay deliver the electoral votes to John Quincy Adams that allowed him to claim the presidency, with the Secretary of State's job as Clay's reward; in the days before the new Congress convened and the electoral votes were officially counted, rumors of a new corrupt bargain began to circulate.

One of the most popular speculations was that the two Californians, Brown and Reagan, would somehow team up to seize the presidency from McCall. On the surface, it didn't make any sense. They were from different generations (born twenty-seven years apart) and resided at opposite ends of the political spectrum. But they were both from the Golden State, and one of the oldest clichés on the books is 'politics makes strange bedfellows.'

The stalemated election was a journalist's dream. The period around Christmas time is traditionally a slow one in the news business, but not in 1976. Every broadcaster and newspaperman was weighing in with speculation on what would happen when the Congress would get to the business of picking a president.

The uncertainty over the country's leadership sent the stock market into a year-end tailspin, but the expectation was for a quick recovery once the identity of the man who would take the oath on January 20th was resolved.

The 95th Congress convened on January 4, 1977, and immediately opened the electoral votes. The historical magnitude of the moment was underlined by the fact that for the first time in history, Congress allowed live television coverage of its proceedings. The House immediately began its first vote for president, and the initial ballot produced a result that reflected November's deadlock. The network commentators were ready to begin speculating on what would happen next; but they didn't have much time for guesswork, because the country was able to watch the next act in the drama play out in real time. At that moment, Brown stepped up to a bank of microphones that had been quickly set up in the rotunda of the state capitol in Sacramento to make a dramatic announcement, carried live on television from coast to coast.

As Brown strode across the black and white tiles toward the podium, NBC's David Brinkley said, "The country is holding its collective breath. We're about to find out whether or not we can exhale." Then Brown spoke:

"I am asking the delegations from the states that supported me in the first round of voting to support President McCall on the second ballot," he said. "I make this request for the good of the country. The nation's business must be allowed to move forward. We cannot stand weeks of gridlock and uncertainty. Although the people did not speak with one voice on November Second, the single largest bloc of voters made it clear that they want President McCall's leadership to continue.

"Many will ask if there's any kind of secret deal been made to secure this result. In the interest of openness and candor, I will disclose that I spoke to the President while the House was balloting. I asked him if he would be

willing to ask Governor Atiyeh of Oregon to replace the sign at the Oregon-California border, which now reads, 'Welcome to Oregon, enjoy your visit,' with one that simply reads, 'Welcome to Oregon.' I also proposed that he join me and Governor Atiyeh at a ceremony to unveil the new sign. The President laughed and said he would happily comply."

McCall told his closest aides that Atiyeh had initially proposed blowing up the sign, but he had quashed the idea. "I said, 'Vic, don't you think a little paint would be more civilized?''

When the California delegation caucused prior to the vote, they stubbornly stuck with their Governor. One member, speaking anonymously, later said "Jesse (California State Treasurer Jesse Unruh, the unofficial boss of the state's Democrats) threatened the fires of hell for anyone who dared vote for McCall."

The second House ballot: McCall, thirty-one states; Reagan, eighteen states; Brown, one state.

Brown was hailed from coast to coast for putting the good of the country above his own interests. Those of a more cynical turn of mind observed that at age thirty-eight, he still had decades ahead on the national scene. His time would come.

17

As always, the beginning of a presidential term brought a host of changes in the cabinet. Hickel, his sense of vindication complete, told McCall he wanted to return to Alaska. McCall tried to persuade Morris Udall to take the job once held by his brother Stewart, but he didn't want to give up his House seat. McCall eventually chose Idaho Governor Cecil Andrus as the new Interior Secretary.

The January tenth announcement that Secretary of State Henry Kissinger, the last of the Nixon holdovers, would depart was a signal that further change was ahead now that McCall had won it outright. The selection of Democrat Cyrus Vance as the nation's new chief diplomat was seen as an even stronger sign that party labels would have little meaning in the new administration.

Vance and McCall had several private meetings in the weeks following the election, and speculation was already beginning to appear in print and on the air that he would replace Kissinger long before the official announcement. A *New York Times* editorial had already spoken of Kissinger's tenure in the past tense, suggesting he would be remembered as one of the most powerful secretaries of state in the twentieth century, and celebrating his accomplishments like the opening of relations with China and the détente with the Soviet Union.

But with the "on the other hand" tone that is the hallmark of so many newspaper editorials, the paper also acknowledged that Kissinger's "lone ranger" approach to diplomacy could have its drawbacks and agreed it was time for McCall to put his own stamp on foreign policy.

Vance was a lawyer, diplomat and bureaucrat, and a product of the WASP (White Anglo-Saxon Protestant) elite. In a Washington climate where self-promotion was almost as important as actual achievement, if not more so, he seemed content to stay in the background and let his accomplishments speak for themselves.

McCall and Vance had hit it off. McCall liked the low-key Vance and assured him that he would be the administration's chief spokesman on foreign policy. Before Kissinger's elevation, he had been Nixon's national security adviser, but he had supplanted Nixon's first secretary of state, William Rogers, as the point man on foreign affairs.

The two men were already developing a new approach to the decades of war and stalemate in the Middle East that they hoped could set those countries on a path to peace. Although McCall's focus on foreign affairs wasn't nearly as intense as his interest in domestic policy, he began to develop a sense of opportunity and excitement. Yet he didn't feel comfortable making any announcements during this period of limbo after the election when he didn't know if he would remain in office.

From the New York Times (January 21, 1977)
By James Naughton

> *Half a million people watched in person yesterday as President Tom McCall took the oath of office for a second time, and millions more partied into the night from coast to coast.*
>
> *A series of "people's balls" from coast to coast were just one of the innovations that signaled McCall's remaining four years in the White House would be about shattering precedents. Yet in his inaugural address, the President reached far back into history to back up his message of conservation.*
>
> *"Some people say Theodore Roosevelt was the first conservationist," McCall declared. "And that may be true in a modern sense. But the call to be good stewards of the earth is at least as old as the Bible."*
>
> *McCall became the first president to take the oath of office in a simple*

dark business suit, forsaking the morning clothes that have been a staple of previous inaugurations. And he delighted the crowd along the route of the Inaugural parade, estimated at just over 500,000, by skipping the presidential limousine and walking most of the way hand-in-hand with First Lady Audrey McCall. The President and First Lady walked home.

From the Washington Post's Coverage of the 1977 State of the Union address:

The first President of the United States in one hundred and twenty-four years not affiliated with the Democratic or Republican parties received a record standing ovation from members of both of those parties as he delivered his State of the Union address tonight.

Tom Lawson McCall, who ascended to the presidency two and a half years ago following the resignation of Richard Nixon, then won election in his own right in a precedent-shattering campaign that ended with a vote by the House of Representatives earlier this month, appeared to have united diverse political viewpoints—at least for one night. He was frequently interrupted by applause, and received numerous standing ovations.

McCall made it clear he plans to continue to challenge precedent as he moves into a term in his own right. He told the assembled dignitaries and those watching on television:

"As the United States enters its third century, we must not remain bound by old structures and old ideas. That is why I am taking this opportunity to announce the creation of several new cabinet-level departments. These will include:

"The Department of Energy, which will be dedicated to the development of sustainable energy sources that will free us of our dependence on the products of foreign shores and reduce our tendency to despoil our land, seas and air;

"The Department of Peace, dedicated to promoting greater communication, cooperation and understanding among nations; and

"The Department of Culture, which will recognize the importance of the

arts in all their forms to our quality of life."

The President also said he would deliver a proposal for a comprehensive national health care program to Capitol Hill within weeks.

President McCall closed by noting the extraordinary path that had brought him to this moment—his appointment as vice president, his predecessor's resignation, his decision to seek election to a term in his own right, and his eventual selection by the House of Representatives.

"Old paths have been left behind; new precedents have been set. Let us resolve together that our party labels come second; that first and foremost, we are citizens of the United States of America, working together for the common good of those who sent us here."

The new Speaker of the House, Thomas "Tip" O'Neill of Massachusetts, was supportive of the president's initiatives. "We're entering uncharted territory here," O'Neill said afterward. "To have a president not affiliated with either major party is something that none of us have ever seen in our lifetimes. The House literally chose this president; we have an obligation to work with him as best we can."

The selection of O'Neill as speaker brought smiles to many faces in the West Wing of the White House. Although O'Neill was a Democrat and the majority of those who populated those offices were Republicans, or former Republicans, there was a sense that O'Neill was someone they could work with. The President and the Speaker shared Massachusetts roots, while O'Neill and Ford had built a strong friendship over their decades of shared service, despite being on opposite sides of the aisle politically. Their mutual love of golf had been the first bridge to bring them together; many a political compromise had been forged on the links. O'Neill teased Ford about being a spray shooter. Ford and McCall had played a few rounds together, and Ford already was trying to figure out who would be the ideal candidate to make a foursome. He also smiled to himself that he would likely no longer be the poorest golfer in the bunch.

18

Excerpt, McCall Library Oral History Interview with Chris Matthews

At the time this interview was recorded in 2003, Matthews was a well-known political journalist for MSNBC who had authored several books. In 1981, he was the top aide to the newly-chosen Speaker of the House, Tip O'Neill; in that role, he had frequent dealings with the McCall White House. Former Oregon Governor Phil Keisling, who had just taken over as executive director of the McCall Library following Westerdahl's retirement from the post, was the interviewer.

KEISLING: Your boss and the President seemed to get on pretty well.

MATTHEWS: Tom also worked pretty well with Ted Kennedy. But it didn't surprise me. They were three Massachusetts Democrats. Tom, Tip and Ted. I sometimes called them the terrific Ts.

KEISLING: But—

MATTHEWS: I know, I know, you're going to say Tom was an Oregon Republican, but he was born in Massachusetts, and his grandfather was governor of Massachusetts. Anyone who ever listened to one sentence out of his mouth knew he was from Massachusetts. And as for his party, you know Tom abandoned the Republicans only after they had abandoned him. He didn't have a party during his second term, until the Citizens Party was formed, but it was clear that his ideology was a lot closer to the Democrats than the Republicans in those years.

KEISLING: The relationship had more to do with politics, though.

MATTHEWS: That's true. Tip loved to come to the White House and have a drink with the President at the end of the day. Well, they both liked to have several drinks, to be honest about it. They both had pretty lively senses of humor, and they both loved to unwind with a stiff one. I think most of the deals that were brokered between the White House and Congress in those years were agreed to during those Happy Hours. They got a hell of a lot done.

KEISLING: But not national health care.

MATTHEWS: Not national health care.

In an-hour long interview with the three network news anchors as he prepared to leave office in early 1981, the retiring President called his attempt to pass national health care legislation "my most noble failure." It has seemed so promising when he took up the idea in early 1977. McCall teamed up with Massachusetts Senator Ted Kennedy, who had been working toward the prize for years. McCall, elected to a term in his own right, felt further emboldened by the fact that he would never be running for office again.

In mid-1970, Kennedy had introduced his first national health care plan. The bill called for universal, single-payer coverage funded through a payroll tax. It was opposed by Nixon, who didn't want to see health care under federal control. Still, the president who had watched two of his brothers die before he reached adulthood realized there needed to be fundamental changes in the system, and bucked much of his own cabinet by pushing a plan in early 1971, which included an employer mandate for private coverage and federalization of Medicaid, a state-run program. Neither plan gained enough political traction to move forward.

"Time to go for the big play," McCall told Westerdahl, Ford and Schmidt as they discussed the 1977 State of the Union address. This was the opening of talks with Kennedy that led to a plan for universal coverage for every American by the end of McCall's term through employer mandates and expansion of Medicaid.

Almost as soon as the legislation was rolled out, an onslaught began that even the skillful McCall public relations machine couldn't overcome. For all the discussion over the dollars and cents aspects, people were mainly swayed by a fear that an unseen bureaucrat would be dictating their health coverage. Or as Schmidt reflected in his memoirs, "Once they started talking and writing about 'McCallcare' I knew the game was over."

When the dust settled months later, and the legislation was officially declared dead, McCall looked back in an interview with ABC's Frank Reynolds on what had had doomed the effort. McCall said plenty of things contributed—the power of the medical lobby, Congressional inertia, public resistance to change—but there was one issue that loomed above all. "The press decided it needed to take me down a peg. That I'd become too big for my britches. And maybe that was true."

Watching the taping session, Ron Schmidt couldn't help but nod in agreement. He thought the law of averages had finally caught up with McCall. The media that had done so much to make him, both in Oregon and nationally, had finally turned on him. It made him think of the "kill your hero" syndrome. But then he realized it came down to something less grandiose: human nature. Some said it was jealousy on the part of the East Coast press, who felt the Westerner McCall had given one exclusive too many to the *Los Angeles Times*, the *Oregonian* or the *Seattle Times*. Some thought it was a case of too many young iconoclasts with a dream of being the next Woodward or Bernstein. Others believed that after Vietnam and Watergate, the press would never be as uncritical as it once had been, no matter who sat in the Oval Office—even one of their own.

It may have come down to the simple fact that Ben Bradlee and Tom McCall rubbed each other the wrong way.

One day, when the *Washington Post* had published one more front-page analysis challenging the financial assumptions the McCall-Kennedy plan was built upon, Schmidt walked into Penwell's office, picked up the *Post*, scanned the front page, then flung the paper across the room in disgust.

"I don't get it Doris, I just don't get it," Schmidt said. "Bradlee and McCall should love each other. Both from Massachusetts. Both from wealthy families that hit hard times. Both Navy men. Both journalists at heart. What is the problem?"

"Maybe that's the problem," she said with a nod.

"What do you mean?"

"They might just be too much alike."

It was an epiphany for Schmidt. His boss and the preeminent newspaper editor in America were rivals. No doubt Bradlee, if pressed, would say he could do a better job of running the country, and McCall knew in the deepest recesses of his brain that he would be a better editor. Not that either man would ever admit it of course.

No one in the White House would ever know how much Bradlee had reined in some of the wilder excesses of his staff. Early in the reporting of the health care debate, Bradlee met with a newly-hired reporter named Janet Cooke who claimed to have interviewed a former White House intern who had a months-long affair with the president a few months earlier. Although the young woman wanted to remain anonymous for now, Cooke insisted the details were airtight. Bradlee listened as she laid out the story, including an alleged tryst in the Oval Office itself. She painted a vivid word picture of McCall's top aides keeping the Secret Service at bay while the president had his way with the intern.

"Jesus H. Christ," he said when she had finished. "What a load of bull crap. Everyone wants to be a goddamned Woodstein now."

"What are you talking about, Mr. Bradlee?"

"Well, the president and First Lady have been married for thirty-five years, and there's never been the slightest hint, the absolute slightest hint, of an affair."

"But sometimes people don't know. What about—"fortunately for Cooke, the words 'President Kennedy' stuck in her throat. She realized almost too late that the example wouldn't sit well with

Bradlee, who had considered himself a friend of JFK. But the editor got the point.

With a deep sigh and a slight head shake, he said, "I know that during the Kennedy administration it was said that female White House interns needed to bring their knee pads to Washington. But it's not like that now. Did you know, Miss Young Hotshot, that we've got a pretty bright young man named Lou Cannon on the White House beat, and I don't think he'd let something like this slip past him?"

"Yes, but—"

"And did you know that the President had prostate cancer surgery three years ago?"

"Well, yes, but—"

"And did you know that the surgeons removed his prostate and one testicle? That he now calls himself 'One Ball McCall'? That he wrote an article about his surgery and its aftermath for our Sunday magazine a couple of years ago—" Bradlee swirled around in his chair, picked up a file folder sitting in a stack behind him, and pulled out a clipping, which he quickly scanned, then turned back around so he could hand it to Cooke—"and here it is, 'Removal of the prostate and celibacy are synonymous.' So tell me, Miss Cooke, how could he be banging an intern?"

Cooke began to squirm; she could feel the blood rushing to her cheeks. She was sitting in the office of the Executive Editor of the *Washington Post* because she was an uncommonly gifted writer. Unfortunately, her gifts might have been put to better use crafting fiction. She tried to mount a defense:

"Mr. Bradlee, I'm no medical expert, but it's my understanding that some men are able to remain, er, sexually active following this surgery. How do we know the President isn't lying?"

"A man doesn't lie about a thing like that. He just doesn't. Miss Cooke, I really thought you were ready for the *Post*, but you obviously aren't. Good luck back home."

"But Mr. Bradlee—"

As Bradlee sat quietly fuming after he sent Cooke packing, he couldn't help but laugh to himself. The reference to "One Ball McCall" reminded him of another one of the president's nicknames. His staff had gathered exhaustive research on McCall, and many of the anecdotes had never made it into print, including the fact that his KGW colleagues Tom Craven and Paul Marcotte had called him "C.B. McCall." The two men went steelheading with him in the early 60s, and noted that he had a tendency to leave the ball of his spinning reel closed, with disastrous results.

Although disappointed, McCall seemed to take the defeat of his health care plan in stride, compared to the defeat of a tax restructuring plan Oregon voters had decisively rejected in 1973. His closest circle of confidantes had gathered at the governor's residence for what they hoped would be a victory party. When the results became clear, McCall took Schmidt aside and told him he would resign. Schmidt and Clay Myers stayed with McCall until it was nearly dawn to make sure he didn't do anything rash, like a public announcement that he was quitting.

The next morning, a physically and emotionally exhausted McCall arrived at his office. It was clear to everyone who saw his slumped frame, sallow face and pained expression that this was a deeply personal blow, something that went far beyond a political issue. A flood of calls from well wishers, some generated by Schmidt, many others spontaneous, helped cushion the blow. In the morning staff meeting, McCall had stood, slammed his fist on the table, roaring, "Goddamn it, it was for the people!" He dropped back into his chair and began to weep. Some wondered if the governor's need for public approval ran too deeply for his own good.

There were angry recriminations, but no tears, over the defeat of the health care plan. Some thought it was because McCall was a few years older and wiser. Some assumed he was taking the long view of history—after all, it had taken a twenty-year battle to pass Medicare. McCall himself told Frank Reynolds that he knew it was a concept whose time would eventually come—that the idea that anyone could go without basic health care in the wealthiest country on earth would soon be seen as unconscionable. But Schmidt knew the real answer. McCall didn't care about the approval of Congress as deeply as he cared about how he was seen by the people of his beloved state. He could handle a "no" from Howard Baker and Ted Stevens much better than the same message from his own people. It was a simple as that.

19

Once McCall was assured of a term in his own right, he felt more confident in putting his own stamp on the nation's foreign policy. Just days after the House vote confirming his election, he announced that he was accepting Kissinger's resignation, with thanks for his service to the nation. Days later, he held a news conference to announce that he was nominating Cyrus Vance to be the next secretary of state. Vance was a career lawyer and bureaucrat. He served in both the Kennedy and Johnson administrations, and was a delegate to the Paris Peace talks.

More than any other president of the modern era, McCall was truly content to let his Secretary of State handle foreign policy, though he did step forward whenever the president's voice and leadership was necessary, and retained the ultimate decision-making role on key policies. He did encourage Vance to push for completion of a pair of treaties returning control of the Panama Canal and the Canal Zone to Panama. Although California Senator S.I. Hayakawa balked, declaring we had "stolen it fair and square," the majority of the Congress was supportive. Agreement on the treaties was announced in the fall of 1977; they were ratified by the Senate the next year, and took effect the year after that.

It was a moment of satisfaction for McCall, who had concluded it was long past time for the United States to put the Panamanians back in charge of their own affairs. By the time the treaties took effect however, he had taken center stage for the foreign policy achievement that would earn him a nomination for the Nobel Peace Prize: the Camp David Accords.

McCall and Vance had spent many hours going over the current situation in the Middle East and the centuries of conflict that had led to the present moment. Their conversations had started right after Vance's confirmation by the Senate. It was a graduate-level education for McCall in the intricacies of geopolitics; but he realized that he would have to build personal relationships with the key players if he was to have any hope of breaking down the walls of mistrust between the Arab nations and Israel. By the end of 1977, he had met with Egyptian President Anwar El Sadat, King Hussein of Jordan, Haffez Al-Assad of Syria and Menachem Begin of Israel.

The President was invigorated by the challenges and possibilities that were opening up, but realized the enormity of the task he had set for himself. "My God, Audrey, getting John Burns and Hector Macpherson (two powerful state senators who had been on opposite sides of the battle over land use planning in Oregon) together would have been easy compared to this," McCall told his wife as they rested in their hotel after a whirlwind day of ceremonial events and diplomatic meetings in Cairo.

Gradually, McCall and Vance had developed a set of three goals for any negotiations: recognition of Israel's right to exist by its neighbors; an undivided Jerusalem; and Israel's withdrawal from territories occupied during the war of 1967. By early 1978 it was clear that Hussein and Assad had no interest in being part of broader peace talks. But Sadat had become frustrated with the lack of progress and displayed a willingness to take bold measures to break the stalemate, having announced to his parliament in November of '77 that he would go to Israel and speak before the Knesset.

Sadat's historic three-day visit to Israel took place ten days later. It helped pave the way for the historic summit at Camp David the following September. McCall was content to let Vance's team lay the groundwork for the meeting, though he did receive regular briefings. But when the time came for the face-to-face meetings, McCall took charge personally, though he did confide some private misgivings about being out of his element in the world of international diplomacy. He told his mother it was a little scary to be wading into the middle of such a hair-trigger situation.

"You'll be fine, son," Dorothy McCall reassured him in the telephone call. "Just don't let your nerve fail you. Remember the time your father faced down Charlie Colby?

"How could I ever forget?" the president asked.

Colby was a Prineville ranch owner with a reputation for murder. Dorothy McCall's brother Douglas Lawson had been shopping for acreage near his sister's home and Colby expected Lawson to buy his property. When Lawson purchased another parcel instead, Colby, who was deeply in debt, telephoned the McCall ranch and threatened to kill Hal McCall. On a bright morning, the two men met each other on horseback on opposite sides of the river. Colby, astride his big black horse, nervously fingered his gun. Hal McCall calmly invited Colby to cross the river so the two men could talk the matter over. Without a word, Colby turned, rode home and took his own life instead.

"I don't think Begin or Sadat will be packing guns," Dorothy McCall said.

"No mother, but they've got a lot of crazy followers back home who do have guns. And bombs. And they aren't afraid to use them."

"All you can do is try, son. All you can do is try."

It was unusual for a president to devote two weeks to a single issue, even something as momentous as Middle East peace. But before they could get down to the momentous business of making peace, McCall insisted that Sadat, Begin and their entourages join him for some good fun with a powerful message—the first Concert for Peace on the Washington Mall, also known as Vortex II.

One of the original quartet of young people who had hitchhiked to Salem in 1970 to pitch the idea for the Vortex rock festival had made his way to Washington several weeks earlier and asked for an audience with the president. Lee Meier had been reading about the evolving plans for the peace summit. He wanted to suggest to McCall that it might be time for Vortex II. Meier's hair was shorter than the shoulder length it had been that summer, but he had remained committed to his values emphasizing nonviolent change. He still wore the same scruffy beard and John Lennon glasses he had that summer. And more importantly, he still believed in the power of nonviolence and that music and fellowship offered a path toward peace.

Schmidt, Westerdahl, Ford and McCall looked at each other after hearing out Meier's pitch. Ford had his reservations about the idea, but by now had learned to trust McCall's instincts. Everyone nodded their assent, and like the first Vortex, it all came together with astonishing speed. The concert would take place on the Washington Mall, in the expanse between the Capitol Building and the Washington Monument. A crowd estimated at between two hundred fifty thousand and three hundred thousand people turned out to listen to the music interspersed with messages of inspiration and hope.

While Vortex I had relied on unknown musicians and a funky vibe where the authorities turned a blind eye to nudity, drug use and open expressions of love, Vortex II drew on a lot of star power and was a little more conventional. There were no pet cougars or pet anacondas, no naked vendors, no tubs of free LSD. Meier was a bit wistful, but realized it had to be this way. One of the beauties of Vortex I was that it was, by design, at a location close to the mainstream path, yet off of it. Milo McIver State Park was only thirty miles from downtown Portland, but the distance could be measured in light years for those who weren't bound by tape measures and maps. Newspaper photographers and television cameramen wandered the field of Vortex, but their film had to be driven back to downtown Portland and processed, providing a crucial barrier of time and distance. Meier wondered how the dynamic of Vortex I might have changed if it had unfolded in real time on Portland TV screens.

Vortex II would take place in the glare of live television, and on the expanse of ground many thought of as the nation's living room. The stakes were high, to say the least; word went out from the West Wing that a certain degree of order had to be preserved.

Still, it was said afterward that all of the National Park Police on duty that day developed curiously impaired senses of smell, and many reported their fields of vision had narrowed as well, though these problems miraculously vanished a few hours after the cleanup was completed.

McCall set the tone by strolling across the White House grounds and onto the mall. He was dressed in golf slacks and a sweater, about as casual as he felt being comfortable with in public. There were elements of the event that might have caused Meier and the others behind the first Vortex to cringe: Billy Graham offered an opening prayer, and Debby Boone and the Beach Boys were among the opening acts. Almost all reviewers hailed the concert as a transcendent moment, greater than the sum of its acts. If there was one complaint that surfaced, it was the schizophrenic nature of the night. The safe and somewhat bland opening half gave way to a decidedly grittier second act. For this segment, the prominent antiwar activist, the Rev. William Sloane Coffin, presented an impassioned prayer for success of the coming peace talks. The Godfather of Soul, James Brown, brought the crowd to its feet with his set, his screaming, howling animal magnetism in full flower as darkness settled over the mall. It was as if the crowd had received a massive, simultaneous shot of adrenaline. He opened with "Papa's Got A Brand New Bag," rolled on with half a dozen more of his classics, and closed with "Peace in the World."

Paul Simon and Bob Seger followed Brown and kept the energy high. Oregon's own distinguished poet, William Stafford, who had spent World War II in conscientious objector camps rather than take up arms, took the stage as twilight settled over the mall to read his poem "Peace Walk."

The emotional highlight, though, turned out to be the first reunion in several years of the original Weavers, the great quartet that had endured the 1950s blacklist. Ronnie Gilbert, Fred Hellerman, Lee Hayes and Pete Seeger had stayed true to their folk roots and their leftist politics through the decades, and had lived long enough to see the mainstream of the country catch up with them.

When they closed the evening with a stirring rendition of "This Land is Your Land." Almost everyone on the mall joined hands and sang along, along with uncountable millions more who were watching or listening to the live broadcasts of the event on television and radio. Among those on the other side of the screen—a young family in Manhattan. John Lennon and Yoko Ono, who were sprawled out on a bed in their apartment at the Dakota, their two-year old son Sean happily wedged between them. Lennon felt a sense of wistfulness that he had turned down an invitation to perform, but he was still in his self-imposed musical retirement. His mood brightened, though, when Paul Simon led the crowd in a cover of one of Lennon's classics, "Give Peace a Chance."

Lennon turned to his wife and said, "They're playing our song, Mother."

As "This Land is Your Land" reached its conclusion, Sadat smiled broadly, and even Begin, who had sat through most of the evening stoically, applauded enthusiastically. The dynamic of that moment, and those that followed, were captured by photographer Gerry Lewin, who had flown to Washington to record the history-making event for posterity. He won a Pulitzer Prize for the series of pictures which appeared in the *Capitol Journal* and were republished in *Time* and *LIFE*.

Many people thought the concert was over at this point; a lot of them began collecting their trash and folding their blankets. But Lewin, at the end of the stage, saw Pete Seeger in animated conversation with McCall. The president signaled for Sadat and Begin to join them; the four men were soon talking with great intensity. After a series of nods, the three world leaders joined the four Weavers on stage for a Pete Seeger classic, "Turn, Turn, Turn."

On the chorus, McCall joined in for an enthusiastic, if slightly off-key, "A time for peace, I swear it's not too late!" Sadat and Begin didn't sing, but they did sway with the music, and even clapped a couple of times. When it was over, the trio hugged; the moment made front pages from coast to coast and around the globe.

There wasn't a dry eye on the mall. On CBS, Walter Cronkite declared, "We may have just witnessed a turning point in world history."

Hunter Thompson was on hand for *Rolling Stone,* and wrote an impassioned article about the day that is best remembered for this paragraph:

> *I witnessed something that was apparently missed by the hundreds of thousands who surrounded me. A little over a decade ago, Jerry Rubin and Abbie Hoffman, doing battle with the insanity of the Vietnam War, promised to levitate the Pentagon. That didn't happen. But I will swear to my dying day that as the crowd sang "Turn, Turn, Turn," the Washington Monument lifted several inches off the ground and hovered there for at least a minute. Curiously, no one else seemed to notice.*

When he wrote his memoirs a few years later, McCall expressed only one regret about Vortex II: his failure to ask Begin and Sadat to join him in an om circle afterward. Still, the three men did join hands while the President recited the Lord's Prayer, and no one was unhappy with the outcome of the summit.

The three leaders and their staffs gathered at Camp David, the presidential retreat in Maryland. McCall had made less use of Camp David than many of his predecessors, preferring to get home as frequently as possible. If he really needed a fishing fix, and a trip home to Oregon wasn't on the horizon, he'd go to Hunter Creek, a couple of miles west of the camp's entrance, and the same spot Franklin Roosevelt had taken Winston Churchill fishing during a visit in 1943. Although the stream was generously stocked with trout, the president and prime minister came away empty-handed that day, and McCall too often experienced the same result.

But the forested retreat, with its main lodge and numerous guest cabins, provided the right setting for some of the most significant diplomatic exchanges of the McCall administration. Although only 62 miles from

Washington, the remote, wooded setting provided not only relief from the sometimes oppressive Washington heat and humidity but enough isolation to allow all the parties to focus on the task at hand.

McCall sized up the two men quickly; he sensed that of the pair, Sadat was far more eager to achieve a settlement. He and Begin had a deep mutual distrust of each other, and McCall was forced to meet one-on-one with each man frequently in the early going. All the major players gave McCall credit for his common sense, determination and good humor in keeping the talks on track toward an agreement.

"Frankly, I don't think Sadat and Begin knew quite what to make of McCall," one mid-level State Department official said afterward. "The Concert for Peace really set the tone for what followed. He's not like the type of American they've been used to dealing with. And that's probably a good thing."

The agreements reached that September paved the way for Israel's pullback from the Sinai, establishment of self-governance for the West Bank and the Gaza strip, and the opening of diplomatic relations between Egypt and Israel. A famous series of photos taken at the conclusion of the talks showed Begin and Sadat shaking hands, with McCall in the middle, towering over both men and smiling broadly.

The world-wide praise for the Camp David Accords helped propel McCall's nomination for the Nobel Peace Prize the next year. He wasn't at all disappointed when the call came informing him he didn't win.

"It's no shame to lose to Mother Teresa," he told Westerdahl.

"True. But Teddy Roosevelt was the only sitting president to win the prize. You're the two conservation presidents. It would have been nice to put one more parallel into the history books."

"Just don't expect me to lead a charge up San Juan Hill anytime soon," McCall quipped with a sardonic grin.

McCall was committed to continuing Nixon's policy of easing Cold

War tensions; he actually admired his willingness to acknowledge that in the second half of the twentieth century, it was an absolutely necessity for the United States to co-exist with superpowers harboring differing belief systems. "It is absolutely insane that we continue to spend billions upon billions to develop more powerful ways to destroy ourselves," McCall had declared in his 1976 State of the Union address. "We need to continue the momentum of last year's Helsinki Agreement (which saw the major powers finally accept the national boundaries created after World War Two and the eastern European countries guarantee basic human rights to their people). Vietnam has taught us a painful lesson: we cannot be the world's policeman. We must always protect our security, but we cannot impose our values and our beliefs on the family of nations, however noble those ideals may be."

This was seen as McCall's boldest statement yet that he would not be supporting the growing "human rights" movement championed by presidential candidate Jimmy Carter and others. As much as he was in synch with a lot of Carter's thinking about our relations with the rest of the world, and as deeply as it pained McCall to see people in other countries denied the rights too many in the United States took for granted, including free speech and free assembly, he would not take the route of confrontation. Vietnam had taught him, and the rest of the country, the lesson of the limits of our might. Better to continue building good relations with both the Soviets and the Chinese, and hope for a gradual loosening of oppression in the far-flung corners of the world.

Perhaps the highlight of the continuation of détente came with the completion of the SALT II arms limitation treaty in 1979; but McCall was bitterly disappointed when the Soviets invaded Afghanistan on Christmas Eve of that same year, driven by fears of Islamic expansion and a desire to maintain access to the Indian Ocean. McCall felt he had cultivated a relationship of trust with Soviet leader Leonid Brezhnev, but realized that the world geopolitical game was a complex one, driven by economic, political and human forces that were sometimes beyond the control of any individual.

20

Tom McCall was used to being the tallest person in the room.

So it was a bit of an adjustment when he welcomed the World Champion Portland Trail Blazers to the White House in June 1977. Surrounded by Bill Walton, Maurice Lucas, Robin Jones, Lloyd Neal and Bob Gross, the six-foot-five president seemed almost.... diminutive.

Yet he relished the opportunity to celebrate the first major league sports champions from his home state. The Trail Blazers had been National Basketball Association also-rans for six seasons; but with the arrival of coach Jack Ramsay and a host of new faces on the court, they had plowed their way through the NBA playoffs, successively defeating Chicago, Denver and Los Angeles to earn a shot at the Philadelphia '76ers for the league title. McCall's main sports passion was following his beloved University of Oregon Ducks; he wasn't a passionate fan at the professional level in any sport. But this was something different; these Trail Blazers were rapidly becoming hometown heroes, and catching their games whenever he could become a pleasant diversion from the cares of his office. From a distance of three thousand miles, Tom McCall caught a case of Blazermania.

McCall had watched the championship game with Audrey and Sam that historic Sunday. The three of them gathered in the family quarters, and he left stern instructions with Westerdahl not to disturb him for anything less than a nuclear attack. The president felt a real pang of homesickness when he couldn't attend the victory parade through downtown Portland the following day. A quarter of a million jubilant Oregonians packed every available square foot of the streets; many hung from lampposts to get a better view of the parade of limousines bearing the players and coaches through the crowd.

Walton had peeled off his jersey and flung it into the swarm of Memorial Coliseum faithful after the win. It was a gesture McCall didn't get to witness as it happened, because CBS television quickly cut away from the arena following the victory for coverage of a golf tournament. But McCall had read about it in the papers. Walton had brought another jersey bearing his name to the White House, and presented it to the president on behalf of the team. McCall accepted it with thanks and asked, "You think you might need another backup next season?"

"I graduated from the University of Oregon just a couple of years before the Tall Firs won the first NCAA championship tournament in 1939," McCall quipped. "It's been a long time between basketball titles for us Oregonians. I salute Coach Jack Ramsay and all the Trail Blazers for an amazing season."

The moments of celebration seemed to be fewer in number as the McCall presidency passed its halfway point. The stress of the world's toughest job was taking a growing emotional toll, and it was about to extract its price.

The president reached a major personal milestone in March of 1978: he turned sixty-five. Not surprisingly, he wanted to celebrate this birthday at home in Oregon instead of at the White House. Audrey planned a relatively small gathering at the house at Salishan. Both of his sons and three of his four siblings were able to make it along with key staffers and their families, plus a handful of friends from his journalism days, some even coming from his earliest days on the job in Moscow.

"It's going to be nice to see some of the old crowd," McCall told Penwell as she went over plans for the party. His wistful look told her that he wished the break could be a longer one. He had been trying to schedule an extended vacation for a while, but it always seemed like there was something urgent enough to crowd it off his calendar.

Air Force One had landed in a driving spring rainstorm in Portland. Eugene was the preferred landing location for these coastal visits; it was easier to secure the airport, and it was slightly closer to the beach house, but the weather had necessitated a landing at PDX. "Oh well, it's typical weather for March," the president told his wife as the jet rolled to a stop. "We wouldn't feel at home otherwise, would we?"

When he could, McCall preferred to take a helicopter to his coastal retreat; but the heavy cloud cover had forced him to travel to the shore by car. Audrey thought he seemed unusually tired as they made the two-hour trip, but his spirits were good, and they were getting better as they approached the stormy beach. It took more than a good old Oregon rainstorm to dampen his mood; he was home and with the people who mattered to him most.

"Bill Brown's going to be there, can you believe it?" McCall said to Audrey with a broad grin. The two men had been bachelor roommates with the young McCall first moved to Moscow, Idaho, and had remained friends. "I'd probably still be rooming with him if I hadn't met you."

McCall had eaten on the drive down at Audrey's insistence, though he complained he wasn't hungry. Audrey pointed out that there were going to be a few toasts offered at the party, and it wouldn't be a good idea to do a lot of drinking on an empty stomach. He nibbled on a roast beef sandwhich that had been prepared for him on board Air Force One, but didn't seem to enjoy it. Almost as soon as the McCalls arrived at their beach house, he went to the bathroom and threw up. Audrey was mildly alarmed, but he blamed the turbulence of the air and car trips for his upset stomach, and he seemed to revive for a time.

But not long after, as he sat down to catch up with his sister Jean Babson, he complained of pain in his left arm and chest. "You're pale, Tom, and it looks like you're sweating," she said.

"Well, it is warm in here," he insisted. When Jean became alarmed, he tried to dismiss her worries; but her instincts told her that something was seriously wrong. "Call an ambulance," Jean quietly told her sister-in-law. "I think the president is having a heart attack." Within minutes, the living room was illuminated by the flash of red lights and the suddenly-subdued crowd parted to allow the EMTs to enter. Schmidt stood in the home's driveway in his rain slicker, making sure the ambulance found its destination. This moment brought home once more how much he loved the man who was waiting for help. He was glad the rain splattering his face made his tears indistinguishable. Schmidt was orphaned in childhood; he had been raised by loving adoptive parents, but the possibility of losing the man he thought of as another father was gut-wrenching.

The only sounds were the crash of wind-driven rain against the picture windows and the staticy chatter on the paramedic's emergency radios.

McCall was still sitting up in the easy chair he had been in since exiting the bathroom. The paramedics seemed to be in awe, but as poorly as he felt, he tried to engage them in small talk and put them at ease: "Sorry to have troubled you young men on such an unpleasant evening," he said with a weak smile. After checking the president's vital signs, they conferred with his family. They suspected a heart attack, but said a trip to the hospital would be needed to confirm the diagnosis and determine a course of treatment. The small facility in Lincoln City was quickly ruled out; a trip to Portland would be necessary. "Damn it," McCall grumbled. "We just got here. This is a hell of a birthday."

"Maverick is ill," Secret Service agent Robert Sulliman radioed, using their code name for McCall. "Prepare for a ground transport."

As he was being carried out of the room, McCall stopped the paramedics for a moment to give an order to Schmidt: "Let them know everything!"

Schmidt didn't need further explanation; he understood his boss perfectly. McCall wasn't the first president to suffer a heart attack; Eisenhower had a serious one in 1955, the same year that future president Lyndon Johnson had a near-fatal coronary of his own. But McCall was also a cancer survivor, and Schmidt realized that media attention on the state of his health would ratchet up considerably from this point forward.

It was a jarring episode for the entire McCall family, both his blood relations and the staff who considered themselves part of the extended family, none more so than Schmidt, who McCall treated like a third son. As he followed the ambulance to Portland in the rainstorm, he couldn't help but think back to a happier Tom McCall birthday celebration in a Salem restaurant just a few years earlier.

Tom and Audrey had been joined by the Schmidts, Westerdahls and the Darrel Buttices for an evening of good food, good drink and lively conversation. As the evening drew to a close, McCall had stood and tapped his glass with his knife to try to get everyone's attention; unfortunately, he hit the glass too hard and it shattered. Undaunted, the governor exclaimed, "THAT'S the note I was looking for!" and began to sing loudly and slightly off key, "Happy birthday to me..." The rest of the table, and the entire restaurant, soon chimed in.

It was a typical evening out with McCall, filled with lots of good stories, good conversation and laughter. The governor wasn't a jokester, but somehow he always managed to bring an upbeat mood to the table. But this evening was going to be the exception.

It was about three and a half hours after McCall had first taken ill that Schmidt stood before a bank of microphones and cameras in the auditorium of Portland's Good Samaritan Hospital to announce, "The President is resting comfortably after suffering a mild heart attack earlier this evening. His doctors say his heart muscle suffered no permanent damage. Barring complications, he should be released from the hospital in a week or so...after that he will head back to the coast for about a month, and if his recovery proceeds as expected, he will be able to return to Washington and a limited work schedule after that."

The questions came like rapid fire, just as Schmidt had anticipated:

Would the president resign? Who would be in charge in Washington?

Schmidt emphasized that McCall's prognosis was very good, and there was no reason to consider a resignation. He said Vice-President Commoner would preside over staff and cabinet meetings in McCall's absence, but would regularly consult by phone with the president, who would continue to receive daily briefings even while hospitalized.

A little over a week after McCall was hospitalized; House Speaker Tip O'Neill flew to Portland to offer McCall personal wishes for a speedy recovery. There was a renewed buzz of excitement among the staff at Good Samaritan when the speaker arrived. They treated the President of the United States like an old friend, but O'Neill, considered by many to be the second most powerful man in Washington, had a charisma and star power all his own. With his shock of white hair, bulbous nose and gravelly voice, O'Neill attracted attention with every step.

Sitting at the president's bedside, O'Neill told the president, "I tried to smuggle in some vodka and vermouth, but the damn Secret Service stopped me."

"Tip, the Secret Service is one thing, but Audrey's something else," McCall said. "They've told me I've got to limit myself to one drink a day from now on, cut down on salt and meat...damn, Tip, there's not much in the way of indulgence left at this point." He smiled, but it was a sad, wistful smile.

"I'd invite you outside to join me for a cigar, Mr. President," O'Neill said. "But I don't want to incur the First Lady's wrath."

"You're a smart man, Tip," McCall said with a nod. A pause. "You know, my cardiologist, a vice nice and very bright young man, made me laugh yesterday. He told me that in addition to changing my diet and getting more exercise, I needed to reduce stress in my life. I just looked at him. I think it took a minute for what he had said to dawn on him. Then he laughed and said, 'I suppose that would be difficult advice for someone in your position to follow, Mr. President.'"

Schmidt and McCall conferred about a media strategy once he was back in Washington. Their first choice for an Oval Office interview was Hugh Sidey, who had written his column on the presidency for *TIME* Magazine for several years. If the well-regarded Sidey sensed McCall was still in command, that message would radiate out to the rest of the media and the public at large. They were pleased with the column that resulted:

> *The President greeted me in the Oval Office looking noticeably thinner (he said he had lost fifteen pounds during his recuperation) but otherwise fit. His color was good. He wore an open-collared shirt, tan jacket and matching slacks.*
>
> *"I dodged a bullet, no question about it," he declared. "But my doctors have assured me I suffered no permanent damage to the heart muscle, and they had absolutely no qualms about me returning to work. But if the time ever comes when I can't do this job, I won't have any reservations about stepping down and letting Barry take over."*
>
> *McCall said there's a lesson to be drawn from his health struggles, those of past presidents, and the scandals of his immediate predecessor: it may be time to bring the presidency down to size.*
>
> *"A bright young woman, one of the White House interns, used a phrase in conversation a couple of years ago that's stuck with me: 'The cult of the presidency.' Maybe it's time we did away with the cult, and remember this is a job done by men, and I hope someday soon, by women as well. Men who are doing their best, but are as fallible as the rest of us. That's a big reason why I tried to make my inauguration more of a celebration and less of a coronation."*
>
> *Our conversation over the next forty minutes made it clear the president is still in command of the national and world situations and still has things he wants to accomplish in the two-and-a-half years remaining on his term.*
>
> *Most who believe McCall may work his way onto the list of great or near-great presidents believe his achievements in protecting the natural environment may be the reason. But his role in restoring the presidency to*

human dimensions may be equally significant.

The heart attack did lead to a change in the relationship between the First Lady and the White House chief of staff. Audrey McCall no longer felt a degree of tension with Westerdahl; now the two became unspoken allies in making sure that the president husbanded his energies as he gradually resumed a full schedule. Sometimes it would be Audrey whisking him away for an afternoon in the Virginia countryside; then there would be days when Westerdahl would announce that a cabinet member or senator had been forced to cancel a meeting at the last minute. Coincidentally, those situations often cropped up on Fridays.

McCall had now survived cancer, an assassination attempt and a heart attack. Some days those who loved him most wondered if he was immortal. On other days, when the fatigue of the job sat heavily on his shoulders, they saw just how fragile he really was. He had never fully embraced life on the Potomac; he now talked with increasing frequency of a longing to go home.

21

After a couple of years of resisting the idea, McCall finally consented to support the formation of a third political party in 1978. Commoner had persuaded him that if the goals they were working on were to have staying power, there needed to be some kind of organizational structure to run candidates not only for president but for Congress, governorships and state legislatures.

"But the third force is more than just a conventional political party!" McCall had pleaded.

"Who says it's going to be a conventional party?" Commoner asked. "We've broken the rules all along the way so far, so why stop now?"

"Yeah," said Ron Schmidt, who had sat in on the meeting to talk about media strategy. "Why call it a party at all? Call it the Citizens' Force. You know, like in *Star Wars*, 'May the force be with you?'

Both men gave him blank looks.

"Come on, you guys saw *Star Wars*, didn't you? It was only the biggest film in the country last year!" McCall and Commoner looked at each other, shrugged, and turned their puzzled gazes back at the press secretary. Schmidt sighed. "I shouldn't forget who I'm talking to."

The organizing convention of the Citizens Party took place in Los Angeles that summer, and the first candidates with a "C" after their names instead of an "R" or a "D" appeared on ballots that fall. It was a token effort, and only four House members were elected, but Commoner, who was the first chair of the party, pledged to field a full slate of candidates in 1980.

Ken Kesey had accepted the presidential appointment as Secretary of Counter-Culture with the promise that he would never have to sit behind a desk in Washington, D.C. or anywhere else. He embraced McCall's vision of his role as a roving ambassador to children, students and those on the fringes of the mainstream. He was a born storyteller and performer, developing a magic act as a youngster, traveling to Hollywood to seek fame on the big screen one summer. That wasn't meant to be, so he applied himself to the craft of fiction and created two of the twentieth century's acknowledged masterpieces. Once he had done that, he turned his art into his life...and vice versa. Yes, it seemed like a perfect fit.

The appointment had been suggested by Sam McCall. When Don Jarvi, who was still working in the West Wing at the time heard the news, he couldn't help but smile. He remembered Kesey as a frequent visitor to the governor's office in Salem, as the novelist was active in local educational issues. One day he heard McCall call out: "Jarvi!"

Jarvi responded to the summons and found himself face-to-face in McCall's small office with the author of *One Flew Over the Cuckoo's Nest* and *Sometimes A Great Notion.* Kesey wore work boots, faded jeans, a red-and-white checked lumberjack shirt and a huge grin. The governor introduced Jarvi as the man who invented the odd-even gas rationing system.

With a broad smile, Kesey responded, "That's like meeting the man who invented the cockroach."

Kesey brought his own brand of irreverence and magic and wonder to the role. It worked for almost three years, until the moment that would always be remembered in Kesey lore as The Interview.

Harry Reasoner and a crew from the CBS newsmagazine *60 Minutes* spent weeks following Kesey around. When the program aired the resulting piece one October Sunday night in 1979, it set off a storm of controversy. Most of the piece was positive, even innocent. There was footage of Kesey in costume, telling stories to rapt schoolchildren; Kesey in dialogue with students on a college campus; Kesey and his entourage in Ho Chi Minh City—they were the first official United States emissaries to set foot in the country since the fall of Saigon in 1975.

Viewers saw Kesey and the latest edition of his Merry Pranksters loading into his famous psychedelic bus Furthur. He had resurrected Furthur when he took on the job, and when people assumed that it was the same bus he had taken on the cross-country trip with the original Pranksters in 1964, he didn't lie...he just didn't bother to correct the misconception. But the CBS crew stumbled across the original bus, gently decaying on the Kesey farm, and that was that.

Nothing to stir people up at all. But then reporter and novelist sat down for a one-on-one conversation. Kesey's head was cocked to one side, and his intense blue eyes twinkled with delight. He wore a tie-dyed t-shirt and faded, ripped jeans. He had refused the offer of the CBS makeup artist to apply powder to his bald scalp to reduce shine. His ear-to-ear grin throughout the conversation reminded more than one viewer of the Cheshire cat.

The most memorable part of the conversation went like this:

REASONER: What do you think of President McCall?

KESEY: He's a good man, the best president this country has had in my lifetime. I just wish he would show a little more courage at times.

REASONER: What do you mean?

KESEY: When he was governor of Oregon, he signed a law that decriminalized possession of marijuana. That was a good first step. I wish he'd get Congress to pass such a law...and then take it a few steps further.

REASONER: Are you calling for legalization of some recreational drugs?

KESEY: All recreational drugs.

REASONER: Including LSD?

KESEY: Yes, including LSD. I've been using it since 1959. You have to be careful with it, just as you have to be careful with the so-called legal drugs.

Used properly, it can help you experience amazing things.

REASONER: I guess we shouldn't be surprised to hear this from the man who made Acid Tests famous.

KESEY: (Smiling) I guess not.

As he watched the broadcast at home, Kesey found himself quietly infuriated over the way the conversation had been edited. Gone was any semblance of context, including his call for responsible use by adults. Left on the cutting room floor was his discussion about the use of hallucinogens in religious rituals for hundreds, and probably thousands of years. He quickly forgot his anger as he switched off the set. He didn't foresee the firestorm that had just been ignited.

At a news conference the next day, Moral Majority leader Jerry Falwell slammed Kesey and McCall for contributing to the moral decline of the country. Falwell said: "This shouldn't come as a surprise from a man who, as governor, sanctioned a state-sponsored music festival which became an unprecedented orgy of drugs, nudity and sex." While McCall tried to ride out the angry tide of conservative outrage that followed Falwell's blast, he accepted Kesey's resignation four days later.

To put it mildly, Falwell had irritated McCall to an unusual degree. That irritation turned to anger. The man who, in 1971, called for a more enlightened drug policy but wasn't ready to push for marijuana legalization now came to the brink of doing just that. In his final State of the Union message in January, 1980, he asked Congress to approve an act to decriminalize possession of less than an ounce of pot—essentially, the same measure he had signed into law in Oregon in 1973.

"It's been eight years since the National Commission on Marijuana and Drug Abuse delivered its recommendations to my predecessor," McCall told the Congress. He noted that the body had supported decriminalization and a social control policy focused on discouraging heavy use. He read from the report: "Looking only at the effects on the individual, there, is little proven danger of physical or psychological harm from the experimental or intermittent use of the natural preparations of cannabis."

McCall looked squarely into the cameras and declared: "It is time to replace decades of misinformation, prejudice and fear with a new, more enlightened policy. It is past time for an approach that replaces paranoia with rationality."

The address was met only with silence from the Nixon residence in New Jersey, but the former president no doubt seethed when he heard or read his successor's words (and probably downed a few stiff ones as well). Nixon had been infuriated by the commission's findings; not surprising from a man who said "homosexuality, dope, immorality in general" were the "enemies of strong societies. That's why the Communists and left-wingers are pushing this stuff; they're trying to destroy us." This was the man who told his long-time chief of staff, H.R. "Bob" Haldeman, that every advocate for legalization was Jewish.

The network commentators had all but declared McCall's proposal dead on arrival in their on-air comments immediately after the speech. "This country is probably not ready to legalize marijuana," CBS's Bob Schiffer had offered. Then a funny thing happened. A groundswell, quiet at first that soon turned into an unstoppable juggernaut.

It didn't surprise anyone that the *New York Times* and the *Washington Post* editorialized in favor of legalization. But then the *Deseret News*, the largest paper in one of the most conservative states in the nation—Utah—did so as well. "Prohibition hasn't worked," the paper declared. "It's time to try education and moral persuasion. Ultimately, if those don't work, nothing will work."

The letters that had been arriving in Congressional offices grew from a trickle to a torrent. Telegrams started to pile up. "It was like nothing since....the bottle bill," marveled one House member. McCall signed the legislation in a Rose Garden ceremony in early April. That night in Pleasant Hill, the former Secretary of Counter-Culture dropped acid in celebration. He called it his "Trip for Tom," and offered a silent prayer that he would see LSD become legal again sometime before he departed the earth.

The very next day, after the trip had ended, Kesey sat down and began making notes for what would be his first full-length novel since the publication of *Sometimes a Great Notion* in 1964. He thought his experiences as Secretary of Counter-Culture just might provide the building blocks for the next Great American Novel.

McCall had used that same State of the Union address to announce another decision he had agonized over for years: he granted amnesty to the young men who had evaded the draft during the Vietnam War. Some 30,000 of them had fled to Canada rather than take up arms in Southeast Asia. There would be a requirement for those who wanted to take advantage of the amnesty would have to request a pardon and perform community service, but this offered them a path to return.

The fate of those men had been an issue in the 1976 elections, with all the leading Democrats pledging to offer an amnesty. The push for an amnesty had continued in the years since. McCall had stayed silent on the matter, and couldn't bring himself to act in large part due to his love and respect for Tad. "Every time I think about it, I can't help seeing Tad on that swift boat," Tom had told Audrey one night. He finally proposed an amnesty program to Congress in 1977, but the Democratic majorities found his proposed requirements for alternative service to be too harsh, and matter hung in limbo for more than two years.

So it wasn't a surprise that it took Tad McCall to persuade his father to change his mind. During the family's 1979 Christmas gathering at the White House, he asked his father: "Isn't it about time that those boys have the chance to come home, Dad?"

President McCall used Tad's very words in announcing that he would offer a pardon to any draft evader who requested one. The wounds of the war were still raw; the conservative denunciation of the move was fierce, while many on the left pointed out that requesting a pardon required an admission of wrongdoing.

22

"The Fate of the Earth" was a landmark four-part series by Jonathan Schell that appeared in the *New Yorker* magazine in February and March of 1980, and was published as a book that spring. It provided significant legitimacy to Commoner and the Citizens Party; it also offered an assessment of McCall's career to this point, with a focus on his environmental legacy.

Schell provided a mini-biography of McCall, and speculated that his love of the outdoors could be traced to the natural beauty he grew up surrounded by in Central Oregon. His public interest in natural protection could be traced at least to 1936, when, as a newly-minted graduate of the University of Oregon, he relocated to Moscow, Idaho to accept a newspaper job, and became chair of the Idaho Wildlife Association.

McCall's environmental credentials were solidified in 1962, when he produced and narrated the landmark documentary, *Pollution in Paradise* for his employer at the time, Portland television station KGW. As Schell noted in his first installment, 1962 was the year of publication for Rachel Carson's *Silent Spring,* considered the seminal work of the modern ecology movement. It was an act of foresight and courage, Schell wrote, to turn the spotlight on the pollution fouling the Willamette River and the skies over Portland when industrial activity was looked at by most Americans as an unqualified good.

"But McCall had seen enough of what unrestrained dumping of wastes had done to the east coast," Schell wrote. "He wanted to sound the alarm before it was too late for Oregon. Slowly, Oregonians rose to the challenge. The 1963 session of the state legislature enacted laws to begin the process of cleaning up the Willamette River."

Schell ticked off the environmental record of the McCall years in Salem, and it was breathtaking: the replacement of the relatively toothless state Sanitary Authority with a far more powerful Department of Environmental Quality; further measures to clean up the Willamette; the first bottle bill, mandating a five cent deposit on soft drink and beer containers; the Bike Bill, setting aside a portion of road building funds for bike lanes; the removal of Harbor Drive, the freeway that skirted the Willamette River in downtown Portland; the Beach Bill that secured the public's right of unimpeded access to all 363 miles of the state's spectacular coastline; and the measure that McCall considered his most lasting legacy, the statewide land use planning program.

When the energy crisis hit, McCall had ordered non-essential electric lights turned off, imposed a 55 mile per hour speed limit on state highways, and ordered thermostats turned down in state buildings. To combat long lines at gas stations following the Arab oil boycott, he advanced an ingeniously simple system of allowing people to buy gas on specific days based on whether the last number on their license plate was odd or even.

When the 1979 gas shortage developed, President McCall had pulled a page out of his Oregon playbook, signing an executive order imposing the odd-even system nationally. He found himself wishing that Treasury Secretary Bill Simon had been willing to listen to him in early 1974 when, as the newly-appointed vice president, McCall had argued against a plan to print five billion gas rationing coupons. The coupons used the same portrait of George Washington that appeared on the dollar bill and it was discovered too late they would trigger change machines. This was why the coupons now sat gathering dust in a government warehouse.

It still staggered him how fuzzy-headed bureaucrats could be, even after so many years in and around government. The contrast with odd-even was amazing. The decision to print rationing coupons was slow, cumbersome, expensive, and ultimately a complete flop. Odd-even had happened quickly and hadn't cost a cent; most important of all, it had worked.

Don Jarvi, then the director of the state's energy information center, had the inspiration while driving from Portland to Salem one day. McCall himself had been caught in one of the snakelike lines that had sprung up once the boycott hit, and his staff was spending the better part of their days fielding calls from every corner of the state wanting to know where they could buy gas. As the shortages and fear intensified, the problem threatened to spiral out of control.

Jarvi thought the system would cut down on panic buying, and he was soon proved to be right. He ran the idea by Chief of Staff Bob Davis at 8:20 that morning. Davis liked it, and put it on the table at the daily staff meeting ten minutes later. Sixty minutes after that, it was before the Emergency Board, a committee of legislators empowered to act between sessions, and they signed off on it. Jarvi met with a group of service station owners in Portland that afternoon, and they were on board; by 6:30 that evening, McCall was making the announcement on the evening news.

Part two of *The Fate of the Earth* was laudatory of McCall, but wasn't an act of hagiography. Schell talked to critics in Oregon who said McCall's policies had hurt the state's economy. Supporters of forest conservation said McCall had been mostly silent on the issues of clear cutting and riparian protections. Others assailed McCall for an outsized ego and accused him of being quick to appropriate credit for the ideas of others, especially Bob Straub, the former state treasurer who had lost to McCall in the 1966 and 1970 races for governor.

"The chairman of the state Highway Commission is a man named Glenn Jackson, and he is widely regarded as one of the most powerful men in Oregon," Schell wrote. "In 1966, Jackson gave his wholehearted support to a plan to extend Highway 101 across an environmentally sensitive sand spit, the Nestucca Spit, on the north-central coast of the state. McCall, to his later shame, threw his support behind Jackson. Bob Straub, to his everlasting credit, led a grassroots campaign that stopped Jackson and McCall in their tracks. Some say Straub was an essential element to McCall's environmental successes, because he allowed McCall to stake out a claim to the territory of the moderate."

Schell also allowed McCall to make his case on forest issues. "You can't take on the leading industry in your state TOO directly and expect to survive politically," he said with a touch of defensiveness. "But we accomplished something significant with the Forest Practices Act."

The 1971 Oregon Forest Practices Act had replaced a thirty-year-old Forest Conservation Act that had required replanting after harvests. The 1971 law was the first of its kind in the nation; it introduced protections for the soil, water, air, fish and wildlife, however limited they might have been. The bill also gave state foresters the ability to inspect logging operations for the first time, and they were empowered to shut down violators. Critics said the bill lacked sufficient teeth to be effective, but McCall insisted it established a critical precedent—that the government can regulate an industry that had operated largely free of oversight to that point.

McCall even drew a parallel between the Forest Practices Act and the 1957 Civil Rights Act, pushed through Congress by Senate Majority Leader Lyndon Johnson. Most in the civil rights movement called the bill almost laughably weak. In private, Johnson agreed that he had to allow it to be gutted of its strongest provisions in order to win its passage. Yet he would passionately argue that getting the first civil rights bill since Reconstruction through Congress was an important step; and the 1957 bill did help pave the way for much stronger legislation in the 1960s.

Though there may have been weak spots, Schell argued that McCall's record in Salem had to be considered in its totality; and he said when the scales were added up, no U.S. governor in the twentieth century, with the possible exception of Gifford Pinchot, could claim such an impressive record of environmental achievements.

Schell described McCall's foresight in addressing the energy crisis as governor "remarkable." On August 21, 1973, he had declared a statewide energy emergency, saying: "We've had the idea that energy in abundance would forever be at our fingertips. We've become careless. We've installed all the modern conveniences, used them without regard to energy supply, and now the piper must be paid. It takes six hundred pounds of coal to operate one sixty-watt bulb for a year. Turn off that bulb!"

Plenty of Oregonians had complied voluntarily, and he made sure state agencies were on board, directing a series of steps, including the disabling or removal of hot water taps in washrooms. But he soon decided a more dramatic step was needed, ordering outdoor display lighting to be shut off. As McCall later told E.J. Kahn of the *New Yorker*: "You couldn't expect anybody to snap off his lights at home if he could look out of his window and see a used-car lot so ablaze with lights you could see it from Mars." Although there were some questions about the legality of the ban, no one challenged it in court, and compliance was high. Not everyone was on board right away, though: the state's Public Utility Commissioner put together a list of six hundred and eighty six businesses that weren't on board, and was prepared to order their power to be shut off, but no order ever came.

McCall's record in Washington had been less spectacular, Schell concluded, blaming a variety of factors including a sluggish national economy, a dysfunctional Congress and a national press corps that was much more skeptical than the admiring band of reporters who remained close to their former colleague. "Still, there's been impressive progress on the environmental front. The national land use planning program, the Beach Bill, the Bottle Bill and the Energy Independence 2000 Act are all regarded as measures of lasting impact," Schell wrote. "When the historians write the record of the McCall presidency, they will likely rank him alongside Theodore Roosevelt as a great environmental president, and they may even place him ahead of T.R."

But he concluded that the greatest change President McCall had brought about was a new shift in the overall tone of the political landscape. What had begun under his predecessor, Nixon, was now on its way to becoming a lasting element of national life: any political decision would, from this point forward, have to factor in environmental issues.

The selection of Commoner as his vice-president and heir apparent sealed the deal, Schell suggested. The senators who had worried about breaking precedent when they let McCall run the Environmental Protection Agency (a post he had relinquished nine months later, after having given the bureaucrats in charge what he privately called "a good swift kick in the rear") were right. When he created the Department of Energy, he tapped Commoner to be the first Secretary of Energy. "I know from experience how little of substance a vice president has on his plate," McCall told Walter Cronkite. "I can't think of a better man to lead us toward our common vision of energy independence."

The article recapped the tribulations of the year just concluded, 1979, which McCall would later rank as his most trying time in office when he sat down to write his memoirs. Energy and the environment, and their impact on the economy, were front and center for most of the year. McCall didn't try to evade responsibility, but made it clear that it was set in motion by a sequence of events largely beyond his career.

In November, 1978, a strike of workers at Iran's state-run oil refineries dramatically reduced oil production and set in motion the Shah's downfall.

It wasn't apparent immediately, but March 1979 was the month the nuclear power industry in the United States died. Two events, twelve days apart, signaled the death knell. The first was the release of the film *The China Syndrome,* the fictional account of a nuclear plant meltdown that starred Jane Fonda, Michael Douglas and Jack Lemmon. The story made for gripping drama, and the producers said the story was a mosaic piecing together actual incidents that had occurred at nuclear plants. The industry's public relations machine struck back hard, calling it "the assassination of an entire industry."

Then came Three Mile Island.

In the predawn hours of March 28, the Unit 2 reactor at the plant near Middletown, Pennsylvania partially melted down. A stuck valve, a failure of monitoring instruments and human error contributed to the near-calamity.

For those with a sense of irony, a line in *The China Syndrome* seemed prophetic. Although the fictional power plant in that film was located outside of Los Angeles, one of the characters said an accident could render an area the size of Pennsylvania uninhabitable. The TMI accident was the most serious in the history of the commercial nuclear power industry. In reality, the release of radiation was negligible, with no health impacts on plant employees or the general public.

But perception and reality are often very different.

McCall had tried to walk a middle ground on the industry as governor, declaring, "build 'em sparingly;" but by 1979, President McCall had been swayed into an anti-nuclear position by his vice president, who persuasively argued that inadequate safeguards were in place to deal with the power plants' toxic waste products.

The president also continued to lead by example in encouraging Americans toward greater conservation, ordering the thermostats in the White House and other federal buildings turned down, and offering incentives to workers to carpool or use public transportation. Although he had posed for publicity photos working in his gubernatorial office by the light of a kerosene lamp, he resisted a suggestion that he address the nation on television wearing a cardigan. "You can only push things so far," he said. "The people don't want a president who is nothing but the national scold." Jarvi had encouraged more creative approaches, including an energy saver's kit and calendar that was distributed to school children from coast-to-cast and an "undrive" public service campaign that played on the popular 7up "uncola" marketing effort of the time.

McCall gave the green light to a plan to gradually deregulate oil prices. He was candid in calling it a short-term solution to a long-term problem. As expected, oil imports decreased, domestic production increased, and gas prices spiked. Fears of gas shortages were dealt with via the odd-even rationing plan. But McCall knew he had to encourage the public to "stay the course" toward permanent energy independence. He was more convinced than ever that renewable sources had to replace fossil fuels. For this reason, he stubbornly resisted Secretary of State Cy Vance's urgings that he proclaim a "McCall Doctrine," which would promise the use of military force if needed to protect the country's strategic interests in the Middle East.

"I'll be damned if I'm going to ask American boys to die for a bigger Buick," McCall told Audrey in the privacy of the second floor family residence of White House. It had been quite a political journey for the governor, who, just a decade earlier, had been an unabashed hawk on Vietnam. But biographer Brent Walth might have concluded that it made perfect sense in the context of McCall's unswerving support for the underdog: this time, the underdog was the planet itself.

Schell closed this installment with this observation: "Near the end of McCall's time in Salem, a reporter asked him the key to his success in advocating for persistent innovation and change. McCall replied: 'There's a spirit here that says let's dare to try things. Let's see why you can do things, rather than let's see why you can't.' If President McCall hasn't been able to move the entire nation quite as far as he moved Oregon during his time as governor, he's still managed an impressive adjustment in our course."

23

From Maverick: The Memoirs of Tom McCall

Sometimes your best decisions only become apparent with time. One of those was my refusal in October of 1979 to allow the former Shah of Iran to enter the United States for treatment of gallstones. I had plenty of pressure on me—Henry Kissinger and David Rockefeller were among those who called—but I held firm. Since the Ayatollah Khomeini had deposed the Shah a few months earlier, anti-U.S. feeling in Iran had reached a fever pitch.

Our embassy had briefly been occupied and the staff held hostage. I shuddered as I pictured angry crowds swarming the embassy, once again taking hostages—or worse. I remember telling Rockefeller that it's never wise to wave a red cape in front of an angry bull. When I pressed Kissinger on whether we were really the only country with adequate facilities to treat the Shah, he equivocated. I had my answer. The safety of United States citizens had to be my first priority. Although our relations with Iran remained rocky until the end of my term and beyond, I can't help but believe that we averted a major international incident.

The Shah entered a hospital in Cairo for treatment. He died in Egypt the next year.

•

He was four years older, only five pounds heavier, but his hairline had receded considerably since his last visit to the Oval Office. Oregon track and field legend Steve Prefontaine had asked for a meeting with McCall because he had heard rumors that the President was being pressured to declare a boycott of the Olympic games in the wake of the Soviet Union's invasion of Afghanistan a few months earlier. He hoped to talk McCall out of it.

In the four years since Montreal, Prefontaine had kept busy with coaching, endorsements, work for Nike and TV commentary. McCall told Prefontaine he had heard rumors he might be interested in going into politics someday, and wondered if there might be any truth to that?

"Not a chance in hell, Mr. President," he replied with a derisive snort. "Not a chance in hell."

Prefontaine launched into his pitch: hundreds of young men and women had spent the better part of their lives training for these games. A boycott would break their hearts, as well as dashing the hopes and dreams of their families, coaches and friends. And what would really be accomplished, he asked? It wouldn't get the Soviets out of Afghanistan; it was better to show them on their own turf which country was stronger.

"Remember a guy named Jesse Owens in Berlin in 1936, Mr. President?" Prefontaine asked. Owens, an African-American, was the most successful athlete at those games, winning four gold medals. "It seems like he did a pretty good job of getting in Hitler's face over all that Aryan superiority B.S." Prefontaine smiled, and the president wondered if he was proud of himself for restraining an urge to say bulls--t. McCall also grinned. The Owens analogy had occurred to him as well, and he thought it was a valid one. Owens himself had sent McCall a letter opposing a boycott.

"You're right on the money Steve," he said with a nod. "As far as I'm concerned, the United States will not be a party to any boycott of the games."

•

President McCall was in an upbeat mood. Only six months left in office. Then he could finally go home. Home to Oregon. There were days when he felt like a prisoner about to be paroled. Then there were other days, like this one, where he knew he would miss being at the center of things.

Air Force One had touched down at Denver's Stapleton International Airport early one Friday afternoon. From there, he was part of a low-key motorcade that took him to a farm about a forty-minute drive out of town. The outdoor setting that was his destination would be the site of one of the most memorable political gatherings of the twentieth century, the first nominating convention of the People's Party. He had wanted this event to take place on his native Oregon soil, but this was going to be Commoner's show, not his, and he had to agree the geographic symbolism of a location closer to the center of the country made sense. He had heard the grumbling of the television networks, who had to go through some complicated and expensive technical scrambles to make the site suitable for gavel-to-gavel coverage, but he also figured, correctly, they wouldn't want to pass up history in the making.

Here McCall would pass the torch to his vice president, who would be the first candidate to run under the party's banner. The formal business of nominating a candidate and adopting a platform would begin tomorrow. Today was all about building a sense of community.

And about having *fun*.

McCall would offer welcoming remarks to the gathered delegates, a collection of young, old, white, black, red, yellow, rich and poor Americans never before seen at a national political gathering. Then he would hand things off to the master of ceremonies for the day, former Secretary of Counter Culture Ken Kesey, who had arrived to great fanfare in the replica of his famous psychedelic bus Furthur. Kesey would in turn introduce a parade of musical performers, starting with the Grateful Dead.

The headlines were generated by the last guest of the night, who hadn't been announced to the press beforehand.

A whippet-thin forty-year old walked out on stage as the hour approached 9 p.m. He wore a guitar around his neck and a tee-shirt that read, "Working Class Hero."

The screams began even before Kesey could bark into the microphone, "Ladies and Gentlemen, John Ono Lennon."

It was Lennon's first time on stage since an appearance with Elton John at Madison Square Garden almost six years earlier, and it signaled his return to music after a self-imposed retirement to "bake bread and tend to the baby."

"This is for the president, let's all tell him thanks," Lennon shouted to the cheering crowd as he launched into "Power to the People." The set continued with a high-energy rendition of the Beatles classic "Come Together." He then reached into his bag of favorite oldies for "Money," which he introduced with a joke about everyone giving to the Commoner campaign until it hurt. A piano was wheeled out on stage so Lennon could accompany himself on his moving anthem "Imagine." That was the end of the brief set, though Lennon returned to the stage for an encore that brought the crowd to another emotional peak—a brand new version of his classic, "Give Peace a Chance," with new lyrics. This time his message was: "Give Earth a Chance."

McCall was a bit nonplussed to learn that Lennon was enough of a fan of his to support the Citizens Party, but happily posed with the singer and Commoner for publicity photos after his performance. He appreciated the cultural significance of the Beatles, but was quietly grateful no reporters asked him about whether they were his favorite musicians. He would have had to acknowledge that his taste ran more to Glen Miller or Artie Shaw. As much as he had enjoyed the Captain and Tennille in the East Room a few years earlier, even they were not of his generation. If one of the reporters had been allowed to venture into the private family living quarters, they would have likely found the First Lady putting a Nat King Cole record on the turntable.

The convention marked Lennon's reemergence both as a musician and a political activist. While his early seventies music had been overtly political, this time around the new album he would record with his wife Yoko Ono, titled *Double Fantasy,* was an unabashed celebration of domesticity. His politics would no longer make their way onto vinyl. Nevertheless, the culture of the McCall years and the candidacy of Commoner inspired Lennon to speak out on behalf of the planet's health and those who supported it.

Commoner had shown a gift in his writing explaining complex issues in terms that were simple and understandable to mass audiences, yet he always showed respect for his readers and listeners. He put the problem of pollution in very basic terms: man had existed in harmony with the earth for about a million years before the industrial age. People thought the supply of clean air and clean water was inexhaustible, so it made sense to assume the planet could act cleanse itself and dilute and degrade any pollutants—but it had quickly become clear there wasn't enough clean air and clean water to absorb the wastes being produced.

It wasn't surprising, therefore, that Commoner took a greater hand in crafting the first platform of the Citizens Party than any presidential candidate before or since. The title itself came from Commoner: "Making Peace with the Planet." The section on the environment represented a restatement and updating of his message across more than two decades of public advocacy.

The platform declared that humankind was at war with the planet, and "we have just begun to reverse course." Although some criticized the document's apocalyptic tone over issues like global warming, millions seemed ready to heed the party's call for fundamental changes in the way goods were produced. Commoner said efforts like catalytic converters on cars and scrubbers in smokestacks were ultimately doomed to failure; until our shift from a containment model to a prevention model was complete, our planet would remain in peril.

From the diary of White House intern Bill Hall, September 27, 1980:

Today's my twenty-first birthday. Never, in my wildest of dreams, could I have imagined I would be spending it three thousand miles away from my family in Washington, D.C., or that the reason for that would be that I was a White House intern for President McCall.

Although I arrived at National Airport a little over a month ago and got settled into my rented apartment in Arlington, some part of me still can't quite believe I'm actually here. I've been dreaming of seeing Washington since I was about five years old.

I'm living in a townhouse just half a block from the southern border of Arlington Cemetery. Of course, I've been through there a couple of times already, visiting the Tomb of the Unknowns, the Marine Corps Memorial, the graves of John and Robert Kennedy, and the many other celebrated people buried there. What the photos can't adequately convey is the sheer immensity of the place. It's humbling to realize that we're all equal at the end.

I have a walk of about a mile to the Metro stop at the Pentagon; the sleek Washington subway whisks me to the downtown area, and the White House, in minutes. It all still has the quality of a dream.

I am so grateful to my professors at Pacific University, Leigh Hunt and Russ Dondero, for making this possible. Although they're both faithful Democrats, the world of Oregon politics is small enough that everyone knows everyone else, and party labels don't matter as much.

Although Oregonians may have a leg up in the selection process, it's still highly competitive, and I'm honored to be here. Right before I left, I attended a reception at the McCall home in Portland with some of the past interns, and that really helped me see the doors this experience could unlock for me. I met as many of them as I could; two who really made an impression on me were Emily Palmer, a recent Lewis and Clark law school graduate who is practicing environmental law, and Phil Keisling, a 25-year-old Yale alum who interned in the fall of '78 and is now a candidate for the state House of Representatives. Some people are even talking about him as a future governor.

Hunt and Dondero warned me that the final months of a presidential term are largely about marking time. People working in the West Wing are more focused at this stage on finding their next gig than on the job at hand—if they aren't already gone, replaced by a chair warmer. I don't get that sense here. Tom (everyone calls him Mr. President, but it's hard not to think of him as Tom) seems determined to keep things moving forward right until he hands off to his successor next January. He has one last legislative priority, the "Superfund" legislation that will put some added federal muscle and resources behind the cleanup of some of our worst environmental messes.

Because the Superfund bill is the big priority now, we're seeing a lot of Energy Secretary Don Jarvi in the West Wing these days. Jarvi moved up from the assistant secretary's job at the beginning of the year after Bob Davis received a job offer that brought him back to Oregon. Most of the rest of the inner circle—Schmidt, Westerdahl, Penwell and the rest—are sticking it out until the end, through I sense a restlessness among them to get back to Oregon after more than seven years on the east coast.

The reminders that the McCall administration will soon be history are everywhere. Just the other day I picked up the latest Rolling Stone. The cover story is a lengthy interview with Sam McCall, the president's troubled younger son who has battled addictions for years and celebrated his thirtieth birthday earlier this year. The main news to come out of the interview was that when Sam returns to Oregon with his parents early next year, he plans to open an addictions treatment center on the coast.

Still, I can't help but sense that the McCall influence on the Capitol will remain long after he's gone. The rumor mill says that Commoner will retain Jarvi as energy secretary if he wins the election, and I'm sure there will be other holdovers. But even more important than the individual players, I get the feeling that McCall has changed the Washington dynamic in fundamental ways.

There's plenty of excitement about the presidential race, even though Tom isn't on the ballot. I'm voting for Commoner, but with a sense of wistfulness—I grew up admiring the Kennedy brothers and always thought I'd be voting for Ted Kennedy for president someday. Meeting the senator has only confirmed my positive feelings for him, but electing Commoner is the best way to make sure the McCall policies are carried forward.

What a thrill it was to finally meet McCall in person. I could feel my heart pounding in my chest when Doris, his secretary, escorted me into the Oval Office. It was hard for my mind to absorb the fact that I was actually standing in this room where so much history has been made. Not that the Oval Office is all that old—the original Oval Office was added to the West Wing by President Taft, but this one was the product of a remodeling project under Franklin Roosevelt. So this Oval Office is less than fifty years old.

But what amazing things have happened here. I felt the ghosts of FDR and JFK as soon as I walked in. Seeing the giant presidential seal on the rug beneath my feet helped bring home the fact that this is the country's seat of power. I couldn't believe I was actually looking at the famous Resolute desk, a gift to the U.S. from Queen Victoria, built from the timbers of a ship that bore that name and used by so many presidents.

Tom put me at ease right away with a friendly handshake, a warm smile, and a heartfelt, "Good to meet you, Bill. It's a long way from home, isn't it?" That's one of his gifts. I've been watching him from a distance for more than ten years. I've been able to sit in on a handful of meetings with staff, Congressional leaders and others, and I've marveled at the president's ability to engage with groups. He puts his experience behind the microphone to good use; he can read from notes, often index cards typed out for him, as if he's speaking off the cuff. After one meeting where he worked a room of disgruntled businesspeople then left the details of resolving the problem to his staff while he headed off to another meeting, I wondered if he was still doing the heavy lifting on issues. Schmidt soon set me straight.

"Never underestimate the value of setting the right tone and putting people in a frame of mind to reason. There are a thousand people who can iron out the details of a resolution, but there's only one Tom McCall who can put them in the frame of mind to get there in the first place." An important lesson for me in practical politics.

Now that the two of us were sitting across from each other, I finally got to learn first-hand what has made him one of the most compelling political figures of the twentieth century.

First off, I was struck by his size. He's six-five, but he sure seems taller. His presence is that commanding. We sat down together, and he began asking me all kinds of questions about myself—family, education, why I was here, where I wanted to be in the future—standard stuff. What impressed me, and what I've heard from others, is his ability to be completely focused on the person he's with. During our scheduled fifteen minutes together (which stretched to almost thirty), I felt like I was the most important person in the world to him. Not Brezhnev, or Westerdahl, or Ted Kennedy, or even his family. Me.

I saw other things that people comment on. His sense of humor. His lack of pretense. (Penwell told me that when he was governor, and she was making his travel arrangements, he said he would be happy to fly coach, apparently forgetting that most seats in an airplane's economy section aren't designed for someone his size.) His ability to laugh at himself. He's imaginative, a dreamer and a risk taker. Most of all, he's compassionate. He genuinely cares about other people. You can't fake that, at least you can't do so successfully for very long. People can tell the difference.

I couldn't resist asking a question that's been the topic of a lot of speculation in the media—namely, what was the president going to do when his term was up next year?

"Write my memoirs!" he answered almost too quickly. "I'm probably going to call the book Maverick, although I was considering Visit But Don't Stay," he said with a smile.

"Yes sir, and then what?" I swallowed, and then went on. "Have you given any thought to running for governor again in '82? I know no former president has ever become a governor, but you could be the first."

The look on his face told me I had struck a nerve; just the hint of a sad grin, and a faraway look of longing in his eyes.

"I'd love to be governor again, Bill, I'd love it! Please don't tell anyone, but in some ways, being governor is a better job than being president. It's easier to move the people and move the bureaucracy, to actually get things done. But Audrey would kill me if I even thought about it. And I'm tired. It's time to step off the stage." He smiled at me, but it was a wistful smile, and when I looked closely at his face, I could see that he was tired. His hair was almost completely white now, and the bags under his eyes were pronounced. He had survived cancer and a heart attack. I thought about a magazine article I had seen, illustrated with side by side pictures of presidents at the beginning and ends of their terms. Lyndon Johnson had been the most dramatic case study; his five years in office, carrying the strain of Vietnam, had engraved deep craters into his forehead, stolen the last traces of color from his hair and etched an expression of permanent sadness in his features that would remain until his death. Although it wasn't nearly as dramatic a transformation for McCall, being president for six years had extracted its price. I found it hard to accept that my hero is mortal.

It's a little ironic for me to have a top-level political internship like this, since I'm not even a political science major-- I'm a communications student. But I've taken a lot of poli sci courses, and it was an interest in politics and government that drew me to journalism in the first place.

I'm in the press office, working under Ron Schmidt. His creativity and passion are amazing. Most of what I'm doing is grunt work—making copies of news releases and delivering them to cubicles, double-checking travel arrangements for the press pool-- but just getting to see the White House media operation up close is amazing. I've gotten to meet the celebrities of the White House press corps, people like Helen Thomas of UPI and Ed Bradley of CBS, but the ones I deal with on a daily basis are the anonymous members of this crowd, the radio stringer from a group of Midwestern stations; the guys from the minor newspaper syndicates; the men and women from European newspapers and TV networks no one stateside has ever heard of. One of the nicer people I've dealt with is Sarah McClendon, who has been around the White House since FDR was in the Oval Office, running her own news service for almost the entire time. I think she's sensed my homesickness, and has almost become a second mother. She keeps asking me if I'm getting enough rest and eating right, and she's treated me to lunch a couple of times.

I am so eager to drink in every second of this experience I have a hard time sleeping at night. I'm rarely home before 11 and usually am back in my office (o.k.—it's a cubicle) by 7 the next morning. On the weekends, I'm up early to see every museum and monument that I can. But all that's on hold tonight. Because it's Saturday night, and I'm heading to Georgetown to party. The Schmidts are taking me out for dinner, and my first drink. Well... my first legal drink, in any event.

•

On Monday, December 8, 1980, John Lennon and Yoko Ono took part in a photo shoot with Annie Liebowitz for an upcoming *Rolling Stone* cover. They also sat for an extended interview with Dave Sholin of RKO radio. During that conversation, Lennon disclosed his plans to become an American citizen; Commoner's November victory had sealed the decision. Even though he had called the United States home for nine years, he knew the news would set off shock waves.

"I'll always love the Mother Country and the Queen, but this is my home now," Lennon said. He was so eager to act on the decision, he persuaded Ono to postpone a recording session they had planned that evening at the Record Plant for Ono's upcoming single, "Walking on Thin Ice." He wanted to stay in and study for the citizenship test he would take in a few days. Although Lennon would never know it, that decision saved his life.

An emotionally disturbed Beatles fan who had flown into New York several days earlier and had been stalking Lennon had finally gathered the courage to shoot him. When Lennon failed to emerge from the fortress-like Dakota Apartments as promised that evening, the fan became so despondent that he returned to his hotel room and took his own life instead.

McCall agreed to Lennon's request that he personally swear him in as a citizen; Yoko and Sean would join him for a ceremony at the White House.

The cover of the next issue of Rolling Stone featured Lennon, naked and in a fetal position, curled up at the fully-clothed Ono's side. It was Lennon's favorite picture from the photo shoot with Liebowitz. He knew the magazine wanted him solo for the cover, but he had insisted the public would accept them as a couple or not at all. Inside the magazine was an editorial from Publisher Jann Wenner:

Citizen Lennon

The decision by former Beatle John Lennon (sorry John, but that's how people are going to know you until the day you die) to become a United States citizen marks not only a milestone in his own journey but in how far we've come as a country.

John took up full time residence in the United States in 1971. It's hard to look back and remember—really remember—the mindset that prevailed in 1971. Our young men were still dying in a pointless war in Vietnam and Lennon was showing up at peace rallies and singing "Give Peace a Chance." The paranoia that had ruled in the White Houses of Lyndon Johnson and Richard Nixon had permeated every facet of American society. John Lennon, never shy about speaking his mind, continued and intensified his political activism, to the point where it landed him on the White House Enemies List.

The FBI became convinced that Lennon would be part of an effort to disrupt the 1972 Republican National Convention in San Diego. That led to several far-reaching consequences. The GOP convention was shifted to Miami and the Immigration and Naturalization service began an effort to deport Lennon, which only ended after McCall replaced Nixon in the White House.

Lennon received his green card four years ago, and that looked like the end of the battle. But the most amazing chapter was yet to come.

The singer has spent much of the last five years out of the public spotlight, in his words, "taking care of the baby and baking bread." But now young Sean is five and John and Yoko are making music again. John, like the rest of us, has been watching the remarkable transformation of the political landscape, and he's liked what he has seen.

As have we.

Welcome to citizenship, John. We're glad to have you aboard.

24

From the diary of White House intern Bill Hall, December 18, 1980

After four months in Washington, I like to think I've lost my sense of being star-struck. Working a short distance from the President of the United States and seeing the most famous and powerful people in the world every single day has been an amazing experience. I like to tell myself that the 20-year-old kid who arrived here last summer in awe of his surroundings is now a world-weary 21-year-old who can't be easily impressed any longer.

Then there are days like today, and I'm that kid again. Because today I met John Lennon.

John, Yoko and their son Sean were in the Oval Office today to meet the President and for John's swearing-in as a U.S. citizen. I tried my best, believe me I tried, not to be a fawning fan. The first time I met Tom, I was struck by how much larger than life he seemed; with John, his physical presence was so much smaller than I had imagined; he's probably four inches shorter than me, about five-ten, and I doubt if he weighs much more than 140 pounds. I guess I had expected an artistic giant to be a physical giant.

What did strike me about John was his playfulness; he seemed delighted to be in the White House, especially with his wife and son; he was curious about his surroundings, asking about the history of all sorts of artifacts. He held up the tie he was wearing, and explained to the President that it was from Quarry Bank School in Liverpool (the school he was attending when he founded the Quarrymen, forerunners of the Beatles), and that his Aunt Mimi, who had raised him, had just sent it over to him at his request.

John and Yoko signed my copy of Double Fantasy for me, and I think I managed to keep from making a complete fool of myself. Well, there was the brilliant moment when he asked me my name, and in a perfect imitation of an echo chamber, I answered, "My name?" I swear for a tenth of a second I had forgotten it.

John and Yoko told the president they would have another album out next year and would be going on tour. I can't wait.

After experiences like this, it's going to be hard to settle back into life at home. I suspect that life is going to seem very slow and ordinary for quite some time to come. Still, I am looking forward to seeing my family, and to my final semester at Pacific University. It will be interesting to continue in person the debate I've been engaged in with Professors Dondero and Hunt via phone and letters. Dondero agrees with my view that Commoner's victory represents a permanent shift away from the two-party structure in national politics, while Professor Hunt still maintains this is an aberration, traceable to the upheavals of the past decade; he fully expects the two-party system to reassert its dominance once the McCall-Commoner era is over. We'll see.

I'm going to have my degree from Pacific in another six months, and then what? I might try to find a journalism job back home, or something in the political realm, although I do have the bad luck of graduating in a political off-year. There won't be any campaign jobs until 1982. I wouldn't be surprised if I find myself back here a year from now. No, not in the White House; those jobs are very hard to come by, but maybe helping with press and constituent relations in a Congressional office.

Maybe, just maybe, the former president will need an eager young staff member to help him with research on his memoirs or in getting his presidential library established. I'm here because of Tom McCall in the first place, so that would be very fitting. And if the right opportunity comes along at the right time, I just might think about running for office myself someday. Would there be a better way to honor the man and his work than by carrying his legacy forward?

•

Audrey McCall was just as happy about being headed home as her husband; maybe even more joyful. She put extra effort into making sure their last Christmas in the White House was a memorable one. In addition to overseeing the details of the decorations and menu, she was also starting to pack their personal belongings.

She removed the president's russet-colored baby shoes, made of the finest kid, that had hung on the bedpost of their Oregon home and, for the past six years occupied the same place in the White House. "Isn't it ironic, Tom, that Tad's headed here just as we're leaving?"

Tad McCall had been sent by the Navy to the University of Washington's law school for a year of post-graduate study in ocean law, and was slated for an assignment in D.C. that spring.

The president wished he could see his eldest son more often, but was proud of his achievements. Public service, though, did extract its price. "Maybe we'll all be on the same coast someday, Aud," he said wistfully.

•

As 1981 began, John Lennon the newly minted U.S. citizen, faced yet another round of questions from the media about the potential for the Beatles to get back together. Lennon continued to push all such questions aside, choosing instead to focus on completing his next album with Yoko, *Milk and Honey*. But the Commoner candidacy had inspired a historic musical reunion.

Paul Simon was moved by the Commoner candidacy. He was coming off the disappointing reaction to his film and album *One Trick Pony*, and wanted to do something that would make a positive statement about what Commoner represented. He decided to finish a song he had been toying with for some time called "Citizen of the Planet." He would record it and pledge all proceeds from the sales to the Commoner campaign. Although he had spent most of the past decade establishing himself as a solo artist, he knew there was one way to insure that the single would get the widest possible exposure and sales.

Simon hesitated only a moment before picking up the phone and dialing his childhood friend. "Artie?" he said. "Want to make another record?"

Soon the radio airwaves were dominated by the first new Simon and Garfunkel song in five years. "I am a citizen of the planet,' they sang, their voices blending in the magic harmony beloved by millions. "I was born here. I'm going to die here. We are entitled by our birth to the treasures of the earth." The good feelings engendered by the recording session led to a coast-to-coast Simon and Garfunkel reunion tour in 1981, and the duo even announced plans for a new studio album; but the same creative differences that led to their 1970 breakup forced them apart once more.

•

Ronald Reagan made another run at the Republican nomination that year, but he was sixty-nine, older than any man ever elected to the presidency, and it was clear that his moment had passed. John Connally emerged as the GOP nominee within a few weeks of the opening of the primary season. The Democrats chose Ted Kennedy, hoping that the magic of the Kennedy name could help them recapture the White House for the first time in a dozen years, but the Commoner-Harris ticket had the momentum from the start.

Connally (who McCall had compared to "a cross between Simon Legree and the mad bomber") finished a distant third, the second consecutive third place finish for the GOP, causing some to speculate that the party of Lincoln had run its course; but others realized that the conservative movement would always have a voice in American politics, and predicted that the country was evolving toward a European-style multi-party system.

Excerpts from the Farewell Address of Tom McCall, broadcast Sunday night, January 18, 1981:

"If there is one lesson to be learned from the decade just past, one message that we must carry forward into the future, it is the need to overcome

the fierce tyranny of the now. When I speak of the tyranny of the now, I am talking about the impulse that causes us as individuals to constantly seek that which is bigger, newer, faster without ever stopping to ask if it is something that we truly need or merely something that we have been programmed by Madison Avenue to want.

"As your government, this means we must constantly look beyond the pressures of the moment for the simple and popular solution and instead seek the solution with the best outcomes for the long term; what's best for our fiscal health, our physical health, our social health, and the health of our planet. We are at a pivotal moment in our history. We can continue to consume a disproportionate share of the earth's finite resources and ignore the reality that someday the cupboard will be bare. We can do that because that day will not arrive in most of our lifetimes. But it will come in our children's lifetimes, or in their children's lifetimes.

"As my predecessor John F. Kennedy once said: 'we all inhabit this small planet. We all breathe the same air. We all cherish our children's futures. And we are all mortal.' On that sunny afternoon, President Kennedy was speaking about the effort to slow our collective rush toward self-annihilation with nuclear weapons. Our progress in that regard has been remarkable. We have begun to show the same self-awareness toward the living ecosystem of our small planet. May that trend continue in the years to come. Thank you, and good night."

When the broadcast was done, the outgoing president's family and key staffers filed into the Oval Office for a low-key celebration. Someone had a bottle of champagne in an iced bucket and handed it to the president. He looked at the label, "Dom Perignon 1966. The year I was elected governor! A great choice!" McCall opened the bottle, but not skillfully; the cork ricocheted off a wall, leaving a small dent, and came perilously close to hitting the precious model of the *Thomas W. Lawson*. But no serious harm was done, and everyone laughed it off.

Many toasts were drunk that night. McCall saved his tribute to Westerdahl and Schmidt for next to last: "It was seventeen years ago this month that the three of us started down this path together, gentlemen. Who would have ever thought it would lead us here?" he asked lifting his glass and making a circle in the air to mimic the shape of the room. A round of claps and cheers followed.

Schmidt found himself remembering the lunch meeting the trio had at the Aladdin Restaurant overlooking the ice rink at Portland's Lloyd Center. The two had been working for a while to persuade McCall to enter the race for Oregon secretary of state. Westerdahl offered to leave his position in public relations at Portland General Electric to run the campaign. Schmidt said he'd have to keep his P.R. job at the Lloyd Center for the time being because there was no money to pay him. Schmidt's memoir picked up the story:

> *Tom said, "Ron, since you're going to head up fund-raising, you can pay today's lunch bill as your first effort." I didn't have any money. Tom didn't have any money. We ended up on a Meier and Frank credit card, which kicked off the campaign and away we went.*
>
> *The skaters below had no idea of the political rocket that was being launched above them that day.*

Seventeen years from the Aladdin to the Oval Office. Schmidt thought: What a ride it's been.

The mood in the Oval Office immediately shifted as Tom McCall signaled for his wife and sons to move to his side. His voice softened, and there was a slight catch in his throat. "As much as you all have meant to me, without—" he paused, glancing at Audrey, Tad and Sam; his arm was already around Audrey's shoulder, and he drew her closer; "without these three, truly, none of this would have been possible."

From Maverick: The Memoirs of Tom McCall

> *In the more than a year since my term ended, countless people have asked me how I felt on January 20, 1981, when I laid down the burdens of office for the final time.*
>
> *When I consider that question, I reflect on the fact that eight of the thirty-*

six men who preceded me in office never got to experience life as a former president, because they died in office.

It is in part for this reason that I felt a profound sense of gratitude and relief to see my term of office arrive at its natural end.

But I would not be honest if I did not concede that I also felt a sense of sadness, for I knew that my time of service and my time at the center of action were also at an end. When I had taken office as Oregon's secretary of state slightly more than sixteen years earlier, I could not have ever envisioned in my wildest imaginings that I would be seated on this podium, preparing to hand the reins of the most powerful office on the planet to my successor.

I was a few weeks shy of my sixty-eighth birthday. I had survived cancer, an assassination attempt and a heart attack. I reflected on great victories and painful defeats in both Salem and Washington, D.C. I knew there might still be battles ahead, but also acknowledged that I had entered the phase of life when it was time to begin the summing up process; the biblical three score and ten was in sight.

It was a beautiful January afternoon, one of the mildest since the inaugural ceremonies had been shifted from March to January. The sun was shining and it was 55 degrees as President-elect Commoner stepped forward to take the oath. It was a grand day for beginnings. But it was a grand day for endings as well.

I looked at Audrey and smiled. I knew this was a grand day, because it was the day we would be going home.

Home to our beloved Oregon.

25

Audrey McCall sensed the end was near. Her husband's cancer had recurred just a few months after they came home. That was in the spring of 1981; then, surgeons removed his remaining testicle and a new round of radiation therapy was launched. But the sobering news in the summer of 1982 that the malignancy was now in his spine meant that a cure was no longer possible. Not surprisingly, the former president wasn't willing to concede anything to the disease, launching himself into a flurry of projects.

The first months of 1982 had brought one milestone after another. The former president completed the manuscript of his memoir *Maverick* and sent it to his publisher. He presided over the inaugural conference of the McCall Institute for Environmental Policy in Portland, which focused on the mixed success of the national land use program. Western states and New England had embraced the law, but most southern and Midwestern states had been resistant; a handful of them had even banded together in a challenge to the law that was working its way to the Supreme Court.

The former president broke ground for the McCall Library and Museum, which would rise next to the University of Oregon campus in Eugene. Schools around the state and across the country were renamed to honor McCall. He attended the weekend festivities that marked the dedication of Tom McCall Waterfront Park in Portland and accepted dozens of awards and honorary degrees; he had to turn down four times as many tributes as he accepted. There simply were not enough hours in the day.

He also made himself freely available to his successor whenever

President Commoner picked up the phone. McCall only visited Washington once after leaving office; he said he thought he ought to let the new president settle into the job without having him skulking around. "But I want to be there for Barry whenever he thinks he needs me," he told a close friend. "That son-of-a-bitch Nixon only talked to me four times in six and a half years. Talk about holding a grudge."

When his book hit the stores in the spring, he went on a publicity tour to support it. Reviewers praised it as the most candid and entertaining presidential memoir in history. The contrast with the turgid, overwritten books some of his predecessors had produced, such as Truman and Eisenhower's two-volume doorstops and LBJ's *The Vantage Point,* couldn't have been greater. Reviewers were even more amazed that McCall had actually written the book himself, holed up in the study of his Southwest Portland home, pounding it out on his sturdy old manual typewriter. He did have research assistance from one of his former interns, Bill Hall, but every word was his own. No ghost writers for this former president.

"I'm a writer, damn it," he groused to Audrey as he slammed down a laudatory write-up in the *New York Times Book Review* that had expressed astonishment at his literary skills.

"Oh Tom," Audrey said. "Don't look a gift horse in the mouth. It's a great review."

The book cracked the best-seller list, despite competition with the first serious work of biography on McCall's presidency, by the *Washington Post*'s Lou Cannon. Cannon's *The Man From Oregon* was praised for its even-handed, detailed look at McCall's amazing rise to power.

An early round of scheduled publicity interviews and book signings for the former president was delayed by an event that hammered home his own mortality: the colorful Dorothy Lawson McCall died in April at age ninety-three. As he presided over her funeral, the one-time most powerful man on the planet was suddenly a little boy growing up in central Oregon once again, listening to a young Dorothy regale him and his siblings with tales of growing up in the grandest of grand styles. He was transported back sixty-plus years as she read to them from the classics every night. The regular doses of Tolstoy, Shakespeare, Thackeray and Poe had sparked a passion for words and ideas in young Tommy McCall that blossomed into something beyond his most vivid dreams.

The great English elms surrounding Westernwold, imported from back east, withstood Oregon's greatest windstorm, on Columbus Day, 1962. But one of them blew down right after Dorothy Lawson McCall died, almost as if the estate was mourning the loss of its matriarch.

McCall had renewed relationships with old friends in the news media when he returned to Oregon, but he wasn't stuck in the past. He cultivated the up-and-coming generation as well; among those he formed a bond with was KGW anchor Kathy Smith, who shared his Massachusetts roots.

•

McCall's post-presidential life had been so busy he had, with some reluctance, turned down an offer from old colleague and friend Tom Dargan to join Portland television station KATU's news staff as commentator. Dargan had assembled the original news team at KGW, and had lured anchor Richard Ross over to KATU; he loved the idea of bringing another member of that crew on board at K2, but the press of demands on McCall's time was too great. Still, he was a frequent interview subject on the station, and got to know many of the staff, including political reporter Paul Hanson.

Hanson and producer Bill Weaver had been assigned to produce an hour-long documentary about McCall's life, with a tentative air date in early January, 1983. Hanson had just begun research and scheduling interviews when he was jolted by the news of Dorothy McCall's passing. The realization that the matriarch was gone brought home the urgency of the project to both journalists. They learned McCall would be flying into the Redmond airport from Portland for the funeral. They had already made arrangements to interview several McCall siblings at Westernwold, where the family would gather to celebrate Mother McCall's long and memorable life.

McCall happily accepted an offer of a ride with the team from KATU, relegating his Secret Service team to a follow-up vehicle. When he learned that Hanson had brought along vodka, ice and clamato juice, he was convinced of the rightness of his choice.

Just a few days after his mother's passing, McCall traveled to accept an honor he cherished above all others: the dedication of the 167 acre Tom McCall Preserve at Rowena, overlooking the majestic Columbia River Gorge.

Audrey McCall worried that her husband's frenzied pace was jeopardizing his health. Her fears were justified. When the cancer had first returned in the spring of 1981, McCall was still confident he could keep the disease in check, telling reporters he felt "as audacious and outrageous as ever." He had defied hospital rules to walk out of the facility under his own power, and the newspapers carried a photo of a fit-looking McCall kissing his wife. His remaining testicle had been removed, causing him to quip to reporters that he wouldn't be riding any camels or porcupines for a while.

This time, the mood was decidedly darker. As he exited Portland's Good Samaritan Hospital in August of 1982 after a stay of several days, a haggard-looking McCall told the reporters who encircled his wheelchair, "I feel like I'm headed for Valhalla like a bat out of hell." The news had been sobering; the cancer that had reappeared the year before in his spine was now at the base of his skull.

Even before the news was made public, a call from a member of McCall's team to KATU management caused a change in plans for Hanson and Weaver. They were pulled off of all other projects and told they now had a September airdate. They didn't have to directly be told why. As the finished program came together, Hanson found himself dealing with a couple of challenges. No one wanted to say anything negative on camera about the former governor and president, knowing that his time was short. But that wasn't a problem; this was a tribute, not a warts-and-all expose. The more difficult problem was what to put in and what to leave out. There were so many great stories about McCall, so much beautiful scenery, and so many memorable words from the man himself that telescoping it all into the available television time proved to be an almost impossible task. Even a decision by Dargan to extend the program from a single hour to two hours didn't make it much easier. Hanson and Weaver decided the first hour would take McCall from birth through the governorship, while the second hour would cover the Washington years and his homecoming.

As the production neared its rushed completion, McCall told Hanson that Audrey had enjoyed getting to know them both, and he hoped she was prominent in the finished product. Hanson winced; yes, Audrey did appear throughout, but she wasn't as prominent as she might have been, given the volume of raw material and the haste with which the finished product had been assembled.

Tom McCall had the perfect suggestion. A dedication, at the beginning, much like the dedication of the book. The program would be for Audrey, carrying Tom's declaration that she was "a fount of common sense" who had been part of every major decision in his life.

Left unspoken by all was the reality that the program was, in every sense, a final memorial, a loving farewell.

But Audrey's husband had had one last fight left in him, and it had been a splendid one. A third attempt to repeal the state's historic land use law had qualified for that November's ballot, and this one seemed to be gaining momentum in a way the first two measures had not. McCall knew in his heart he had to do all he could to save the law, no matter what the price. He poured his last energies into the campaign, including his moving talk at the University Club about loving Oregon more than he loved his own life.

It resonated so deeply, because Oregonians realized it was *the truth.*

When Hanson and Weaver's documentary, "A Nice Place to Visit: The Legacy of Tom McCall" aired, it was the final blow that sent the already staggering Measure 6 to the canvas, never to rise again. Despite the limitation of time, the journalists had woven McCall's own eloquence with pictures of the landscape he loved to create a powerfully evocative portrait of the man and his times. Every ABC affiliate in the state picked it up, further enhancing its reach and impact.

Not only had McCall turned the tide against the measure to abolish land use planning, he had also helped elect Oregon's first governor to run under the Citizen's Party banner. The eight-year run of Vic Atiyeh in the statehouse was coming to an end, and it had been a lively fall as Republican Secretary of State Norma Paulus and former Portland Mayor Neil Goldschmidt vied with the first Citizens Party candidate for Oregon governor.

Paulus had lobbied hard for McCall's endorsement, and he felt great personal warmth and political loyalty toward her, if not to the Republican brand. The idea of her becoming the first woman governor in the state's history also appealed to McCall. As president he had put the first woman on the Supreme Court. But in the end, he stuck with the party he had helped create, and his backing helped to elect Portland Mayor Bud Clark as Atiyeh's successor. Clark narrowly outpolled Paulus and Goldschmidt.

Clark, who had won the 1980 mayoral election over veteran city council member Frank Ivancie, responded with his signature cry of "whoop whoop" when McCall appeared on the podium at his campaign headquarters to offer his congratulations.

The Portland mayor only carried six of the state's thirty-six counties, all in the Willamette Valley corridor. Oregon journalists began to write and speak about a "rural-urban divide," saying it was becoming clear that only McCall had the persuasive powers needed to bring the state's diverse interest groups together.

Momentum already seemed to be headed in Clark's direction, but

McCall's pre-election endorsement at a gathering on the banks of the Willamette River in downtown Portland helped propel the colorful barkeep-turned-mayor to victory. With Clark's encouragement and blessing, McCall also used the moment to stump for his cherished land use program, and deliver an indirect jab at his successor as governor, Vic Atiyeh, who was in the final weeks of his second term.

McCall's instincts in the 1974 primary had been correct; Atiyeh had spent the past eight years simultaneously trying to embrace the McCall record and distance himself from it. Atiyeh hadn't taken a stand for or against the measure to repeal the land use law, but McCall had been troubled by suggestions from the incumbent governor that restrictions on development and McCall's famous "visit but don't stay" quip had contributed to the state's current economic malaise.

As he hesitantly stepped to the podium, McCall couldn't help but think back to a similar rally, almost six years earlier to the day. That had been a day of triumph; he was the incumbent President of the United States, about to win the endorsement of the nation for a term in his own right. He was still healthy, even vigorous. The future still stretched to the horizon and beyond. It had been a sunny, unseasonably warm day.

Now the setting of the sun was in sight. Fall was in the air, and the overcast skies threatened to unleash moisture at any moment. The end for McCall might be months away, or it might only be days. He had to ration these precious moments carefully, not only to preserve his cherished land use program, but to help define the land he loved. His energies were ebbing, but his command of the language was as strong as ever. He told the crowd:

"There's been a lot of bad mouthing about '*visit but don't stay.*' It served its purpose. We were saying '*visit but don't stay*' because Oregon, queen bee though she is, is not ready for the swarm." McCall paused. Most of those truly feeling and understanding the gravity of the moment thought he was reaching within himself for whatever limited reserves he had left.

They were wrong. He was summoning energy, as he always did, from the people and the natural beauty that surrounded him. His former secretary of counter-culture had once called Oregon a citadel of the spirit. Ken Kesey had drawn on these people, this land, to do wondrous and beautiful things in his art and his life. Tom McCall thought Kesey was right, but he took it a step further: he believed that Oregon itself was a wondrous spirit; that somehow the land, water, skies and people melded to form something greater than the sum of their parts, something almost indescribable in its beauty. He knew how to summon this energy when he needed it. His plea to all who could hear his voice was simple: that they love this fragile place with the same devotion he did.

"I am simply saying that Oregon is demure and lovely, and it ought to play a little hard to get. And I think you'll all be just as sick as I am if you find it is nothing but a hungry hussy, throwing herself at every stinking smokestack that's offered."

There were few dry eyes in the crowd as McCall stepped away from the podium. Clark grasped McCall's hand tightly, then pulled him toward him for an embrace. "Nice job, Mr. President," he whispered.

"Thank you," McCall replied, as he slowly pulled away. "But if you don't mind, I still prefer 'governor.' I think you're going to wear that title well."

Audrey recognized the sense of joy and relief in her husband's eyes that election night, but she also saw the cancer's advance. She knew McCall would not live to see another election, but she prayed he would get to experience one more Thanksgiving and one more Christmas. In the end, those prayers were granted.

Tom McCall died January 8, 1983.

When the graveside ceremony at the Redmond cemetery concluded, the television crews broke down their gear and left, the print reporters tucked their notebooks in their pockets, and the still photographers drifted away. There were planes to catch and deadlines to meet. Eventually only one member of the press corps was left. It was fitting that it was Gerry Lewin, the *Salem Statesman-Journal* photographer who had captured so many iconic moments in the public life of Tom McCall.

When McCall stepped up to a podium, Lewin was there. When he scooped ice cream for a surging horde of delighted Salem grade schoolers, a true Gulliver among the little people, Lewin was there. When McCall was released from the hospital after cancer surgery, Lewin was there. When a group of angry workers from a factory closed by state regulators confronted the governor on the Capitol steps, Lewin was there. It seemed that Lewin had always been there, quietly, unobtrusively, recording an era of Oregon history with his own special artistry.

Now Lewin would record the final stanzas of the symphony of McCall's life for posterity. He captured all the majesty and emotion of the ceremony, the state troopers carrying the coffin with military precision, the moments of sadness as those closest to McCall said their final goodbyes. He wanted a shot of the finished grave, what he knew would truly be the Final Photograph, but the cemetery employee who was assigned that task seemed to be working with an almost painful slowness, and the light of day was starting to fade.

"The huge pile of flowers and wreaths rested near the open grave," Lewin recalled. "I trembled with sadness and sorrow as the president's coffin slowly disappeared, being covered with the soil of the land he once led. I watched as the old man worked, slowly hesitating as if in awe of his chore. Daylight was fading and I began to wonder if I still had enough light to get a meaningful picture by the time the gravesite would be completed. Another shovel was nearby and I told the old man I would feel honored if I could assist him. Together, we finally closed the grave. We laid the flowers and wreaths upon it. I got my shot. The sun disappeared behind the Three Sisters and I returned to Salem, probably at a slower pace than I ever drove before."

Nephew Sandy McCall found a sense of justice the week his famous uncle passed away. A group of Maryland citizens finally forced McCall's predecessor as vice president, Spiro Agnew, to pay back the $268,482 in kickbacks he had taken while serving as the state's governor. In an essay published in The *Oregonian*, he observed: "Four days later you, like your father and grandfather, died a poor, honest, dear man."

The venerable Sam Rayburn, longest-serving speaker of the U.S. House of Representatives, said an honest politician will die broke. McCall hadn't quite accomplished that feat, but he and Harry Truman were the only postwar presidents not to achieve millionaire status; McCall's estate was worth less than a quarter of a million dollars at the time of his death.

Tens of thousands, perhaps hundreds of thousands of words of tribute poured from every corner of the land in the days that followed. But perhaps his life was best summed up by the only words engraved on his tombstone beyond his name and the years of his birth and death:

HE CARED

Epilogue

When Jacob Tanzer witnessed Tom McCall's farewell wave that day in October 1982, he had what he considered an odd thought: he could see actor Jack Lemmon playing out that moment in a movie of McCall's life. But it didn't seem quite so odd nine years later when Tanzer watched that very scene come to life on the big screen in a biographical film about McCall produced by, and starring Lemmon. *The Man From Oregon* took its title from the Lou Cannon biography. The image of Lemmon smiling and waving froze as the closing credits rolled.

Although there had been frequent informal reunions of McCall's Salem and Washington staffs, this was the first great reunion of McCall alumni since the two funerals. The next significant gathering wouldn't come until the centennial celebrations of McCall's birth.

Remarks by Former President Al Gore at the Dedication of the McCall Building, Washington D.C., March 22, 2013.

Al Gore served as the forty-third President of the United States, from 2001 to 2009. Gore's path to the presidency was unusual. In 1992, then-Senator Gore turned down Bill Clinton's request to be his running mate on the Democratic ticket, citing a need to spend more time with his family after his son had been involved in a near-fatal accident the year before. Gore spent the next eight years as executive director of the Commoner Center for Environmental Policy and wrote the bestseller *Earth in the Balance*. In 2000, Gore made a dramatic return to politics, announcing his candidacy for president on both the Democratic and Citizen's Party tickets.

"I have spent the last eight years working to influence policy from the sidelines," Gore said in his declaration of candidacy. "But I now realize that I can best serve the future of our planet by returning to an active role. What John F. Kennedy said almost forty years ago is still true: the presidency is the center of action."

The move sparked a fierce debate within the ranks of both parties. Elements of each party feared a fusion ticket would dilute their 'brand,' and some states still had laws on the books that prohibited candidates from running under more than one party's banner. Gore's strong eco-message ultimately prevailed in both parties and for the first time since 1972, the presidential race came down to two major candidates instead of three. Nevertheless, Gore defeated the Republican nominee, Texas Governor George Bush, by the narrowest of margins.

Gore was joined on the podium by President Hillary Clinton, former President Jesse Jackson and McCall's sons. Tad and Sam still missed their dad all these decades later, and they also couldn't help but think of their mother on this day. Audrey had passed on at age ninety-two just a few years earlier, and they knew how proud she would have been to be present for this event.

Tad had just retired from his second career with the Environmental Protection Agency, which he had joined after leaving the Navy. He had risen to the agency directorship during Gore's second term, and the second President Clinton had continued him in that job. He was quietly proud that he and his late father would go down in history as the first parent and child to lead the EPA.

Many other Oregonians were on hand, including former Energy Secretary Don Jarvi, McCall Library Director and former Oregon Governor Phil Keisling, and Oregon's current secretary of state, Bill Hall. Hall was nearing the point of decision on something he had been weighing for some time: Whether 2014 would be the year he would seek to follow Keisling, Meyers, Hatfield, and of course, Tom McCall, from the secretary's job to the governorship. Steve Prefontaine was there, still looking like he could turn in a respectable time in the

5,000 meters, despite having passed his sixty-second birthday a few weeks earlier.

There was someone else sitting behind Gore who owed the arc of her career to Tom McCall. It was the first sustainability secretary who would call the building home, Oregon native Emily Palmer. She already had a photo from her first meeting with McCall in 1975 hanging on the wall of her new office. The 59-year-old secretary found herself almost drowning in memories. She marveled at the way her life had come full circle, all because of her admiration for McCall and her commitment to carrying forward his legacy.

She traveled back through the decades in an instant; she was once more the nervous 21-year-old being ushered into the Oval Office for the first time. So much was still ahead of her at that moment; a distinguished career in environmental law, the chairmanship of two leading energy development firms, and a little over four years earlier, the call from the president-elect (the first female president, no less!) inviting her to join the cabinet. It had been such a great adventure, and it had gone by so quickly. Too quickly.

Emily found herself having to consciously redirect her attention to the present moment, and Gore's words:

"Today we dedicate a headquarters building for our newest federal department, the Department of Sustainability. This energy efficient structure is a fitting memorial to the thirty-eighth president of the United States, Tom McCall, who was born one hundred years ago today. More than any other president, McCall advocated for sane, forward-looking environmental policies.

"After Tom McCall's passing, his Oregon political rival and personal friend Bob Straub called him mentor to the soul of Oregon. Fortunately for all of us, he then had the opportunity to become mentor to the soul of the nation.

"It's been said that Tom McCall was the Patrick Henry of the environmental movement, a title also applied to his successor, Dr.

Commoner. They sounded the alarm, and their successors have picked up the torch and carried it forward.

"A leader's lasting legacy is often not apparent during his lifetime. Although Tom McCall championed many innovative ideas, his most significant contribution to the American story may turn out to be his willingness to question the previously unquestioned doctrine that growth is good. He helped us look at the price of growth, as well as its potential benefits.

"That is why I believe President McCall's true memorial is not with the walls of this building. It is to be found all around us—in the clean air we breathe, in the clean water we drink, in the soils we walk upon. That is his legacy.

"Forty years ago, then-Governor McCall told the Oregon Legislature: 'We must respect another truism—that unlimited and unregulated growth leads inexorably to lowered quality of life.' It is difficult to appreciate from the perspective of the twenty-first century what a revolutionary statement that was, especially from a political leader. In 1973, we were in the last days and hours of the great postwar economic boom. Until Tom McCall stepped forward, no one in his position had ever questioned the cost of that growth."

The former president was unusually passionate on this afternoon, emphasizing words and phrases with upward inflections and an occasional gesture. Throughout his political career, Gore had been accused of being stiff and unable to bring emotion to his public appearances. Maybe, Hall thought, he's channeling just a little of the McCall spirit.

"Tom McCall has been gone for more than thirty years, but I like to think if he could pay us a visit, he'd be pleased with much of what he would see. Solar, wind, wave and geothermal are our major energy sources instead of fossil fuels. Our cars are powered by electricity and hydrogen. The Dam Removal Act that I signed into law in 2002 is continuing the restoration of waterways large and small. We will phase out all use of coal by 2030 and are well on the path to generating all of our energy from renewable sources no later than 2050. We no longer allow clear-cutting in our federal forests, and seventeen states have adopted similar prohibitions. We have dramatically slowed our contribution to global warming.

"On the other hand, Tom McCall would remind us of the great unfinished tasks before us. Although a similar environmental ethic prevails in some areas of the globe, that is not the case everywhere. Rainforests are still being clear-cut. Toxic chemicals are still being dumped into the air and the sky. This is understandable when we acknowledge that the peoples of so many nations still aspire to our level of material attainment. If we take our obligations as stewards of the planet seriously, we must help these peoples learn the lesson Tom McCall taught us so many years ago."

As Gore neared his conclusion, the sons, colleagues and successors of Tom McCall all felt themselves pulled back through the decades to a time when some of them were younger and some of them had not yet been born. Yet the McCall era was an inspiration to all of them. They knew remarkable things had been accomplished in those days, but as wonderful as the McCall governorship and presidency had been, it was only the beginning, and it was up to each and every one of them to carry their mentor's legacy forward.

"When Tom McCall became president in that dark summer of 1974, some wondered how a man who had no foreign policy experience could adequately lead this country on the international stage. But Tom McCall was a disciple of John Muir's doctrine of interconnectedness—the belief that all of nature is a whole, not just a series of discrete parts. President McCall helped us to see our interconnectedness with our brothers and sisters across the globe. The earth is a smaller place because a giant named Tom McCall strode across it."

McCallandia and the Historical Record

Obviously the fun of alternate history is seeing how things might have taken a different path. Nevertheless, I have tried to use the actual events of 1973-1983 as a template for this work. A brief discussion of some of the points whtere reality and McCallandia diverge, and what really happened to some of the key figures in this story:

Richard Nixon, of course, did not choose Tom McCall as his new vice president when Spiro Agnew resigned. He was planning for John Connally to be his successor in 1977. Besieged by the Watergate scandal, Nixon bowed to Congressional pressure to select Gerald Ford. Ford went on to pardon Nixon, endorse the ridiculed "Whip Inflation Now" campaign and lose the 1976 presidential election to Democrat Jimmy Carter. Ford faced an assassination attempt from Squeaky Fromme on the same day my fictional President McCall crosses her path (there was also a second attempt on Ford's life two weeks later, but that doesn't happen in this narrative.)

After being pardoned, Richard Nixon went on the write several books and become a frequently sought out elder statesman before his death in 1994.

Ronald Reagan challenged Gerald Ford for the 1976 Republican presidential nomination, losing narrowly. Although precedent says candidates don't name their vice-presidential choices until after being chosen as the party standard bearer, Reagan broke with tradition by naming Sen. Schweiker as his potential running mate before the convention began. Reagan easily won the 1980 Republican nomination and the presidency and was re-elected four years later.

Jerry Brown was an unsuccessful candidate for the Democratic Party's presidential nomination in 1976, 1980 and 1992. He won a second term as governor of California in 1978. He lost a race for U.S. Senate in 1982 and left politics for a time, before becoming mayor of Oakland in 1999, the launch of a second act that led to his election as California Attorney General and then winning the governorship for a third time in 2010.

Ken Kesey continued to write (two novels, two children's books, numerous articles) teach, speak, perform and delight his fans until his death in 2001 at age sixty-six.

Henk Pender did paint McCall's official gubernatorial portrait. Like the man himself, it's larger than life and hangs near the door to the state House chamber in the Capitol building. Instead of the scene I describe, Pender portrayed McCall standing on the beach, his hand outstretched in greeting.

Tom McCall's memoir really was titled *Maverick*, but except for the quoted passage about meeting his future wife, all the excerpts in these pages are fictional.

Jack Lemmon really was interested in playing McCall in a film and flew to Oregon for a meeting with Audrey McCall, Sam McCall and Ron Schmidt, but the project never materialized. A credible source told me that Lemmon was unable to interest a studio in the project, possibly because a conservative Republican—Reagan—was sitting in the White House at the time.

Al Haig's thought about never seeing himself working for someone as vapid as Ronald Reagan is tongue-in-cheek; in reality, Haig became Reagan's first secretary of state, earning a page in the history books following the 1981 attempt on Reagan's life by declaring to the White House press corps, "I am in control here."

McCall's October 1973 farewell address is taken word for word from his actual farewell address of January 1975.

Bob Straub was elected as McCall's successor in the governor's office in 1974 and then lost to Victor Atiyeh four years later. He never sought political office again. McCall's comments to Atiyeh on general election night 1974 are adapted from his actual remarks to Atiyeh on primary election night 1978 when Atiyeh ended McCall's bid for a third term.

Although he was endorsed by McCall, Clay Myers lost the 1974 Republican primary for governor to Atiyeh. After completing ten years as Oregon Secretary of State, he was twice elected state treasurer.

Ron Schmidt remained on Governor McCall's staff until near the end of his administration. He, Ed Westerdahl and John Phias did launch one of the state's most successful public relations firms. Schmidt died of cancer in 1992 at age fifty-six. Westerdahl died at age seventy-four in 2010.

Steve Prefontaine died in an auto accident in Eugene on May 30, 1975, more than a year before the Montreal games. Although it was reported that his blood alcohol level was above the legal limit at the time of his death, the circumstances of his passing remain a subject of debate.

Gerry Lewin did not take the photo I describe of McCall's lonely walk following his resignation from the governorship, since that moment didn't happen, but he did take many of the iconic photos of McCall I describe, and he really did help cover McCall's remains following his burial. His memoir of assisting with the burial, slightly edited to fit this narrative, was written for the McCall Centennial Issue of the Newport High School magazine Harbor Light.

The memo from Watergate Special Prosecutor Leon Jaworski laying out the case for the prosecution of Richard Nixon is part of the historical record.

Younger readers may be surprised to read about a Republican president supporting the Equal Rights Amendment. In fact, the Republican Party was originally one of the driving forces behind the measure, and that support continued as late as the 1972 party platform.

McCall's choice of Nelson Rockefeller as his successor as vice president (the same choice Ford made in real life) is based on McCall's longstanding admiration of Rockefeller. He often spoke of him as a potential vice president or president.

Although a national Bottle Bill never became a reality, nine other states followed Oregon's lead and adopted Bottle Bills.

Jim Bouton took the 1976 baseball season off to make a short-lived sitcom for CBS television, then resumed his baseball comeback the next year, finally returning to the major leagues with the Atlanta Braves in 1978.

The Captain and Tennille did play at the White House in 1976 at the invitation of First Lady Betty Ford.

The first presidential debate of 1976 really was interrupted by a twenty-seven minute audio outage. Candidates Ford and Carter stood at their podiums, mute and unmoving, during the entire outage. I couldn't imagine McCall doing the same thing.

David Garth, one of the most successful political consultants of the twentieth century, never managed the campaign of an Oregon candidate, though there were reports Bob Straub wanted to hire him in 1978 if he had ended up facing a third race against McCall for governor.

No presidential election since 1824 has been decided in the House of Representatives.

Theodore White ended his "Making of the President" series with his book on the 1972 campaign. I assume he would have continued it with such an historic election to cover in 1976.

Janet Cooke was a reporter for the Washington Post. Her Pulitzer-prize winning story, "Jimmy's World," published in 1980, described the life of an eight-year-old heroin addict. It was exposed as fraudulent, ending her reporting career.

McCall did not suffer a heart attack in real life. The course of his cancer followed the same progression and timeline as in these pages.

President Carter did allow the deposed Shah of Iran to enter the United States for medical treatment, a decision many blamed for the seizure of the American embassy in Iran and ensuing hostage crisis. He did make the decision to boycott the 1980 Moscow Olympics.

Barry Commoner and LaDonna Harris sought the presidency and vice-presidency on the Citizens Party ticket in 1980, earning more than 234,000 votes. Commoner had founded the party in 1979; it was dissolved in 1986.

Simon and Garfunkel reunited at a famous concert in New York's Central Park in the fall of 1981, which was followed by a tour and the start of work on a new album, which was later converted into a Paul Simon solo project. "Citizen of the Planet," one of the songs put on the shelf when the reunion album was cancelled, was finally released on *Old Friends*, the album of their 2003 reunion tour.

In real life, Sam McCall did not find the healing he found in these pages. He died of an overdose in 1990, aged 40.

John Lennon was killed by a deranged fan on the night of December 8, 1980.

Acknowledgements

This is a work of fiction; it is based on real people and real events. For events prior to October, 1973, I have tried to stay close to the historical record as much as possible, but I have taken the novelist's liberty of changing a couple of things to help the story; for instance, the Arab oil embargo happens in the narrative a few months sooner than in reality so that odd-even gas rationing can be introduced before McCall leaves for Washington. The words, thoughts and actions attributed to the individuals named in these pages from October 1973 onward, both written and spoken, are wholly the product of my imagination. One exception is that many of the words are McCall's own, though edited for time and context.

Anyone who wants to learn about McCall and his times should begin with Brent Walth's exhaustively researched biography, which will stand as the definitive McCall life story. McCall's autobiography, *Maverick*, is also useful, as are the two memoirs by his mother, Dorothy Lawson McCall, *The Copper King's Daughter* and *Ranch Under the Rimrock.* He inspired lots of great journalism; my three favorite pieces are E.J. Kahn's "Letter from Oregon" that appeared in the New Yorker on February 25, 1974, Tom Bates' "Decision at Roads End" which was published in *Oregon Times* magazine in March 1978, and "Of Passion and Pragmatism: The Legacy of Tom McCall" by Ann Sullivan, published in the *Sunday Oregonian*'s "Northwest Magazine" on November 7, 1982. Veteran broadcast journalist Paul Hanson's "A Nice Place to Visit: The Legacy of Tom McCall," which aired on KATU in 1982, is a moving tribute that has stood the test of time. All of these sources were immensely helpful in researching my story; they were supplemented by a stack of four thick folders containing clippings, press releases and campaign documents I've collected over the past forty years.

In addition to Matt Love, I want to thank others who read drafts of this manuscript in various stages of completion and provided helpful feedback: Lisa Nowak, Sharron Kelley, Kip Carlson, Onno Husing,

Kimberly Herring, Janet Harrison and the members of my writing critique group, Theresa Shivers-Wisner, Dorothy Blackcrow Mack and Sue Fagalde Lick. A conversation in the Capitol Building cafeteria with one of my former political science professors, Russ Dondero, helped focus my thinking on several potential scenarios of a hypothetical McCall administration. Russ also provided a detailed critique of the manuscript which helped me sharpen many of the political aspects of the story. Russ has been a significant contributor to keeping the McCall legacy alive; he founded the Tom McCall Forum, which Pacific University sponsored for many years. (I am grateful to Russ for making it possible for me to have dinner with former McCall aide Ron Schmidt many years ago.)

I also want to thank others who haven't reviewed this manuscript prior to publication but have provided great encouragement for my writing: Diane Hammond, Joanne Verger, Ame Kane-Barkley and my aunt, Carole Bakken.

State Representative Vicki Berger was very helpful in sharing memories of her father, Richard Chambers, the driving force behind the Bottle Bill. Gerry Lewin kindly allowed the use of his iconic McCall photograph. McCall described Lewin as a "superb camera artist" when he signed a copy of his autobiography for him; one more example of McCall choosing just the right words.

Former McCall colleagues Phil Keisling, Don Jarvi, Doris Penwell, Darrel Buttice, Jacob Tanzer, Kathy Smith and Paul Hanson also shared wonderful memories of their time with McCall. Tad McCall, Tom McCall's eldest son, generously answered a number of questions about his father. All of their comments and suggestions helped make this a much better book; all opinions, conclusions and any errors or lapses are mine.

The biggest thank you of all goes to my children, Chris Rogers and Rachel Rogers and my wife Carol Hall, for their love and support. It was Carol who said since I've spent so much of my life reading books I might as well write one.

Bill Hall is a native Oregonian who has served as a Lincoln County Commissioner since 2005. Prior to that, he spent thirty years in broadcast and print media. He's been an admirer of Tom McCall since he was a child, and volunteered in McCall's 1978 campaign for the governorship. He lives in Newport with his wife and daughter. *McCallandia* is his first book.

Contact Bill at billium@newportnet.com